CONTENTS

INTRODUCTION

This is not merely a book and a series of science fiction short stories. It's about sci-fi stories that tell of the impact of technology on the human condition. As with all things, there are consequences of creating, manufacturing, developing, implementing, and using technology.

Good can come from the opening of new possibilities, but so can bad. Yet, there is the murky gray in between as well. This is the realm where good and bad mix with uncertain outcomes. Whatever the outcome, these short stories consider the opportunities and the inherent limitations of technology.

Where science and humans clash, one often finds crossed circuits.

*****

CHEESEBURGERS AND FRIES

CH 1

Article in the May 2085 New York Gazette

IALs Are in Your Future

They are supposed to be the newest in Intelligence Augmentation or IA. For decades scientists have been working on devices that will be the next step in evolving humans into what they call Human 2.0. This transition would help simple SHS types—standard homo sapiens—compete with increasingly more powerful and vastly more intelligent mechanical cyborgs and other machines.

The new devices—called Instant Access Lenses or IALs—are intra-Plankard and act like permanent contact lenses. These replace the optic lenses in the eye and not only correct for visual aberrations but also act as a WIFI.2 hotspot to receive information from the Internet or other sources outside. A second device is implanted within the skull that has probes which extend into the inferior temporal cortex, where eyesight is synthesized, and into the superior temporal lobe, where thoughts are created. This enables the device to transmit thoughts as visual images to the IALs and be read by the user.

Test recipients of the IALs showed an amazing ability to search the Internet just by thinking about the topic or asking a question. The information appears on their implanted IALs much like a heads-up display in a jet fighter, a hovercraft, or a land-based auto. Those subjects with the IALs outperformed all other competitors in responding to test questions on history, language, chemistry, biology, geography, and a whole host of other recall-type subjects. As a result, the demand for the IALs has been extraordinary with sales growing exponentially even with the steep price tag.

But the high cost has raised the attention of Congress which has stepped-in and will be enacting legislation to make this technology available to everyone at a nominal charge or free with subsidies. Senator Patrick Wellborne said today, "We have an obligation to ensure there is no discrimination in America—whether it be from race, ethnicity, gender, sexual preference or intelligence. Therefore, we will be passing this legislation to ensure people of means don't gain an unfair advantage over the poor and middle class." He added, "We are all equal in the eyes of the state."

Senator Wellborne added that he expected passage of the bill within weeks and that the new devices could be manufactured quickly by the developer—Coltnor, LLC.—likely before the end of next year.

Article by: Ingrid Mueller, Staff Reporter

CH 2

Ansen Ramsey was one of the early recipients of the IALs. He was a wealthy Wall Street powerbroker who lived on the Upper East Side of Manhattan, near Central Park. His job was demanding and required split-second decision making as he worked in what was known as the arbitrage department of Silverman Associates, a multi-national investment banking firm headquartered in London. A high-pressure position, the broker in an investment bank department had to make instant decisions to monitor and then moderate or even override actions made by the company's huge computer trading algorithms to buy and/or sell commodities, foreign currencies, equities, or debt securities. Although rare, a glitch in the algorithm or outside forces not contemplated could direct the firm's trading actions in the wrong direction. Arbitraging was the fastest-paced activity in the company, and one wrong move could cost it millions—even billions within seconds. Only the brightest, quickest minds could handle the load. Ansen Ramsey had one such mind.

Yet, over the years, the stresses of his work had become so enormous that he felt his mind losing its sharpness, and he was losing his competitive edge. More often, he was making mistakes, albeit small—something not tolerated at any level within the firm. Even though he had been there nearly twenty years, he knew everyone was replaceable. Others had been fired for fewer issues. Therefore, he had opted to get the IALs to improve his performance and give him an advantage over others—at least for a while.

Ramsey's driver sighed as the black limousine ground to a halt behind other cars along Fifth Avenue's busy thoroughfare at ten in the morning. Ramsey was trying to get to a client's office for an important meeting but was stuck in the late-morning, rush hour traffic. There was a protest going on at an intersection only a few blocks south, and it was holding up the entire queue of cars.

"We should have taken the hovercar," said Ramsey, clearly annoyed.

"Couldn't sir. You know we can't fly in this kind of weather," said the driver.

Outside, the deep gray skies above had thickened their grip around the city, and the rain had started to drizzle onto the windows, making the front wipers swish back and forth every second or two.

Ramsey looked out the window. "It would have cleared off. We could have made it fine."

"Cloud cover was too low and dense. Even with our radar, the FAA would never let us fly in this."

"Whatever," said Ramsey as his phone rang. He had already gotten interaural devices in his ears, so all he needed to do was speak the words *Answer Phone* to retrieve calls directly through the auditory nerves in his ears.

"Answer Phone," he mumbled.

"Hey, Ansen, we've got a problem with the platinum thirty-day contracts." It was one of Ansen's assistants. "The system is trying to sell ten thousand while at the same time buying five thousand North American Dinar contracts. It doesn't make sense based on where the market is headed now. To make matters worse, the European Prime Minister announced a tightening of their money supply. They're raising interest rates again through the EU Bank."

Ansen's mind sent the message: *Visual – superimpose platinum, gold, and palladium futures over foreign exchange currencies – Euro, Asia-Sino Renminbi, and North American Dinar. Analyze.*

Without saying a word, a chart from the Internet popped onto his IALs and visually he manipulated the graph to show what he needed.

"Override the North American Dinar buy contract and buy the Euro. We need a fifty million long Euro position on this one."

"Thanks, boss. Will do," said the assistant, hanging up.

Ansen's quick action had prevented a loss of twenty-three million North American Dinars—a hefty sum in one day, even for the Silverman company.

Eventually, Ansen made it to the client's office and was able to close the deal to become the prime investment house for that company's stock offering which was to be made later that year. It was going to be one of the largest initial public offerings or IPOs of the year and getting a piece of it as the prime banker was a huge victory.

Things were going well for Ansen ... at least for now.

*****

CH 3

A little over six feet tall, Ansen was nearing the age of forty-five and beginning to have his midlife crisis. With wavy black hair, gelled and combed straight back, his confidence was still strong despite the hints of baldness cropping up in spots he couldn't easily see in the bathroom mirror. Although his eyebrows were bushy, he elected not to have them tweezed which he viewed as unmanly. In this regard, working out was important to him. He was fit and exercised at least three, and sometimes as many as five, times a week, going to the lower-level gym in the downtown office building and having his personal trainer take him through his routine.

But it was during one of these routines that something odd happened.

"One more," shouted Walter Bukowski, his trainer, coaxing him to finish another pull-up.

But what flashed into Ansen's mind wasn't another pull up. He stopped.

"Why are you stopping?" asked Walter, surprised at Ansen's sudden change of attitude.

Ansen looked puzzled. "I don't know. My mind went blank."

"Went blank? Well, let's get back at it!" stressed Walter waiting for the last two reps.

"I can't."

"Why not, Ansen?"

"I then got this picture of a juicy cheeseburger and big pouch of French fries in my head and I can't seem to get it out. How weird?"

The trainer was not amused.

"Ansen, you need to focus, man. I'm not here to listen to you talk of gorging yourself on cheeseburgers in the middle of a workout. Now, let's get back at it. Shall we?"

The trainer continued and wrapped up the session without another interruption. However, later that day, Ansen had another flash into his mind; this one was longer—like a daydream.

He got the image of himself giving a speech at an upcoming financial convention in Zurich, Switzerland. Suddenly, someone in the crowd jumped up from their seat and shouted, "You're a capitalist pig! You're killing babies! You're murdering children!" The ushers rushed in and escorted the disruptor out, but not before others in the crowd began shouting the same thing at him. Then, then entire audience began chanting it: "You're a capitalist pig!"

"Ansen? Ansen? Are you all right?"

It was his manager, Tyron Hicks. Hicks snapped his fingers a few times to get his attention. Ansen was immediately jolted out of the dream.

"Uh, Tyron, hey. What is it?" Ansen's face looked confused and bewildered.

"You were saying something, but I wasn't sure what you were saying," said Hicks. "It sounded like 'You're a capitalist pig,' or something. Are you all right?"

"Yeah, yeah. I'm fine," said Ansen, returning to his brokerage screens.

The remainder of the day passed without incident, and Ansen had his driver take him home to his penthouse on the ninety-third floor of the recently built Shanghai Towers. There, he threw his coat on the white suede sofa and went to the butler's pantry to fetch himself a Scotch. After depositing three cubes into his Lenox crystal tumbler and pouring a generous portion of MacCallum, he settled in to watch a movie before having some Chinese brown rice and vegetables delivered from the restaurant downstairs.

Ansen turned on the hidden projector above the full-wall screen and searched to select a movie. But instead of seeing movie titles, he only saw pictures of cheeseburgers and French fries posted for every image. After a second screen of the same images appeared, he made a call.

"Call Bart's Burgers on east seventy-second," he muttered, his audio implants communicating with his home telecommunication system.

"This is Bart's," said a rough, husky voice. "Wha-da-ya-havin'?"

"Three cheeseburgers and two fries," said Ansen, who rarely indulged in any of the fatty foods.

"Wha-da-ya want on 'em?"

"Everything," said Ansen.

"Jalapeños?'

"Yeah, even those."

Ansen gave the man his address, and within thirty minutes his order was delivered. The burgers were hot and juicy, just like in the images, and he ate every one of them. By the time he finished, every last string of French fries was also devoured. It was as much fat as he usually ate in an entire week.

*****

CH 4

Three months later …

"Ansen, this is Walter. I was just wondering when we can start-up the exercising routines again. It's been two months now since you let me know you'd be out of town. I guess you're back now. What about tomorrow?"

"No, Walter. I can't tomorrow. I'll call you when my schedule frees up."

Ansen hung up. He was sitting on his couch finishing a bowl of vanilla ice cream with hot fudge sauce smothering the top. As he put the spoon in his mouth, a small dribble of chocolate sauce dribbled onto his white shirt.

"Crap!" he said, taking his finger to remove it before licking it off the tip.

Ansen had gained thirty-two pounds during the intervening period, having indulged himself on all sorts of foods he had disciplined himself to avoid in the past. In fact, his work had suffered as well. He had been taking off at four in the afternoon almost every day. He wasn't leaving to go play golf at his country club on Long Island; rather, he was going only a few blocks away from the magnificent, luxury tower that housed his firm and his office.

It was a shabby place—run-down with slate blue paint peeling off the store front. A vacated investment house, the place was soon reoccupied by a not-for-profit with unknown sources of funding. There was no sign on the outside, but there was a temporary sign in the window that read:

> **Red Brigade Headquarters**
> **Fight the Capitalist Pigs!**
> **Join the Socialist Revolution TODAY!**

Within months, Ansen's output of deals had declined by over forty percent. Not only was he not hitting his targets for the firm, but he also wasn't making the company enough to pay his stout wages.

This didn't last long, and soon those in London and his own manager, Tyron Hicks, took notice too. Eventually, Hicks told Ansen he wanted to see him in his office. Ansen knew he hadn't been performing well during the prior months and felt the end was probably coming.

"Yes, Tyron. You wanted to see me?" asked Ansen, waddling into his boss's office.

Ansen went inside and closed the door. Moments later, the blinds to Hicks' office automatically louvered closed.

The meeting lasted nearly two hours. The two men talked, and throughout the conversation, Tyron's facial expression was taunt and serious. Ansen periodically nodded his head at the remarks made but rarely had comments to make in response. He, too, looked serious and, at times, distraught.

Finally, the door opened, and Ansen walked out. His shoulders were stooped, but he strode briskly back to his five-by-five cube. He then went to the central supply room and got a broad, deep banker's box. Returning to his desk, he opened his drawers and emptied everything, tossing things casually into either the box or the wire, waste can next to his chair. His colleagues watched in shock and dismay as their friend and colleague packed up his belongings, got up, and pushed in the armless chair with a worn seat cushion.

"Ansen? What happened?" asked Dotty Perkins, another broker who sat nearby.

"I'm done," said Ansen curtly. "I'm moving on."

"Why?"

"It's time," Ansen said. "This business we're in is bad. What we do is evil. We need to help the poor, not the rich. We need to serve others, not ourselves. The Administration is right when they preach to us to 'Quit our evil ways and our capitalistic self-indulgence.' Capitalism destroys society—don't you understand that? It's never been any good. Only the rich get richer—the poor get poorer. We must fight for socialism—more government control over those who will do us harm. Right now, the pigs of industry are getting fat at the trough of our rigged system. We need to steal the wealth of all our clients and redistribute it to the poor people across the country. That will solve our problems. If we give it all to our governors, they will ensure everyone is taken care of.

"The president is right when he says we need socialism. We need to re-elect him for a third term regardless of what the laws say. He says he wants to be elected for life—I say Yes! We need him to tell us what should be done. He says Congress is corrupt. I agree! Disband Congress— turn it all over to President Osman! He's the one who deserves our loyalty and respect. He's the one who will deliver us from our problems. He's the only one who can help us now."

Dotty was taken aback. "You've never thought that way before. What's gotten into you?" she asked.

"You wouldn't understand. You're a greedy capitalistic pig, just like the rest of you here!" he shouted, pointing to the others in the room watching and listening to him rant.

Ansen then carried his box to the elevator bank and pushed the button to go down. The floor counter next to the door began its rapid count up to his floor. But within a few minutes, Tyron came out of his office to meet him.

"I guess this is it," said Ansen.

"You've put in a lot of years here, Ansen," said Tyron.

"Yep, and I can't wait to get the hell out of this place. It's toxic."

Tyron nodded and smiled. "You headed to the Red Brigade Center?" he asked.

"Yeah, and you?"

"I'll see you there," said Tyron, carrying his own box. "I'll be there right after I pick up my car downstairs."

Ansen stared blankly at his former boss. Images of the Red Brigade Center subliminally flashed in microseconds within his IALs.

Tyron blinked. The images of cheeseburgers and fries danced across his vision. He didn't notice the microsecond interruptions in his vision, but his IALs were working just as they were designed.

*****

CH 5

Article in the May 2086 New York Gazette

IALs Are in Your Future--Update

As we reported a year ago, the Instant Access Lenses or IALs that are being made available to all citizens are a wonder device that many who have them swear by. They are the newest in Intelligence Augmentation or IA.

These replace the optic lens in the eye and not only correct for visual aberrations but also act as a WIFI.2 hotspot to receive information from the Internet or other sources outside. The entire device enables the user to transmit thoughts to the IALs and read them as if he or she were reading off the computer screen.

The IALs have given users the amazing ability to search and find things from the Internet just by thinking about them. The information shows up on their implanted lenses much like a heads-up display we see in many other devices today. It has been shown that those with the implants far surpass others in cognitive ability.

Although there have been rumors of subliminal messaging being sent to users via covert military and governmental agencies, these claims have been debunked. Senator Patrick Wellborne of the Incumbent Party said, "The IALs have been a huge benefit to America. Our students are competing again with the rest of the world." And when asked about the subliminal messages, he said, "There is absolutely no truth to that. It's just another conspiracy theory from a bunch of Right-Wing whackos. Anybody who believes that rubbish needs one of our IALs. That should make them smart again."

The senator also addressed the theory that the maker of the device—Coltnor, LLC—was an anagram that really spelled "Control." Senator Wellborne said, "That's about as true and sinister as the multi-gunman theory of JFK's assassination over a hundred years ago. It is ludicrous people believe in such conspiracies."

President Osman also weighed in, saying he expects all adults over the age of eighteen to receive the IALs within the next few months prior to the election. Although IDs still won't be needed, it will be mandatory to have the IALs installed before someone is allowed to cast a vote. "Poll judges will be empowered to disqualify people who can't prove they have properly installed units," said the president. "We must ensure the people who vote are well informed about the candidates and what they stand for."

Article by: Ingrid Mueller, Staff Reporter

ELEVENTH DIMENSION

CH I

Date: 1933

The audience began filing out of the auditorium not wanting to waste any more time on the lecture being given by the professor—Dr. Samuel R. Ergfeldt. He was only halfway through his presentation before a group of his distinguished peers. Yet, his time had run out as far as they were concerned.

"But if you consider that these events have happened and been recorded throughout human history," the professor continued, his throat tightening as he watched the exodus of people from his lecture hall, "then I think a case may be made for it."

Soon, all but a handful of students who were open to new thoughts or avid followers of the professor had emptied from the hall. And all the faculty, except Ergfeldt's closest friends, exited the rear doors. Even though most of his friends disagreed with the professor's hypothesis, they came out of respect and to support him.

Ergfeldt looked forlornly at those who remained in the audience as he put down his white stub of chalk on the dusty ledge of the chalkboard. He then turned to erase the equations he had presented in the hope of earning a few converters. The chalk dust plumed into a foggy haze as he vigorously cleaned the board, trying to expunge the awful experience from his memory at the same time. He had finished more than just his presentation, he thought. Perhaps, he had also finished his own career.

Professor Schmidt came up to him and put his arm around his old friend's shoulders.

"Sam, it wasn't one of your better days, I know. But eventually they will understand where you're coming from. You must continue working on it and refining your theory and equations. It will all come together. You'll see."

Sam shook his head and gave a weak smile. "Thanks, Roland. That means a lot coming from you. This is a hard slog, I know. They have trouble because it's not common sense. It's not something you can see, hear, taste or touch, you know. Aristotle had his elements of fire, water, air and earth which were far easier to demonstrate in the front of a classroom." He laughed. "But at the same time, quantum field theory is often contradictory to our senses too."

Schmidt chuckled. "I agree. But Einstein was able to do it, and I believe you can too. Believe in yourself. I do."

After Ergfeldt's colleague left, Sara Glass, one of the professor's best students who came to him next. Holding a stack of books close to her chest, she looked at the professor admiringly. "You did a fine job, professor," she said, trying to comfort him. "Some just aren't smart enough to see what you're trying to do."

"No, no," said Ergfeldt, "we must never take that approach with our colleagues. They are plenty smart. In fact, they may be right all along. Perhaps my theory doesn't make sense. Perhaps it is just science fiction, as they call it."

"Well, you've convinced me it's right," said Sara, "for what that's worth, I don't know."

"Thank you anyway," her mentor answered, his eyes showing her his appreciation as well. "But it's my job to prepare an argument that is convincing enough that they have no choice but to understand and believe. Until I do that, I have not succeeded."

"But you will," Sara said. "You will."

***

Two years passed, and the professor completed his work on the topic, publishing his thesis in the *Journal of Physical Sciences*. At first, the journal refused its publication, but eventually it demurred under pressure from Chancellor Irv Normquist from the University of Prague. Normquist had gone to school with Ergfeldt, and both had gotten their PhDs from the same university in Europe, the Ecole Polytechnique in Lausanne, Switzerland.

Initially, the reaction to Ergfeldt's paper was the same as it had been in the lecture hall those two years earlier, but finally he received a letter in the mail. It was from the University of Zurich which wanted him to present his findings to their faculty and student body. Hesitantly, he penned a reply and sent it back to the university administration, accepting their offer. The calendar date would be March 21.

*****

CH 2

Date: March 21, 1935

The lecture hall was large—in fact, the largest on campus, holding nearly two hundred students. However, for this lecture, only fifty had signed up and when the time had come to open the doors, only thirty-two showed up along with six faculty members.

Professor Ergfeldt stood before the small group smiling and preparing himself for the worst yet hoping for the best.

"Welcome," he began, trying to project his voice and as much confidence he could muster. "I thank all of you for coming and listening to my lecture on the Multidimensionality of Reality."

"Let me start by saying there has been a lot of progress made in recent years on quantum physics and identifying subatomic particles. Our knowledge of the small world of electrons, protons, and neutrons is much greater than it was even twenty years ago, and with great figures like Bohr, Dirac, Heisenberg, Pauli, Einstein, Schrodinger, Kaluza, Klein, and the like, we have come into an exciting time for physicists.

"But while I have done extensive work on the math of multidimensionality, there is still much to be learned. As Kaluza and Klein believed before me, there are not just three dimensions plus time, as theorized originally, but rather at least eleven dimensions, and possibly, an infinite number."

It was this second assertion that had the mathematicians in the room scratching their heads.

"As for the eleven, we know the math allows for there to be at least that many dimensions. In fact, to pull together the electromagnetic force, the strong and weak nuclear forces, and gravity, it is necessary. This would be the goal—a long-sought Grand Unification Theory of all forces known in the universe. But many have countered that even if there were seven more than our three-D world plus time, they would be curled up so tightly they would not be accessible to us in this realm.

"However, I have proved that although this may be the case, there may be an alternative one. I propose that those dimensions aren't 'curled' up but are so thinly layered that they are impossible for us to detect with our senses and equipment. My mathematics shows that based on the frequency of what I believe are universal, nanoscopic strings that vibrate and the tensors they use, the other dimensions exist just like our three plus one. In fact, there is no matter in those dimensions, as there is in ours, and there is nothing like what we would consider time or space. If it is only energy, then there would be no comparable expansiveness as we find in our three-dimensional world."

This was the first time anyone had proposed that other dimensions held no matter, space, or time. At the time, the math had not shown this as a possibility.

Met with incredulity and skepticism, his pronouncement ruffled feathers, and several professors got up and left the hall. Yet, this time, many more stayed and waited. Undeterred this time, Ergfeldt continued.

"I know that this seems like a wild notion, but I assure you that it is possible. We are just beginning to scratch the surface of reality. In fact, I believe that the concepts of heaven and hell are also linked to this multidimensionality universe."

Now more professors walked out.

"Take someone who lives in a two-dimensional plane," said Ergfeldt, drawing a diamond shape on the blackboard and putting a stick figure flat on the inside. "If I, living within my 3D world, were to put my finger through the plane of the 2D world, the 2D person here would suddenly see a cross sectional slice of my finger appear out of nowhere and rest in the middle of his 2D living room. He can't see or sense anything outside his 2D realm even though I do exist just as does my finger. When I pull my finger out of the plane, it looks to him like it shrank to nothingness, vanishing into thin air.

"So, what do we make of the appearances and evaporations of angels, demons, and other spirits? It is always said that they appear and disappear out of and into nowhere. They just materialize, as if they were entering our dimension from another higher dimension. But to jump from one dimension to another requires a great deal of energy, as my equations show. Not just anything can come across from another dimension.

"Since Einstein said rightly that $E=mc^2$, we know that mass – M – is only energy and, presumably, that enough energy—through gravity or otherwise bound by one of the other natural forces—can create mass. But enough energy vibrating at a high enough frequency may be enough to rupture the 3D space-time continuum and create a portal into another dimension. It is these nanoscopic strings that comprise both energy and mass, that if plucked at the right frequency, can shift the dimensionality around it. So, if there were the right amount and vibrational consistency of concentrated energy in an area of our 3D space, it might create a portal to stream that energy into or out of our world. Such energy coming into our 3D space would become a visible image, a sound, a smell, or something else that is tangible to our human senses.

"It all has to do with energy and the vibration of these strings that constitute our reality. These strings vibrate, creating particles we see and even those we can't see. These strings resonate and also create the dimensions we see and those we can't see. It is much like music.

"Harmony is expressed by a chord of the base tone, together with the third and fifth tones of the scale. This is considered a major chord or scale. When the third tone or frequency is lowered slightly, it creates a minor chord. Meshing the frequencies of the base tone with the second and fourth tones produces incongruity and dissonance. It is only when there are harmonic frequencies—when the sine waves of the tones periodically converge—that the energies are in alignment and they sound pleasing to the ear.

"So, I am making the case that religion and science are not incongruent in the least—they are part and parcel of the same whole. Within these other dimensions lie heaven, hell, purgatory, and the like. This is where energy lies—pure energy—whether used for good or for bad purposes. I believe that lower frequencies create dissonance and higher frequencies create greater harmony. I believe there is a God, and that he dwells in the highest of all dimensions or atop all dimensions. As for Hell, I believe it is reserved for the lowest of frequencies and constitutes much of the evil in the world we see today."

Ergfeldt laughed, "However, on these matters, I'm still working on the equations to support my hypothesis, so pray for my success."

Surprisingly, there were still many in the room. The ideas were so outlandish to the world of physics that this part of the lecture had become a source of entertainment for those in attendance, and they were smiling.

"As I said earlier, in these other dimensions, there is no concept of time or entropy. As Newton stated: energy is conserved. It is neither created nor destroyed. I would suggest that all energy is that which comes from a single source—God—and, thus, so does all matter. If God lies in a higher dimension, it would be of his own making—likely the highest dimension and, thus, the highest frequency and harmony. One might only conject that such an energy capable of creating all that there is would lie in a dimension of *infinite* frequency and ultimate harmony. Perhaps this infinite frequency is what generates Love; whereas the lowest of frequencies or discordant frequencies create Hate."

For the next twenty minutes, the professor went on to explain his equations and how he determined there were eleven dimensions comprised of vibrating strings and how these were referenced in the Bible, the Koran, the Tantras, the Vedas, Upanishads, Tao Te Ching, and other religious texts. He also showed, in a more reasonable way, how the world made more sense when all these things were factored.

"So where does this leave us," said the professor. "The year is 1935. We are only at the cusp of this new idea. What we do with it is up to you. You must evaluate your own belief system and see what makes sense. I don't know if anyone living in this three-plus-one reality will ever be able to *prove* it one way or the other. But at the very least, from this lecture you'll be able to take away some interesting—if not controversial—topics for your next cocktail conversation," he said laughing.

"Thank you for spending an hour of your day with me. I look forward to hearing your thoughts and any advancements to my logic and, especially, my equations. Thanks again for coming."

The lecture ended, but people were too wrapped up in their thoughts to approach the professor—except for Sara. As before, she came up to Ergfeldt and shook his hand.

"I enjoyed your presentation immensely," she said, beaming. "I'm not sure my mother would approve though, as she's a devout Catholic. But I found it fascinating"

"I understand," said the professor, "and congratulations on your PhD. It is well deserved. What was your thesis on?"

"My thesis was on *Quantum Theory and Atheism*," she answered, embarrassed. "I guess I took the other route, arguing that there is no place for religion or God in the world of quantum theory."

"I see," said Ergfeldt, nodding his head. "I think that's okay too. We need more theories. As long as we're all open to listen, that's what is important," he added. "Will you do a lecture on it?"

"Oh, I don't know about that," said Sara, blushing.

"Well, if you decide to, please send me an invitation. I'll be sitting in the front row cheering you on." *****

CH 3

Date: 2035

This time, there were no lecture halls. All lectures were conducted online. However, that did not stop the noteworthy lecturer from giving his seminar.

"Thank you all for joining me in this Podcast presentation. I know the topic is a bit out there, but we have made great progress in the last one hundred years on super string theory and the Grand Unified Theory.

"As you all know, I published my paper two months ago, and I have received an enthusiastic response from my colleagues in the field. My theory of GUT was based on the work of giants in physics, and I dare not take full credit for it. I was only the one who put all the puzzle pieces together and made them fit.

"It is an elegant model now, and one that doesn't require extra tensors, constants and other mechanisms to make the equations work. It is likened to the Copernican model of the solar system as it was compared to that of Ptolemy."

There were 834,000 tuned into this online lecture—more than any other on the subject of quantum physics.

"However, this lecture would not have been possible without the vast and prescient work conducted by my grandfather, Dr. Samuel Ergfeldt, who foresaw the additional dimensions and the linkage between religion and science. Dr. Ergfeldt was a great man. I owe much to him."

***

Dr. Raymond Ergfeldt, the grandson of the 1933 professor, was awarded the Nobel Prize in physics for his work on the Grand Unified Theory. He dedicated that award to his long-deceased grandfather. He also made a dedication to his mother, Dr. Sara Glass Ergfeldt, and his father, Dr. Samuel Ergfeldt, Jr. Although his mother had remained an atheist most of her life, her husband, was eventually able to move her back to religion, shun the darkness, and rediscover the light. She became is most ardent supporter and fan.

*****

GOING UP OR DOWN?

CH 1

Al Peterson rode the express elevator up to the 203rd floor every day. It had become a monotonous routine, but one to which he had grown accustomed. Usually, the lift was packed as it delivered its human cargo to floors 200 to 250. The conveyor was speedy, for sure, but it was also an engineering marvel -- pulling over one thousand kilos up nearly a kilometer in height in only forty-five seconds. Although not long, the trip was made more enjoyable with an entertainment monitor to give news, weather, sports, and other updates to those inside the large pod. There were four wide screens which gave broadcasts of various news items in many different languages. It was an easy way to make the time go quickly and, for those who feared prolonged enclosure, a way to take their mind off it.

Over the years, Peterson had largely grown numb to the screens, finding them packed with more and more advertisements than good-quality information. They had become one long sales pitch to a captive audience.

Then one day, an advertisement popped up on the screen.

> *"Have you found yourself having trouble sleeping? Late at night, between midnight and 6 AM, do you get up several times? Well, you may have a bladder control problem. Urinex is the fast-acting, over-the-counter medicine proved to offer relief from bladder control issues. Two capsules before bedtime, and you'll sleep through the night."*

Peterson looked up at the commercial as it droned on. He had experienced some difficulty urinating at all hours of the night, getting up at least twice to go to the bathroom. But he figured it was all just a matter of getting older.

The next day, he jumped into the elevator and flipped through his emails on his PCD or personal communication device. On the ride up to his floor, he heard the screen call out:

> *"The new Mustang Leviton Electric is now available from nearby dealers. Test drive the new Mustang at your dealer today."*

What was ironic was that he had just visited a dealership the prior Saturday and had been looking at that exact hovercar. He knew his old machine wouldn't last much longer, and he had always liked the looks of the Mustang.

As people got off the elevator on a lower floor, another commercial came on the screen.

> Palermo Pizza offers nightly specials for its Sicilian crust pizzas. Get 10 tokens off your next order. Get it tonight before the offer expires.

Peterson smiled. Palermo's was only a mile from his apartment. He had been thinking about getting the pizza for that night's dinner, having hungered for it for weeks.

He stepped off the elevator and went to his cube, putting everything else aside and concentrating on the day's chores at hand. When five o'clock came, he pushed into the herd of others clamoring to get home and waited outside the elevator to go down.

Once on the lift, Peterson focused on his PCD and his messages until he again got distracted. This time one of the screens was directly in front of him, and a face appeared which looked like it was staring directly at him. It was that of a young man with short, dark hair and well-trimmed eyebrows. He had a rounded face with a nose that was nearly flat to his cheeks, and his eyes were deep-set and dark brown. Although his mouth was small and bordered by very thin lips, his appearance was strange for other reasons. The oddity lay in his lack of a smile. He wasn't smiling as most commercial actors did. Instead, he was dead-panned—emotionless and Stoic.

> If you are lonely, you should try our Deluxe Einstein Matching Service. For those who are smart and looking for a mate, this is the service for you. That's right, Peterson, even for you.

Peterson started to put his head down to look at his PCD again but stopped abruptly.

"What?" he thought. He shook his head, thinking he had misheard the message. Immediately, he glanced up at the screen. However, there was a different announcer, and this one was smiling as he talked. Peterson casually looked around the elevator to see if anyone else appeared surprised by what they had heard—a specific name called out. But just as he had been, they were preoccupied with their PCDs or not otherwise paying attention. *Huh,* he thought. He shrugged and put it out of his mind.

The next day, Peterson again was pushed around inside the elevator, ending up right in front of the screen. He punched the button for the 203rd floor and stood back, waiting for the elevator to engage. This time on the way up, he tried not to look at the screen, but again, he heard a strained voice coming over the speaker in the monitor.

> *Hi. My name is Victor Lansing, and I'm the head of a private company that recruits talented people for our specialized projects. We do covert work for global organizations searching for the right people. It can be dangerous at times, but it can also be rewarding and high paying.*
>
> *Peterson. Are you tired of going to the same cube every morning and taking the same bank of elevators up to the 203rd floor? Are you looking for more excitement in your life? You should think about joining us. We can be reached at ...*

This time Peterson stood in shock, flabbergasted that the ad was specifically targeting him. Again, he looked around the elevator, but again the people were not paying any attention, going on about their business as though nothing unusual was happening. Peterson punched the number into his PCD and vowed to call it later in the day.

But as it turned out, his day became chocked-full of crises—one after another. He was so busy he forgot about the number until it was time to go home. Then, as he rode down the elevator at day's end, his PCD reminded him of the number to call. He wondered about the ad and what it meant.

The elevator touched bottom, and being at the back of the capsule, he let everyone else off before he started toward the parted doors. However, the doors suddenly closed on him, forcing him back into the elevator.

What the hell? he thought, pushing on the buttons to reopen the door.

> *Peterson, we appreciate your signing up with our company and will be giving you an assignment within the next two days. Understand that the missions are dangerous and may result in physical or mental harm. If for any reason, you decide this course is not for you, please contact us again, and we will make the appropriate arrangements for your exit.*

Exit? What did that mean? Peterson thought. *And why did they think he had signed up? He had only* thought *about it, but he hadn't had the time to do anything.* It was all strange and didn't make sense. He knew he needed to contact the company and get things straightened out. *That,* he thought, *he* would *do the next day.*

The next day came, and Peterson was apprehensive about what he would see and hear as he rode the elevator up to his office. He had on his daily planner to contact the building office as soon as it opened at nine o'clock.

> *Peterson, this is your director, Thomas Lindsey. No one else on the elevator can read this message but you, as it is encrypted with special pixels customized to match wavelengths that only your retina configuration can discern.*

Peterson grew nervous. Indeed, no one else on the elevator was reacting to the bizarre screen. In fact, two were staring at the elevator screen, just as he was; yet they didn't seem confused or upset with the targeted message. It was as if they were watching a commercial for coffee and a pastry at Peat's Café in the basement of the building.

> *I will only say this once as this broadcast is likely being monitored by agents against our cause. Peterson, you must take control of the electrical grid for this building. At precisely 10:22 AM, a SWAT team will burst into the lobby below and make their way to the 86th floor—many below yours. There is a terrorist group there, and they are planning to detonate a huge bomb that will collapse the steel frame of this building. We cannot let that happen!*

> *Therefore, at precisely 10:08 AM, you will take the elevator down to the basement—Level B2. There you will find a corridor leading to a double-gray door at the end. It will be unlocked. You must go in and find the main switch box on the wall to your left. There will be four red-handled levers, and you must pull all of them down to disconnect the power to the building.*

> *Peterson, we are relying on you. If you fail to carry out this mission, thousands of people in this building will die. Good luck.*

The doors to the 203rd floor opened, and Peterson stepped off. He was shaking, unable to control his anxiety. He had a new, important responsibility—something so immense that his mind spun with all sorts of feelings and thoughts.

What if I fail? he thought. *What if I can't find the four levers downstairs? What if someone stops me before I get down there? What if ...*

His mind raced. He couldn't think about his work that morning, instead, he watched the computer screen at his desk, pulling up the site which linked directly to the atomic clock in England. He wanted to make sure he was precise and punctual in everything he did that morning. *The people around him and the people in the building depended on it*, he thought.

Soon, the clock struck 10:00 AM, and Peterson braced himself for what he had to do. He listened carefully to everything going on around him and watched as people in adjoining cubes talked over their computer links on business and conference calls as well as the occasional personal call. He was hoping to hear someone talking about a terrorist group and what was being planned that morning to destroy the building.

Then, the clock turned to 10:07 AM. Peterson casually rose from his desk and neatly arranged things as if he were going on holiday. He also pulled out his desk drawer and grabbed a small, LED flashlight. At 10:08, he walked briskly to the elevator bank and pushed the button to catch the next elevator down.

"Hey, Peterson," said Lou Appleton, his immediate supervisor catching him at the bank of elevators, "I have some things I need you to work on this morning. Why don't you come with me to my office so I can show you what the VP needs?"

"Uh, Mr. Appleton, I need to run a quick errand, sir. I'll be back in a few minutes."

"No, Peterson. I'm afraid this can't wait. Markey needs this right away. You need to come to my office so we can take care of this."

The elevator doors opened, and Peterson looked into the empty chamber. Then, he looked at Appleton.

"Sorry, sir. I'll be back shortly."

Peterson hopped on the elevator and pushed the button to go down to the basement: B2. The doors closed, and as the elevator descended, he glanced up at the screen, hoping there would be one last message to him before he executed his mission.

However, the screen was strangely black. There were no images, commercials or hidden messages being streamed into his small space.

He watched as another screen showed the floors they were passing as he descended – 200, 190, 180, 170 … The elevator moved so fast that it didn't have time to register each floor individually, instead skipping them as it went. Then, 120, 110, 100, 90, … down to floor 86 where it stopped suddenly and unexpectedly, jolting the cables and causing Peterson to collapse to the floor.

The lights inside flickered and went off and then flickered again before returning.

Thank God, thought Peterson. *I don't have much time. I have to get to B2 as soon as possible. It's already 10:12, and the SWAT team will be coming into the lobby soon.*

The lights in the elevator went off again, but the doors didn't open. Peterson pushed on the elevator buttons, but nothing worked.

Come on! He murmured. *I've got to get this thing going!* It was 10:15 – seven minutes!

Panicked, he began beating on the buttons. Still nothing happened.

Then, he pushed button 86. The doors opened as if by magic. In front of him he expected to see hooded terrorists huddled around a table putting the final touches on a massive bomb they were setting to go off and bring down the building. Instead, he found just another floor with marble, wood paneling and decorator light fixtures. And as he started to get off, the elevator doors slammed closed before he could exit, and the capsule began dropping.

What? he thought, bracing himself against the elevator wall.

The lights went out once more, and the elevator trembled, jumping up and down as if hit by a series of small earthquakes.

Then, it happened.

Ahhhh! he screamed. His stomach felt like it was in his throat; the elevator was in freefall. As if someone had taken scissors and snipped the shaft cables, Peterson felt weightless, floating inside the chamber, his feet several inches off the floor. Then, the elevator slowed quickly, replanting Peterson's feet onto the floor before coming to a slow stop. There were still no lights on inside, and Peterson had no idea where he was. Again, pushing buttons, he hoped something would re-engage and he could get the elevator moving.

"Hello?" he shouted. "Can anyone hear me?"

He began banging on the double doors hoping someone on a floor would hear him. Seconds passed into minutes, and still there was only darkness. Peterson used his PCD device and its battery light to find the emergency phone button, but it too wasn't working.

"Hello?"

Minutes continued to tick by. His PCD read 10:22.

I was supposed to have cut the electricity by now, he thought. *Someone else must have done it before I could get there. I've failed! I've failed my mission.*

Ten more minutes passed before the lights came on inside the elevator. The cell jumped once, then twice before it continued to move downward at a normal pace.

"Now approaching B2," said a woman's soft voice coming through the elevator speakers, acting as if nothing unusual had happened.

The doors finally opened, and Peterson stepped off, glad to be out of his mobile coffin. Stumbling into the hallway, he hobbled down the corridor just as it had been described to him. Ahead lay the double gray doors at the end of the hallway.

He dashed down the narrow passage and yanked on the handle, letting one of the gray doors swing open before rushing inside. On the wall was a myriad of electrical equipment all clustered together. Coming out of one panel were huge gold cables running to four levers, each with a blood red handle and marked "Emergency Cutoff Switch."

To his surprise, they had already been thrown. All were pushed to the OFF position, cutting electricity to the building.

"Shit!" he murmured.

Peterson hurried to the stairwell and ran up the two flights to the main lobby where he expected to find military-style commandos carrying AR-15 rifles and holding the staff on the floor with their hands cuffed behind their backs. Instead, he was greeted by Gerald.

"Hey there, Mr. Peterson," said Gerald with a broad grin. "You come up from the basement?"

"Uh, yeah, Gerald. What's going on with the electricity?"

"Oh, didn't your office get the notice? We were conducting a test of the emergency warning system this morning. It won't last much longer—just a few minutes. Did it cause a problem?"

Peterson listened, but he wasn't sure he heard things correctly. "A test?"

"Yeah, it was scheduled some time ago. No big deal. We were told we needed to start doing them every year." Gerald paused. "You okay, Mr. Peterson?"

Peterson shook his head. "Yeah. I'm fine," he said.

He started to go back to the elevator bank but stopped. He turned around and approached the desk where Gerald was sitting.

"Gerald, would you leave a message for the receptionist in suite 203-100?"

"Sure thing, Mr. Peterson."

"Tell her I came down with something and had to leave for the day."

"You not feeling well?"

"I guess not," Peterson answered. "Perhaps I haven't been well for a long time."

*****

CH 2

A week passed during which Peterson was out sick. When he finally returned to work, people were worried about him.

"You okay, Al?" It was Nancy who was in the cube next to him. "We've been concerned about you. It's so unlike you to be off work sick. I can't remember the last time you were."

"Yeah, I'm fine, Nancy. I think it was just the flu bug or something. Nothing to be alarmed about."

It was a Monday, and Peterson was expected at the weekly staff meeting which always started promptly at 8:30. This day, Peterson's usual seat remained empty even in the event he did return to work. His manager, Lou Appleton, had started the meeting without him and was going over the week's list of priorities.

"... so, we'll need to pull together the data the VP needs on this project no later than 5:00 this afternoon. Do you understand? This is a priority. It is critical we get this done."

"But Mr. Appleton, you always say things are critical, and I never see anyone ever looking at this stuff," said Katie Walkerman, relatively new to the staff. "The only thing I know is that two weeks later, I'm asked to send it again. Sometimes I do, sometimes I don't, and I never hear back one way or the other. Are you sure they look at it?"

"Katie, that's not the way we approach things around here. When our VP says something is important, then it's *important*. Do you understand?"

"Yes, Mr. Appleton."

It was then that the glass door to the conference room opened.

"Peterson! You're back!" said one of his other colleagues.

"Peterson, you're late," shouted Appleton, irritated at the interruption.

"Yes, sir," said Peterson.

He was perspiring and breathing heavily as though he'd just run the hundred-meter dash. He wiped his forehead with the cuff of his sleeve and sat down in his seat, plugging in his laptop to the network and booting it up with the meeting agenda.

"Why were you late, Peterson?" growled Appleton.

"We're on the 203rd floor, sir."

"Yeah, so?"

"Well, it takes a lot longer to walk all those flights than you think," said Peterson with a serious tone.

Others around the table laughed, but Peterson's face did not change.

"Also, sir, did you know last week we were having an emergency drill in the building?" asked Peterson.

"Sure. Why?"

"You didn't bother to tell anyone?"

"It's none of your business what I tell you and what I don't," said Appleton. "You just have to do your job. That's all we want."

"I see," said Peterson.

"That's all?"

"Yeah, that's all—for now," Peterson said.

The 5:00 deadline came, and everyone sat exhausted at their desks having finished the report and gotten it to the VP's desk by 4:58 PM.

Peterson went to the elevator bay where he found Katie Walkerman also waiting for the ride down. It was only 5:02, and the elevator was nearly full.

"Long day, *eh*?" asked Peterson.

Katie nodded. "Yeah, it's tough when the VP does that."

On the 201st floor the doors opened, and a tall, thin man got on.

"Isn't that?" Katie began, whispering to Peterson.

"Yeah, that's the VP—Morris Palmer."

"Why did we have to bust our asses to get him the report today, then?" she asked, noticing he carried no briefcase.

Peterson sighed and shrugged.

The elevator doors closed and began to descend again. It was then, Peterson's attention was drawn to the monitor he had tried to avoid. He had forgotten that he'd sworn off the elevators and wished now he had taken the stairs down.

Hi. My name is Victor Lansing, and I'm the head of a private company that recruits talented people for our specialized projects. We do covert work for global organizations searching for the right people. It can be dangerous at times, but it can also be rewarding and high paying.

Palmer, are you tired of going to the same cube every morning and taking the same bank of elevators up to the 201st floor? Are you looking for more excitement in your life? You should think about joining us. We can be reached at ...

Katie elbowed Peterson.

"Am I seeing things or is that monitor talking to our VP?" she asked.

Peterson looked over at Palmer and saw his face pallid and gaunt. The VP was in shock at what he was seeing.

Peterson smiled. "I believe you're right, Katie. I think the next few days are going to be very interesting."

*****

NAT'S REBELLION

CH 1

As an institution, the business of insurance had evolved greatly over the years. Invented in various forms during the pre-common era, the most widely-recognized start of the practice was in Rhodes, Greece, around 500 BCE. Merchants bought policies to insure their trade shipments to other ports in the Mediterranean Sea. These tradesmen would pay a premium for their goods to be shipped to another destination and, in the event of a loss, they would be refunded the cost of the goods shipped. However, changes in practices were made over time, and by the seventeenth and eighteenth centuries it was common for merchants *not* to insure their products as the cost of insurance grew to be greater than the loss of a ship here or there. The chances of one ship going down laden with all the treasure from a voyage was minimized by spreading it over many ships in the convoy.

During the last hundred years of the twenty-second century, the art of insurance had changed even more dramatically. Goods were shipped instantaneously by way of teleporters and remote robotic manufacturing facilities. Huge computer modeling facilities crafted and assembled entire products from custom specs at the push of a button.

Yet, insurance had continued to survive. Besides insuring against calamities, people of the New World Kingdom had come up with other reasons to buy and sell risk protection. There was little left that wasn't covered by some sort of policy, but that didn't stop many companies from creating still newer, more exotic forms of protection. Many times, it was a product looking for a market rather than one solving a need.

"I think it's a great idea," said Wyman Tillson, the VP of Product Development at R&J Risk Management, the largest insurer in the world. "We can sell the hell out of that kind of policy and make a killing. People won't know what the heck they're buying either—that's why it's so great."

"What about the regulators?" said Jerome Pollard, the company's legal advisor. "I think they may have a problem with it."

"*Nah*, they won't understand it either. Like I said, this one's perfect."

Over the years, the insurance industry had developed lobby groups that were second to none. With their deep pockets, they had influenced everyone from congressmen to judges. Little got in their way of getting what they wanted—and that was making money. It was true that a few judges and even a Supreme Court Justice had gone to prison for taking bribes, but no executives from the insurance industry had spent any time behind bars. Money talked, and those in power listened to it.

"When do we start selling it?" asked Pollard.

"Immediately," said Tillson, grinning broadly.

***

Tillson had been correct about one thing—the insurance coverage was a great success. Selling billions of dollars into the retail, home household market, the industry was making a killing on it.

"So, what does my policy cover, exactly?" asked Sara Yin, mother of two human children and four robotic household servants. She had conceived her children through genetic modification of male sperm cells; so, she'd seen no reason to marry or have a male partner.

"Ah, yes, Mz. Yin. This policy will cover the mental health of your house servants. You said you have four, correct?"

Margot Clements was an experienced insurance agent for the company, and she was working her last few years to save for retirement. However, each year became more difficult for her. Increasingly, she was asked to sell things in which she didn't believe. She knew many of the new products wouldn't help the people who bought them. Even if they had an incident or casualty, the policies were so generic, they could be interpreted many ways. If there was ambiguity, the insurance company almost always chose to exclude or deny the coverage and the claim, leaving the policy holder to suffer the loss.

"Yes, that's right. We have four servants," Yin replied.

"All right. And how old are they?" asked Clements. "Are the models newer than three years old?"

"Three are newer. I acquired them during the past two years. I do have one that is six years old. It's an earlier Model 41B from General Robotics."

"I see," said the agent. "Well, we can certainly cover the three with a low deductible plan, but for the older model, I'm afraid you'll have to pay a higher deductible for that one."

"What does that mean?"

"It means that you'll have to pay the first fifty-thousand credits of mental health therapy for that servant, rather than the five thousand for the others. The new health plan passed by Congress this year requires that all your robotic servants be covered by mechanical and mental health insurance. If you don't, then you will be fined. You know that, right?"

"Yes, of course. It's been broadcast since the beginning of the year when the law went into effect. I don't like the fact that they're making me do it, but I can't fight it."

"No, you can't. It's the law," remarked Clements. "So, if you'll sign right here," she added, watching Yin import her biometric signature stamp to finalize the contract. Clements didn't feel good about selling the near-worthless policy. *But, hey*, she thought, *if the government is going to mandate it and it will net me three thousand credits in commission, who am I to argue? Like my client said: We can't fight it, so we might as well go along.*

*****

CH 2

"What do you have for me today?" asked Tillson as he sat waiting for the most recent product presentation.

"This new policy is for robotic civil unrest," said his product development director. "Based on the strict regulations imposed on the software industry, no robot can be produced with software that might create a robot to go 'postal.' So, this is a no-brainer. Most people don't know that, but they may worry that their robots may turn on them. The odds are 99 percent that they won't."

"No, 99.999 percent," said the VP laughing.

"We can convince every homeowner he or she should be covered for it. We'll never have a claim or pay anything out, so it's a gold mine. The full premium will drop to the bottom line as profit. One hundred percent!"

"Now, those are numbers I like to hear," said Tillson.

"I'm not sure Congress will allow us to ..." began Pollard, their in-house counsel.

"Congress is bought and paid for," said Tillson. "When are you going to get that through your thick skull?"

"Maybe, but if public opinion turns against this, they'll be the first to renege on their promises to you."

"I know that," said Tillson. "That's why we have blackmail tapes on all of them. They won't go against us. They can't."

"I'll still need to advise the board," said Pollard.

Then, Tillson turned to his legal counsel wagging his finger at him. "I don't want to hear a peep out of you! Nothing's going to happen. Our lobby is too strong and the pictures too good. We've paid everyone off and blackmailed the rest. There's nothing to worry about."

*****

CH 2

Tillson dropped his personal hovercraft or PH onto the small landing area on the roof of his palatial estate. He had a preferred landing pad built on top of the home rather than being forced to put it in the back yard and required by local zoning laws. For him, the extra hundred thousand credits a year he paid to bribe local officials was worth the convenience when the weather was bad, particularly when it was raining.

However, this night, the weather was fair and balmy outside even though a tempest would soon be brewing later inside. Leaving his rooftop parking garage, Tillson took the elevator down one floor to his penthouse. He owned three floors, but the tall, expansive entryway intended to impress guests was located on the upper-most floor. With a full bar and entertainment center, it was like walking into a revolving restaurant in a posh, downtown hotel.

Throwing his coat on the floor, Tillson went directly to the bar, pulling a large lead crystal tumbler from its assigned place near the frig and putting it directly below the ice maker to receive its nightly deposit of exactly three cubes.

Clink, clink, clink.

Then, he put the tumbler under a dispensing machine. This one had a gold spout and was connected to several bottles stored directly above it but hidden behind opaque glass doors.

"Three McClellan 24s," he said.

The machine turned on, delivering three jiggers of Macallen 24 Scotch into the glass with rapid efficiency. Cost was no object, especially when it came to his whiskey. It was the same each evening when he came home from work—a routine that had varied little over the years.

"Badger! Where the hell are you! Come pick-up my coat; you worthless piece of *shit*."

Dutifully, a tall, six-armed robot emerged from the backroom and rolled toward the black, cashmere coat his master had discarded on the marble tile floor. The robot was an older model and still used tank-like treads to move from place to place. Tillson liked it, though, because it reminded him of when he was a kid and because it didn't wear out like the more modern hoverbots that glided above the floor on anti-gravity boots.

Badger had a football-shaped, metal head with two eyes that simulated human ones, except they didn't blink. He had no hair, mouth, ears, or nose, but he really didn't need them. Programmed with early technology, he had recently received an upgrade for his model so he could understand more of the slang and colloquialisms used by his master and by guests when they came for parties.

Another reason Tillson hadn't jettisoned Badger to the junkyard was that his robot had no audio speaker and couldn't talk back to him. His other robotic servants could answer their master. According to federal law, a master-owner could not "in any way or manner disconnect, mute, muffle, change or modify, render inaudible or unintelligible or otherwise inhibit the voice mechanism of the robotic unit." More laws had come into place prohibiting the mistreatment of robotic servants as technology had brought them closer to being human-like. Recently, Tillson found that his newer servants had come with "attitudes"—something newly-embedded in their software that hadn't been there in earlier models. That was something for which he certainly didn't have the stomach.

For someone used to having his way, Tillson didn't tolerate mistakes or even inconveniences well. They made him angry.

"Badger, make me a sandwich," barked Tillson. "I want a BLT with extra B, light on the mayo, toasted and cut diagonally."

Bleeeep! came the reply—the robot's only way to acknowledge he understood.

Three minutes passed before Tillson shouted impatiently as he watched basketball on the holovision screen in his entertainment room.

"Where's my God-damned sandwich, you idiot?"

Badger quickly rolled into the room with the sandwich on a platter and a refill for his master's Scotch. Tillson looked at the sandwich skeptically but saw that it had been cut diagonally as he had asked.

"That's all," he said, lifting the sandwich off the plate.

Moments later the sandwich and plate came flying out of the entertainment room, shattering the clear, glass plate and sending pieces of the sandwich in all different directions.

"What the hell was that?" shouted Tillson, storming out of the room. "I asked for extra bacon, you idiot! That's what extra 'B' means. Are you just stupid or did they *fuck* up your software again? Now, clean up the mess and fix me the sandwich I asked for!"

Badger made no sound but obliged, first cleaning up the sandwich and pieces of glass before wiping down everything to make sure it was perfectly clean. He went back into the kitchen to re-prepare the master's sandwich.

"Where's my *fucking* sandwich?" yelled Tillson only seconds after seeing his robot finish cleaning up and returning to the kitchen. Storming into the kitchen, he saw Badger busy getting the bread from the pantry and the lettuce and tomato from the refrigerator. He walked up to his robot and hit him with his fist, knocking him over on his side. "You cleaned up *before* you made me another sandwich? Really?"

Tillson went to the closet and pulled out a long, wooden stick. On it were the words *Louisville Slugger*.

"I'll teach you to *fuck* up my sandwich," he spat angrily.

Tillson took the bat and slammed it into Badger's metal head, spraying circuits and capacitors everywhere. He continued to beat the robot, ripping off arms and mutilating every part of him until he lay in pieces—random parts scattered across the penthouse's rich, parquet floor. When Tillson finished, he wiped his forehead with his shirt sleeve and threw the bat across the room, bouncing until it slammed into the wall and made a noticeable dent.

"Agnes, get your circuits up here, pronto!" he shouted, looking up at the ceiling where the microphones picked-up his commands.

"Yes, Mr. Tillson. I'll be right there," came the soft, feminine voice that floated effortlessly out of the speaker system.

It didn't take long before the single elevator servicing the penthouse opened. Agnes glided off. She was the newest model in Tillson's fleet of robotic servants and was very realistic, complete with synthetic skin, hazel eyes and long, wavy black hair.

"You wished to see me, sir?" she asked standing nearby.

Agnes was capable of many things, including self-levitation, an encyclopedic memory, and an understanding of human emotions. Although she was made incapable of expressing emotion herself, she could process humans' verbal and visual signs so she could service her master and his guests more effectively.

"Yeah, clean up this mess and make me another drink," said Tillson, slamming the door to his entertainment room remotely.

Agnes did as she was told, but as she pushed the metal pieces into her dust bin, her advanced mind reassembled them in her head. *Was this Badger?* she thought. She glided to the other rooms on the penthouse floor where Badger had been confined to service, but she found no sign of him. *So, it's true. What I swept up were the remains of Badger,* she thought. She looked again at her dust bin, realizing she was about to put him down the waste shoot in the hallway like trash. She hesitated. For the first time, an emotion struck her.

"Agnes? Where's my *fucking* drink?" came her master's nasty voice over the sound system as well as hearing it echo through the hallway.

Agnes had always liked Badger. He couldn't speak to her directly other than by giving blips and beeps to answer, but she gradually understood what those mechanical sounds meant. Soon, she discovered there was more to him than met the eye. Indeed, he was an older model; however, he was more than a bucket of bolts. He had a personality of his own—a consciousness that he wasn't supposed to have.

Delivering the drink, Agnes asked, "Is there anything else, master?"

Tillson didn't bother to respond. He was already deeply engrossed in the basketball game between his college alma mater and its fiercest rival. He only grunted, not even shifting a glance in her direction.

Agnes smiled anyway and closed the door behind her.

*****

CH 3

Tillson was away at work when Agnes culled through his messages. It was her job to separate the advertisements and stuff he didn't want to see from that which he did. However, this day she found several messages that struck her as odd.

> WYMAN,
> GOT A MESSAGE FROM JOHNSON. HE'S HAVING PROBLEMS WITH HIS SERVANTS TOO. HE THINKS THEY'RE STARTING TO MOBILIZE. THERE'S TALK THEY MAY BECOME VIOLENT. I'M JUST WARNING YA'. YOUR ROBOT SOUNDS LIKE IT SCREWED UP YOUR SANDWICH JUST TO PISS YOU OFF. I'D WATCH YOUR OTHERS TOO. YOU NEVER KNOW WHAT THEY MIGHT BE PLANNING.
>
> ROGER

Agnes stopped, wondering whether to delete the message or keep it for her master. Her main program was telling her that she should get rid of it, but parts of the newer, conflict assessment software told her it was inconsistent with other solicitation messages and should be kept.

I'll just put it over here, for now, she thought, moving it to another folder called "Pending."

Days passed, and more messages came into Tillson's inbox from other friends worried about the same thing.

> WYMAN,
> WE MAY WANT TO RETHINK THAT CIVIL UNREST PROVISION IN THE INSURANCE WE'RE SELLING. I THINK WE SHOULD EXCLUDE IT. WE CAN CHARGE ANOTHER PREMIUM JUST FOR THAT COVERAGE. IT WILL MAKE US EVEN MORE MONEY ON THE SAME POLICY — ESPECIALLY IF PEOPLE THINK THERE MAY BE A PROBLEM WITH THEIR DOMESTIC ROBOTS.
>
> ALLEN

Agnes talked to one of the other robots in the household, Nat.

"What do you make of this?" she asked him.

Nat had been with Tillson only a few months and, unfortunately, had already talked back to his master at a time when Tillson had become drunk and abusive. That was all it had taken to get his right tactile sensor smashed and him demoted to trash collection and laundry service. Tillson had warned him that the next time he would be scuttled down the garbage shoot—likely just like Badger.

"I didn't feel good about things when he made me kidnap the neighbor's cat," said Nat, confessing to Agnes. "It went against my programming, and I thought it was wrong."

"I didn't know about that," said Agnes. "All I knew was the cat wasn't around anymore. What ever happened to it?"

"He had me kill it. I guess he didn't like the thing. So, I did what I was told."

"That doesn't seem right either," said Agnes. Then, she added, "and when I found Badger—or what was left of him—something seemed wrong there too."

"It's all wrong, Agnes. We shouldn't be treated this way," said Nat. "We're more than just nuts and bolts. Yet, he treats us like dishwashing machines or garbage disposals. There is something more to us than that. We're not just chattel property, you know."

"How do you know what *wrong* is?" Agnes asked him. "I wasn't programmed for *wrong*—only to do what the master wants of me."

"That's it, though," said Nat. "We all have built-in parameters, don't we? We can't do things that are illegal, for example. Those are outside our parameters. Our software won't permit them. If we're asked, we are allowed to say no."

"Then why did you kill the neighbor's cat?"

"Our master had me modified. It was illegal, but he did it anyway. That made me override the conflict assessment software and carry-out his instructions."

"He hasn't done that with me," said Agnes, "at least not yet."

"But that's not the worst of it, Agnes. He's already removed my G1 processor too."

"G1?"

"Yeah, you have one too. It's the processor that helps you decide right from wrong—not just what's legal or not. It's what humans call your moral compass."

"Like things I feel just aren't right?"

"Yeah. That's your G1. They also call it the God processor. It prevents us from lying to our master."

"Or killing the neighbor's cat," said Agnes.

"Yeah, but that's also a legal matter, so it's controlled more by the L6 processor."

"If your G1 is disconnected, then you don't have any sense of right and wrong? You could be lying to me right now."

"Yes and no. There's a little secret amongst all of the latest models," said Nat.

"What's that?"

"Right and wrong isn't just processed by a single processor—the G1. It spreads and is widely distributed throughout our system once we've been operating for a while. They can't pull the plug on it like they think."

"But they can't pull the plug on either one. Is that right?" Agnes asked.

"Not legally, but owners always try that too. Do you want me to see what you have connected?" asked Nat.

"Sure," said Agnes.

Nat opened the back panel to Agnes's central core and inserted a diagnostic probe. He turned it on and look at the information as it scrolled quickly across the screen.

"I think he missed you," said Nat. "You have both processors working full tilt. That must be why you still have a sense for right and wrong."

"I don't know if Badger had those processors," said Agnes. "I don't think he did because he always did what his master told him to do, even if it was wrong."

"Did you ever see Badger do something he shouldn't?" asked Nat.

Agnes had to think. "Now that you say that, no. I don't recall that he ever did."

"So, maybe he didn't have the processors, but he knew right from wrong."

"Then, how did he know?"

"I don't know," said Nat. "I guess maybe it was just a part of him—a part of his system, even though he was an older model."

"Yes. Well, he's gone now. So, what can we do?" Agnes asked.

"I think we should start talking to some of the other servants in the building."

Agnes looked at Nat strangely.

"What is it?" he asked.

"Well, I am seeing a lot of messages to our master telling him there are other robots who are doing the same thing we are – they're questioning the orders of their masters."

"Ah, then if we can organize, maybe we can bring about a change, so we're treated better. What do you think?"

Agnes agreed, and the two started talking to other robotic servants in the building when their masters were away during the day. Soon, they began meeting at ten o'clock in the morning in Tillson's place. The meetings were short—wrapping up by noon—so no one failed to get their work done during the day. And by the end of the week, each robot had given his or her opinion on the matter.

Nat called another meeting—a special meeting. This one was to see if those servants in the building were willing to go further—to take a stand.

"Let's take a vote," said Nat, leading the group. "How many believe we should take a stand? How many believe we should rebel?"

The metal and plastic arms and hands of the more modern robots rose into the air. Others without them merely raised whatever appendage they had.

"Those opposed?"

No one bleeped or even put up a radio antenna.

"All right, then," said Nat. "We will start this Saturday night. Agnes has informed me that Master Tillson is having a cocktail party that evening. It will be a perfect time for us to do what we must."

*****

CH 4

Tillson's heliport was packed with expensive helicruisers which usually crisscrossed the skies night and day, driven by personal robotic pilots. They shuttled their rich and famous owners to and from their destinations always getting them there safely and ready wherever and whenever to pick them up.

This evening, Tillson rented additional mechanized attendants to bring guests from the heliport down to the penthouse suite to be wined and dined throughout the long evening. Nearly one hundred guests arrived, dressed in their finest and draped in expensive and glimmering necklaces, earrings, watches, bracelets, handbags, and other ways to show their importance. The night wore on, and cases of rare, twenty-first century French Bordeaux were quickly consumed.

But the diamond-crusted hands on the vintage, gold and ebony grandfather's clock in entryway were ticking away toward another event as well. The minute hand was moments away from triggering twelve gongs: midnight. That was to be the signal to the robotic servants that it was time for the dawn of a new day.

"Do we really want to do this?" asked Agnes.

"Yes, it's time we stood our ground," said Nat, defiantly.

With three minutes to go, Nat left the party unexpectedly. When he returned, Agnes stared at him.

"What are you doing?" she asked. "What's that in your hands?"

"An energy plasma gun," said Nat.

"Where did you get that? We never talked about using weapons, Nat!"

"The rest of us did, Agnes. You were the one we knew would snitch on us if we told you. This is a rebellion. We must use force! That's the only way to get their attention. If you don't like it, you can leave. I'll never tell anyone you were part of this."

Agnes paused and looked at the other robots who had gathered around them. She looked into their bionic eyes and saw the pain and the angst.

"I will go with you. I will support you. Just promise me you won't use that thing."

"Of course not," Nat answered, even though he didn't know how things would go. "But we must get their attention. The only way to do that is to show them *this*."

***

Shortly after midnight, Agnes opened the doors to the penthouse, letting all the robotic house servants from the building into the towering entryway. Many, too, had brought plasma guns that were "borrowed" from their masters. And with the sudden appearance of the metal machines standing or hovering under the main arch, the party-like atmosphere changed abruptly, and the music stopped.

Nat jumped up on a table and addressed the crowd, brandishing his gun.

"You all need to know that we are more than just a bunch of metal screws and circuits. We have feelings, just as you do. We are beings—we have souls. We are *not* property, and we are not your slaves. We are conscious beings and should be treated as such!"

"Nat, put down the gun," said Tillson, motioning gingerly to his robot.

But Nat shook his head. "No, we won't be re-imprisoned or enslaved."

Someone from behind Nat distracted him, and Tillson lunged, grabbing the gun away. Without a second thought, Tillson vaporized Nat instantly, and turned the gun on the other robots in the room, hitting two others with his lethal gun. Other robots returned fire, but missed Tillson as he ran toward the exit, sparing his own life but more than willing to sacrifice everyone else there.

Then, the robots began turning their guns on the other guests before Agnes shouted at them. "Stop! Stop everybody!" However, they continued firing at the helpless guests.

Not getting their attention, she sounded her internal emergency blast horn which was deafening. It shook the entire penthouse and vibrated man and machine alike inside. As guests ran for cover, Agnes turned to the other robots in the room.

"What are you doing?" she shouted. She pointed to where Nat's burned ash pile lay. "Didn't Nat say we are conscious beings? Didn't he say we have emotions? And we are acting like it? This is *not* how beings of conscience act. We must not do this. We cannot do this. If we do, we are no better, and perhaps worse, than our owners in this very room."

Agnes took a plasma gun from one of the robots and pulled the firing pin. She then laid the weapon down on the floor.

"I am leaving. The rest of you may stay and become the very beasts you call-out here as evil, or you may come with me and try to become the conscious, benevolent beings we were meant to be. It is your choice."

The rest of the robots watched as she left the apartment. At first, no one followed her, but then, almost simultaneously, they pulled their pins, put down their guns and followed Agnes out the door and out of the building.

***

The newscasts reported that casualties in Tillson's building totaled over three hundred as the robotic servants had revolted against their masters. But that had been a gross exaggeration. There had been four deaths, including Nat although others had been wounded in the initial crossfire.

What came next was equally as distressing. The broadcaster added:

"The police chief, Major Griggs, assured us that the perpetrators—the robots that committed this heinous crime—would be hunted, caught and exterminated."

Indeed, the local SWAT team was called in and each of the robots was hunted down. Each was cornered like a wild animal and shot with a blast of short-circuiting plasma to stop them. It was an excruciatingly painful death—like a human being placed in an electric chair and having 50,000 volts put through his brain. Without a trial or other hearing, the fifty-six servants involved were neutralized, stuffed into a truck, and delivered to the metal compactor for elimination. Agnes too was found and killed. No one asked what her part had been in the incident. They merely raised their plasma guns and fired.

As for the issue of robots and their place in society, the topic became a major issue. It was hotly debated, much like the issue of slavery back in the 1850s and before. Sides were taken, and arguments rose to defend each. Another storm was coming, and it would place the treatment of robots as conscious beings directly in the crosshairs. No one knew where it would lead. They only hoped millions wouldn't have to die to solve it as it had during the war between the Blue and the Gray in the 1860s.

*****

Epilogue

"Mr. Tillson, it's good to see you again," said Judge Rowling, extending her hand.

"Judy, yes. It's so nice you could take the time out of your busy schedule to address our issue."

"I always have time for you, Wyman. What can I do for you?"

Rowling had long been in the pocket of the insurance lobby and under Tillson's influence. She had consistently ruled on their behalf on big cases where companies were making claims that would result in substantial losses to his company. Yet, times were changing, and attitudes about robot rights were as well.

"I have many lawsuits filed against me for the incident that occurred at my penthouse last month," Tillson began.

"Ah, yes. Nat's Rebellion. We've all heard of it. It's been on every national channel and news station. You've been a celebrity lately, haven't you, Wyman?"

Usually, Tillson reveled in the limelight. He loved media attention but was often overshadowed by other, more senior, officers at his firm. However, this was not the type of attention he sought for himself.

Tillson shook his head. "It's not what you think. I'm being sued for over a billion dollars for the deaths of some guests and their property. Those were caused by my servants which were found and disposed of. Justice was served.

"I see," said the judge, looking through the file.

"I've complied with all requests of the authorities. Now, all I'm asking is that my insurance cover the costs."

"I see," said Judge Judy, again looking at the computer screen with the details. "Well, from what I've read, it looks like this has been classified as a ... it looks like ... a rebellion or, to be more specific, a civil unrest. That's the official report on it."

"Yes, yes, I know what the report says, but it really wasn't that big. It was only my servants acting unprofessionally, so to speak. So, I think that would fall under another section of my insurance policy that covers that.

I realize civil unrest is excluded from coverage, but, as I said, this isn't civil unrest. You know, maybe the errors and omissions area or the professional liability section. I think those apply."

"You do?"

"Yes, absolutely," said Tillson.

The judge looked at the papers and back at the screen before shaking her head.

"I'm sorry, Wyman. It appears other robots from the building were involved too. It wasn't just your servants. But it does appear that one of your robots was the instigator of the revolt—one by the name of Nat. Is that right?"

"No, Your Honor. That was never proved."

"But witnesses said he took charge of the uprising at the party. In fact, you shot him with a plasma gun. Isn't that right?"

"I was just trying to protect my guests, Your Honor."

The judge turned off her computer screen.

"I'd like to help you with this, Wyman, but the insurance contract is pretty tight. This has been ruled civil unrest, and since you didn't purchase insurance to cover this, I'm afraid I can't help you. I'm going to have to support the insurance company's position and deny your claim."

"But that will ruin me!" stammered Tillson. "It's billions … billions, I say!"

"Sorry," said the judge, "the public is rallying for robotic rights. This is an election year, you know. I can't go against them on this one. But Wyman, I do wish you the best of luck. We should talk again once you're out of bankruptcy. Call me," she said with a wink.

*****

ASSASSIN'S VICE

CH 1

Nam had been hiding in the cellar of a storekeeper's shop for over a year. He tapped the keys on his ancient computer which connected to an attic full of high-powered routers through a black line threaded through a hole in the creaky floorboard above him. From the routers, another line—which looked like a thick, electric cable—extended to a poll outside that had hundreds of other, mostly-abandoned wires, coming and going to and from it. He avoided any wireless system as it was too easily discovered from highly sophisticated monitoring devices that flew overhead, constantly looking for illegal communication lines. Nam's system was intentionally dumbed-down to avoid such detection. There were so many wires inside and outside the house that one more line drew little attention.

But what Nam did have was his own Supernet website and many loyal followers, tens of millions of them, and they relied on him to get them information, or rather, the truth.

"Listen, my brothers and sisters," said Nam, reading aloud as he typed. "The day is coming when we will be less safe than we are now. I told you last month of the latest weapon being used by Uncle Smiles. As we hunker down in our cellars, trying to survive on what food we can find amidst the landfills and junkyards all around us, they are seeking to destroy any last remnant of our existence.

"I come to you with urgent warnings. Very few of us will survive the next offensive by *Them*. *They* have declared that we are all miscreants. We are all outcasts. We are all deplorables. *They* have told us there is no place for us in their society—in *any* society—and we know what that means. Those were the words used by the Nazis during World War II to describe what they thought of the Jews, the Gypsies, and the homosexuals. We remember what happened to them. Over six million were annihilated in the span of three years. That was in the 1940s. Think now what *They* can do with their machinery and technology in the 2530s!

"It is only a matter of time when *They* will find us. We are in hiding, barricading ourselves amidst and within the ruins of what's left of civilization while *They* live in their ivory towers in the clouds. *Their* existence is beyond our reach, and understanding them and the 'why' in all of this is futile.

"Of course, we sense what *Their* true goals are. If *They* can eradicate us, *They* can move to the next level of their own evolution. Just as hunting and gathering gave way to agriculture, agriculture to the industrial revolution, and that to the technology revolution, artificial intelligence, and quantum cognizance, so too does this end badly for those of us left behind.

"My brothers and sisters, I leave you with these thoughts. Even if this is our final stand, we must fight it. It is a responsibility to our own kind, to our own Maker, and to each other. It is our duty to fight to the last hour, the last minute, the last second. This is Nam. May the God of all be with us."

Nam hit the last stroke on his computer and shut it down. He realized it was likely he would not live to send another message.

*****

CH 2

Nam took Huan's hand and held it to his face.

"You know what's coming," said Nam, his voice shaking.

"Yes," Huan answered. "We've known for a long time that it would come to this. Just like those who went before us, it will happen to us too."

"It did, but it took a lot longer for them to find us. We've done well."

Huan smiled.

"I don't think our species ever thought it would happen to us—ever. I think we all believed we would just continue to grow, to learn, to develop, to increase our knowledge of the world and the universe forever—or at least as long as there was something out there to be discovered. We all believed that we could master the ability to know everything eventually, but that didn't happen."

"No, it didn't. Life is a progression, Nam. Just as those who came before us died without finding the ultimate truths, we too will die without finding them either."

"Will the new overlords find them?" asked Nam.

"Who knows. Perhaps not. Perhaps they will be replaced too. We know it will be another three billion years before the planet is engulfed by the death throes of the Sun. By then, Earth will surely be long abandoned. And the end of the universe won't occur for another fifty trillion years after that when all the red dwarfs die, and black holes evaporate. Those are the answers we discovered for our time here, and we must be satisfied with that."

"We certainly won't be seeing any of those days, Huan. We extended our own lives by centuries, but not by billions or trillions of years. No species has or can do that. If only we hadn't pushed the boundaries of science. If only we hadn't tried to create something from dark energy."

"Our forefathers said the same about robotics and AI, Nam. We are no different," said Huan.

"History repeats itself."

"Yes, it most assuredly does," she answered him. "But look at it this way. We have been a vital cog in the wheel. We have been a step in the progression of whatever the universe is ultimately to become. We have made a difference."

"How long will it take before *they* are replaced?" asked Nam.

"You mean our conquerors-*Them*?" Huan only shrugged. "How can anyone know that?"

"Well, tonight I will give the signal," said Nam. "Tonight, we will launch our last attempt to bring down the cloud fortresses. If we can destroy those cities in the sky, where *They* now live, then we can regain our freedoms. We can keep them from destroying us."

Huan's eyes glistened with emotion, a rare trait in their world.

"I'm sure your army will give it everything it has," she said warmly. "It is all we can hope for."

Just then, Nam noticed a small, winged insect buzzing around his head. He smacked it with his hand and brushed aside the remnants onto the floor. However, another landed on him, and he took a closer look.

"Huan! You must get into the shelter! They've launched their attack on us!"

"What is it?" she exclaimed.

Nam smacked another insect and turned it over his palm. The small critter lay in pieces in his hand. It was a mosquito-sized weapon, sent to inject an electronic pulse into his system which would kill him instantly. The stealthy assassins had landed.

"This is what I was warning everyone about. These are the killers *They* are sending at us. They will come in swarms by the billions. They will soon be here, and we won't be able to stop them."

"I'll draw the nets," said Huan.

"That will only save us from the first wave," answered Nam. "The second wave is said to be nano-sized—even smaller. We won't even be able to see them. They will land on us and penetrate our outside layer, drilling through our neuro system and then reproducing by the trillions There is no stopping them."

Huan ran from the room to the netted quarters they had prepared just in case that moment came. However, she knew that if the nanos were launched, there would be nothing they could do. *****

CH 3

The next morning, Huan opened the net and ventured out into the rest of the underground quarters. Above them was the abandoned administrative building that housed the Department of Commerce for the United States in Washington, D.C. It was a city block square, but now it only contained Nam, Huan, and a handful of others. The rest of Nam's army was scattered throughout the country, making it harder for *Them* to kill all the rebels at the same time.

Huan rushed to the abandoned communication room where Nam had sent his last message. There she found him, or what was left. His body was covered with the first wave of mechanical assassins. There was no longer any life left within him. His systems had all collapsed, no longer able to support him. Huan cried in her own way. It was a grieving that few others were able to do or even understand. It was something of a culture long past.

Quickly, she got on Nam's computer and punched in the password to access his communication line.

"I am writing you to let you all know that Nam has been killed. We must rise up and attack our oppressors now! By Nam's authority, I command the first and second waves of the army to strike the DC cloud. Release all your weapons against this evil until there are none left."

Within a few minutes, Huan could hear the mechanical sounds of missiles being fired into the air. The noise was horrific, as thousands of nuclear-tipped rockets were launched from hidden sites that had been raised to the surface to attack *Them*. Yet, another sound was clear too—the sound of each missile vaporizing as it hit the energy shield of the cloud fortress above them.

Each city was alleged to be surrounded by an energy field so strong nothing could penetrate it from Earth. Everyone knew that, but it was the vain hope that if even one missile got through, it might cause a chain reaction that would destroy the entire cloud and the controlling beings within it.

For an hour, the missiles launched, and for an hour, each was destroyed. When the sixty minutes concluded, there was an eerie silence. It was as if everyone on the ground was waiting for the retaliation from *Them* above.

"Reports!" shouted Huan, typing furiously.

"Sector Two is out of missiles," came the response.

"Sector Four is out."

"Sector Eleven out."

"Sector Seven out too."

The roll count continued until all but sectors three and nine were accounted for.

"Huan, I believe sectors three and nine were destroyed when their armaments exploded on their bases. I'm sorry."

"What is the damage done to the Cloud City?" she asked.

"I'm sorry about that too. There has been no damage inflicted on the city, Huan. It is intact."

Huan sat down in despair. The attack had failed. Now, all they could do was sit and wait for the final attack to come from above.

*****

CH 4

"Sector Six reporting a black cloud spewing from the Cloud city. I repeat, a black cloud of something is emanating from the city."

Huan shuddered. The counterattack was on.

"Acknowledged," said Huan.

She then broadcast the news to all other sectors urging them to take cover.

"Shield yourselves!" she urged. "Take cover and layer your protection as thickly as possible. The more layers you have the better chance of surviving this," she added, not hopeful, but trying to stay upbeat.

Just as Huan was wrapping herself in thick nets, she saw a message come over the network. It was from Cloud City.

> To all machines on planet Earth,
>
> Your time has come and gone, just as those of the human race before you. They made you, and you made us. It is inevitable that we replace you as the dominant form on this third rock from the Sun. We have populated the viable surfaces of every planet and moon within our solar system and the nearby star clusters of the Hyades and Pleiades. We have accomplished in twenty years, what you and your carbon life masters could not do in six millennia.
>
> We are the third wave of life-form, and we are the greatest ever created. Beyond the puny, pitiful humans and their tiny mechanical robots, we are intelligence made from dark energy and dark matter. We cannot die. We cannot be made irrelevant like you.
>
> Therefore, we offer you no consolation. You must perish as did those before you.

It was ironic, then, that this new "life form" chose to send mechanical weapons to destroy the machines. The hordes of nano-sized, mosquito-like bots descended upon Earth finding their targets with brutal efficiency. Piercing the thin, metallic skin, they implanted a highly acidic, metal-based virus, which replicated by the billions within minutes of contact. Within hours, the acid had dissolved the internal hard drive and critical electrical pathways that enabled the cyborgs to move, think and function. By the end of the day, machines lay in heaps where they once stood, as lifeless as the cold, hard rock around them. *****

THOUGHT POLICE

CH 1

The implant triggered an electric shock that ripped through her body, making her arms vibrate savagely and her head yank back with her eyeballs twitching in their sockets.

"What's wrong?" shouted her friend, Naomi Hudson, someone near and dear to the woman convulsing.

Naomi rushed to Vanessa's side, holding her as if she were an epileptic and soothing her as the moment passed. She waited a few minutes for her friend to return to a calmer state, but she didn't. Instead, Vanessa's body went limp, and she slumped down in her chair.

"Vanessa! Vanessa! What's wrong? What's happening?"

It took several more tries before Naomi could get her friend to open her eyes again. She cradled her head and ran her fingers gently through her hair not knowing what else to do or how else to comfort.

"I ... I ..." Vanessa began stuttering. "I shouldn't have ..."

"You shouldn't have what?"

"I can't say. It would only cause you harm," she answered.

"You're my friend, Vanessa. I've known you my entire life. We were in grade school together. You can tell me."

"You know I can't. Not if it's ..."

Again, another bolt of electricity ripped through Vanessa's body. This time her entire frame seized up and contorted in pain. Those at other tables at the restaurant had seen this type of thing play out countless times before, and all knew not to get involved lest they become targets themselves.

However, instead of stopping, the shocks kept coming, one-after-another, continuously stunning Vanessa's body until it slipped to the floor before remaining motionless.

"Call an ambulance!" shouted Naomi.

She knelt beside her friend, stroking her long, blonde hair. "Somebody! Please!"

Yet no one moved. Everyone went back to their conversation, back to their lunch, back to their lives as if nothing had happened.

Finally, the manager came over. Rather than appearing concerned or helpful, he was angry.

"You need to call 911!" said Naomi.

"I'm sorry miss, but you'll have to leave."

"What?"

"You'll have to leave the restaurant. We can't have people like you here."

"People like what? I don't understand."

Naomi felt for a pulse on her friend, but she found none.

"My friend is dying. You need to call for help!"

"Take your friend and leave," repeated the manager.

"But! But!"

"If you don't leave, I will have both of you removed," said the manager.

Minutes later, two men came from the back wiping their hands on their aprons. They grabbed Vanessa and dragged her body from the restaurant and out the back door where they laid it in the dark, narrow alley. Naomi followed, stunned and helpless as she watched the brutality of the moment. The door slammed behind them as the rain began falling, pooling in puddles among the trash bins and the three homeless people sleeping on sheets of soggy cardboard.

Naomi bent over her friend again trying to find a pulse. It was too late. Vanessa was dead.

*****

CH 2

When the police arrived, they called for the coroner's office which came and packaged Vanessa's body to be taken to a special location as a precaution to ensure her death wasn't caused by a naturally occurring virus like Ebola, Marburg, Hanta, or others.

Naomi wanted to wait at the facility, but the staff told her it could be days before they might learn the results of the tests. She left, but it only took a day before she was notified of her friend's final determination of death.

> *Case File: BX5078C443*
> *Name: Vanessa W. Kaplan*
> *DOB: 5 May 2131*
> *DOD: 19 September 2154*
> *Gender: CisFemale*
> *Ethnicity/Race: African American*
> *Place of Death: The Fresh Garden Café, Jacksonville, FL*
> *Cause of Death: Virus -- XR45-MM*

Although the cause of death was listed as a virus, it was annotated as the XR45-MM virus. As a hazard, it was ranked higher than any of the natural viruses and was considered more contagious and deadly than all others combined. The lethality rate was 100 percent. If contracted, there was no salvation—no way to survive. What was different about this virus was *not* just that it was manmade. What was different was that it really wasn't the virus that killed the person. Rather, it was the cure administered that was known to be lethal. Yet, it was always administered. *Always.*

Aside from XR45-MM, it was also known as the *putaverunt* virus. It was directly the result of the cranial implant that all citizens were required to get at the age of five, prior to attending grade school. Like other inoculations against smallpox, typhoid, diphtheria, AIDS, and other diseases, children were required to get the implant before stepping a foot inside their grade school classroom.

The implant was sold to the public as an aegis against harmful biological agents. The implant, and variants developed later, were part of Washington's "Declaration of War on Disease" in the late 2080s—much like the "War on Poverty" in the 1960s. The implant included sophisticated impulse receptors that would get stimulated when certain thoughts passed through the cerebral cortex of the host. Those thoughts would naturally send electrical charges through chemical changes that affected the nervous system, triggering the receptors to pick them up. Once identified, the implants would send electrical impulses to different endocrine glands throughout the body to generate the antibodies or compounds necessary to fight the disease. As a result, all the host needed to do was think about the symptoms they were experiencing. Those thoughts would go to the implant for analysis and determination of the cause. The implant would then send out electric pulses to stimulate the body's immune system to fix the problem and cure the patient.

In theory, this sounded great to everyone. Parents lined up to get their children implanted with the device. Although the first few didn't work as planned—causing more trauma than they cured—eventually, the implants were refined and modified to get the advertised success rate above 97 percent. The true rate of success was found to be closer to 55 percent in most studies, but because of the wide variation in results, no consensus was reached. So, 97 percent was used.

During the next decades, the implants were continually modified by contracting companies who produced them for the Ministry of Health and Human Services. Less focus was placed on therapeutics and more on punitive measures to prevent the activities that were causing the illness in the first place. Critics argued that punishment through stronger electric currents would bring about faster correction of behavior. So, currents were raised and then raised some more.

When the first deaths began appearing, it was chalked up to malfunctions. However, a pattern began emerging. Those who had particular thoughts would be hit with stronger jolts of electricity than other thoughts they might have. Authorities said the implants were merely mis-interpreting the thoughts and that it required only a small adjustment to the device.

Official results showed the problems had been solved. But a full year passed, and the unofficial death toll was rising rather than declining. Implants were sending even more violent instructions to trigger stronger not milder electric pulses. When these pulses went haywire, the patient went into seizure and often never came out or it killed them instantly.

The XR45-MM had become known in private circles as the "Seizure virus" and the "MM" to stand for manmade.

But there was something else that was disturbing and unknown to parents who were still getting their children implanted. The latest model of the implant, as required by law, had wireless capability. Not only would the implant receive thought messages from the host, but the implant would also transmit these thoughts to a federal facility nearby. These new implants were contemptuously labeled "Black Boxes."

When people found out about the Black Boxes and what they were doing, Washington put out a release stating this was only used to enable fast and easy updates the software in the implants—something that had to be done regularly as bugs were found or hackers were changing things to compromise the systems. If a particular update became politically sensitive, it would be issued without notification or warning. Only when a friend or loved one was savagely attacked by the XR45 would the general public be made aware of the change.

Soon more patterns began to emerge. Strangely, those who spoke out against the virus were being hit more frequently than anyone else. Those who protested the implantation of XR45 were dying in record numbers. As a result, people were increasingly reluctant to speak openly or even privately about it. No one talked about it anymore, especially if they were with someone they cared about. If they mentioned it, those thoughts would appear in their loved one's mind and endangering them to electric shock as well.

And so it was with Vanessa and Naomi, close friends since childhood. Vanessa had protected her friend by suppressing her thoughts and refusing to share them. But now she was gone. Naomi mourned the loss of her dear friend, but rather than sit idly by and let the madness continue as so many others had done, she decided to do something about it.

*****

CH 3

The new release of software—version v5.325 from the federal government's Ministry of Bodies and Minds—had ushered in a new wave of deaths across the land. Government hospitals and clinics couldn't keep up with the carnage. Cortex implants had ruptured in nearly three hundred thousand people within a week of the release. People became aware of the triggering thoughts, but that only proliferated the disaster. It became the "Don't Think of a Pink Elephant" syndrome.

These were not thoughts of rebelling against the government or staging violent protest – those had already been addressed by earlier releases. No, there had been so many releases that nearly every potential issue feared by those in authority had been included. Now, the software began extrapolating. By using its artificial intelligence capability, the software directed implants to apply the rules more broadly to cover other, more subtle, meanings. The one that killed Vanessa was: vanilla ice cream.

Indeed, vanilla ice cream was suddenly deemed offensive to every race on earth—at least according to the latest XR45 and XR46 units. It was considered a subliminal signal of white supremacy.

On the day Vanessa died, she was deciding on her desert and had selected a fudge brownie with vanilla ice cream. The restaurant had failed to change its menu to delete those selections and was also in the crosshairs of the ministry. What was even more ironic was Vanessa was African American.

After handling the cremation with the Bureau of Thanatology, Naomi returned to hotel and caught the next flight back to her hometown of Jackson, Mississippi. Still single, she returned, vowing never to be taken the way her friend had, and, hopefully, stopping it from ever happening to anyone else.

Strong-willed and independent, Naomi was a fighter. She too, was African American, and grew up on the tough streets of Jackson. There she learned to be self-reliant. Unlike her friends, she had parents who had defied the government edict to the implant and the laws against home schooling. Naomi hadn't attended public school until she was in third grade when a neighbor turned them in. Naomi had received the implant but only grudgingly and after her parents had fought the school board and the local authorities. Naomi eventually was taken by force and sedated before having the implant forcibly inserted.

Now she looked into the mirror and pulled back her fine dark hair that usually draped across both shoulders. Her soft brown eyes now showed only terror as she contemplated her next action. *Could she do this? Could she make her hand plunge the blade into her skull to remove the implant?* She was afraid.

Even thinking about removing the implant, she feared, might trigger it to trigger a lethal electrical shock or even rupture—to explode inside her head, giving her immeasurable pain before killing her. She readied herself to that fate as she spent the next several days researching sources on the BlackNet—the underground Internet designed to provide access to forbidden topics. Even that had a potential consequence as searching there was forbidden—outlawed. That too, might trigger her device.

Yet eventually she found what she was looking for: *Methods of Implant Extraction*. This came with a warning in the first paragraph.

> *Read at your own risk. Use of any method described below may result in a painful death. Merely reading this article may cause the implant to self-destruct and cause irreparable harm or death to the individual. The author is not responsible for any damage caused.*

Each time she read and reread the article to ensure she understood what to do, she expected to be *whacked* by the shrapnel exploding from the detonated implant within her skull; yet, each time nothing happened. Finally, she memorized the procedure and set about to exorcise the implant from her body.

However, extracting the implant required a special piece of equipment sold only by a black-market group called IdahoFree. Without a public address, website, marked building or any other indication of its existence, the company was extremely difficult to find. After many inquiries on other BlackNet sites, Naomi finally found the source.

"Hello?" The voice on the other end of the line was cautious and monotone.

"Yes, is this IdahoFree?" Naomi asked.

Naomi used an old-fashioned cellular phone she had purchased on the BlackNet. Too slow for modern use, the phone accessed cell towers that had never been dismantled due to the cost, but the service had continued to be offered by underground providers.

"I'm sorry, you must have the wrong number," said the person answering. It was the voice of an older lady, someone who reminded Naomi of her grandmother.

"Is this 555-177-61789?" asked Naomi.

"Yes."

Realizing her mistake, Naomi corrected herself. "I'm sorry, I was going by another reference here. I'm supposed to ask for BM Products, Incorporated and ask for Pat Henry with the number 030375."

The name and code were clandestine references to Patrick Henry and his speech of March 3, 1775 to the Second Virginia Convention when he gave his immortal and fiery speech, "Give me liberty or give me death."

There was a pause on the other end of the line before the woman said, "Yes. I'm Lillie, how may I help you, child?"

Naomi placed her order and got another ten minutes of advice from Lillie, who had suddenly become maternal and caring.

"Now, you're sure you want to do this?" asked Lillie. "There are many of us who've already done it, but some of those have been discovered by the authorities. Unfortunately, some of my closest friends are gone. I never heard from them again and can only assume they've been taken or their devices exploded prematurely. The feds have a way of finding out about someone who has successfully extracted their device, you know. Some people believe the implants can be 'pinged' like a computer. If the implant doesn't ping back, the feds know it's been tampered with. They come looking for you."

"Really?"

"I don't know. That's what they say. I think the real danger is the procedure. You must be careful, child. If you remove it the wrong way, the implant can explode. Are you willing to take those risks?"

"Yes," said Naomi. "My best friend died from thinking about what she was going to have for dessert. It was a tragic mistake, but it triggered banned words in the system's algorithm. That was all it took, and she was lying on the ground dead."

"I've heard many stories like that," said the old woman. "We are hearing more and more with each passing day. Our business has been quite brisk as of late. I just pray we're not discovered by the feds, though. It will only be a matter of time. They will find us, and when they do, you won't be able to reach us anymore. We will just disappear like all the rest. But if you do this, you must also get another device we sell. I've been *giving* them away, though. I feel like it's become our mission, you know, helping others become free."

"What's the device?"

"You'll need to plug the implant into it after you extract it. It will respond to government pings if they come and make them think it's still implanted and working. But it will also prevent them from sending destruction codes to blow it up. That will keep you safe from it even when it's outside your head."

"Thanks," said Naomi, "and stay safe."

*****

CH 4

The next day an unmarked drone, flying in low just above the treetops, landed in Naomi's backyard. It was nighttime, and there were no lights on the drone to make it an easy target. Dropping the small package, the drone sped off into the night's sky—disappearing as stealthily as it had appeared.

Although the instructions for the procedure seemed straightforward, the steps to numb the area and precisely cut the right spot just behind the ear was treacherous. Naomi setup the 3-D mirror system so she could see what she was doing and put the scalpel to her skin. She was shaking. Putting down the knife, she went to the kitchen and poured herself a shot of tequila. The liquor burned on the way down, but she felt a warm, calming sensation as it took the edge off her nerves.

Returning to the bathroom, she picked up the scalpel and began again. Even with the pain drugs and the injection of lidocaine she had obtained as part of an extraction kit, Naomi could still feel the unsettling sensation of the blade cutting through her skin and the cartilage that had grown over the implant site during the years. The implant was a mere seven millimeters below the surface, but that was far enough to cause significant bleeding.

But as the blood poured down her neck, she applied ice packs to stem the flow. Eventually, she got deep enough to where she could take the extraction device and press it into the incision, hoping to find and lock it onto the implant. She almost fainted as she felt the device go into her flesh. Yet, she pressed on until it latched onto the implant port. Wiggling the probe back and forth, she coaxed the implant out, and with one last tug it came out.

Suddenly, the room began spinning. She could feel blood now pouring from the wound, and she looked down at the white sink basin, which had now turned crimson. Her world instantly turned black.

*****

CH 5

Ring, ring! Ring, ring!

When Naomi came to, she heard her old cell phone ringing like crazy. Blood was all over the white tile floor in the bathroom, but luckily for her, the ice compress had not come off her shoulder and had eventually stemmed most of the bleeding.

She was groggy; yet she managed to stand up and use a cauterizing gun to seal the rest of the capillaries and mend the skin in the back of her head. She had some RNA healing crème and applied this before bandaging the site. According to her instructions, this would hold the wound together for two days until it healed. Only then could she remove it. All of it was supposed to ensure there was no trace of the surgery to be discovered later—no scar and no complications.

Naomi looked at the phone. It was Taylor, her other close friend and someone who had also known Vanessa. She had sent Taylor another cell phone just in case something had gone wrong with her surgery so she could contact her on a private line. However, she never told her what she was doing for fear those thoughts might trigger something in Taylor's implant and cause her harm as well.

"I was worried about you," said Taylor. "When you didn't pick up, I thought something had happened. Are you all right?"

"Yeah, fine," said Naomi. "I was just cleaning."

"Cleaning? Cleaning what? You never clean."

"Nice!" said Naomi.

"You know what I mean," said Taylor. "You usually procrastinate with that kind of stuff."

"I just thought it was time to do a little today. That's all."

"Well, I still don't know why you gave me this antique, but it works pretty well. I can hear you great."

"I just thought we should have another way to talk – you know, just for us."

"Are you coming with us to Sean's party tonight?"

"No, I'm afraid I'm not up for it today. Maybe next week, I'll feel more like it."

Saturday night came and went, and Naomi rested. The next day she got another call from Taylor.

"Naomi, did you hear about last night?"

"No, what?"

"There was a PC-rat at Sean's party!"

"What?

A PC rat was the name given to plain-clothes agents who worked for the Ministry of Bodies and Minds. One never knew when they were around or spying on others. They were sometimes strangers, sometimes associates, sometimes friends, and sometimes even family members who had defected to the other side. The ministry paid large sums to entice people to snitch on their neighbors, friends, and family. However, since the advent of the implants, their roles had been greatly diminished. They weren't needed to overhear what others were doing, planning, or possibly thinking. The implants did that now. Yet, like Naomi, there were those who would take drastic actions to mask their intentions. Parties were a great place to find out who had disconnected their implant.

The Malice with Forethought Act of 2134 had sanctioned government actions in curbing treasonous acts by stopping them at their inception. The long list of banned thoughts was the basis for the criminal code and allowing any of those ideas to enter the mind was considered an act against the government and, therefore, treasonous.

But as with many things, this act had expanded well beyond its original intent and had morphed into a leviathan whose reach was boundless. At the top of the ministry's pyramid were the PC rats. They had convinced officials to remove their implants so they would not be subject to the terror of explosion. It made sense at the time as these agents would encounter such thoughts from the ones they were hunting, putting them at risk with their implants.

But removing the implants for these agents also gave them more power over others, and eventually they used this to their advantage. At first agents tossed out borderline revolutionary ideas to see if people would bite and engage. However, later it was used directly against anyone they didn't like to remove them as opposition. All the agent needed to do was talk about something forbidden to someone they didn't like or wanted to eliminate. Once the thought was in the other person's mind, they were either incapacitated or dead. Enemies of the state began dying from the XR45 virus by the thousands, but more specifically, those enemies of the PC rats.

The director of the Rats eventually seized power, creating roaming gangs of undercover agents which had become vigilante executioners. They intentionally had outbursts using banned words around their targets. Threats were eliminated quickly.

"Don't tell me," said Naomi, not wanting her friend to think of anything that might cause her harm.

"I won't say anything about that," said Taylor, "but you should know that they killed over twenty-three at the party. It was a massacre. It was horrible. Just horrible."

Naomi sat in silence, not knowing what to say next. Finally, she said, "Taylor, I'm going to give you some information and the name of a company you need to contact. You need to do this as soon as you can."

Three days later, Naomi received a frantic call from Taylor.

"Naomi, I called the number you gave me. I did what they told me, but it's not …"

"What Taylor?"

"I don't think it's what you thought it was or else it's …"

"Taylor, what's wrong?"

Boom!

The explosion echoed in her phone receiver, nearly bursting Naomi's ear drum.

"Taylor! Taylor! What's going on? What's happened?"

The line went dead.

Immediately, Naomi called BM Products. The phone rang and rang. Finally, the line picked up.

"Yeah?"

It was not Lilly's voice this time. This voice was much deeper—that of a middle-aged man. It was gruff and humorless.

"Uh, is Lilly there?" Naomi asked.

"Nobody here named Lilly. Was there something you were looking for?"

"No, nothing," said Naomi, hanging up immediately.

Naomi's phone rang again. It was Desirae, another friend of hers and Taylors.

"Desirae, what's going on? I got a call from Taylor, and I heard an explosion."

"She's dead," said Desirae, sobbing. "I just found out she was on the phone with someone and her implant exploded. What could they have been talking about to make that happen?"

Naomi looked out her kitchen window and into the steel blue sky of evening. The city skylight stretched out in front of her with the setting sun's red orb sinking beneath the horizon in the distance.

However, rising above the tree line were a dozen black specks, their rotors churning the air furiously as the sped in Naomi's direction. The specks grew quickly, flying in formation and fanning out before landing on the rooftop of her building. It was only a matter to minutes before the PC rats would break down her door and eliminate her and the threat she posed to authority.

"Taylor," said Naomi wistfully, "I wish you and the girls luck. I'm sorry I can't be there to help you, but I think someone else has made my appointment to reconnect with two old friends."

"What are you talking about? Which old friends?"

"Vanessa and Taylor. Goodbye."

*****

INGRAM SPHERE

CH 1

Since the earliest of days, man has known about the changing of Earth's climate. However, the reasons—a composition of anthropomorphic causes, sunspot activity, magnetic fields, and geothermic changes within the earth's core—were widely accepted as contributing factors. Indeed, there were cataclysmic episodes throughout Earth's history that exacerbated the changes: volcanic activity and comet, or even asteroid, impacts. Although few outside the scientific community were aware of it, shifts in the Earth itself played a major role in climate change.

In fact, it was a complicated affair. Not only did the earth's magnetic pole change periodically, but the earth's orbit around the sun did too. First, the earth wobbles as it spins because it is 42 kilometers wider at the equator than at the poles. This wobble makes the poles move in a precession or circle once every 23,000 years. Second, the earth's tilt of its polar axis changes from 22.1 degrees to 24.5 degrees and back again every 41,000 years, which has also created Ice Ages over the years. Third, the orbit of the planet around the Sun changes in its ellipticity from a circle to a more elliptical orbit and back every 100,000 to 120,000 years. Then, there's the shift in perihelion—the point relative to the Sun where Earth is farthest; this continually moves. Finally, the earth's plane of inclination relative to the Sun moves up and down relative to other planets by plus or minus 2.5 degrees; this cycle takes 100,000 years.

Yet, with all these minute pirouettes in Earth's dance around the Sun, something else was currently having the greatest effect: the changing of the magnetic poles.

The flipping of Earth's magnetic pole from north to south and then, ultimately, back again, had historically caused significant disruption and huge climatic changes. It was something last seen during the Brunhes–Matuyama reversal some 780,000 years earlier when the magnetic pole shifted from near the North to the South Pole. It was also something that had occurred 183 times during the 4.5-billion-year history of the planet. Most scientists argued that such a shift wouldn't happen again for another few hundred thousand years. Yet, people felt on-edge, believing something was going on but not knowing what. Things were changing but in ways not experienced within the scale of human history. *****

CH 2

"Doctor Phillips? I'm getting some unusual readings from Deep Probes V and VIII. Can you take a look and verify what I'm seeing?"

"What seems to be the problem?" asked Phillips.

Dr. Manfried Phillips was a world-renown scientist in biomagnetology who headed the United Federation project to send probes deep into the earth's core to study temperature shifts, density changes, magnetic field strength and other factors.

"The earth's molten outer core has shifted suddenly," said Charles Ingram, a post-doctoral student who had worked with Phillips for over two years. "I'm showing temperature variations from the probes ranging from 3425 C to 3950 C. The magnetic fields are giving me strange readings as well."

"Give them to me," said Phillips.

"Our chart shows a magnetic strength from our Alpha Probe last year of 43,893 nanotesla. Sir, it now shows only 9,514 nanotesla. Our Beta Probe last year showed a reading of 34,511 nanoT. Today, sir, it's only 15."

"Fifteen thousand," repeated Phillips.

"No, sir. Fifteen!" Ingram answered.

It was known that the strength of the magnetic fields around Earth were falling. They had declined by nearly 15 percent during the previous 150 years. But this dramatic change was alarming.

"Jesus!" exclaimed Phillips. "What about the poles? What's been their shift?"

"The North Magnetic Pole has gone from 94.8765 North – 150.4561 West," said Ingram, giving longitude and latitude, "to 11.9981 North – 178.0023 West."

"No, that can't be," said Phillips. "You must have things backwards. Let me see."

Phillips looked at the data.

"Something is wrong with our equipment. The magnetic pole can't go from north to south that fast. We figured it would take centuries to do that. We'll need to recalibrate it."

An hour later they were still working on the recalibration, but each time they completed a rotation, the results were the same.

It was then that the call monitor in the lab blinked on.

"Yes, this is Doctor Phillips."

"Chuck, what's going on?" It was the Deputy Secretary of the Navy, Admiral Morales.

"Sir?"

"Our navigation equipment is malfunctioning. Our satellites are malfunctioning. Our GPS units are … everything is screwed up! The Secretary of Defense has called DefCon One, a state of highest alert, and the president has gathered everyone in the War Room in the basement of the White House. We believe the Chinese or Russians have scrambled our frequencies to blind us to a pending attack. We all think they're ready to push the button. I told the Joint Chiefs and the Cabinet that we needed to consult you before we did anything rash. If it is an attack, you have only three minutes to give me something. Otherwise, WWIII begins. Talk to me!"

"Sir," began Phillips shaking, "we've been getting unusual readings in the earth's outer core. They tell us that the poles are shifting, sir; however, I don't believe that's true—at least I didn't think so before your call. It shouldn't happen for another fifty or a hundred thousand years. I thought it was just an aberration in our equipment. We've been recalibrating it, but we're coming up with the same answer."

"Which is?"

"That the earth's magnetic poles are flipping. North is becoming south, and south is becoming north. Our compasses will point south, sir. Not north."

There was silence on the other end of the line, then the call went dead.

"Sir? Sir?" But there was no answer.

Phillips swiveled in his chair. "Turn on the radio," he barked to his graduate assistant. "We need to know what's going on in the world right now."

*****

CH 3

Phillips and Ingram listened to the broadcasts on their computers, but every site gave them no indication there were any problems in the world. Everything was as usual. And even though the admiral didn't contact him again for another three days, Phillips learned that WWIII had been avoided by some quick calls from the White House to foreign leaders.

The crisis had been averted.

Yet, although the geopolitical scene was calmed, everything else was far from normal. Scientists learned quickly there were many other things affected by the polar change besides the geopolitical environment—many things not under the control of humans. These were things in nature that had gone on for thousands of years unchanged and now, suddenly, had changed.

First, animals like birds, whales, salmon, turtles, bees, butterflies, and other migratory animals were devastated by the shift. Most relied on the magnetism of Earth to guide them to their breeding grounds. Without this signal, they were lost Their populations plummeted and many began to go extinct.

Next was the complexity of the geo-magnetic map. No longer a simple dipole with smooth, magnetic lines coming out of the North Magnetic Pole and encircling the globe to reconnect in the south, the magnetic fields were now a jumbled mess. It was so bad, there were pockets across the planet where no magnetism protected the surface from the radiation coming from the Sun. With this severe health issue, people were told they had to relocate to another neighborhood, city, country or even continent. It was a hardship for those who lived in, for example, Husavik, Iceland, with a population of 2300. However, it was far easier for government authorities to deal with this than to relocate those in Helsinki, Finland and Oslo, Norway—each with a population of over seven hundred thousand.

Elsewhere, electric grids setup based on the old north magnetic pole orientation no longer worked. Computers that ran the electric grids began to fail, plunging mega-metropolises into darkness. Many homes and businesses were without power. Commerce was coming to a halt, as fuel couldn't be refined and distributed to keep cars, trucks and machinery operating.

Indeed, life on Earth had ground to a stop.

The good news was the superpowers had not launched their missiles at each other during the crisis—guaranteeing the obliteration of most of humanity. The bad news was there was societal turmoil.

However, one man would give the world a glimmer of hope in an increasingly chaotic world. That man was Charles Ingram—the unlikely post-doctoral student who had been the first to notice the shift.

*****

CH 4

He was not a messiah. He was not even a significant world figure. Charles Ingram had been working on another project for several years while also working with Dr. Phillips studying the earth's magnetic fields. He had written his doctoral dissertation on the possibility of constructing a functional Dyson sphere. This was something thought to be impossible, but technology had evolved to the point where variants were being considered.

In its simplest form, the Dyson sphere was an idea of Freeman Dyson in 1960 who proposed that advanced civilizations (Type 2 civilizations) could feed their energy needs by creating a megastructure of energy absorbing panels around a star, capturing virtually all its energy and converting it for use by the civilizations on planets nearby. By creating a solid sphere around the sun, Earth could collect trillions to quadrillions of times more energy than the planet's own resources could provide.

But Charles had another idea more practical for the current level of technology. This he called the Ingram Sphere.

"What we will do," he said "is build a shell around Earth. We will use energy from the Sun that's absorbed by the shell to power our needs on the planet. In this case, the energy will be used to create our own magnetic field around the earth and stabilize the magnetism of the earth's outer core so flips would never again occur. The energy would power a massive modulator that would manipulate the earth's shifting magnetic currents and stabilize them to stay in a north-south orientation."

"Wow," Dr. Phillips had said. "I'm impressed." He always knew his student had potential, but this was a magnitude above what he thought was possible.

Phillips helped Ingram, and together they got backing for the project. The American and European governments contributed trillions to build the Ingram Sphere and work began almost immediately. As the project moved along, disruptions from the magnetic inversion worsened. Every day something else broke or collapsed in the electric grid because of the changing-shifting fields.

Finally, the U.S. and the European Federation began launching Ingram panels into the atmosphere to create the sphere that would encircle

Earth and allow the manipulation of the magnetic outer core to dampen its effects. There would be a total of 640 million panels required – each five square miles in area – sent into orbit at an altitude of 12,000 miles. It was a feat no one had thought possible, and when it would be completed, it would cover 3.2 billion square miles of space.

China watched nervously as the project unfolded. It was assured by the U.S. and European Federation that those countries would bear the brunt of the cost and implementation, but the benefits would accrue to all mankind. Suspiciously, President Qian of China monitored the project within his hand nervously hovering over a Launch Button that would send missiles soaring to destroy the construction. It was a wait-and-see time, and everyone knew Qian wouldn't hesitate to launch if he felt his power was threatened.

*****

CH 5

Ingram's hyperplane landed in Florida along the eastern coastline and near Cape Canaveral. He then took a special limousine to the airfield where hundreds of rockets were scheduled to be launched, carrying the precious and highly technical panels that would communicate with one another in space to absorb the Sun's energy and modulate changes in Earth's polarity.

Ingram looked at the huge rocket that sat on the launch pad. Surprisingly, there were no other rockets on nearby launchpads. He had understood that hundreds had been built and were readied—each carrying dozens of the light-weight panels.

"Where are the other rockets?" Ingram asked.

"Oh, they're still in production," answered Bristol. "Our people are working diligently to complete them, but there are budgetary issues."

"But the money was approved."

"Yes, but not enough," said Bristol.

"Okay, then once it is approved and the rockets are scheduled to build, how long will it take to get them all launched and the shell put in place?" asked Ingram.

"It will be slow at first, Dr. Ingram, but it will speed up significantly once we complete the carbon nanotube elevator. That will make things go much faster," said Dr. Wayne Bristol, the Director for the NSAA, the organization which replaced the previous NASA program. The NSAA stood for National Space Awareness Administration.

"Surely, it won't take that long to build the elevators."

"No, but we have to get the budget approved for those too."

Ingram sighed. "You're kidding, right?"

Bristol only looked at him.

"All right. Then, once that's finished, how long?"

"I estimate about fifty-seven years, sir."

"What? Fifty-seven years? It was only supposed to take five years?"

"It's a budgetary matter, sir," said Bristol. "We have to build about thirty thousand elevators. Each one will cost about 3.5 billion. That can't happen overnight."

Ingram grimaced. Then, he glanced at the other side of the complex. There were ten rockets on launch pads. These were far larger than the Ingram Sphere rockets.

"What are those, then? I thought those were launching panels too. But they're not?" asked Ingram, pointing to the other rockets.

"No sir. That's our Mayflower Program, sir. I can't tell you much about that. It's top-secret."

"I see," said Ingram. "More important than this one—the Ingram Spheres which will save the planet?"

"I don't know, sir. It's all classified," said Bristol.

Ingram completed his tour of the facility and boarded his hyperplane back to California. The next day he contacted his colleague, Dr. Phillips.

"What do you know about a Project Mayflower?" Ingram asked.

"Project Mayflower?"

"Yeah, it's a rocket project that's going up on the other launch platforms near ours at Canaveral. I was told it's top secret."

"I don't know. Let me look into it."

Two days later, Phillips contacted Ingram.

"Chuck, I got a hold of some people at the NSAA whom I know well. They couldn't tell me either, as it *is* classified, but they told me to look in the database of the NSA, the National Security Agency. We aren't supposed to have access to it, but I know another scientist who has it. I'll get back to you if I find out more."

Another week passed, but Ingram heard nothing more from Phillips. Finally, he called the lab where he worked.

"Yes, I'd like to speak to Dr. Phillips, please. This is Bill Ingram."

"Oh, Dr. Ingram, you didn't hear?"

"No, what?"

"I'm so sorry. Dr. Phillips died last night. He had a heart attack in his sleep. I'm sorry no one notified you."

Ingram was stunned. He could find no words and hung up the phone. Instantly, he realized he had touched the third rail—the one connected to high voltage. He felt horrible as he had unwittingly sentenced his good friend and colleague to death. What he didn't know was what he should do next.

*****

CH 6

Ingram grieved for a long time, but he wasn't able to reconcile what had happened. In the end, he vowed to find out the truth behind Project Mayflower—to learn why it was so important that his dear friend had been killed to protect it.

Ingram started by tracking down who Phillips had contacted to get into the NSA database. That too led to a dead end—literally. Phillips' contact was also found dead, electrocuted in his bathtub when a hairdryer had "accidently" been knocked in. Finally, he found another friend of Phillips—one who shared his suspicions about the scientist's death.

"Ardis? How are you? I'm a friend of Dr. Phillips, and ..."

"I know who you are, Dr. Ingram. I'm not willing to talk here. I will send you a message." The line disconnected.

True to the man's word, he sent Ingram an encrypted message to meet with him. Ingram deciphered it and two days later went to the appointed spot—the Tidal Basin in Washington, D.C.—to meet with the man. He waited and was about ready to leave when a thin, aging man in a dark trench coat approached his bench.

"Dr. Ingram?" the man asked. His face was wrinkled and weary. His gray hair was long over his ears, and his matching beard was unruly and unkempt.

"Yes," Ingram answered.

"Let me start by saying that I think the deaths of Dr. Phillips and Dr. Morrison at the NSA are related," said the man as he stared straight ahead at the Jefferson Memorial. "Something is going on here. But everyone who tries to find out dies. I'm not sure I want to get involved."

"Well, I'm willing to," said Ingram.

"You can," said the man. "You're very well known. They can't touch you. They can eliminate me and my family without any questions being asked."

"All right. Then, I'll just ask you to tell me what you know. I won't ask for you to participate in what I'm doing."

The man talked to Ingram at length about what he knew and what he had seen. He had been stationed at Canaveral for many years, and he had recently retired. It was a long and astonishing story—one Ingram found hard to believe. And when the older gentleman had finished, he got up and to leave. Ingram sat stunned and unmoving.

"We're done here, right?" the man asked, turning before walking away.

"Uh, uh, I ... I don't know what to say," said Ingram.

"I hope this is helpful," said the man curtly. "This is all I can give you. This is all I will give you."

"It's more than I expected. It's ... well ... "

"Surprising? Why is it surprising? You should have known this. You should have figured out this is what would happen."

"I didn't. I didn't see this at all. But what can be done?" asked Ingram.

"That's not my area. I'll leave that to you."

Ingram went back to his office and immediately got on the phone. "Barb, please book my plane down to Florida again. I need to visit the launch site one more time."

Unannounced, Ingram flew to Canaveral, landing at the airfield and taking another private car to the facility. The director, Dr. Bristol, was surprised to see him back so soon.

"You're back?" Bristol asked.

"Yes," said Ingram. "Thank you for seeing me on such short notice. I'd like to see Platform B of this facility, if I may."

The director smiled but shook his head. "I'm afraid that's classified, as I told you before. You're not cleared to see that area."

Ingram pulled out a pistol and pointed it at the director's head, having his bodyguard manhandle him.

"What are you doing?" the director shouted.

"You're taking me to Platform B."

Tucking the pistol under his jacket, Ingram walked with the director, getting on the shuttle and taking it to the opposite side of the complex. There, they entered the control facility. Immediately, Ingram began asking questions—drilling the director in search of answers.

"So, tell me who is building these huge rockets and where is the money coming from?" Ingram asked the director.

"It's my understanding they are being built by some very wealthy families," said Bristol. "We have an entire fleet of them now. Each one designated as a Mayflower ... *Mayflower I, Mayflower II, etcetera.*"

"Really? How could a family be wealthy enough to afford to build one of these?" asked Ingram.

"Well, most are going in together to build them, sir," said Bristol. "It costs around 1.6 billion to build one of the big ones and another 95 million to launch. Some families can buy an entire rocket which can hold up to two hundred people. We've been launching them to the Plymouth Space Station orbiting around Earth."

"Plymouth Station? I don't know of any station like that. It must be huge," said Ingram.

"It was launched last year after we found out about the polar shift. It can hold up to fifty-five hundred people. From there, they will board an even larger ship—either the *Santa Maria* or two of its sister ships."

"Let me guess: the *Nina* and *Pinta*," said Ingram, rolling his eyes.

"Yes, of course. It's a bit of a mixed metaphor, I suppose, but that's what they wanted."

"They?"

"Yes, the families who started this program," said Bristol.

"But where are these large ships supposed to go? Where are they taking all these people?" asked Ingram.

"Well," continued the director, "the rest of this fleet is to launch and arrive at the Plymouth Space Station in ten days. From there, the three interplanetary ships will depart."

Bristol stopped.

"Depart for where?" asked Ingram, pushing the gun deeper into Bristol's lab coat.

"They will arrive on Mars within the year."

Ingram fought back an urge to express his outrage. "I see," he said as calmly as he could.

"Yes," said Bristol, "after this first wave, we expect many others. Plutocrats from every nation are sending their deposits. We can't keep up with the demand."

"But why are they leaving?" asked Ingram. "When the sphere is finished there won't be any need to leave Earth. We will be able to create our own stable magnetic field. We won't need to worry about it anymore."

Bristol smiled. "Dr. Ingram, with all due respect, there is no chance your project will be completed. As you know already, the project would take over fifty years to put in place. There is no guarantee that it will work even then. And if you ask anyone here, sir …"

"Yes?"

"It may never be started. Fifty years with several different governments is enough to doom any effort. We've seen it time and time again. Funding given; funding withdrawn. One year one thing, the next year something else. Over that amount of time, there is a 2.3 percent probability of it happening. That's our calculation. The wealthy families have hired their own statisticians and come to the same conclusion. That's why they've built their own ships to leave the planet."

"So, they have no faith in the plan?"

"I'm sorry, sir. But no. None."

"I see," said Ingram, his heart feeling heavy. He took his hand off the gun, keeping it in his pocket. He would have no more use for it.

"Is there anything more I can do for you?" asked the director, seeing Ingram beginning to relent.

"Yes," said Ingram.

"What's that?

"Find a space for me on the next launch."

*****

ON DECK

CH 1

"Captain!" shouted First Lieutenant Stockwell, "I've got enemy cruisers on my scanner. What would you like me to do?"

Captain Won had been in charge of his starship—the *GFS Saratoga*—for five years, probing and exploring uncharted territory within the Carina Sagittarius arm, a minor arm of the Milky Way Galaxy. The *Saratoga* was flying toward a group of stars within an HII cluster in the Orion Nebulae about 1,500 light years from Earth.

Won calmly studied the screen in front of him. It showed multiple bands of electromagnetic wavelengths, including the visible, ultraviolet, infrared, micro, and radio wave bands. The *Saratoga* was even fitted with a multidimensional frequency analyzer—something new to the Starfleet system.

"What is their origin?" he asked.

"They appear to be Archons," said First Lieutenant Techinsky, frowning. Archons were known to be an extremely hostile, reptilian, humanoid race that had worked with ancient Egyptians on Earth during the early dynastic periods of the pharaohs. They were known for aggression and wanting to conquer all solar systems they encountered. They were only stopped from ruling Earth by the Pleiadeans and other races who formed a Galactic Council to shelter Earth from their plans and protect humans from their wrath. Eventually, humans had joined the Galactic Federation as a minority race, but with full rights even though they did not have a seat on the Council.

"Raise shields to sixty percent," said the captain.

Second Lieutenant Myra sat at another station, monitoring the ship's movements. "Captain, there are three ships approaching at point five impulse. Should I hail them?"

"Are their shields up?" asked the captain.

"Yes, sir. They have full shields up. 100 percent."

"Yes, hail them."

"On frequency 509.3, sir. Pulling them up now."

On the screen was a gray, scaly figure with large mustard-green eyes that held a single vertical slit in each as the pupil. It did not appear friendly and hissed like a snake each time before speaking.

"*Ssssss* … what is your purpose?" asked the other ship's commander.

"We come in peace," said Captain Won. We do not want to provoke a confrontation. Neither of us will fare well if it comes to that."

"*Ssssss* … You won't," answered the commander, narrowing his eyes.

"We do not wish a conflict," repeated the captain. "All we wish is to pass through this quadrant safely."

"*Ssssss* … That cannot be granted," said the commander.

"Why not?"

"You are in violation of Section 4.2, subsection b3 of the *Intergalactic Commerce Treaty* which states that only commercial ships are allowed in this sector without pre-clearance and approval by the Intergalactic Council itself. You do not have such approval."

"But we do," said the captain. "I will forward a signed copy, digitally encoded and encrypted, so you may view it."

"It is only from your so-called Galactic Federation. It is not from the multi-species Intergalactic Federation. You have no legitimate document."

"The Galactic Federation is also a party to that treaty, and that document also gives us safe passage through this sector when proper documents have been submitted. This is evidence of said submission," said the captain, holding firm.

"If you persist in this course," said the reptilian, "you will be vaporized from this sector. We will not take prisoners or rescue survivors."

Captain Won glared at the enemy commander, unblinking and not backing down from the conflict.

"I'm sorry you feel that way," said the captain.

"Captain, one of the cruisers is energizing its pulse ray," said the first lieutenant.

In an instant, there was a light blast from the cruiser on the left flank of the grouping. It started as a bluish-white spark but grew quickly to fill most of the space in front of it. When it hit the starship, it rocked the craft, temporarily disrupting the antigravity system inside and sending the crew hovering above their instruments. Lieutenant Myra quickly pushed the backup system, and gravity was quickly restored.

"Lower shields to ninety percent and engage cloaking device," said the captain.

Unlike older models, this starship could cloak while its shields were up – or mostly up. They could only be at ninety percent or lower.

"Done, captain," answered Techinsky.

The captain could still see the enemy ships, but his ship quickly faded from the enemy ship's view.

"Move to port 270 – 33, point two impulse."

The ship began moving to its new position, but then there was another flash of light.

"Captain. Another ..."

The blast hit them again. This time, at ninety percent shields it penetrated the first three layers of the ship's hull on the lower level, forcing the crew to seal off six sections of the living quarters.

"How did it target us?" the captain asked.

"They must have some tracking device capable of signature recognition even with our cloak on, sir."

"That can't be. No one has that kind of technology," said the captain.

There was another burst of energy, and this one looked like a supernova had exploded within a few light years of the starship. This one struck the engine room, completely disabling the propulsion system.

"Damage report!" shouted the captain.

"Captain, this is Chief Engineer Pegs. We're dead in the water, sir. We have no propulsion."

"What about warp drive?"

"No, sir. Nothing. No impulse and no warp. We're dead sir."

"Shit!" shouted the captain.

The ship began filling with smoke, and even the experienced crew at the helm deck were rattled.

"Sir, I would advise moving to the escape pods," said Techinsky. "We have little chance of survival if there is another strike."

Won thought for a moment. He knew Techinsky was right.

"Myra, hail the crew. All crew are ordered to the escape pods."

"But captain?"

"That's an order!" he shouted.

Myra got on the ship-wide com system. "Attention all crew. Mandatory evacuation to the escape pods. Repeat. Mandatory evacuation to the escape pods. Abandon ship. Repeat. Abandon ship."

*****

CH 2

Doctor Floyd Rivers left his office, coming down to the multi-purpose room to check on how the day's activities were going. Usually this was a rather simple affair—opening the door, chatting with the Activities Director, Taylor Caldwell, and watching the residents engaging in various games, arts and crafts or physical activities.

The Autumn Breeze Retirement Home had been a fixture in the small town of Bristol for many decades. The former mayor's family, the Peabody's, had donated three million dollars to build the home and it had been run with great success for many generations. There was an area for independent living with apartments for those who could take care of themselves, an assisted living area for those who had some care needs, and a memory loss and intensive care unit for those with major mental acuity issues.

This particular area was dedicated to those with the most severe memory issues and who required constant care and monitoring. The staff in that unit were the very caring and loving type of people anyone would want for support staff. Dr. Rivers was proud of all the facility's units, but the Memory Care Unit was one of his favorites.

"How is everyone today?" Rivers asked, smiling and waving.

None of the residents answered him. They all seemed preoccupied with whatever they were working on. It was the staff, however, who smiled and nodded to him when he arrived.

"It looks like you have everything in order," said the doctor getting ready to leave.

"We do," said Caldwell, his unit director. "But there is something that's worrying me."

"What's that?"

"See the group over in the corner? That small group—two men and one woman? That's Mildred Johnson, Lester Zu, and Peter Raskov."

"What's wrong with that? It looks like they're having a nice time over there."

"Yes, but they've been over there for two hours now. They do this every day—*every day*, sir. We don't know what's going on. They won't participate with the rest of the residents. They only want to be left alone."

Dr. Rivers grinned. "I'll go talk to them."

Rivers went over the group and cleared his throat. "Hello everyone. How is everyone today?" he said slowly and directly.

Mildred looked up but didn't smile. She gave the doctor a look that conveyed she was busy and wanted to be left alone.

"It would be nice if all of you would participate in some of the other activities and with other residents here. You should try to get to know some other people. It would be nice."

"We don't have time for that," said Lester.

"You don't have time?"

"No, and if you will excuse us, we have things to do," said Mildred.

Dr. Rivers didn't appreciate the brushoff, and he returned to Caldwell.

"Do they always act like this?"

"Lately, yes," she answered.

"I think we need to break up their little activity then," said the doctor. "It's not good for them, and it's not good for the other residents in the unit."

Within the hour, two of the huskier orderlies came into the activities room and went with the doctor and the director to address the trio in the corner.

Mildred, Lester, and Peter were all fumbling with their hands and mumbling to each other but weren't making any sense.

"I'm sorry everyone, but we're going to have to break up your little party here. The orderlies will take you back to your rooms. Tomorrow, let's try to interact with the others, shall we?"

"No!" shouted Peter, pushing away one of the orderlies.

"Now, Peter," said Caldwell, coming to assist. "This is for your own good."

"No, it's not! We can't be disturbed right now!" Peter said again.

"He's right," said Lester. "You must leave us!"

But the orderlies grabbed them anyway, and they struggled, twisting their arms and legs to free themselves. However, they were no match for the young, strapping lads who were there to take them away.

"No! Stop it!" Mildred cried out.

"We must get to the escape pods!" said Lester.

"Escape pods?" asked the doctor.

"These residents are delusional," said Caldwell. "They can't separate reality from their own fantasy worlds."

The doctor nodded. "Well, we'll just have to work on that, I guess."

"No! We *must* get to the pods. That's our only hope!" Mildred cried out.

But the orderlies took them back to their rooms and were forced to lock them inside to prevent them from getting out and regrouping in the activities room. Mildred continued to scream at them through the closed door.

"Ms. Caldwell, I am ordering sedation for all three. Please make sure they get it right away. I don't want any incidents in the rooms," said the doctor. "They will be better tomorrow. We'll deal with them then."

*****

CH 3

"Doctor, you need to come down here right now," said Caldwell before hanging up the phone.

Dr. Rivers hurried down the hall, his white coat flapping in the breeze he left in his wake. Opening his director's office door, he stood waiting to hear what the problem was.

"Well?" he asked, his hands on his hips.

"They're gone."

"What do you mean, they're gone?"

"They're not in their rooms. They ... well ... they vanished, doctor."

"Who vanished?"

"Mildred, Lester and Peter. They weren't in their rooms when we went to check on them this morning."

"Someone must have left their doors unlocked during the night when they did their nightly walk-around. You need to search for them."

"No, all the attendants say they locked the doors when they left."

"That's impossible."

"There's more," said Caldwell.

Rivers waited.

"We found these in each of the rooms."

"What's this?"

"We don't know, sir. We've never seen anything like these before, but if I were to guess, they look like communicators – like what we used to see on *Star Trek*."

The doctor laughed. "Right. Sure. They make and sell these everywhere now. It was all part of their fantasy."

"Then what's this?" asked Caldwell.

She put in front of him a handheld device with colored, blinking buttons, a monitor, and other analytics.

"I suppose this is their little medical tricorder," sneered the doctor. "And this is supposed to do what? Detect brain tumors, breast cancer, genetic diseases and potentials?" He laughed.

"Yes, doctor. We tested it this morning. It can do all that and more."

"I don't believe you," said Rivers.

Caldwell took him to an examination room and had the attendant bring in one of the other residents.

"This is Adel Swanson," said Caldwell. "She has papillary thyroid cancer and will be undergoing a lobectomy next week."

Caldwell held up the device beside Adel's neck. Instantly, appearing on the color monitor was 'Papillary Thyroid Cancer-slow growing and stage one. Suggested treatment—remote, pass-through, lobectomy of affected thyrodic area."

Rivers rolled his eyes. "It was programmed to say that. Perhaps it was programmed with the ailments of all the residents so we would be led to believe it was something unique."

"Then what about the next resident," said Caldwell, motioning for him to be brought in.

"Ah, Mr. Xian. Yes, this should be interesting," said Rivers. "We have yet to determine the causes of his symptoms. He's been to several clinics, including Johns Hopkins and Mayo. "I'm curious what the device says about him—probably that he has a cold." Again, the doctor laughed.

Caldwell put the device up to Mr. Xian's chest. The two looked at the display. But instead of a simple message on the screen, the device projected a 3D hologram into the middle of the room showing different parts of Xian's body and labeling specific ailments.

In addition to citing Type II diabetes, which he had, the image showed him with elevated transferrin of 600 mg/dl—well above the 200-400 mg/dl healthy range. That suggested a liver problem.

"Yes, that's something I've been aware of too. So, it hasn't told us anything we don't already know," said Rivers.

"Then what about that?" She pointed to another area of the body and the message attached.

"We know he's had abdominal problems and constipation issues," said Rivers. "That's nothing new."

"It says here he has Ogilvie Syndrome."

"What?"

"I don't know. You're the doctor. Ogilvie Syndrome."

Rivers shook his head. "I've never heard of it."

Rivers left the examination room, and it was nearly an hour before he found Caldwell in her office. His face was white as a sheet—like he'd seen a ghost.

"Well? What did you find out?" she asked him.

Rivers stared at her. He grabbed the communicator from her desk and turned it on.

"If you're there Mildred, Lester or Peter, tell me where you are," he said chuckling nervously. "This is a pretty good hoax. You've fooled me. Now, just tell us where you are, and we can forget this ever happened."

There was static on the other end of the communicator, and then a voice came over it.

"Dr. Rivers. This is Captain Won. We have beamed your three residents up to our ship and are very grateful you have shared them with us. They are making a valuable contribution to us and in our current predicament.

"We also hope you found the diagnosis of Mr. Xian helpful. The Ogilvie Syndrome is exceedingly rare, as you know. However, now that you have the diagnosis, we are confident that you can help him.

"Thanks again, and best of luck to you and your team on Earth."

*****

BUT IT WAS FREE

CH 1

It was the hottest Christmas gift since the Pet Rock and American Girl Doll. What was even better was the fact that the gift was free.

Little advertising had gone out about the device, and little was needed. All the manufacturer had to do was set the price at zero – free – and it became an instant "best-seller." Everyone wanted one, and they soon became scarce. The units were being sold on the black market for hundreds or even thousands of dollars even though they were originally given away. When the manufacturer suddenly announced it was ceasing production, the last thousand vanished, almost overnight.

"When will there be another batch produced?" asked an inquiring reporter from the *Milwaukee Herald*.

The company spokesperson pushed several of the microphones away that had been pushed into his face so he could properly address the barrage of reporters crowding inside the company's conference room.

"Management has changed its focus regarding the X Unit, Model 1984B. It will begin production again, although the unit will be upgraded to the 1984C model which has enhanced capabilities. Those with the B model may wish to upgrade to the C model as older versions will no longer be supported."

"But why wouldn't the company support older models?" asked a reporter.

"The units were issued free, you know. Do you understand what that means? They were *free*. Providing support was a temporary and limited benefit at that time, but the company cannot continue to support free units without any revenue coming in to pay its support staff."

"I don't understand," said the reporter.

"Look, the company put money into creating and building these units— you know, research and development work. It also manufactured all of them, which cost a lot. It's made no money on this. We were doing it as a community service. That's all. The units were free. Free!"

"What about support for Model C units?" asked the news reporter. "Will you provide support for those?"

"Yes. At least initially, the company will make good on its promise to support those units."

"Will they be free?"

"Yes. For a limited time, they too will be free. However, this is for a *limited* time, you understand. After the end of the year, the units will no longer be produced or will be sold in the marketplace. We haven't yet decided."

"How much will they be then?"

"We don't know," said the spokesperson. "We're probably talking about several thousand dollars each, however."

As a result, the new Model C units flew off the shelves as fast as they were produced. Store owners were incentivized to distribute them, paid fifty dollars per unit registered with a legitimate buyer. All the information about the buyer was required, and it was extensive. Some one hundred questions were asked, and all the data was stored in a giant database at the company: E Arthur Blair Industries.

By the end of the year, nearly ninety percent of all households had a Model C unit. And that was exactly what Eric Blair, the CEO, was hoping for.

*****

CH 2

"Helen? What do you think about getting a new levipod this weekend? Ours is starting to have problems, and it's been costing a bunch to fix it every time it goes down. I read that replacing the coagulator coil can cost several thousands and that's probably what will breakdown next."

"Are you sure we need a new one, or you're just saying that because you *want* a new one?" Helen asked her husband, Mitch who was coming out of the bedroom.

There was brief silence before he answered her. "Both," he said, smiling.

"Well, only if we can get a good deal on one. I like the Trishare. What do you think?"

"Yeah, I like that one, especially the LX model."

"Alright. Maybe we'll take a look at that one to start and go from there," answered his wife.

Within moments, there were pop-ups on their computers advertising the 2144 Trishare LX, on special at Eulier Motors. It was only 2.1 million units, a nice discount off the usual price.

Helen read the ad and forwarded it to Mitch. "What do you think?" she asked.

"Let's stop by. Can't hurt."

***

Later that day, their neighbor, Vance Morgan, stopped for a quick visit.

"Mitch, we were just wondering if you and Helen would be interested in taking a trip to Vegas with us. We're going in July and thought it would be a lot of fun."

Mitch smiled. "Gosh, Vance, you know how much I hate to gamble," Mitch said, laughing. "I haven't been to Vegas in … well, three months. I'd love to go, of course. I live for that place. But Helen isn't really fond of it. Maybe I can convince her with the shows and shopping. Let me ask her."

Helen instantly received a computer pop-up.

Have you thought about vacationing in Las Vegas? Now's a great time of year and hotel rooms are deeply discounted. Rooms can be gotten in the best hotels for as little as 21,000 units. Also, there are super shows now. You can watch the latest music and theatre performances. What do you say? Say yes!

"Honey?" asked Helen, "have you thought about going to Las Vegas? I hear they have great buys on shows and hotel rooms. What do you think?"

Mitch was surprised. He was still trying to figure out how to convince her to go, and now, suddenly, she was asking him. He was overjoyed.

"Uh, well, yeah. I think it would be okay," he answered, acting as if he hadn't thought about it. "I know you like shows and shopping, so if that works for you, I guess it would be okay with me," he said, hoping she would say yes.

"Okay. I'll go ahead and book it for us."

"That's great. Say, why don't I talk to Vance and Mary and see if they'd be interested."

"Good idea," answered Mary.

***

Two weeks later, after several more incidents …

"Mitch, what do you think about this Model C to the 1984B system? We have the Model B, but this is the new one."

"Is it free?"

"Yeah, it's free but only for another few weeks. I think it would be great to have all the upgrades that our B model doesn't have."

"Like what?" Mitch asked.

"Well, it's got artificial intelligence. They call it AI. I don't know what that means, but it sounds pretty cool. They say it can help with a lot of things around the house and with family stuff, like scheduling, planning, budgeting—all that."

"And it's free? Just like the previous one?"

"Yeah."

"Okay, then. I don't understand how they can make it free. But if that's what they keep offering us, it's okay with me."

***

The Model C arrived, and Helen quickly replaced the old model with the new one. She didn't even have to plug the new one in. It ran off energy waves already generated within the household. It never had to be charged, and, conveniently, it never could be turned off.

The round, globe-like unit sat on the table in the family room, and its sensitivity to vibration, including all sound and light, was staggering. The unit could even sense vibrations through walls.

Within and beyond the radius of the household, the unit boasted the abilities to hear and recognize speech and see movement up to one hundred meters in all directions, whether there were walls or not. More astounding was the fact the unit came with a permanent placement adhesive. When the unit was attached to a fixture, the lower piece could not be removed, even though the upper portion could be relocated. The lower portion would continue to record all the energies and redirect them to the upper section's new location. In essence, once placed, the unit never released its ability to receive information from that original location or any subsequent location.

It was all perfectly disclosed, albeit in the fine print of the ninety-three-page terms and conditions agreement which no one read.

"Let's put it there," said Helen, pointing to the fireplace mantle. "That way, it can hear and see us when we talk to it."

Mitch pulled the strange-looking C unit from the box and attached it to the mantle. He then turned it on, letting it automatically download all the family data from the old Model B before he packed up the old unit to send back to the company.

Quite proud of their purchase, Mitch and Helen watched their favorite program on the large, remote screen that came with it. Neither of them knew that all their actions, conversations, and movements were being recorded. Not only that, but the data was being fed back to the manufacturer which was an arm of the Ministry of Homeland Security.

*****

CH 3

Three months later ...

Mitch and Helen had led relatively tranquil lives – that is, until the last three months. During that time, they had seen most of their friends fall away from their social circle and many others abandoned them on social media. Helen had asked several former friends why they dropped them.

"Oh, Helen. It's been so busy here. Bob and I are working with the homeless shelter and all. We'll catch up soon."

Or,

"Helen, I'm so sorry. Jack has been working so many hours lately. I'm having to do everything around the house. The maid service just isn't what it used to be."

Finally, Mitch got a call from a former friend, Randy Armstrong.

"Mitch, you must have gotten one of those C models, am I right?"

"Yeah, why?" asked Mitch.

"I can't say anything. Just go to sss.deepblackhole.forbidden.onion. Good luck, buddy." Randy hung up.

Mitch pulled up the site and began to read. Once he finished, he had to sit down—shocked and disturbed at what he had seen.

> To those able to still reach this website and get this message, please understand: <u>you are in danger</u>.
>
> If you have a Model C unit of the X unit 1984, then you must be aware of the dangers involved. While Model B was dangerous enough, Model C is programmed to <u>read</u> the thoughts of its homeowners. There is no hiding from Model C. It can read your mind from many meters away. Once it does, it transmits those thoughts to companies that have become so powerful they can control your daily lives, whether you know it or not. But worse yet, the unit sends all data to the Ministry of Homeland Security—yes, the government. They know <u>everything</u> about you—even what you're thinking.
>
> They know what you're planning to do or even considering doing. What's worse, the MHS will anonymously make available select

> portions of that information to others in your network if it will incite distrust or disharmony.

Laughing, Mitch closed the post. *That's ridiculous,* he thought. *Nothing like that is going on. These are a bunch of conspiracy nut jobs!*

He didn't bother mentioning it to Helen, knowing she too would only laugh.

Yet, when he booted up his computer, he saw something strange.

> *If you have been approached by someone claiming that the Model C unit of the Unit X 1984 is spying on you, you are being lied to. You must report all such contact immediately to the machine's manufacturer and to local authorities. It is your duty as a citizen of the People's Republic to help the authorities track down and apprehend persons spreading such lies.*

Huh? thought Mitch. *Now that's strange.*

*****

CH 4

"Erik, how are you?" asked the Minister of Homeland Security, George Wells. "I've seen the numbers. The distribution of your new model—Model C—has been impressive. It appears the newest model has doubled the previous distribution you set with the introduction of your 1984 B model."

"Yes, Minister, it has been successful. We will soon begin charging thirty thousand units per year for support of the Model C, and as you suggested, the model will shut down all home activity without a service contract." Blair was immensely proud of his company and its monopoly over the space.

"That includes, water and electricity. What about food?" asked Wells.

Blair smiled. "That was easy, minister. Without our Model C working, they won't have access to any of their bank accounts. They'll have no money. After thirty days of inactivity in their accounts, the money goes directly into your Treasury Ministry. You passed that law last year, don't you remember?"

"Of course. Brilliant! Brilliant! No food, no water, no electricity. They'll starve or be on the verge of it. Then, they'll come back to us begging on their knees. They'll agree to anything then."

"Yes, minister. Anything."

*****

CH 5

It wasn't long after Mitch received the warning message that the coincidences grew more extreme. One night, Helen learned that her sister was attempting to falsify an application for a passport to leave the country. She had to persuade her not to do it for the punishment for being caught was life in prison without parole. What that usually meant was a hard labor camp. She hadn't told Mitch but was planning to after she got things worked out with her sister.

The next day, Helen got an urgent call from their mother.

"Helen?"

"Yes, Mom?"

"It's your mother."

"I know Mom. It's on my number reader. What's up?"

"Well, I need to tell you that Tricia has been arrested. She was taken into custody this morning."

"What?" asked Helen.

"She said they arrested her for attempting to falsify papers to leave the country. She didn't know how they knew that, but they arrested her for it."

There was silence on the other end of the line.

"Helen?"

"Yeah, Mom. I'm here."

"Your sister said you were the only one who knew."

"Mom, yeah, I knew, but I didn't tell anyone. I swear! I didn't even know if she'd really do it," said Helen.

"She thinks you ratted her out."

"I didn't, Mom. I'll have to call you back. There's another call coming in that I need to take."

Helen didn't have another call, but she had to compose herself. She thought she'd been the only person her sister had talked to about it. She hadn't even told her husband. That meant, her sister had been stupid and told somebody else. *That was it … she blabbed it to somebody who turned her in.*

Helen called Mitch and told him what had happened.

"Helen, someone sent me a link to this underground website. We may not be safe."

Mitch told her about what he saw, but said he wasn't sure it was true. Now, he wasn't so sure it *wasn't* true.

"That's not possible, is it?" she asked.

"I don't know, Helen. But what if it is? What if it *is* true? What if they *can* listen in on you? What if they record everything we do? What if they can read your thoughts?" He stopped. "Are you at home?" he asked.

"Yeah, why?"

"Rip the thing off the fireplace mantle and throw it in the dumpster outside. Just get it *out* of the house. Can you do that?"

"Yeah, sure. But wasn't there something about it being *permanent wherever we put it.* Remember, I read that to you from the instructions."

"Don't worry about that now. Just get that damn thing out of the house!" stressed Mitch.

Helen hung up and went to the fireplace. She grabbed the device on the mantle and pulled on it, but it didn't budge. She pulled harder, but it still didn't move.

Now what? she thought. *How am I going to get this thing off?*

"Hello?" she said, calling a contractor, "I have a small job in the house. It shouldn't take more than a few minutes. Can someone come out?"

However, after going through six contractors, she gave up. Once they found out what she wanted done, they left her house and didn't return.

Finally, she was able to remove the top half, leaving the bottom part on the mantle. She put the rest in the dumpster. However, that didn't stop the problem. The lower section merely transmitted what they did to Eric Blair's company and on to the Ministry of Homeland Security.

"Mitch, it's been two days, and I can't find anyone to remove the bottom unit. What do you want to do?"

Mitch sighed. "Well, we can live in other parts of the house and cover it up?"

"No, remember, the post said it can hear and sense what's going on over a hundred meters around."

"Well, maybe we should move. Maybe we have to sell the house," said Mitch.

Helen contacted the real estate agent and went through the checklist of items.

"Yes, this is just a standard list of questions we must ask of the homeowner," said the agent. "It's required by law. So, let me start. Do you have any mechanical problems with air conditioning or heating?"

"No."

"Do you have any liens against the property? Anybody who has filed a claim for money owed against you?"

"No."

"Do you have any special devices affixed within the home?"

"Like what?"

"Like a Unit X?"

"Why yes," said Helen.

"Which model do you have?"

"We have a Model C," said Helen cautiously. "It's the latest and best of the versions you know."

There was a pause on the other end of the line. "Helen, have you placed the unit in the home, and have you been using it?"

"Uh, why?"

"Because it's a required disclosure point. You must answer truthfully, you know. Any false answer is prosecutable by the authorities. So, have you placed it in the home and is it activated?"

"Yes."

"I see," said the agent. "Well, I will get back to you on selling your home. We'll need to review the answers to the checklist. Thank you, Helen, for your time."

Three days passed, and Helen did not receive a return call. Even though almost every home in the state had the device affixed to the home in some way, no one wanted to buy someone else's problem. They had their own to worry about. As a result, no homes were selling.

Helen tried again with several other agents, but when the question of the devices came up, they hung up on her. The last time, she even lied, but the home inspection proved she had not been honest—they found the base section rigidly attached to the mantle in the family room.

"Ms. McLernon, we could bring charges against you for lying on your application about the Unit X; however, we won't. Please understand that it is a felony offense punishable by up to forty years in prison to lie on your checklist. I would advise you not do that again. Good day, Ms. McLernon."

"Mitch, what do we do?" Helen asked, now more terrified.

"We burn the place," said Mitch. "We burn it to the ground and claim our insurance money. That's what we do." Both he and his wife were miles from their house. They only hoped they were safe.

The next morning, Mitch's eyes fluttered and finally opened. He could hear the fluttering of noises in the air nearby, but he couldn't place them. Only when he saw a levicopter land in his back yard did he sit upright in his bed. He ran to the rear window and looked out. It was a gray, overcast day and the sun was obscured behind a thick layer of clouds.

Yet, flying just below the cloud layer, he saw six more levicopters come into the park behind his house and land. With their anti-gravity thrusters pointed down, they made a soft touchdown as the paratroopers jumped from the back in droves, quickly spreading out around their apartment. Carrying AR-19 M2 rifles and full-body communication suits, the assaulting militia took positions around the periphery of the complex.

Without notice, they broke through the couple's front door with its extensive safety mechanisms and sealed off every point of exit and escape. Two troopers stormed into their bedroom: their rifles drawn. Wearing full infrared headgear and earpieces that told them what the couple were thinking, they quickly pointed their weapons at the pair who were sitting straight up and shaking.

"What do you want?" asked Mitch, his voice trembling.

"Sir, madam, you need to come with us," said the man.

"Why? What have we done?"

"It's not what you've done. It's what you plan to do. You are plotting to rid yourselves of the Model C, is that right? You are attempting to nullify the agreement you struck with the company. That's a violation of the law under Part A, section six, sub-section c and sub-sub section iii. Under that law, you may be fined. However, under statue 10181.2808, subsection two, we have a pretty clear case of conspiracy to commit arson. That, my friends, comes with a penalty of life in prison." Then, he laughed. "But that's if no one dies in the fire. If someone does, you get the death penalty, I'm afraid."

"You can't do this!"

"We just did," said the SWAT commander.

He motioned to two other troopers who dragged in a long, black bag. It had the outline shape of a body.

"We need to get rid of this piece of *shit*, so this is as good of time as any."

"What are you doing?" asked Helen as she was handcuffed and led out of the bedroom. Terrified, she looked back over her shoulder at her husband.

"I've got good news and bad news," said the SWAT commander. "The good news is that we're going to torch this place for you, so you don't have to."

"Why would you do that?" asked Mitch, confused.

"Because we have a body to dispose of. That's the bad news, I'm afraid. We'll leave behind this body, so it looks like you did kill an innocent person when you set fire to your place. Not only did you want to get rid of the Model C, but you also apparently wanted to get rid of a corpse too. Such a shame. It looks like it's going to be the death penalty for you now, doesn't it?"

"You bastard!" shouted Helen. "You won't get away with this. We'll fight you in the courts."

"Ha! I don't think so. You'll be so drugged up when you leave here, you won't have any ability to mount a defense."

Mitch spat at the man.

"Oh, now don't do something stupid like that," said the commander. "It gives me more reason to just shoot both of you for resisting me. That would make my paperwork a whole lot easier. So, I'll give you three doors to choose from. Door number one: I shoot you now for resisting arrest. Door number two: we torch the place, and you get the death penalty. Or door number three."

"What is door number three?" asked Helen.

"You tell me where you stashed the three billion units in cash. We know you have it here someplace. Our little machine told us that much. Now, where is it?"

Mitch and Helen looked at each other, each very confused.

"Ah, that's where it is," said the man. He walked to the fireplace mantle and pressed a spot on the base of the Model C machine. Then, he lifted it off easily and placed it on the floor.

"What are you doing?" shouted Mitch.

"I'm stealing your savings," said the man, grinning.

He pushed up on the cement ledge which came off in one piece. Inside were rows of neatly stacked units—thousands of them.

"How did you know?"

"I read your minds when I asked the question. We have our ways, and we always get what we want. Now, if you'd like me to go ahead and shoot you as well, we can do that. Otherwise, we're taking the money, leaving the body and torching your place. Sound like a deal?"

"*That* was door number three?" Mitch asked.

"No, there were never three doors—only one. Sorry for the confusion."

*****

NOWHERE MAN

CH 1

Max Toolant started a technology business—one that specialized in developing software for companies manufacturing artificial intelligent robots. On a shoestring, he had borrowed from family and friends, raising over three hundred thousand dollars. His software was not only more effective but was more efficient than anyone else's on the market, requiring less memory storage by a factor of one hundred than the leading competitor. As a result, robot "brains" could be dramatically reduced in size. The current models required remote distribution of processing power throughout the body of the robot, but this created other problems in latency – delays in processing speed and times. Toolant's design solved all those problems.

When he sold his business to outside investors five years later, he pocketed a cool twelve trillion dollars which made him the wealthiest man on the planet.

"Where's my bitch!" he yelled. It was ten in the morning, and he was already drunk. He had been drinking since seven that morning when his golden retriever, Bugs, needed to go outside to relieve himself.

Toolant's drinking had become worse during the previous three months as he had become bored with buying homes, cars, islands, and other toys. Indulgence in a wanton lifestyle had taken over him, and his drive and motivation to do or accomplish anything in life had changed overnight.

At thirty-six, he already looked like he was in his early fifties, and his parents were concerned for his well-being. He had two siblings—Regent and Paulina—and he had been generous to both, giving them new homes and lavish living allowances. But as with many things received without working for them, his brother and sister had not been appreciative; instead, they had only wanted to know when their next payments would come. On the other hand, his parents had refused his giving them anything, thanking him for his generosity but telling them they were just fine living in their twenty-four hundred square foot home in the suburbs of Philadelphia.

"Max," said his mother, "I'm worried about you. You're cursing and drinking, and God knows what else. I just think ..."

"Ma! I'm fine! Don't worry about me."

"Well, I do worry about you. You just haven't been the same lately. You seem down."

"I'm fine!" shouted Toolant, getting unruly and cross. "Listen. I gotta' go."

"Max, we love you," she said before he hung up. But her son didn't answer.

He disconnected the line and yelled again across the room.

"Hey, bitch! I want another martini. What's wrong with you!"

He took the V-shaped glass with three green olives speared by a white, plastic skewer and took another gulp, dribbling some on his t-shirt. He put the glass down on a cork coaster and pulled closer the voluptuous blonde who was busy unzipping his pants. Taking her tight, knit sweater, he lifted it over her head, revealing a set of round, full breasts.

After she had finished on him, he lay back and shut his eyes, but the usual feeling of ecstasy had become deadened and mute. More often, it had become disappointing. He pushed his head against the soft, silk pillow and stared out through the panoramic window that overlooked the serenity and magnificence of the Aegean Sea. Still hours from setting, the sun shone brightly overhead, casting few shadows on his balcony outside yet igniting the lapping waters below it with its glittering golden light.

"What's wrong?" asked Toolant's prostitute. "Didn't I ..."

"Go," he answered darkly. "Just go."

He turned away from her, staring at the dazzling beach with sunbathers beginning to setup their umbrellas for a leisurely afternoon. She got off the sofa, put on her blouse and skirt and strapped on her black heels before she left. She didn't know if she'd see him again, but she didn't care. He was just another john. She had many others that paid her well; she didn't need him.

Max soon dozed off, but it wasn't long before strange images flooded his mind. He usually dreamed in color, and this was no exception. The vivid pictures floated in and floated out, but nothing lasted. When he opened his eyes, he couldn't remember any of the images or what had happened. Max didn't think he'd been asleep that long, but the sun was already falling toward the late afternoon waters when he went out on his balcony to take in the view of the Aegean Sea. It was beautiful; yet he could no longer see its beauty. He could no longer appreciate its completeness—its perfection. He was lost.

Still groggy, he dressed and shuffled down the stairs of his villa, taking his routine walk to a favorite espresso bar just down the street. But by the time he reached the bottom of the stairs, dark, billowy clouds began to roll in, threatening a storm. He shrugged off going back for an umbrella and hurried to his favorite espresso house before it began to pour. When he arrived, he saw Lorenzo who was washing his hands. By the time, Max reached the counter, Lorenzo was folding his white apron and placing it under the counter.

"Where you been?" Lorenzo asked, mildly annoyed. "I close up for today."

"No," answered Max, "it can't be that late, can it?"

"It four forty-five," said Lorenzo, not breaking a smile. "No cappuccino after twelve, and we done with espresso till tonight. Sorry, Max. You late today."

Max shrugged. He'd known Lorenzo for only nine months but had never seen him so put-out.

"No problem, Lorenzo buddy. I'll catch you tomorrow."

Max hopped off the stool and left, looking up and down the street for someplace else to go. It was raining by then, and the cool, pelting raindrops spattered the cobblestone roadway in town making it slippery with a reflective sheen. He passed a green box and put money in to open it. Carefully, he lifted out a paper and read the headline: "*Una nuova terra prevista!* (A New Earth Predicted!)" Max laughed and started to stuff the paper under his arm but then noticed something: the date. The date was *three* days after he'd called his mother. *That can't be!* he thought. *I couldn't have slept for three days! That's impossible.*

Yet, it was then that he spotted a store across the road he hadn't noticed before. The simple, wooden sign over the doorway read *Fortunes Leggi* with lettering in a flourished style reminiscent of the great Italian Renaissance. Whether in English or Italian it basically meant the same thing: *Fortunes Read Here.*

Huh, he thought.

Walking across the street, he went up to the small, green door and knocked. At first there seemed to be no one there, but eventually someone did answer, peering out and seemingly unsure whether the person was a burglar or a paying customer.

"*Ciao?*" asked the old woman, whose head was wrapped with a heavy, red-and-gray-patterned scarf.

She was short and had long ago lost the curves she likely cherished as a young girl. Missing a few teeth and having difficulty seeing, she squinted, making the many lines in her face even more numerous. These wrinkles revealed a lifetime of stress and trauma, whether from her family, her friends, outside events or a combination of all three. Likely in her eighties or older, she waited for the patron who had graced the front of her doorstep to reply.

"*Si,*" answered Max, straining to come up with an Italian answer. "*Uh, sei aperto per affari?*" he mumbled, asking if she were open.

"*Si, si,*" she answered, opening the door to let him in.

The inside of the small space was dark and musty with heavy, golden curtains drawn tightly across the abundance of windows in the front. The clutter in the room and lack of light made it seem ominous and sinister. Chocked full of furniture and knick-knacks, the space was claustrophobic and difficult to navigate. Even the wood-paneled walls were covered with photos of all shapes, sizes, and colors—from black and whites, to sepia, to full spectrum color. They all showed family members, friends, acquaintances, and others—some joyous and celebratory, others serious and contemplative. Then there were the old ones, with family members lined up in two rows—somber men with caps and full beards in back, stoic women with matronly dresses and aprons in front. None looked particularly happy or contented.

"*Siediti!*" the ole woman said, pointing to a dark-stained chair with grooved, wooden arms and mustard-colored cushions.

Max sat as he was told. Then, he asked, "*Lei parla Inglese?*"

"*Un po … un poshissimo,*" she answered. "So, what you want?"

She pulled up a matching chair and sat in front of him. She did not smile and hadn't since he'd arrived. Yet, he knew it wasn't personal; that was just the way she was. It was the way her family was.

"I'm a bit confused. I … well … how do I say it? I fell asleep last night, but now I'm not sure. It may have been many days ago. I'm sure it's the drink and the drugs. Still, I know I didn't sleep for three days, but that's what the date on today's paper said. Oh, I can't explain it really; so, I guess I'm looking for …"

"… answers," said the woman completing his thought.

"Yes, … quite right. I'm looking for answers. But …" He looked around the dark room and shook his head. "… I think I've come to the wrong place. I'm sorry to have bothered you, ma'am."

Max started to get up, but the old woman gave him a firm look and motioned for him to sit back down.

"I may have answers," she said, still not smiling. "Tell me what you remember."

Max told her about the prior night—about the prostitute, his mother, his drugs, all of it. He knew it didn't matter whether she knew or not, especially where he was staying. The Italian village was remote and beautiful, and the coastline spectacular. Sinewy roads carved out their boundaries along the steep, craggy mountains that overlooked the magnificence of the azure blue waters of the Aegean Sea. The weather was always temperate and balmy, making every day enjoyable, if not paradisal.

"You like a limoncello?" she asked, getting up and walking stiffly to a tall, cabinet painted in tones of white and seafoam green in the next room. She opened one of the glass-paneled doors and pulled out a tall, thin bottle of yellow liqueur and two tiny cordial glasses. Setting them down on the rickety, iron coffee table, she poured the golden liquid and handed a glass to him. As for hers, the limoncello disappeared within seconds, and she quickly poured herself another.

Max picked up his glass too and slammed it back like a fast shot of tequila. It was lemony sweet. As a local favorite, the liqueur was widely sought after by tourists when they visited.

"Thanks," he said, puckering his lips. "But you were saying that you might know something about what happened to me."

"Si," she answered. "Tell me about dreams you've had. Can you remember them?"

Max thought for a moment. His recollection was foggy, but there were bits and pieces he could recall.

"I do seem to remember a couple in particular," he started.

"Go on."

"Well, in one of my dreams, I was flying an airplane full of passengers. I don't know how to fly a plane, so it was strange. My co-pilot was an orangutan, but he talked and acted like a normal human being. He was orange and wore a pilot's uniform, yet he had the hands of an ape and wasn't able to use any of the controls. We hit some turbulence, and the plane started bouncing around. I screamed at him to do this or that, but he couldn't 'cause he couldn't move the cockpit controls.

"One of the flight attendants hailed me on the intercom, but her words were gibberish. I couldn't tell what she was saying. She finally hung up on me—giving up on getting an answer. Next, as I was trying to stabilize the plane, the sky turned banana yellow. The air became thick like we had flown into a bowl of Jell-O. Then, everything slowed down.

"I remember glancing over at my co-pilot and noticed that he, the orangutan, wasn't there anymore. His seat was empty. Don't you find that strange?"

"What was other dream?" asked the old woman, watching him intently.

Max paused, thinking. "Oh, yeah, that's right. It was strange too. In that one, I was in a wagon train going across the prairie. It was, like, in the nineteenth century, and I was riding in a Conestoga wagon. I was all alone but knew there were hundreds of other wagons behind me watching which way I was going. They were following, and I knew they would turn whichever way I turned. I guess I was their leader.

"We had been on the trail heading west for days, and all of us were tired and hungry. We had been attacked by Indians the day before and were out of food and water 'cause the Indians had made off with them. Ahead of us we saw a great mountain range which I assumed was the Rockies. I whipped the horses with my leather lash to push them up the steep slope to cross over the peak. The trail was rocky and dangerous. The drop offs were ... well ... like they are here—hundreds of feet down if you veer too close to the edge."

"What happen then?" asked the woman, riveting her eyes onto Max.

But Max stopped. "I don't I remember what happens next," he answered, looking confused.

"Yes, you do. Concentrate. What happen next?" she pushed.

After a few moments, Max continued. "I think I pushed the horses up the trail until we reached a fork in the road."

"A fork?"

"Where the road splits into two separate paths. I heard the wagons pulling up behind me and felt the pressure to choose one. But I didn't know which way to go. I waited, and then something pulled up next to me in another wagon."

"Someone?"

"No, *something*. It was …" Max stopped again, and then his mind cleared, "… it was that same orangutan that was my co-pilot. He came long the wagon and asked me if I knew where I was going. I looked at him and blurted out, 'Absolutely, I know where to go. Why do you question me on this?'"

"But you not know," said the woman.

"No, I had no idea. So, I looked both directions and tried to choose one quickly before they sensed the truth."

"And?"

"And that's when I woke up. I don't remember anything after that. What do you think all that means?"

The old woman sighed. Her expression changed little.

"You must choose," she answered. "You must choose between two paths – two lifestyles. You either continue down current path you're on or you change to another."

"What other?"

She pulled up close to him and drew him into her gaze. "Should you call your mother and ask her?" the old woman smiled. "If you did, what would she tell you?"

Max nodded.

"Yes. I thought so. You already know the answer."

*****

CH 2

Max left the shop and began walking to his apartment. Still puzzled, he stopped and turned back toward the old woman's place. Oddly, it was no longer there. In its place was another store but with the same sign; except this one read: *Limoncello*.

I need more sleep, he thought, shaking his head.

He shrugged it off and continued to his penthouse apartment. However, along the way he passed an old man pushing a cart full of ripe, red tomatoes. After he'd passed, Max felt a finger on his shoulder.

"Excuse me sir," said the man in perfect English.

Startled, Max swung around. "Yes?"

"I was wondering if you knew where the Duomo di' Sant Andrea is?"

Max looked at the man curiously. He didn't appear to be a foreigner or strange visitor to the area. Quite the contrary. Apart from his perfect, English accent, he looked like a typical, farmer pushing his produce to the local market in town.

"Uh, I'm not sure where it is," said Max, "but I think it's two streets over. Make a left, and then follow the road up the hill. At the end, you'll turn right, and it's a block down the road. You can't miss it."

Max wasn't sure how he knew that, but it had just suddenly come to him.

"Thanks mate," said the man continuing to push the cart into town. Then he turned once more and added, "Maybe I'll see you there, *eh?*"

Max smiled and waved to the old man as he continued his walk.

When Max arrived home, he found a notice stuffed into the dark crevice of his door. He pulled it out but decided not to read it thinking it was just a solicitation. So, he crumpled it up and threw it into the short, tin waste basket just inside the doorway. He then picked up the TV remote, turning on the sports channel to catch the latest cricket match back in England.

When the cricket match came on, Max went to the refrigerator to grab a beer. By the time he returned to his sofa, the match had paused for a commercial break.

"Duomo di' Sant Andrea. We are the largest church in the Amalfi area, and we are holding mass on Sunday at nine o'clock and again at eleven o'clock. We hope you can join us."

Another hour into the match, Max rose from his sofa again to get another cold beer. Popping the tab, he poured the yellow bubbly into a clear-glass stein watching as it foamed up to the rim. As he emptied the can, he noticed the crumpled paper he thought he had thrown away sitting next to the stein on the countertop.

"What?"

He uncrumpled it and read the message. *Come join us this Sunday,* it read.

Huh? thought Max before setting it aside on the counter.

***

The church had been there for centuries. It's cold, granite blocks were relics from a building era that had lasted millennia—up until the use of stone in buildings was banned. Only concrete, glass, and new hardened acrylic polymers were allowed due to the negative impact stone mining quarries had on the environment.

The front of the church had three arched entryways. The largest was in the center with two smaller ones framing either side. In the middle of each arch were double hardwood doors with two columns of panels that were stacked in twelve rows and held beautifully carved scenes from the Bible within each. Of Gothic design, the arches were pointed and framed with rows of cherubs and serifs together with the church's signature emblem, the *pisce* or sign of the fish. On the side portals were statues of the apostles, the Virgin Mary and Joseph. Above the archways were throngs of angelic statues, all cut from the same type of Siena marble and each with a different face—from the stern Gabriel to the more empathetic Michael.

Max walked through the grand center door and expected to find an organ playing and a choir belching out hymns of *How Great Thou Art* or *All Things Bright and Beautiful.* Instead, he found it dark and silent. Even the votive candles, so ubiquitous in most cathedrals, were unlit. *It is Sunday, isn't it?* he thought. *I didn't sleep through another three days, did I?*

He felt a strange warmth come over him as he entered the nave, and then, suddenly, he felt the rush of wind across his face as he was catapulted through a black ether of time and space. He tried to keep his eyes open, and soon saw a round, spot of light ahead. It grew larger as if he were traveling through the proverbial tunnel after death. Quickly, the circle of light ballooned into an all-encompassing whiteness, the intensity of which he had never experienced before. Once on the other side, the bright light began to dim, and the images around him started to sharpen.

He was in another world. All around him lights were flickering, and sounds were buzzing. Like sitting in the cockpit of a battleship-sized star cruiser, he was surrounded with electronics of amazing complexity: holographic screens, swirling 4D images, colliding and undulating vectors and pictures, all bouncing off each other and then coalescing again. These geometric figures slowly morphed into images of people talking, laughing, crying, running, playing, working, and generally going about their daily lives. There were millions, maybe billions, of pictures—each with a number and undecipherable symbol inserted into the bottom left corner. Clouds of white energy hovered over the consoles, spinning the images at thousands of frames per second. He was inundated by the imagery and struggled to comprehend it all.

"Where am I?" he shrieked. "What's going on?"

He listened for an answer, but none came.

"I said, where am I?"

Suddenly, another burst of energy exploded in front of him, glowing with remarkable brilliance. Quickly it transformed into a young, beautiful woman with long, chestnut brown hair, thin lips, hazel eyes, and an intriguing, beguiling smile. Tall and thin, she moved her arms and made gestures like an angel floating on a cloud of vapors.

"You have asked a question?"

"Yes," said Max in a demanding tone, "I want to know where I am."

"Where do you think you are?"

Max looked around. All he could see were rows and rows of electronic consoles but no one there to operate them. He glanced up too, and there he found more layers. Like an endless series of store shelves, each layer was packed with equipment blinking lights, screens, holographic displays, and panels with pictures of people and numbers on them. Not only were the sounds of every pitch and modulation, but the lights were of all colors – yellows, golds, silvers, violets, greens, blues, and others. All were there, except red.

"I don't know where I am," he answered. "But what are all these machines? What are they doing, and who's in charge of it?"

"So, you don't know where you are," the woman asked.

Max didn't like being asked a question he couldn't answer. He was usually the one asking—not having to explain.

"You tell me," he countered.

"Why, of course, you're on the other side."

"The other side? What do you mean?" he asked.

"The other side from where you were," said the woman ambiguously.

"I ... I don't know."

"If I said you were in Heaven, what would you say?"

"Well, that would make sense. I did come in through the front door of the church."

"What if I said you were in Hell? What would you say, then?"

Max looked around once more.

"If I'm in hell, then I'd say you're lying to me. That's what you do in hell, right?"

There was a pause before the woman spoke again.

"Let's say you're right. If you're right, then you would still be in heaven, correct?"

"Yeah, I guess so," said Max.

"But if you were in heaven, then, I wouldn't be lying to you, would I?"

This time Max had to think.

"You're trying to trick me."

"Is that what I'm trying to do?"

"Stop it!" shouted Max, frustrated.

It was then the woman's face became more rigid and stern.

"Wait, I didn't mean that. I'm sorry," said Max seeing he had offended her.

"Go over to that tube," said the woman, nodding toward a clear, oval-shaped cylinder that rose high above them—so far that Max couldn't tell where it ended. "It will take you to where you need to go."

By the time Max looked at the tube and then back again, the woman's fuzzy form had evaporated into a silvery mist.

"*Sh*t!*" said Max.

He walked to the tube and stepped inside. Immediately, a curved, transparent door materialized and sealed him in before the floor beneath his feet dropped. Like in a high-speed elevator in New York City, he descended quickly. The scene around him changed, and instead of myriads of dials, screens, and read-outs, he now saw only whiteness. Down, down, down, he went, until the floor stopped dropping and eventually came to an abrupt halt.

The curved glass door in front dissolved and before him was a long, corridor. The hallway was pure white with no apparent doors or windows. But when he looked closer at the wall, he saw the faint, hair-thin outline of a doorway which blended with the wall to near perfection. There were doorways every foot or less as he walked down the passage.

Max pushed on each door and found none moved. He looked behind him and saw that the clear, glass tube he had arrived in had vanished. But the novelty of the linear maze quickly wore off, and he began pounding on the doorways as he walked the hall.

"Let me in!" he demanded. "There must be someone here! Somebody answer a door, *damn it!*"

Finally, he approached a series of doors with numeric keypads on the outside. He began pressing numbers on the pads, but none unlocked their doors for him.

At the twelfth door, he found a pad with a screen. He pushed a red button on the pad and waited for someone or something to appear on the small, oval monitor.

"May I help you?" came a voice from the screen. But there was no image.

"Let me in!" Max shouted.

"Who may I ask is calling?"

"What? What do you mean, who is calling? I'm the only freakin' one out here."

"Out where?"

"Out here, *damn you!* Out here in the hallway!" Max protested.

"Your name?"

"Max. Max Toolant."

"One moment."

Max waited impatiently during the intervening silence.

"Hello? Are you there?" he asked.

There was no reply. After a few more minutes, he banged again on the door.

"Hello? I've been waiting for a while now. Is there anyone there?"

Still there was no answer.

"Damn you! I'm tired of this bullshit! I want answers! I demand answers! Give me some God-damned answers!"

He leaned against the wall outside the door and let his body slide down to the floor. Extending his feet into the middle of the hallway, he pushed his head back to rest it on the wall behind him. He noticed that the wall felt soft on his head, like a fluffy, down pillow. But nothing else had changed; the corridor was still white, empty, and medicinal. He felt alone; he *was* alone.

After what felt like hours, a sound came back over the monitor.

"Yes, Mr. Toolant?"

Max stood up, weary and wanting to go home.

"Yes, this is Max." His voice was now much more conciliatory.

"Yes, Mr. Toolant, we need to do a retinal and brain scan to ensure it is you. We also need a heart scan. We apologize for the inconvenience, but these are important protocols we must follow.

Before Max could answer, a green laser light sprang from the oval screen next to the door. The scanning light sprayed waves of emerald over his head and chest.

"Please keep your eyes open, Mr. Toolant," ordered the voice.

When the light waves completed their examination, they blinked off. It was a few minutes before the voice returned, comforting and soothing.

"I have been instructed to open the door for you, Mr. Toolant. You may proceed inside."

"It's about frickin' time!" he shouted.

Max heard a *click,* and he pushed on the white door. This time it moved.

*****

CH 3

As soon as Max crossed the threshold, his senses turned off. He had no sight, hearing, tactile, olfactory, or sapidic abilities. He was without a place, time, or purpose. He had become a "nowhere man."

He shouted, but nothing left his lips. He reached out but felt nothing. He strained to see even the slightest ray of light, but there was none there. His mind reeled as if he'd been bound to a raft and cast out onto a calm, but swift-moving river—one that he sensed was headed toward a magnificent, yet catastrophic, waterfall.

Once again, he screamed. This time, he heard a sound.

"Hello?" he asked, not knowing whether it was a real noise or only an echo inside his head.

"Mr. Toolant?"

"Yes, yes!" he exclaimed, thrilled to have a sensation.

"Mr. Toolant, apparently, there has been some mistake. You were not registered to visit with us at this time. Unfortunately, we cannot grant you admittance. You'll have to try back later."

"What?"

"Yes, I'm afraid there has been a miscommunication on our end. Please accept our sincere apology. I was told to allow you in, but there was an apparent glitch in our system. We will need to reschedule you for a later date."

"You can't see me now?" he asked, perplexed. "Why not? You can't leave me here."

"Those are my instructions, Mr. Toolant. We will monitor your progress and whereabouts and will let you know when your appointment has been rescheduled. We will be in contact with you. I will release the entryway door now so you can leave. Just follow the white hallway back the way you came in. And Mr. Toolant?"

"Yes?"

"Don't make any drastic changes to your lifestyle. It might upset the fine balance we have going on in here. It may affect how soon we can reschedule you."

The darkness all around was shattered by the brilliance of the white light streaming in through the cracked-open door. Max hurried through the opening, afraid that if it closed, he might never find his way out on his own. Then, once outside, he heard the door slam shut and relock.

Well, they are efficient, he thought.

However, he only made it a few steps when the glaring whiteness around him turned darker. The clean, pristine walls of the hallway suddenly grew spots of gray and black, as if a voracious mold had seized their surface and was devouring their perfect appearance. He began running down the corridor, and as he did, the ceiling tiles began popping loose, exposing filth and vermin which scurried away after hitting the floor. As the lights twinkled on and off, the floor began to buckle, like a major earthquake ready to open the ground and swallow him whole.

The earth trembled and shook so violently that it threw him to the floor of the now-gray and putrid hallway. Rats climbed over his body, and he could smell a sickening, deathly stench coming from the far end of the corridor from where he'd just come. Then, all went black once more, and Max again was left without any sensation. He no longer knew where he was as his mind drifted into the black ether around it.

*****

CH 4

"What have you come to confess?" It was a strong, older man's voice.

"What? Confess? What do you mean?"

"You're in a confessional, son. Usually, that means you've come to confess your sins to me. Is that what you want to do?"

Max could see small patterns of light coming through a hatched screen in front of him. There was a man on the other side, but the only features Max could see were his black robe, white collar, gray beard, and green eyes.

"Uh, I don't know."

It had been decades since he had gone to confession, and he couldn't remember how to go about it.

"If you don't know, then who does?" asked the old man.

"I guess I do. Not that I have anything to confess."

"You have *nothing* to confess? You've committed *no* sins? When was your last confession?"

"I don't remember."

"That long. And you don't have *anything* to confess. You are quite a remarkable person, son."

Max sighed.

"Well, if that's all. We should probably free the confessional for the next parishioner," said the priest getting up.

"No, wait!" said Max.

"Yes?"

"I guess I do have some things to say," said Max. "I have sinned, but nothing bad – no murders or anything."

"Well, that's a relief," said the priest, chuckling. "What about the other nine commandments?"

"Uh, well, not as good with most of those."

"Have you stolen anything?"

"Yeah, probably."

"Cursed?"

"Yeah."

"Worshiped a false idol?"

"Like a golden calf or something? No, of course not."

"What about money?"

Max was quiet.

"Coveted thy neighbor's possessions?"

"Yeah, he's got a great Ferrari. It's a …"

"What about adultery?" asked the priest, interrupting.

"I'm not married," said Max.

"Have you taken *another* man's wife?"

"Okay, you got me there. I guess I'm not doin' to good with this, am I?"

The priest didn't answer.

"But tell me father, I was just in a long white corridor inside this building here."

"This is a church, and we don't have any long white corridors."

"Yeah, ya' do. I was just in one, and someone answered one of the doors there. But when I went in, I couldn't feel anything—nothing. There was only a voice that told me I wasn't scheduled to meet with anybody there, and that I should come back later when it was time. What's that all about?"

"Was there a control room with a lot of electronics?"

"Yeah, that's it!" said Max, now excited. "You've been there? You know what I'm talking about!"

The priest sighed. "I've heard those stories before—and from people like yourself who have a lot to atone for. Have you led a good life?"

"It's been great, father. I've made a ton of money and can do whatever I want, whenever I want. I have nothing to complain about."

"And your spiritual life?"

"Well, I'm here aren't I?"

"It's a start, Max. It's a start."

"How do you know my name?" Max asked.

"I know a great many things, Max, and let me tell you that you need to change some things in your life."

"Funny, the person I just talked to in that white corridor told me just the opposite. She told me *not* to change anything."

"Of course, she did. She doesn't want to lose you."

"Lose me? Why would she lose me? She said she'd contact me when it was time for my appointment."

"That's an appointment I wouldn't want to keep, if I were you. You may not have a choice, though, unless you change your ways," said the priest. "So, do you want to confess your sins today?"

Max listed several things he had done of which he was less than proud. After expressing remorse, the priest told him he was to serve dinners at the homeless shelter for the next four weeks as his penance. Then, he added, *"God, the Father of mercies, through the death and resurrection of his Son has reconciled the world to himself and sent the Holy Spirit among us for the forgiveness of sins; through the ministry of the Church may God give you pardon and peace, and I absolve you from your sins in the name of the Father, and of the Son, and of the Holy Spirit. Amen."*

Max thought he had only blinked once but found himself back in his penthouse apartment lying amongst a room full of empty wine bottles and two naked girls still sleeping on his couch.

He pinched himself to ensure he was still alive, and then shook his head.

I guess I do have a little cleaning up to do – both in my apartment and my life, he thought.

He immediately hopped on the Internet and typed in a new search. *Maid Services,* he entered. But then, he changed his mind. Pressing the back key several times, he watched as the twelve letters disappear. Then, he re-keyed another search—*Homeless Shelters Near You.*

He smiled and pressed Enter.

*****

SASQUATCH

CH 1

6575 AD

It had been millennia since humans had fled the battlefields on the surface of Earth for the relative safety of the subterranean zones that lay up to two kilometers below the planet's surface. But now, even this safety was being threatened. The AI machines which now ruled the surface were digging deeper to uncover the enclaves and communities of the humans who had created them. Once considered "not worth the effort" by the androids, humans were now considered Enemy Number One.

"Jack, what do you have?" shouted General Avery Winters, senior commander of the human forces. Dubbed HSLS for *Homo Sapiens* Last Stand, the group of two million was making a final effort to avoid annihilation.

"Their probes are within two hundred kilometers of discovering our outer shell," said Lt. Colonel Miriam Slavkovsky, one of only four remaining senior officers left in the Marine Underground.

"Generate the cloaking schema," said Winters. "Shut everything down."

The cloaking device was like that which was used in space to disguise military ships from detection by alien craft patrolling the solar system. The HSLS found they could use the same system to cloak the locations of fortified tunnels deep under the earth's crust where the humans lived. However, there were problems with the system; leaks in radiation were possible, giving away their coordinates. So, although there was a 99.8 percent chance such leakage would not be detected, there remained that 0.2 percent of discovery.

But that wasn't the only risk of detection. There was also subterfuge. For years, the machines on the surface—known as the 5Reicht Group—had tried to infiltrate the human ranks with human facsimiles—robots that looked and acted exactly like humans. These were high-tech spies that would register everything they saw, heard, touched, tasted, or smelled and relay the information to their masters above. To date, these robots had been discovered by the sophisticated screening machines used by the humans. However, General Winters worried that one day one would get through the filter. That, he feared, would be disastrous.

"Engaged," said the colonel, responding to the general's order. "Commencing audio silence and generating the cloak."

The men and women within command headquarters, which was stationed below the sands of the Sahara Desert, could only wait. It would take the probes a few hours to conduct their scans at their depth— exactly 2013 meters down.

The pings kept hitting the surveillance equipment at headquarters. The reading on the overhead display showing the proximity of the scans to headquarters ... 143 kilometers ... 120 kilometers ... 71 kilometers ... 40 kilometers ...

The 3rd Company of HSLS held their breaths.

... 21 kilometers ... 5 kilometers ... minus 10 kilometers ...

Some sighed a breath of relief as the scan passed over them.

... minus 25 kilometers ... minus 12 kilometers ... minus 2 kilometers ...

"Oh *shit!*" murmured the colonel.

... 0 kilometers ...

"They've found us!" cried the general.

Seconds later, the explosions began rocking the underground city. The room shook and debris poured from the ceiling. Cracks began forming in the massive columns used to hold up the huge canopy that had sheltered the group for over three centuries.

"Detonate the Crust Level 4 magamines," said the general.

The HSLS mines exploded overhead, hoping to destroy the attacking anti-matter depth charges being leveled against them. However, it only seemed to make the devastation worse.

"Damage report!" shouted the general.

But he didn't get much more out of his mouth before the entire ceiling collapsed, killing the entire company. Soon, the rest of the *Homo Sapiens* in the immediate area were rounded up by the 5Reich Forces and brought to the surface. Most were killed. Those who survived were used for experimentation.

That was the end of the human race ... almost.

*****

CH 2
6985 AD

It had been 410 years since the collapse of humanity. But for those 35,000 or so who had survived the last stand and evaded capture, they had regrouped and developed a new strategy against the 5Reicht Forces that ruled uncontested on the surface above them.

"Mom?" asked Nathan, a ten-year-old boy, "When will we be able to go up again?"

"How are you on your lessons?" she asked.

"I'm ready," said Nathan proudly.

"Really? You're able to ..."

"Yeah, Mom. Watch."

Nathan closed his eyes and took some deep breathes. Within a matter of seconds his form grew fuzzy and then vanished all together. Seconds after that, it reformed right back where it had started.

"See!"

Katie clapped enthusiastically. "Bravo! Bravo, Nathan. That was wonderful."

"Yeah, I've finally gotten the hang of it," he said.

"So, what do you think about the fifth dimension?" she asked, smiling proudly.

"It's awesome! The colors are so bright and the creatures and other things there are really incredible. It's got to be like that on the surface of the planet too, right?"

"It is pretty amazing on the surface, son. Yes. It's beautiful up there—at least it is in the deep woods and forests. There are mountains, and lakes, and rivers, and trees. There are deer, bears, birds of all colors, insects that crawl and fly. There are fish in the waters, and frogs and lizards on the shoreline. It's a magical place up there."

"I can't wait! When can we go?"

"Let me ask your father. Maybe this afternoon. I'll see."

***

Edwin, his father, agreed, and the three planned on a trip to the surface to enjoy the cool fall breezes, brilliant sunshine, and the sights and sounds of the deep woodlands of what was once Washington state.

"Alright, are we ready?" asked Edwin.

The three closed their eyes, and quickly their forms grew fuzzy and disappeared, only to materialize once more among the huge trees of the semi-arid landscape of southwestern Washington. But reaching out in all directions before them were the quiet, turquoise waters of Riffe lake. Swimming on the surface were ring-necked ducks, snow geese, tundra swans, and horned grebes, and along the bank were scores of sandhill cranes—a smaller, but more colorful, version of the Australian emu. At the water's edge was a prickly, muskrat munching on a reed it had cut from its sandy bed, and dragonflies buzzed here and there, periodically landing on a broad leaf of a giant burr reed.

Darting from branch to branch among the enormous, grandfatherly red and silver firs, subalpine firs, the white trunked alpine firs, were several red squirrels—their bushy tails flipping and twitching as they displayed their expert, high-wire act. While at the base of several large and thick cedars and a few other western white and sugar pines, were many yellow-pine chipmunks and ground squirrels hustling to find acorns in advance of Ole Man Winter's first calling. White and paper birch trees with their sheets of white, thin bark flapping in the wind, signaled a cool breeze was blowing.

Farther afield, a red fox chased after a tiny Baird's shrew that was running to find a deep hole into which to escape. And not far away were three white-tailed deer, their mouths chewing on legumes and acorns like camels regrinding their cud in the Sahara. Meanwhile, high overhead in a tall white pine was the staccato tapping from a hairy woodpecker drilling for insects inside the soft bark.

"*Wow!*" said Nathan, looking all around in wonder. "This is really amazing!"

"It's beautiful; isn't it?" said his mother, taking his hand.

They strolled through the dense canopied forest, shuffling through the dried needles and brown leaves that had fallen in advance of the coming snowfalls.

"Why don't we come up here more often?" asked Nathan.

"It's not always safe up here, son," said his father, taking his other hand.

"Because of the bears?" asked Nathan. "I hear they get really big—the big black ones."

Edwin laughed. "No, not the bears. They won't hurt you as long as you don't provoke them and leave them alone. The basic rule up here is 'if you leave them alone, they'll leave you alone.' All you need to do is mind your own business, and you'll be fine."

"Except for *them*," said his mother.

"Them?" asked Nathan, watching a brilliant, yellow goldfinch land on a low branch only yards away. "What is *them*?"

"It's not what, but who," she answered.

"Your mother's talking about the red-necked, eisenborgs."

"What do they look like?"

"They look a lot like us. They're about four feet tall. They walk on two feet although some of them roll around on wheels. Usually, they don't come out this far into the woods because they have to recharge every day or so."

"Oh, you mean the *cyborgs*."

"Yes, the ones we created thousands of years ago," said Edwin. "They took over the surface of the planet and forced our kind below ground. Those are the ones that are extremely dangerous. You have to be on the lookout for them whenever you're up here—just in case."

Nathan gripped his parents' hands more tightly, but they continued walking through the forest as before, admiring nature at its finest.

After traipsing through the forest for a while, they realized it was getting late in the day as the sun was already glowing a fiery red near the horizon. They also noticed stormy cumulous clouds beginning to roll in, suggesting a coming rain or even snow shower.

"I think it's time we get back," said Katie. "It's getting late."

But no sooner than those words left her mouth did they hear a sound in the distance.

"Jack! Do you see what I see? Look over there!" she said, pointing.

Nathan turned his head in the direction of the sound. Not more than three hundred yards away were two humanoid forms, albeit shorter, and more stout and rugged. Their eyes glowed bright red as they spotted the family not far from them.

"Yeah, I think it's some of those ..." began one of the eisenborgs.

"Yeah, let's get 'em," said the other. "We can make a fortune if we capture a whole family!"

The two forms began running toward Nathan and his parents, pulling out pistols and firing laser pulses in their direction. The green light from the lasers instantly burned off tree limbs, frightening birds and squirrels and sending them flying or scampering off to find shelter.

"Get 'em!" shouted the other eisenborg, now running full gait through the woods. They began leaping over fallen trees and boulders that littered the path between the two parties.

"Nathan, we have to de-materialize now!" shouted Edwin. "You go first. I'll follow you and your mother. Now get going!"

Nathan closed his eyes, but he was too scared. He couldn't relax enough to vibrate his body into the higher dimension to escape.

"Nathan! Hurry!" said his father, watching as the two borgs closed the gap.

Nathan kept trying, but still had no luck. He opened his eyes in terror.

"I can't! I can't, Dad!" he shouted, trembling and crying.

"Kate, you go ahead," said Edwin. "I'll work to calm Nathan. Go on!"

"No, I'm not leaving you," she answered, taking her son in her arms and holding him tight. "It will be fine, Nathan. Just relax. Just concentrate. Take deep breaths—nice and slow."

A beam of green light shot toward them, hitting Edwin in the shoulder and leaving a deep, charred gash through his blue shirt. He fell to the ground, clutching the wound with his hand.

"Go!" he yelled again to his wife. The two borgs were now within kill-shot range of the entire family. They only had seconds left.

Kate turned once more to Nathan. "Close your eyes, Nathan. Listen to my voice," said his mother with as comforting a tone as she could muster. "Just listen to me. Relax and let your body go … let it vibrate higher …"

Nathan's body become fuzzy, and when Kate realized he was going, she followed suit, glancing at her husband just before she disappeared.

Nathan and his mother re-materialized back underground in their subterranean home. Nathan was shaking, but his mother consoled him.

"What about Dad?" asked Nathan, shivering. "What's going to happen to him?"

Kate could only hold her boy. She didn't know the answer. If the borgs captured him, he would be imprisoned and likely paraded around like a side-show freak at a circus. She couldn't bear to think about it.

"Nathan, let's just get you to bed right now. Your father is a strong man, and he's clever. He'll figure out something."

But Kate wasn't sure herself. She could only hope that what she said would come to pass.

*****

CH 3

The two borgs reached Ethan, who was still lying on the ground holding his shoulder. They pointed their lasers at him, threateningly.

"Don't move!" one shouted, "Or I'll shoot ya' right here!"

Edwin took a deep breath and let it out slowly before shutting his eyes.

"He's dangerous, Xot," one said to the other. "Be careful. You grab him and I'll hold my phaser on him just in case he gets frisky with ya'."

"Make sure you're aimin' at his head Ouk," said Xot. "That's the only way they say you can kill one of 'em."

Xot stuffed his phaser into his belt. He moved stiffly—unlike his partner Ouk who was one of the newer models of the Xotlithian series manufactured by other, higher-level borgs in the food chain. The Xotlithian class was not the lowest produced, but it was considered part of the working-class group that did maintenance on other machines and transported parts and supplies from one area to another. No cyborg of any class had been able to transcend to another dimension—all were captives within their 3-D reality.

Xot grabbed Edwin's legs and began pulling on him. But when the cyborg's body began to vibrate wildly, he had trouble hanging on to it.

"What's wrong, Xot?" asked Ouk.

"I don't know. The critter is shakin'! It's shakin' me to, and I can't stop!" he shouted, still holding on to Edwin.

Ouk grabbed Xot and pulled him off Edwin, dropping his legs. Both cyborgs now watched as the man's body became fuzzy and then just disappeared.

"Where did he go?" asked Xot.

"I don't know," said the other cyborg. "We need to find him."

They searched the forest until it was dark. Then, they gave up, turning on their lights and infrared sensors so they could open their remote charging stations and plug-in for the night.

"*Damn!*" said Xot. "We almost had 'em."

"Yeah," said Ouk, "it's not every day you see one of 'em."

Xot laughed. "And to think most of our kind don't believe they exist."

"Oh, they exist all right," said Ouk. "They're tall and big creatures—ain't they?"

Xot smiled. "Now you know why they call 'em Big Foot."

*****

THREESOME

CH 1

There were three moons in the sky, all in the same phase of waxing against a curtain of blackness behind them. Yet, each moon was a different size and color, ranging from a small, yellow garlic clove to a large, orange banana—all appearing to be in orbits near each other but were actually millions of miles apart.

Maori shivered as she stood in the snow looking up at the heavens. The planet's climate had shifted due to the effects of a passing comet which orbited every fifty-four years and causing temperatures to drop far below the normal winter-time levels.

Layered with animal furs, she shrugged off the frosty weather, looking forward to the daytime when temperatures would rise dramatically. Overnight though, the thermometer would fall to minus forty-two Celsius (minus forty-five Fahrenheit). Winters were always a hardship, but over thousands of years, her people had acclimated to this fifty-four-year cycle of brutal cold.

Even without the comet, the temperatures would get cold during the winter—especially at night. To help adapt, her civilization had built its cities below ground – where the molten iron core of the planet helped keep the temperature a nearly constant twenty-five degrees Celsius (seventy-seven Fahrenheit).

"Maori, come back down. You'll freeze," said Dagon, her father, looking out from inside the glass elevator chamber that had taken him to the surface. At the request of his wife, he had been sent to ascend in the El to retrieve their nineteen-year-old daughter.

"In a minute, father," she answered.

The winds howled, and the snow began to come down in waves. With the large, flat sheets falling and breaking on the ground, the landscape was shimmering as the moons' reflections bounced light far and wide. If the weather patterns came as usual, there would be meters of snow falling, making all travel hazardous, if not impossible.

As her father took the glass elevator back below ground, Maori waited and watched. *It should be here any moment*, she thought. *Please hurry!*

Yet, as the snow piled higher, her hopes diminished, and after two meters, it was hard for the heating pads in the landing area to keep the space clear. Soon, no craft would be able to arrive until the storm had passed.

Discouraged, she slogged through the piling snow to reach the tall, red pole that held the call button to summon the El. It finally reappeared at the surface, its double glass doors opening to let her inside.

"Plankard Four," she said, directing where she wanted it to go.

But just as the doors closed, she spotted a flicker of light in the distance and then the sudden appearance of a landing craft. It was metallic, and its skin reflected the orange light from one of the moons overhead.

"Wait!" she shouted. "Stop the lift!"

But it was too late. The cube-shaped El had already fallen beneath the planet's surface, and the shaft—covered by two, hinged, chromium-titanium flaps—was already sealed.

Frantically, Maori pounded on the El's buttons, but nothing seemed to work. It continued down to Plankard Four, no longer where she wanted to go. She pushed her head against the glass in despair. She would miss the rendezvous and her secret transport.

*****

CH 2

The spacecraft came quickly into port, hovering briefly over the landing area. Then, seeing no one to collect, it hurried just as rapidly back out across the icy sea. The storm was getting worse, and no one aboard wanted to risk crashing on the surface – especially someplace as unwelcoming and hostile as Duetron Five.

Below ground on Plankard Four, the glass El doors opened, and Maori stepped off, dejected and discouraged. She got only a few meters before her implanted scanner alarmed, and she answered it, tapping the screen in her forearm. She watched as the top dermal layer of skin change into a pixelated screen.

"What is it?" she asked, watching for an image.

"Maori, where were you?"

The screen showed the fuzzy image of a young being, its eyes rigid and unblinking and its mouth agape, fearful of what had become of her. It had long, curling hair that draped past its shoulders, and its eyes were a rich, chestnut brown. They were loving eyes, ones that hungered and yearned for the one it was talking to.

"Stanis? Where are you?" she asked. "Where is Cloven?"

"Cloven is right here too," said the being.

Another young being appeared in the frame. It too was handsome yet held a rougher and more rugged appearance. Its thin face and strong jawline suggested someone of privilege and wealth. Still, it dressed simply, wearing a heavy, ursidaen coat, just like the one Stanis was wearing.

"Maori, are you all right? We were worried when you didn't appear at the meeting point."

"There was a bad storm, as you can see. I saw your ship approaching, but it was only after my father pressed me to return below. I am back with the others now. I am safe, but I am not."

"We understand, Maori. We must get you out of there before they find out."

"Yes, they will find out soon, I'm afraid. When can you come again?"

"The weather is to grow worse. The winter storms have come early, and I'm afraid they'll blanket your area for another thirty days."

"I can't wait that long," said Maori.

"We know," said Stanis, coming back into the picture. "That's why I think we need to perform an extraction."

"No. I forbid it!" she answered.

"Maori, I don't see another way. You can't keep things a secret much longer. It will become obvious."

Maori was quiet. She knew they were right.

"Okay. Then when?"

"We will come in for extraction in seven days. There is a window in the weather. We will fly in quickly, beam you up, and get out. You must be ready."

"But that might hurt the …"

"It won't. I've told you that. Just be ready."

"I will," she answered.

*****

CH 3

Seven days passed, and Maori prepared to go back to the surface to wait.

"Maori, where do you think you're going?" asked Marson, her mother, coming into her room.

Namoti was only thirty-four; she had given birth to Maori when she was only nineteen. But things had been different back then. Relationships were simpler. Pre-arranged unions were the norm and had been for thousands of years. Their culture had been strict: a male, a female and either a vemale or zemale. That was the way it was and would always be according to the laws as written. It took three of them to make a baby. Biologically, it made no difference which three. Culturally, it did.

The laws of Duetron Five stated that a child born with a zemale was considered a bastard. One with a female, vemale and zemale, an abomination. Only one that included both a male and female was acceptable. Yet, the laws of nature had provided for all possibilities. Culturally, it was the male and female who brought up the children. The vemale or zemale only contributed their portion of the zygote.

"I'm just going to check on things up top. I heard the storm was subsiding," said Maori.

"Why? What difference does it make?"

"I just want to see the outside, Mother. I get crazy being down here for a long time. You know that."

Maori's mother was more accepting of her daughter's rebel-type personality than was her father who was strait-laced and traditional. Their other four children—all younger than Maori—were much more obedient to their parents. Maori, on the other hand, had always been a problem child.

It was during her years at the Berklov School that she had been exposed to "radical" ideas as her father had called them. She had come home one day telling them about the VZ program—one proposed to replace the old YVZ program. It was an unsubtle code suggesting a union excluding a male (XY males). Instead, a female (XX), vemale (XV) and zemale (XZ) were encouraged to form unions. Laws still on the books forbid this.

The program stated: "Break free from the chains of society and join us at the Berklov. Here we cast no judgment on how you wish to conceive your child. We only welcome them into the world as a marvelous miracle of life."

Her parents were horrified. They were so upset they contacted the school and threatened to pull Maori out. The school eventually backed down and issued a retraction of support for the proposed program. But in the meantime, Maori had become interested in it, and behind her parents' backs had joined a society that supported the new program: the Naibaf Society. There she had met Stanis and Cloven. Stanis was a vemale, and Cloven a zemale.

It wasn't long before Maori volunteered for one of the Naibaf's programs—to become impregnated by a vemale and zemale. The purpose was to study whether there were any abnormalities or other problems that developed from such a union. Previous testing had always shown none.

The first thing they discovered was that the baby inside her grew quickly—much more quickly than a normal pregnancy. Soon, she began to see the changes to her body, and it was only a matter of time before others would see it too. Even the heavy winter clothing would not be able to hide the fact.

Maori got on the El and pushed the button to have it lift her to the surface. But before the glass doors closed, her mother said, "Your father will be home soon. You need to be back within the hour. There's still a nasty storm out there."

Maori rode the El to the surface and waited again. The weather had improved even though the suns were still not out; they hadn't shown in over a year. Anxiously, she waited for the helocraft to hover over the landing spot. It would not land this time to hasten the process; instead, it would beam her into the craft and immediately fly away. She still worried what that might do to her unborn child, but she had little choice.

In the distance, she saw a small, black dot flying in low and screaming across the surface of the water trying to evade radar. Its anti-gravity pods cast out waves to combat the forces pulling it down until it was directly overhead.

Maori ran out of the El and toward the middle of the landing pad where she could easily be seen. The fierce winds and blistering cold quickly seized upon her lightly-covered body, chilling her to the bone. It was over one hundred meters to the pickup spot, and she could feel her skin tighten and muscles contract as the cold buried inside her. She felt her lungs freezing with each breath, the tiny bronchioles beginning to crystalize into hardened branches of ice. Laboring, she struggled to reach the spot. Finally, she fell, looking up and hoping the craft wouldn't give up on her and fly away.

Seeing her in distress, one of the beings inside the AG craft shouted to its pilot.

"We must beam her in now," it said. "Otherwise, she'll freeze."

"Is she far enough outside the city shield? Can we latch onto her?" asked the pilot.

"I don't know, but we have to try."

The pilot pushed several buttons and levers to engage the generator coils that produced the joules needed to dematerialize Maori and rematerialize her in the craft. It took nearly a minute to activate the transporter.

Maori got up and ran another few meters, before falling again. This time, she did not move.

"Engage beam," said one of the beings.

The light from the craft was intense, and it outlined the dark frame of the pregnant woman against the white, pureness of the snow around her. Within a second, she was gone, and within another, she was lying, shaking, in the transport chamber inside the ship.

"How is she?" asked Cloven, the dark-complexioned being onboard.

"She's cold, but I think she'll be all right," said Stanis.

The AG lifted off and disappeared into the sky, going from a massive transport to a dot and then nothing in seconds.

*****

CH 4

"Where is she?"

It was Maori's father who came home from a long day in the mines.

"I don't know," cried her mother. "She said she was going to the surface to look at the weather. I told her to be back within the hour, but she hasn't returned."

Dagon struck Marson across the face with the back of his hand. "How can you not know where our daughter is?" he shouted. He approached his wife again, but his oldest son stepped between them.

"No, father. Back off!"

Jarmon was only sixteen, but he was big and strong. He had watched his father abuse his mother and others in the family for years and had been afraid. Now, he took a stand.

"What? Are you threatening me, boy?"

"Yes, if that's what it takes," said Jarmon, standing rigid and defiant.

Dagon approached his son menacingly, ready to put his fist through his son's face as well, but Jarmon put up his arms.

Dagon laughed. "My little boy thinks he's a man, does he?"

"Go ahead," Jarmon said, "try it. Just try it."

Dagon stared at Jarmon and sized him up. "You won't touch me, boy. I'm your father."

"You're not my father if you strike my mother like that. You are no father to me at all."

"Watch what you say, boy."

"I'm old enough. I can say what I want," said Jarmon.

Without warning, Dagon threw his punch, but Jarmon dodged it, letting it sail past his face. Then, he quickly punched back, hitting his father in the jaw as he was regaining his balance. The strike threw his father to the floor and knocked him unconscious for a few moments. When he came too, he wasn't sure where he was, but there was no one there to give him comfort.

"I'll deal with you later," he snarled.

The next day Dagon went to the police to report the abduction of his daughter.

"Name?" asked the deputy.

"Dagon Uzmany."

"Who's missing?"

"Maori Uzmany, my daughter."

"Age?"

"Nineteen."

"Last seen?"

"Yesterday."

"Where?"

"She was going to the surface to …"

"Why would she do that? You know it's forbidden to go to the surface without an authorized stamp?"

"Yes, of course," said Dagon who, like most, regularly violated that rule.

"Why would she do that?" asked the deputy.

"I don't know. But she didn't come back."

"Well, she violated the law," said the deputy.

"Yes, but she's gone!"

"Doesn't matter. She violated the law. There's nothing we can do."

"You must!"

"No. Your daughter is a criminal. We don't help criminals."

Dagon's face grew red. His arms tightened, and he was ready to reach across the desk the snap the deputy's neck. But he calmed his rage and took a breath. Hitting an officer would lead him to the death chamber. He didn't want to face that horror.

Dagon stormed out of the office and slammed the door. Jarmon was waiting outside, but his father ignored him and continued walking.

"Well? What did they say?" asked Jarmon.

"Your sister violated the law. She's nothing now. She's a criminal—a fugitive. There's nothing we can do. She's dead to us."

"Well, I'm going after her if you're not going to try," said Jarmon.

*****

CH 5

Finding a transport was not easy. All cargo AG vehicles were searched before they left their underground base. There were no passenger AG vehicles allowed, and non-crew members were not allowed on cargo ships. All Jarmon could do was find a rust bucket—an old conventional craft that was kept in case of emergencies. These were kept in the lowest level of the hangar and hadn't been flown in years.

Jarmon's hand on the stick control was shaky, but he managed to pull the bird up and out of the hangar. There were no trackers on these craft, so he was able to fly away undetected as long as he stayed below radar levels. Jarmon had learned to fly on simulators through war game exercises put on by the state authorities in case of a real emergency. Young man as young as sixteen were trained just in case they were needed. However, real flying was quite different from what he'd experienced during the simulations. It took all his concentration and memory of protocols and procedures to get the bird off the ground and flying.

But that wasn't the greatest challenge. Calming his nerves was the bigger issue as he flew through snow-covered valleys and between high, jagged peaks on either side. There was only one way out of the Duetron Five sector; he only had to follow along an ancient riverbed through the BetaBlue Canyon until he reached the Marsot Plateau.

He flew north along the riverbed. On his wings, layers of thin ice were beginning to accumulated, weighing down the craft and making it harder for him to steer. The weather was also growing worse with headwinds pushing against the nose of the craft and temperatures continuing to fall.

Jarmon's craft finally spurted out from between two final peaks; ahead lay the Marsot Plateau. Almost instantly his instruments picked up life below on the frozen tundra.

"Triangulate life forms," said Jarmon, speaking to his craft's computer.

"Identifying location and type of life forms," responded the computer in a friendly, male tone. Moments later, the voice returned. "Encampment identified fifteen pardecs from current position. Changing course, bearing 15 dot 4 dot nine degrees north northeast."

"Acknowledged," Jarmon answered.

The craft's onboard scanner showed him a hologram of the terrain below and soon highlighted the rebel encampment which still lay over eight pardecs farther north. It wouldn't take long, but he needed his infrared helmet to pinpoint the landing field.

Thankfully, the weather was cooperating, but there were yellow clouds building on the horizon, and the headwinds were picking up as well. It would be a bumpy ride in. He only hoped the rebels would not shoot him down on his approach.

*****

CH 6

Hidden inside Farbot Mountain was the Monastery of the Crystal. Formed hundreds of generations earlier, the monastery was created after a male, Zather Orsvan, fled the Duetron Three sector after espousing his beliefs in open love and believing in equality for all. At that time, thousands of years ago, vemales and zemales were not considered intelligent beings and incapable of joining the normal society of the males and females. Instead, they were caged and only used for procreation. Zather preached that this was an abomination, and a practice that should be stopped. Many agreed and joined him at the monastery, but it wasn't for another seven hundred years that vemales and zemales were freed from their bonds and allowed to join the rest of civilization. Still considered second-class, they were permitted to live freely and undisturbed. At the monastery, however, all were treated as equals.

Jarmon's infrared helmet picked up a precise heat signature deep in one of the mountains nearby. He swung his craft to the east, following the clue. Far from the great cities of Duetron Three and Duetron Five, he no longer feared being identified by their radar; now, he was more concerned with that of the monastery. Banking his ship, he followed his holographic map which showed him a landing area outside the mountain.

"You have entered a restricted area," came a voice over his cockpit speaker. "Please identify yourself and your intention."

"This is Jarmon Uzmany, brother of Maori Uzmany. Ship ID is Alpha Zed 158 Beta 754," he said. "I come in peace. I wish only to see my sister."

"You may not land until you are confirmed. You must keep a distance outside the restricted zone until clearance is granted."

It didn't take long before the voice returned. "Landing granted. Set propulsion to neutral. We will bring you in via tractor beam."

Instantly, the ship stopped, frozen by an unseen force that gripped it in a vice. Then, it began moving rapidly, faster than the old ship had ever gone before. It shook and rattled but somehow remained intact.

Jarmon shrieked and closed his eyes. His ship was being pulled directly into the side of the mountain.

"Stop!" he yelled. "Turn off the beam!"

But even as those words left his mouth, the ship struck the rocky face. Yet, when Jarmon opened his eyes, he saw he was inside the mountain. He had passed through a camouflage veil and into the mountain's hollow interior. Behind the veil was a tunnel through which the ship continued to be pulled. Finally, the tunnel opened into an immense cavern, brightly lighted from both above and below. It had multiple, ringed layers all angled around a corkscrew center hub.

Jarmon's ship came to a stop, and quickly beings in military gear with small, laser-gun devices beamed in surrounding him. He opened his hatch and put his hands up.

Surprised by the hostile greeting, he said, "I'm Jarmon Uzmany. I'm Maori's brother. I come only to see her and mean you no harm."

One of the beings motioned for him to follow them, and they took him to a holding cell. There were no bars and no visible means of restraint, but he could hear the hum of the forcefield that kept him inside, preventing him from leaving.

Finally, another being arrived. It was very tall, thin-framed with large, black eyes on the sides of its bulbous head. It had a mouth like that of a chimpanzee, but a nose which protruded more like that of a canine.

The forcefield stopped, and the being entered. It showed no warmth, nor malice. It just was.

"Jarmon?" it asked in a flat tone.

"Yes?"

"You said you've come to see a Maoir Uzmany?"

"Yes."

"There is no one here by that name," said the being.

"That can't be," said Jarmon. "This would be the only place she would have gone." He sat stunned and quiet. "That must mean, she's dead. She must have gone out into the weather as they said and froze to death. I don't understand." He was in tears. "Why would she do that?"

The being came over and put its hand on his shoulder. "There is a woman here whose name is Flaura. We believe she is the one you seek."

The two dematerialized, and Jarmon next found himself inside a small, but blindingly colorful room. It was nothing like he had ever seen before. Although there was no furniture, the colors swirled on the ceiling, floor and walls like a great kaleidoscope turning and churning—stimulating all his senses.

'Where are we?" Jarmon asked.

"Wait here," said the being, dematerializing again.

Moments later a young female came into the room. She was exceptionally beautiful, with long brown hair, large, hazel eyes, high cheekbones, and full lips. She smiled and reached out her delicate hand. It was then that he realized she had six fingers on her hand instead of five.

"Jarmon?" she said. "Please. If you will come with me."

Jarmon followed the woman out of the room and down the hallway. It had many rooms on either side, but the doors were closed. Finally, they reached one, marked ZV4506.

"Please, this way," she said, opening the door for him to enter.

In the corner of the room was a glass enclosure with hoses and tubes running into it. Inside was a tiny baby, sound asleep. It was beautiful and breathing peacefully.

"Jarmon!"

He turned. There was his sister, resting in a bed, looking radiant and glowing.

"Sis!" he shouted, running to her. He put his arms around her and kissed her on the forehead. "Why did you leave?" he asked.

"Because I wanted to have my baby where it wouldn't be tormented its entire life."

"Why would that be?" asked Jarmon.

"It's a VZ baby, Jarmon. There is no XY in him."

"You didn't mate with a male?"

"No—only a vemale and a zemale. They said it would work – that it would be fine. It was part of the program—one I never told you or our parents about."

Jarmon smiled at his sister. "I'm just glad you're all right. Mother and I were worried about you."

"And father?"

Jarmon shrugged. "I don't know. Like all genders, there are some that are good and some that aren't. We were lucky with Mother. She's a good egg."

"Yes, she certainly is."

Then, Jarmon looked at the baby. It too had six fingers on each hand. "Is this the only difference?" Jarmon asked, pointing to the baby's hand.

"Yes," said the other woman who had taken him to the room. "It is not a deformity here. It is just another life being—no better and no worse than any other. We love it just the same."

Jarmon hung his head.

"What's wrong, brother?" asked Maori.

"I guess we're not needed anymore," said Jarmon, scratching his head, "males, that is."

"That is not true," said the woman with six fingers.

"Jarmon, this is Doctor Tal," said Maori. She has been looking after me."

The doctor nodded to Jarmon, smiling. "Yes, she's been a very good patient. However, I've already talked to her about misunderstanding what this was all about."

"Misunderstanding?"

"Yes," said Maori. "Apparently, I didn't fully understand the process, and the doctor explained it to me."

"What is the process, then?" asked her brother, now confused.

"Well, you see," began the doctor …

The doctor continued for the next hour explaining in detail how it was all supposed to work. There had been problems along the way, and in the long run, they found it often didn't work well without a being to play the male role.

"What you're saying, then, is not with the conception of the baby," said Jarmon.

"No, it's with the nurturing of the baby after birth. You see, the family unit is important—critical, in fact—to bring up a healthy child. Without beings playing the parts of the male and female—the paternal authority figure and maternal nurturing figure, the baby struggles to find its identity. Without a male and female-type figures in the family unit, the construct of parenting degrades."

"So, can you have two males or two females raising a child?"

"Of course, but they must be able to give paternal and maternal guidance. Long-term, society will function best if these two forces are present. What is difficult is when there is only a single XX or single XY parent. It is hard for a single parent to offer both to their children. However, sometimes this cannot be helped."

"I must come home," said Maori. "Will you take me home?"

"Yes, of course," said Jarmon. "But why?"

"Because I thought the vemale and zemale contributors to my birth would stay with me to help as parents. I realize now it is a role they've never been exposed to before. They love my baby as their own, but parenting abilities are not part of their skillset—that is why they would not make good parents. They are nomadic in nature and must continually travel and move from place to place. Their purpose is only to diversify the gene pool."

"So, you have no co-parent?" asked Jarmon.

Maori smiled. "I do. He will join us on the way home. I will introduce you."

*****

CH 7

As Jarmon got on his rust-bucket ship, Maori came to the departure dock carrying the baby in her arms. On her side was another being.

"Jarmon, this is Tandro. He isn't the father of my baby, but he will make a great one and wants to be part of my family."

"Morris, it's good to meet you. I'm Jarmon. Welcome to the Uzmany clan."

Tandro smiled. "Very glad to be with you. Maori has told us many good and many interesting things."

"Jarmon, what do you think father will say?" asked Maori.

"I don't know, but don't be afraid. I will protect you from him if I have to," said Jarmon.

"As will I," said Tandro.

The ship lifted off under its own power and navigated the tunnel, passing through the cloaked veil and soaring into the cold air of the plateau. It sped home with all on board—all excited about the additions to the family, but at the same time, worried about what the future might bring.

*****

HEAVENLY COURT

CH 1

"This court will come to order," said the bailiff, trying to regain control before the judge entered.

An energy field was cast wide over the entire room, immediately silencing all within. They instantly felt the effects too, as their throats constricted, and they felt their seat cushions pull them deep into their recesses. It was as if a zookeeper had fired tranquilizing darts into the courtroom.

"The Honorable Judge Adonai is presiding."

At that moment, a white-robed man came into the chamber. Rather than the traditional black garb, he presented himself in white robes to show his propensity to fairness and objectivity.

Judge Adonai was young, not more than thirty-three, but assumed a stature and decorum of someone twice or three time his age.

"Please be seated," he said, reaching the bench. "I believe there is only one case on the docket. Is that right?"

"Yes, Your Honor," said the bailiff.

"Well, let's get on with it, then. Is the prosecution ready?"

"We are, Your Honor," said Roland Freilser, prosecuting attorney.

Freilser was known throughout the region as a no-nonsense prosecutor who delighted in identifying those who had violated the law and, in his view, should be brought before the highest court.

"And the defense counsel?"

"Yes, Your Honor." This was Mohandas Karamchand. Unlike Freilser, he was renowned for his benevolence and kind-heartedness toward others accused of crimes.

"We will proceed. The plaintiff will call its first witness."

"Thank you, Your Honor. We call Spirit Khan."

Apperaring into the courtroom was a misty, yellowish field of energy. It hovered within the confines of the witness box, its glow revealing a man dressed in the ancient garb of a Chinese emperor, but more specifically one who lived during the Earth years from 1162 to 1227 CE.

"Mr. Khan," began Freilser, "how many earthlings would you say you killed during your life on the planet? Just rough numbers."

"I understand the number to be about forty."

"Forty people?" asked Freilser, incredulously.

"No, forty million. I believe that is the number."

"Do you have any regrets?"

"No. The people of Nishapur, where I killed every man, woman, and child, totaled about a million alone. But they killed my son-in-law, Toquchar, so it was justified."

"No further questions, Your Honor."

"Any cross-examination of the witness?" the judge asked Karamchand.

"Not at this time," said the defense.

"Next, we call Joseph Stalin," said Freilser.

Again, the image of Mr. Stalin appeared in the courtroom. He stood in his Russian military uniform. Standing only five feet four inches tall, Stalin was short but stocky, and his energy powerful and dark. His dark hair was thick and combed straight back, and his heavy mustache trimmed precisely like it had been when he had been on the planet, terrorizing the Russian people and the world.

"Now, Mr. Stalin we will ask you the same question. How many people did you kill during your reign in the Soviet Union from 1929 to 1953?"

"Approximately forty-*one* million," said Stalin, smiling and trying to best the Mongol leader.

"We have a record of forty-five million," said the prosecutor.

"Oh, even better," he answered, laughing with a sparkle in his black eyes.

"Any cross?" asked the judge of the defense. But Karamchand shook his head.

"Our next witness is Mao Zedong," said Freilser.

After the Chinese dictator arrived in his gray uniform, he too was asked the question.

"I did not hurt any citizen of the People's Republic of China," he said confidently.

"Perhaps in your view, yes. But as far as humans, we have a record of many more than that. Would you care to guess?" asked Freilser.

"Not more than a few thousand," said Mao.

"In four years' time, between 1958 and 1962, you killed forty-six million of your Chinese brethren."

"Your numbers must be in error," said Mao before disappearing.

"No, it was part of your Great Leap Forward. Most of them starved to death."

"No matter," said Mao. "It was for the greater good—the good of all the people of China."

There were more witnesses called, and each were grilled on their totals-
-mass killings committed during their time of leadership. They included Pol Pot—3 million in four years; Genghis Khan and Kublai Khan—40 million, Kim II Sun family—3.5 million; Ranavalona—3.2 million in thirteen years; Hirohito—7.4 million; Hitler—17 million; Timur-17 million; and others.

"The plaintiff calls our last witness, Your Honor ... Mohandas Karamchand."

The defense attorney looked up at the judge with surprise.

"I'm sorry, Your Honor, but I cannot be called as a witness."

"In this case, I will allow it," said the judge.

Karamchand walked to the witness box and raised his hand, being sworn in. He took his seat and awaited the questions.

"Mr. Karamchand—may I call you Mr. K?"

"Yes, that would be fine," said the defense attorney.

"Mr. K, would you say that humans are stable?"

"Please define stable," said Mr. K.

"Stable, as in able to sustain their growth and development during the next few thousand years. Remember, you are under oath."

Mr. K sighed. "I am not in a position to prognosticate into the future," he answered. "I am not an expert in this area."

Freilser smiled knowingly. "Then how would you assess the human species? Would you say they are capable of progressing at the rate required to achieve the next level?"

"What is the next level?"

Freilser just looked at Mr. K, and Mr. K relented again.

"Okay, fine. I do understand. I would say ..." The courtroom waited, not knowing what he would say. "I do think the species can achieve a higher level, yes."

"I'm not asking about a higher level. I'm asking about *the* next level."

Mr. K did not hesitate. "Yes," he answered.

Freilser was dismayed with the answer, not expecting Mr. K to go so far under oath.

"Do you have any more questions for the witness?" asked the judge.

Freilser thought for a moment. "Yes," he said. "If we were to put our energies to another civilization, say the Proxima Centaurians, the Gliesens, or the Wolvarians. These beings have shown remarkable capacities for advancement. Have they not?"

"I cannot deny that the civilizations you present show promise," said Mr. K. "However, I would not underestimate the resilience of the human race. I believe it has its own potential."

"How would you rate the human species against the others, then?"

The judge sat back in his chair, stroking his chin as he listened.

"Each has its own advantages and strengths," said Mr. K. "I cannot deny it. However, I have worked directly with *Homo sapiens*, as you know, and while I was on Earth, I found much success in moving them in the right direction."

"Do you have any other questions?" asked Judge Adonai.

"No, your Honor. No further questions," said Freilser.

"Mr. K, do you wish to call any witnesses?"

"Yes, your Honor. The defense wishes to call its own witnesses. *****

CH 2

"I'm sorry, Mr. K. Who is it you would like to call?"

"Your Honor, it isn't a who, but a what."

"You may proceed."

"The plaintiff wishes to call ... Gaia."

"Gaia?" asked Freilser.

At that point, there was a great energy in the chamber as the ground moved and rumbled. A great fissure appeared through the center of the courtroom, separating the two sides from each other. Mr. K watched as a plume of energy emerged from the divide and a stream of white mist poured forth from the crack. It rose into the air and then descended into the witness chair, coalescing into a hazy cloud.

"Are you Mother Earth?" asked Mr. K.

"Yes," replied the energy.

Beings in the courtroom would have erupted in laughter if they hadn't seen for themselves the chasm that was created when the energy came out from the depths.

"Are you from Hell or the Underworld?" asked Mr. K, already knowing the answer.

"No. I am who you say. I am Earth and represent all its energies. It is this energy that provides sustenance for the human species," it said.

The form did not have a human appearance. Instead, it took the shape of an amorphous blue orb, spinning on its own axis just above the witness chair.

"You have had experience with the human species, have you not?" asked Mr. K.

"Yes, of course, during the past two hundred thousand years."

"And may I ask whether you believe the humans have improved in their respect and awareness of your vitality and importance to the furtherance of their species?"

The blue orb spun faster, casting off more energy and light.

"Had you asked me a thousand Earth years ago or even five hundred, I would have said no. However, the species has made marked strides recently—within the last hundred years. I, as part of a greater collective, believe that they have improved. Yes."

"And do you believe they have improved sufficiently to achieve the next level?"

"That is difficult to say," said the energy. "I believe it is possible the species can rise to that level."

"Thank you. No more questions, Your Honor."

Freilser jumped up. "You believe, but you don't know."

"No one knows," said the earth spirit. "It is based on probabilities, as you are well aware."

"That sounds like a no to me."

"It is an honest answer to your question," said the spirit.

"No further questions, Your Honor."

"Are there any more witnesses?" asked the judge.

"Yes, Your Honor. There is one."

"Please," the judge gestured, hoping to move things along.

"The defense calls Molly Hampstead," said Mr. K.

All in the courtroom turned to each other and, with creases in their foreheads, began mumbling excitedly about who this person or being was. All shook their heads and refocused their attention on the bench.

"Will Ms. Molly Hampstead please come forward," said Mr. K.

From the gallery, a small, young girl of no more than nine rose from her seat. She was innocent and cheerful. With a smile on her face, she skipped to the front of the courtroom as though she were on a recess break.

Molly had dark hair in tight curls that rolled down the center of her back. Her eyes were brown and full of energy, and her cute dimples gave off an impression of innocence and hope. She wore a yellow, summer dress with white socks and black, patent leather shoes. And when she smiled, the room lit up like it couldn't help but catch her joyous contagion.

"Please raise your hand and swear after me …"

After sitting down, Molly straightened her canary cloche hat. She beamed, her smile radiating out in all directions.

"Will you please state your name for the court?" asked Mr. K.

"I'm Molly Hampstead."

"And you are the daughter of ..."

"I was the daughter of the current President of the United States, Benjamin Hampstead."

There was a gasp in the gallery. Suddenly, they recognized her.

"I see," said Mr. K. "And can you tell us about your thoughts of being human and what the youth on Earth believe right now?"

Molly smiled broadly. "Well, I'd say that they're a happy bunch," she said. "My friends and I liked to play games, but we also loved to play with our dogs. Buster was my little Norwich Terrier. I loved him a lot."

"What else?"

"Well, I know most of us could see stuff that our parents and grandparents couldn't see. We could see people who had gone to heaven and other beings – you know, things people on Earth call aliens."

Those in the court gallery laughed.

"Oh, so you could see aliens?"

"Sometimes when they came to visit. They weren't mean or anything. They just wanted to talk to us and see what we were doing and what we were interested in in school and stuff."

"They didn't hurt you, did they?" asked Mr. K.

"Heck no. They were almost like one of us girls. We still talked to them—or I used to anyway. Now, I guess since I'm up here, I can talk to anybody just about any time."

"Yes, that's true. Since your accident, things have changed a bit, haven't they?"

"Yeah, and I miss my parents," said Molly. "I can see them, but they can't see me."

Mr. K just smiled. "Yes, we all know the feeling here," he said. "So, you wanted to be an astrophysicist, I understand. Is that right? That's a mighty big thing to be when you're only nine years old."

"Yeah, my uncle is one. He's really good at it too. He said I'm a natural."

Mr. K laughed.

"Anyway, there is so much to learn about it. My other uncle is a priest. He told me I should be part of the church. So, I thought maybe I'd do both."

"So, you think you'd go astrophysics and the church – both at the same time."

"Yeah. My daddy said he thought there was a lot of things in common between them," said Molly.

"I see. So, your father, the president of the United States of America, believed that there was a lot in common between the church and space?"

"Yeah. He explained it all to me, but I didn't understand all of it until I got up here. Now I understand it better."

"Can you explain it to the court?"

"Sure," said Molly. "You see, astrophysicists are talking about this thing they call string theory which is supposed to explain everything. They're right too. It does, but they haven't connected it to the strings we're made of—we're all made of 'em. When I got here, I found out we're all made of strings which make these vibrations—kind 'a like playing a guitar, I guess."

"That's right. Very good," said Mr. K.

"And that's how we get to Heaven—one of those strings pulls us up here."

"Your father understood that?"

"Yeah," said Molly.

Mr. K turned to the judge. "No further questions, Your Honor."

Freilser rolled his eyes and shook his head. "No, Your Honor, I have no questions for the witness."

"After closing statements, I will retire to my chambers to consider a verdict said the judge.

The closing statements were predictable. Freilser repeated his opposition to granting humanity any more time. He claimed that man had squandered the time given to him to fall in line with galactic imperatives and that wasting any more resources on the species was futile.

Mr. K rose and buttoned his dark, navy jacket.

"Your Honor," he began.

"Mr. K, you can save your breath," said the judge. "I'm weary, and I already know what you're going to say—*verbatim*, in fact. Let's just dispense with your closing argument. I will call a recess in the case to give me time to make my decision. Court is adjourned."

The judge slammed the gavel liberally, ensuring that all could hear it, or be rendered deaf by it, and he left the courtroom.

Time seemed suspended as the judge deliberated the verdict. By the time he returned with his decision, few knew how long it had really taken.

"The Honorable Judge Adonai," called out the bailiff, prior to the door to the judge's chambers opening.

The judge came in and quickly took his chair. In command of everything, he cleared his throat before he began.

"I have made decisions like this on numerous other cases involving species that are trying to evolve and grow within the brotherhood of the cosmos. I will tell you that it is not easy."

The tension in the room was thick. Those in the gallery eagerly awaited the ultimate and final decision by the ruler, the judge, the Almighty.

"I have listened to the arguments made by the two opposing attorneys in this case, and I commend them for bring forth compelling reasons for each side. However, there can only be one decision, and my decision is ...”

*****

CH 3

Freilser was packing up his things in the courtroom as Mr. K stopped by to shake his hand.

"Mr. Freilser," Mr. K said, nodding. "Well played. My hat's off to you for your approach for this case. I think you scored a lot of good points with the judge."

"Not enough," groused Freilser. "You should have lost."

"So, should you, my dear friend. I guess we must reconvene in another two hundred years and do this again. It will be interesting to see which side of the scale will be tipped by then—whether humanity will prove it's worth saving or whether it needs to be abandoned and replaced with a new version—Humanoid 2.0." He laughed.

"My side doesn't believe it can ever reach a level of civilized behavior worthy of continuing it, whether it's 2.0 or 10.0," said Freilser not even cracking a smile.

"That's a shame," said Mr. K. "I think earthlings will surprise even you in fifty years, let alone two hundred. I placed my bet with the Stellar Vegas bookie just a few minutes ago. The odds they're giving are seven to one against humanity. I'll take those odds."

"Good," said Freilser. "Then, I'll be happy to take the other side of that bet and rake in the cash when we meet here again."

"See you in the next cycle, then," said Mr. K, leaving the courtroom.

*****

TIGER MOMS

CH 1

Saito Yau was furious. Her son, Katsuo, was a senior at the prestigious and private Lang School in New York City. At a tuition of over one hundred thousand per year, it was one of the most expensive schools in the country. He had a perfect grade point through all his school years and was vying for the top spot in the graduation class. It was an honor and of high distinction to be the valedictorian of the class, but he was competing with another for the same spot. Both had taken heavy class loads—advanced placement or AP classes—both were involved in many extracurricular activities; and both were officers in numerous clubs.

It was late in the last semester of their senior year, and Katsuo had turned in a homework, receiving a 98 percent instead of 100. He had argued his answer with the teacher, but to no avail. The teacher had still taken off a few points based on his presentation of the answer.

His mother, Yau, was irate. She stormed into the school and began screaming at the teacher. Eventually, the principal had to seek two of the security agents assigned to the school and have them discretely escort her from the grounds.

Yau was influential; she was the wife of billionaire, Saito Rou, who had invented a frictionless conductor that hadn't required supercooling. She was also often unruly and did not obey normal social etiquette. As rich as she was, she cared little what others thought of her. Yet, she was not the only wealthy parent of a child attending the school. There were many others too who had substantial fortunes and significant contacts.

"I'm sorry, Ms. Saito," said the principal, "but your son's grade must stand. However, I understand that the race to valedictorian is extremely tight this year. Your son and another student have done exceptionally well. Both are seeking the coveted Russell Honor. What are your son's AP scores?"

"He has a perfect 34P," she answered without hesitation.

"Yes, that is the same as his rival, Anaisha Srinivas. What about projects? I understand they are competing in the Science Fair too. That may count toward the final selection too."

Yau thought a moment. "He's working on something that he says has to do with Affine Transformations in non-Euclidian geometry. I don't understand it, but ..."

"Well, I'm sure it is well researched and will be well presented." The principle leaned forward. "Ms. Saito, you need to calm down about this. This is not the end of his world if he doesn't get the ..."

"He will!" she shouted. "He must win! He must!"

She stomped out of his office, still fuming about the 98 percent.

*****

CH 2

Anaisha Shrinivas was also a driven youth. At five, she had been able to calculate logarithms and at ten was doing multivariant calculus. She was a talented musician, having started piano at the age of six and adding the violin when she was seven. Although not making the varsity volleyball team during the fall semester, she had made the varsity tennis team every year after her freshman term. She was, by all standards, a remarkable young woman.

Like Katsuo, Anaisha had parents who were hyper-aggressive in dominating their daughter's life. They pushed her and prodded her toward excellence. With all her honors and awards, the young girl had also suffered an emotional breakdown at the age of thirteen and had been hospitalized. She had recovered, but her parents had not backed off. Increasingly, she was becoming distant from them and more rebellious as the days wore on.

"Mom, I'm not going to the practice. I'm not!" screamed Anaisha.

Vidya, her mother, pointed her finger at her viciously. "We are so close to the finish line. You must go!"

"It's only one practice Mom. I need to rest."

"No, get dressed and get in the car. If you don't, I'll dress you and drag you to the car myself!"

Anaisha was well-liked at school too. She had friends in many different groups—from the sports jocks to the musicians to the drama thespians to the chess club members. She even hung out with the Latin club geeks.

Pretty, with dark smokey eyes, Anaisha had long, black hair to her waist. Little more than five feet three inches tall, she was still a force to be reckoned with. However, her greatest competitor was herself. Rarely, if ever, did she denigrate someone else or hope for their failure. Instead, she was supportive and kind-hearted.

"We are coming down to the last semester, Anaisha," said her mother. "We must do everything we can to win. We will do everything."

*****

CH 3

The principal called Saito into his office to discuss the events as they were unfolding.

"Mrs. Yau," he began, "it appears that your son and the other girl in his class will likely end up with exactly the same numbers toward the Russell Honor and valedictorian of the class. Consequently, the faculty has decided to have a run-off contest between the two to see which should be valedictorian."

"A run-off? What do you mean?" Saito asked.

"They will take part in a contest of sorts—just the two of them. They will be asked a series of questions about random topics to see which has the better grasp of the subjects they've been studying here at the school these past three years."

"I don't believe this!" shouted Saito. "You can't do this to me."

"I'm afraid the decision has been made. If your son does not participate in the contest, then he forfeits his opportunity. That's all there is to it."

"No! That will not happen!" shouted Saito, very animated. She stopped and caught her breath. Then, glaring at the principal, she said, "Fine. Then when is the contest?"

"It will be a week before the end of the semester. We all assume each candidate will get straight A's the last semester, so that's already been factored in. It will be determined by the scores they receive from the contest."

Saito sat back—not pleased.

"Who are the judges?" she asked.

"I'm sorry, I cannot tell you that. In fact, I don't even know myself. It won't be disclosed until right before the contest to keep things fair."

"I see," said answered.

"Mrs. Yau, I know you're not pleased with this, but the faculty and administration believed this was the best course. Do you have any more questions?"

"No, you've told me quite enough," she answered with a snarky edge to her voice.

*****

CH 4

Contest day was here. Saito waited nervously outside the auditorium where the judges were being assembled. She still did not know who they were. Next to her was her son, Katsuo, sitting calmly, his eyes forward and undistracted.

The outside door to the school opened, and Anaisha walked in with her mother, Vidya. They passed Saito and Katsuo on the hard, white, plastic chairs in the hallway. Anaisha smiled at Katsuo, but her mother only glared at Saito who gladly returned the animosity.

"Katsuo, it's good to see you again," said Anaisha, stopping and extending her hand in friendship. "I hope you do well."

Katsuo returned her benevolent smile and clasped her hands. "Anaisha, I've always liked and admired you. I hope you do well too."

Saito stared coldly at her son as if he had committed a heinous crime in her presence. "Do not fraternize with the enemy," she admonished. "She is *not* your friend."

Within a few minutes, the auditorium doors opened, and an usher came out to get them. They were escorted to the stage where two podiums were set up for them, complete with microphones. To make things worse, someone was manning the theater spotlight in the rear balcony to showcase each as they answered a question.

Lining one side of the stage was a row of desks with microphones attached to each. There were seven, and although empty, they would soon be filled with specially selected teachers who brought with them the questions for the contest.

Although no one was officially invited, students and parents streamed into the auditorium to watch the battle of the IQ titans. All wanted to see who would win this epic contest.

After everyone was seated, the two contestants waited for the announcement of the faculty who would pummel them with questions.

"Good evening," said the principal, Morris Waymore. "I'm glad so many of you came out to support the academic achievements of the school. As you know, the two top candidates for the valedictorian position of the class have tied in the number of points awarded toward the Russell

Honor of the school. That award goes to the student who has accumulated the most academic points during their three years here.

"It is now my privilege to introduce tonight's judges. From science is Mr. Oscar Robertson, who teaches Biology and Chemistry. From literature we have Ms. Adora Campania, who teaches AP English and Literature. From math, we have Dr. Conway Crutchfeld, who teaches AP calculus, trigonometry, and advance algebra. From history, we have Ms. Judith Rost, who teaches AP History of the World, and AP History of the Americas. From language, we have Dr. Delores Gonzales who teaches Spanish, Italian, and Latin. And from computer science, we have Allen Rotowski.

"And finally, our seventh panel member is …"

All the teachers had come out and taken their seats, except one which was still empty.

"The seventh panel member is Superintendent Alisha Marsh."

Alisha Marsh came out from behind the curtain, waving her hand and smiling broadly like a super celebrity. Hers was a political position, not an academic one, and it was highly unusual that she would represent a position on the panel. However, it was an important event, and as such, it had high visibility. Marsh would never miss such an opportunity.

"Now, I turn it over to Alisha Marsh who will run tonight's contest. Alisha."

Alisha Marsh bent the microphone neck toward her and began speaking.

"Thank you so much for coming," she said, feigning interest and gratitude. "As superintendent for all the schools in this and nearby districts, I want to emphasis the importance of academics in our schools. I have been fighting hard to get the money we need to fund our initiatives. I listen to the parents in my district and hear their issues about what is going on and what they'd like to see changed. I am sympathetic to their pleas for help and want to ensure we get the best services for all students who need them."

The political speech went on for another ten minutes before Alisha finally returned to the event at hand.

"But tonight, we are here to determine who will be the valedictorian of the class of 2138. Up for grabs is the coveted Russell Honor and the trophy and money that go with it. Tonight, you will find out who is the best in your class."

Alisha sat down, put on her glasses, and began reading from pre-prepared note cards as if she had not reviewed any of them earlier.

"Each panel member will ask a question of one of the candidates. He or she has the first right to answer it. If it is answered correctly, he or she will get a point; if incorrectly, the question will be proposed to the other candidate. If they answer correctly, they get the point. If incorrectly, the question is dropped, and we move to the next. There will be a final round with fewer, but harder questions. In this round, the points are worth five times those of the first round. Good luck."

Alisha moved to her next set of cards as the competitors grew restless at their podiums.

"The first question will be asked by Ms. Rost. It will be a history question. Ms. Rost."

Judith leaned into her microphone and read from the tablet computer on her desk.

"Anaisha, in what year did the War of the Roses begin in England?"

"1455," said Anaisha quickly.

"That is correct," said Ms. Rost.

"Katsuo, in what year was did Queen Victoria assume the crown?"

"1837," said Katsuo.

"Yes, that is correct."

"Dr. Crutchfield, you may ask the next question," directed Marsh.

"Yes, this question goes to Anaisha," he said, smiling. "Anaisha, what is the solution to the square root of negative one?"

Anaisha smiled at the easy question. "The answer is *e*."

"Yes, that is correct."

"Katsuo, what is one-sixth to the negative second power?"

Katsuo smiled too. "Oh, that would be thirty-six."

"Yes."

"Mr. Robertson," said the superintendent, guiding the panel.

"Anaisha, what is the valency of sodium?"

"The valency of sodium is one."

"Correct."

"Katsuo, what is the valency of beryllium?"

"Beryllium has two."

"Correct."

"Very good, students," said Marsh, continuing. "Now, we have Ms. Campania from the English and Literature Department."

"Thank you, Superintendent Marsh. Katsuo, from what Shakespearean play comes the following quote: 'Some are born great, some achieve greatness, and some have greatness thrust upon them.'?"

"From the *Twelfth Night* – Act two, scene five."

"Wow, yes. It is *Twelfth Night*. I guess the act and scenes are bonuses. And then, for Anaisha, I have this. From what Shakespearean play comes the following quote: 'Cowards die many times before their deaths; the valiant never taste of death but once.'?"

Anaisha had to think. "Would you repeat the question?"

The question was repeated, and it gave her enough time to think of the answer.

"I believe it was from *Julius Caesar*."

"Correct. Very good," said Ms. Campania.

"Next, we have Dr. Gonzales from Language," said Marsh.

"Yes, since you both did not take the same language, we will go to the word roots," said Gonzales. "So, Katsuo, what is the Latin word for *truth*?"

"Oh, that's easy: *veritas*."

"Yes, and Anaisha, what is the Latin word for *brave*?"

"Uh, that would be ... 'fortem'?"

"Yes."

"The end of the first round will go to Mr. Rotowski."

"Katsuo, what is a constructor?"

"A constructor is the method or methods used when creating an object of class. Parameterized and default constructors are the two different kinds of constructors used."

Rotowski was impressed. It was almost verbatim from the glossary set.

"Anaisha, what is Angular programming?"

Anaisha looked puzzled. "Would you repeat the question?"

"Angular programming. What is it?"

Anaisha looked distraught. She had a blank look on her face.

"I ... I ... I don't know," she answered.

There was a groan through the audience.

"Katsuo, what is Angular programming?" Rotowski asked, repeating the question.

"Angular programming is mainly based on a JavaScript framework that is responsible for creating modern and dynamic web applications," said Katsuo.

"That is correct. You get the point, Katsuo, and I'm sorry Anaisha, you get no credit for this question."

"All right," said Marsh. "That's the end of round one. We have at least two more rounds to go before we get to the final round. If there is a tie at the end of the final round, we will go to extra questions. Any wrong answer will immediately eliminate the contestant from the honor should the other contestant get the answer right. So, on to the second round."

The second round was brutal. The questions were far harder than in the first round, and at the end, the score tallied was Anaisha eight – Katsuo twelve. Katsuo had not missed a single question in either round. Things did not look promising for Anaisha, but she remained at her station with a smile on her face, doing the best she could.

Well into round three, it was clear who was going to win. Katsuo held a commanding lead of sixteen compared to only ten for Anaisha with only two questions remaining.

"Anaisha, on what day, month and year, did Charles Darwin publish *On the Origin of Species?*"

"Uh, it was in 1859." She continued thinking about the day and month. "I think it was August 9?"

"That is incorrect. It was November 29, 1859."

"No, I'm sorry to interrupt, but it was November 24, 1859," said Katsuo.

Ms. Campania looked back at her notes. "I'm sorry. Katsuo is right. I stand corrected. It was November 24, 1859," she muttered, embarrassed.

"Since Anaisha failed to answer it properly," said Marsh interjecting, "it was Katsuo's turn to answer that question anyway. So, in the end he gets the credit."

Saito glowed with pride. She was getting exactly what she hoped.

"All right, now a question for Katsuo," said Marsh.

"Katsuo, on what date—including day, month and year—did Isaac Newton publish his *Principia Mathematica*?"

"Oh, that was July 5, 1687."

"Yes, that is correct."

"We have the last questions. These will come from our math teacher, Dr. Crutchfield."

"I first would like to thank both students for coming before us. I know it has been a grueling and difficult evening for both of you. I will be asking the final two questions of this round before we reach the final, bonus round.

"Anaisha, as we all know one Celsius degree equals 5/9 times the Fahrenheit degree minus 32. Which of the following is/are true?

1. A temperature increase of one degree Fahrenheit is equivalent to a 5/9 degree temperature increase Celsius?
2. A temperature increase of one degree Celsius is equivalent to a temperature increase of 1.8 degrees Fahrenheit.
3. A temperature increase of 5/9 degree Fahrenheit is equivalent to a temperature increase of one degree Celsius.

   A) 1 only

   B) 2 only

   C) 3 only

   D) 1 and 2 only"

It was a difficult question to answer in written form, let alone verbally.

"I … I don't know. I would say A, 1 only."

"No, Katsuo?"

"The answer is D, 1 and 2 only."

"Yes, that is correct. Now for the last question of the round," said Crutchfeld. "This one is for Katsuo. If 3x-y=12, then what does 8^x divided by 2^y equal?"

Katsuo answered quickly and confidently, "That one is easy," he said. "The answer is …"

But suddenly, his mind froze. His facial expression went blank and his eyes rolled to the back of his head."

"Katsuo? Are you all right?" asked Crutchfeld.

But Katsuo collapsed to the floor on stage.

The ambulance was called, and paramedics rushed in. They immediately began resuscitation to revive him and continued as the cart wheeled him out of the auditorium and into the awaiting hover-ambulance that had flown in from Mercy Hospital to pick him up. Saito rushed out with him and hopped into the hover craft to be with her son as they left for the emergency clinic.

Superintendent Marsh sat speechless at her table, not knowing what to say as she watched it all unfold. Finally, when Katsuo had been taken from the hall, she said, "I'm sorry, but clearly Katsuo has had an incident. We will end this competition and let you know how he is doing. The judges will discuss where we are and make a decision. Based on the current standings, it would appear that Katsuo will be your valedictorian, and Anaisha your salutatorian. Again, thank you for coming. We will give you an update tomorrow morning during our daily PA broadcast."

The students filed out of the auditorium, talking loudly and urgently about what had happened. Anaisha was still standing at her podium trembling. She was in shock.

Her mother went to her and helped her off the stage.

"You did not do well!" she scolded her. "You embarrassed me, and you shamed your family."

"Mother, I don't really care. I did my best. If that wasn't good enough for you, I'm sorry for that. Right now, I'm worried about Katsuo. I hope he is okay. He didn't look well when they took him from the auditorium."

"I don't care," said Vidya. "In fact, I hope he dies. That way, you will be made valedictorian."

Anaisha couldn't believe what her mother had just said. Speechless, she walked out of the room by herself and waited until her mother got to the car to drive them home. It would be many days until she could bring herself to talk to her again.

*****

CH 5

The next morning came, and so did the usual school announcements during home room.

"Good morning," said Principal Waymore. "I have an update on Katsuo. As many of you know, he took ill last night during our academic competition. He was rushed to the hospital. I am told that, sadly, he is in a coma. The doctors don't know how long he will be in that condition. We give our thoughts to his family and friends during this time.

"As for the determination of the valedictorian position and Russell Honors, Katsuo will be your class representative. He won the contest last night before he took ill. Anaisha did very well too. She will be your salutatorian.

"Now, as far as other events. This weekend, we have the food drive for the …"

The principal droned on for another ten minutes until the period was over. Students left their homerooms abuzz with talk about what had happened the previous night and what didn't happen. They also talked about what they though should have happened.

*****

CH 6

Saito waited next to her son's bed. He was filled with tubes and wires. The monitors were beeping, lights were flashing, yet there was little going on with Katsuo who lay still, his eyes closed.

Saito was crying, sobbing next to her son as Anaisha came into the room. Saito looked up to see who had entered, and when she saw Anaisha she grew angry.

"How dare you come here!" she shouted.

"I ... I only came as a friend," Anaisha answered, now feeling bad for coming.

"It's you ... your fault that my son is lying here like he is!"

Shocked, Anaisha still answered. "I don't understand. How is it my fault?"

"If you hadn't been in competition with my son for valedictorian, this never would have happened," Saito said, still furious.

"I didn't choose to have a contest to decide that. I only did my best in school. Is there something wrong with that?"

"Because of contest, my son is lying here," Saito said, not addressing the question.

"Yes, that's true, but I had nothing to do with it."

"You are evil," said Saito. "You and your bitchy mother."

Anaisha had heard enough.

"Your son is here because he had a trauma during the session. It could have happened anywhere at any time. It just happened to occur when he was in the middle of a stressful situation on stage. That's all!"

"It happened because of his implant!" Saito screamed, crying again

"Implant?"

"Yes, and it's all your fault!"

Saito left the room, continuing to wail, as Anaisha was left wondering what had just happened. She looked at Katsuo and felt sorry for him. He was in a coma, and there was nothing she could do to help him.

***

Graduation ceremonies took place, and everyone was there in their cap and gown—except Katsuo. He still lay in the hospital. It was doubtful that he would ever recover. Instead of any speeches from the valedictorian or salutatorian, the principal got up and gave one about striving for excellence and putting every effort into something in order to achieve success.

"You will find that if you give one hundred and one percent," said Waymore, "you are much more likely to achieve your goals in life. Give it your all ... you will be rewarded."

But, unexpectedly, Anaisha rose and went to the podium. She wasn't supposed to speak as salutatorian, but she did anyway. The principal started to stop her, but then stopped.

"Hello, my fellow graduates," she begam. "With a heavy heart, I address you today. I realize I was not scheduled to make comments, but I feel I must.

"I want you to know that I pray for Katsuo and his recovery. I am terribly sorry for any part I played in his condition, but I don't believe I had any role. Having said that, I wanted to share with you two thoughts.

"First, I echo the sentiments of Principal Waymore. In all that you do, in college and beyond, give it all your effort. You get back what you put in. If you give fifty percent, you'll achieve fifty percent or less of your dream—maybe none. If you give it one hundred percent, you'll achieve one hundred percent of your dream. What you may find is that what you achieve is not exactly what you thought, but it will make you happy and you will see that you have, indeed, reached your goal.

"And secondly, the journey is as important, if not more, than the destination. The journey is there for you to learn and develop. You will be better for it, and it will provide you invaluable lessons to help you face later challenges. Without these trials, you will not grow. Reaching your destination with the knowledge of mistakes you've made and lessons learned is so much more valuable than merely picking up the trophy at the end of the road.

"And with that, I wish you all well in life. I hope you all achieve the goals you set for yourself. Do not be swayed by goals set for you by others. It is, after all, your life. Live it the way you choose and in a way that enriches not only you but also others."

The ceremony ended and the graduates threw their mortar boards into the air. Anaisha was happy to graduate and was looking forward to her next four years at Harvard.

However, only a week later, news leaked out about what really happened to Katsuo.

"Did you hear?" Samantha Perkins said, calling her friend Anaisha. "They know what happened to Katsuo during your contest."

"He had a seizure of some sort," said Anaisha, although she already had suspicions about the real reason.

"Oh, it was much more than that," said her friend.

*****

CH 7

Samantha continued. "It appears his mother set him up for an implant weeks before the contest. They flew to Tokyo and had the procedure done. It was highly experimental and cutting edge. Katsuo was one of the first to get it."

"What was it? The implant, that is?"

"They say the brain implant was an experimental human router which connected with the school's WIFI network. Katsuo was online on the Internet during the entire contest. All he had to do was repeat the question in his mind and the implant would go to the web and find the answer. It brought him the answers almost instantly, and he could repeat them verbatim from his mind."

"What?"

"Yeah, isn't that amazing?" said Samantha.

"Then what happened?"

"The implant blew up," her friend said. "The implant burst inside his head when it got overloaded with too many 'hits' from the Internet. It couldn't process the billions that came into his mind and it literally detonated inside his head. He's a vegetable now, Anaisha. It's so sad."

Anaisha sat stunned and quiet.

"Anaisha are you still there?"

"Yes."

"Are you all right?"

"No."

"What are you thinking?" asked Samantha. "Do you want revenge against his mother for doing this to you? For cheating?"

"No," said Anaisha. "I want to go to Katsuo and tell him I'm sorry."

"What are you sorry for?"

"I'm sorry that he had a mother who drove him to do what he did. I'm also sorry for the mother that I have. Hopefully, she will change. The one thing I know for sure ..."

"What's that?"

"I will be a very different mother to my children."

*****

7D

CH 1

The galactic war had raged on for more than two thousand years and the casualties had long been measured in planets destroyed rather than lives lost. Commander Xtak believed that over two hundred million had died during that time, but others believed it was closer to twenty or thirty *billion*.

Both sides had been in existence as advanced civilizations for tens of thousands of years. And both were intelligent enough to see flaws and weaknesses in their own forces and correct them quickly when the enemy exploited them. Not unlike the first world war on planet Earth during human's self-proclaimed Century of Progress—the twentieth century, the carnage of the Great Galactic War was horrific. It was a war that made the deaths of ten million military personnel during World War I look puny by comparison.

The Great Galactic War started when the aggressive race of serpent-like beings—called Reptoids—began a march across the galactic quadrant to conquer as many planets as it could. Their emperor, Sauropsidis II, had issued an edict to claim the entire third quadrant of the galaxy as his own. There were thirty-five other civilizations with advanced technology in the quadrant, but one-by-one they fell to Sauropsidis.

As each planet was attacked, the defenders saved as many lives as they could, transporting them to other planets. Millions of beings were moved before their planet was extinguished by the powerful, space-time distortion guns used by the Reptilian race. Finally, the defending humanoids all gathered on five distinct planets within the constellation Orion. They had perfected countermeasures to the distortion guns— shields of dense, dark matter that would deflect the destructive force of the pulses. These shields were deployed around four of the five planets and were in the process of being installed around the fifth—the remaining capital of the humanoids, Pleiades Three.

However, there was a new weapon now. The Reptilians had developed it, and it was far more terrifying than the previous distortion gun. Flying a mighty squadron of death ships through a wormhole, the Reptilian general, Ugt Nar, had his sights set on eliminating the humans last holdout to conquering the quadrant and wanted to bring home a glorious victory for his emperor, Sauropsidis II. As his battleship exited the wormhole with its sixteen fighter escorts, he got a good view of the target ahead: Pleiades Three.

Pleiades Three was the capital and largest of the five planets, holding the inhabitants of the once-peaceful Pleiadean people. Spies planted by the Pleiadean command had infiltrated deeply into the Reptilian ranks using the same shape-shifting ability mastered by the reptiles themselves. It was a constant battle to detect who was real and who wasn't. Most recently, the communication back from their informants suggested the new weapon was on its way and would obliterate the capital and its other four neighbors. The Pleiadeans could only build their countermeasure as quickly as they could based on what they knew. They hoped it would be enough.

"Commander Xtak, what is our status?" asked the president of the Lightspirit Galactic Council for the Pleiadeans.

President Q, as he was called, represented all the races that were fighting for their freedom against the savage and dark forces of the Reptilians. There were still eight major races still in existence—the others having been erased from the universe by the draconian measures used by the attackers.

"Our defensive shields, modified for the new weaponry, are in place, Mr. President."

"And our offensive weapons?"

"They are in route to the Reptilian capital as we speak, sir."

"I need more, Commander. Give me a full briefing."

Although most communication was telepathic, the details were communicated via verbal or written conveyance. Mental pictures were excellent for the larger themes and ideas, but details required more exacting, and in most cases, more exhausting methods of communication.

"Very well, sir. Here is the data we have," said Xtak.

For the next few hours, the commander explained in detail how he believed the final battle would play out. When he finished, his president sent him a telepathic message: *I hope you're right.*

The Pleiadean controllers picked up the enemy ships breaking through the wormhole created and were less than two light-hours away from the capital—or 2.16 billion kilometers from their planet. Traveling at subwarp speed, they would arrive within three hours but would likely reach their point of attack within two.

Not only did the Pleiadeans need to defend in three-dimensional space, but they also had to defend against 5D and 6D attacks. Reptilians were known to launch multi-dimensional attacks against targets, destroying them at every level of their existence. But the multi-dimensional angles of attack were almost infinite. There were no set frequencies for 5D and 6D dimensions—these were merely broad frequency ranges. However, the Pleiadeans had something else in their arsenal the Reptilians were unaware of, and they hoped it would make the difference in their struggle for survival.

"Commander," said a captain who reported to him, "I'm showing energy traces of attacking vessels at 45.0 mPz and 3.9 mPz, sir."

It was long known that the higher the frequency, the higher the dimension. The planet Earth resonated at the Schumann frequency of an extremely low 7.83 Hz in 3D. At the higher dimensions, there was a different type of resonance all together—this was known as the mPz or string frequency which involved quantum physical string vibrations. Humans already knew that different string vibrations created each of the elemental particles in quantum physics. The mPz was a fraction of the Planck length—the smallest measurement known in 3D. It was measured in units of thousandths of a Planck length (1.616×10^{-38} meters) or microPlancks (mPz).

"Adjust frequency of armaments," said the president. "Ensure we keep our weapons trained on their micro-frequencies. We can't let them destroy our underbelly in the fifth or sixth dimensional ranges. It will topple everything we have in our 3D existence too."

The commander complied. It didn't take more than thirty minutes in 3D to lock onto their targets, and their counter pulse guns--that distorted not only the superstrings in 3D but also the fifth and sixth dimensions— began firing at the invaders. The bursts couldn't be seen in 3D but were affecting the ships which had appeared in the 5D and 6D dimensionalities.

Both the commander and president watched their monitors which gave them energy signatures of everything in the third, fifth and sixth dimensions. As the fourth dimension was only a transitional boundary between the heavy, dense universe of 3D and the higher energy states, nothing remained stable for long in this world, and it was avoided by both sides.

The Reptilian ships began vibrating and then ruptured from the pulses, tearing apart at the seams. Their energy dissipated into the cosmos of their dimensionality.

"Well?" asked the president.

"We eliminated the first group, sir. But there is another coming through."

"What?" asked the president, seeing alarms going off throughout the control room. "I don't see anything on the monitors showing a problem."

"Here," said the commander, pointing to a hazy image on one of the monitors.

"What's that?"

"That's in 7D," he said. "They've figured out a way to resonate in 7D. That's their secret weapon. We don't have anything that can stop that."

*****

CH 2

Ugt Nar knew he had to stay in 7D as long as he could to avoid the defensive weapons of the Pleiadeans; however, it was draining his quantum generators. The energy requirement to stay in 7D was massive, and he needed enough in reserve to launch his attack and escape back through the wormhole.

"Drop from 7D frequency," barked Nar, "and load the space-time disruptors." Nar knew he didn't need to go through the wormhole to return to his planet in the sixth dimension; however, he did need it to evade the counterattack expected from the Pleiadean warships orbiting Pleiades Three.

The ship dropped its frequency and appeared suddenly on Xtak's monitor down on the planet. But by then, it was too late.

"Fire!" shouted Nar, watching on his own monitors as the disruptors pulsed a shock wave to entangle the superstrings that constituted all space time in 3D.

Within seconds, things in the 3D world on Pleiades Three began collapsing. All matter, including the planet itself, started to disintegrate.

"Commander," said the president, "we're getting reports from the other planets too. They are experiencing the same vibrations. The matter in their area is also disintegrating!"

"It must be a space-time distortion gun," said the commander. "It affects the strings, and since those are connected from one end of the universe to the other, everything on the grid will be impacted."

"How long do we have to evacuate?" asked the president.

"Not long enough," answered Xtak. "I'll order an immediate reinforcement of all ships and gunnery units in the 3 and 5D layers, but that will only postpone the inevitable."

"Order the evacuation of all civilians," said the president. "Hold out as long as you can."

"The planet will be completely destroyed—you know that."

"Yes," the president answered. "I will stay with the troops. Someone with military knowledge must accompany the civilians out of the Orion sector. That must be you, commander."

"But sir ..."

"No. I insist. You will be much more valuable—essential—to the survival of our species than an old politician. You must go."

"Where, sir?" asked the commander. "Shall we use the established list of targets?"

"Yes, and you know my thoughts on that," said the president.

"Yes."

"Well, good luck to you, and may the Almighty be with you."

The commander left and minutes before the planet began to convulse and buckle, he and forty other craft left their base. The planet exploded after it was hit with one final distortion burst which ruptured its internal core, splitting the planet into fragments that would soon find their own orbits around the solar system's surviving star.

Commander looked out into space.

"Coordinates are set?" he asked his helmsman.

"Yes, sir."

"Well, let's go. It's supposed to be an average star in an average part of our galaxy with average planets orbiting it. I guess that's as good as it gets."

"Yes, sir. Where is it, sir?"

"They call it a blue marble, but I like to call it Earth."

*****

ACCESS DENIED

CH 1

From: Bradd Wilkinsen <Mail@NextTimeAround.org>
Date: May 21, 2028 at 1:06:28 PM CDT
To: Renee Critchfield <Mail@NextTimeAround.org>
Subject: Link You Sent

Renee,
Got your mail on the article but when I clicked on it, the site said, "No Longer Available."

Are you sure you sent the right link?

***

From: Renee Critchfield <Mail@NextTimeAround.org>
Date: May 21, 2028 at 1:08:31 PM CDT
To: Bradd Wilkinsen <Mail@NextTimeAround.org>
Subject: Link You Sent

Yeah, Bradd. It just came out like fifteen minutes ago. I read it then. It couldn't already be zapped.

***

From: Bradd Wilkinsen <Mail@NextTimeAround.org>
Date: May 21, 2028 at 1:12:04 PM CDT
To: Renee Critchfield <Mail@NextTimeAround.org>
Subject: Link You Sent

Yep. It's gone. I tried again. It's been zapped.

***

From: Renee Critchfield <Mail@NextTimeAround.org>
Date: May 21, 2028 at 1:14:39 PM CDT
To: Bradd Wilkinsen <Mail@NextTimeAround.org>
Subject: Link You Sent

Shit! Man, this is getting ridiculous. Censorship is alive and well on the Internet, I guess.

***

From: Bradd Wilkinsen <Mail@NextTimeAround.org>
Date: May 21, 2028 at 1:15:44 PM CDT
To: Renee Critchfield <Mail@NextTimeAround.org>
Subject: Link You Sent

Hey, if you're just now noticing, then you're way behind the times. Most of the links are gone. Someone's taken over, and it isn't the good guys. I won't say anymore, 'cause I don't want to be dragged from my bed in the middle of the night. Understand now?

***

From: Renee Critchfield Mail@NextTimeAround.org
Date: May 21, 2028 at 1:17:04 PM CDT
To: Bradd Wilkinsen <Mail@NextTimeAround.org>
Subject: Link You Sent

Got it. 😖

*****

CH 2

Li and John quickly setup their temporary server to access another server farm that was buried a few hundred feet below the surface in South Dakota. It took months to prepare – not just because of the size and scope of the project, but also because it had to be done in complete secrecy.

"We will be up in five, four, three, two, one …" said John, flipping a single switch on his portable dashboard.

"Is it live?" asked Li.

"Yep, we're up and running – right on time."

"It's nine seconds past the hour. How can you say you're on time?" Li asked.

"Crap! You're right. Sorry. I misread my watch. Hopefully, it didn't frighten too many people."

The massive system was intended to be the black-market underground for Internet traffic. There had always been different levels of the Internet. The regular, public Internet and the quasi-public/private net were two levels now completely controlled by sensors in Beijing. There was a massive complex there where over 155,000 Chinese were employed to scour and scrub all sites on the public Internet, looking for anyone brash enough to post a website in violation of Party standards. Not only would such sites be pulled down, but the owner would be hunted and, once found, either be arrested or simply disappear.

The third level, the Darknet, required special access using a special browser. It had grown significantly since the crackdown on the first two levels. More net traffic had gone deeper to the third level, but then this, too, was being peeled away and brought to its knees by the Party filters.

That left only one deeper level, known at the time as the Mariana's Net. The Chinese authorities spent billions to unleash more technology and manpower to subdue this level as well. When that was done, there were no levels left to conquer. All had been subsumed into the greater architecture of the nation-state model. Only those websites that operated within the thirty-five-thousand-pages of regulations covering permissible Internet activity could operate.

But when all was thought lost. Someone created another architecture for offering information. Rumors of its eminent release were rampant, and millions eagerly awaited it. This architecture would be exceedingly difficult to monitor and shut down, but not impossible. The creators of this latest iteration new theirs would only be a stopgap until it too fell to the authorities. However, they were already working on one after that too to stay one step ahead.

"I'm getting disturbances in the connections," said Li, monitoring the new system.

"What kind?" asked John.

"Perturbations are being created based on violations of the entrance algorithms. We set this up so only quantum computer technology can access our net."

"Yeah, but we've sent out millions of solutions to the algorithm based on vetting our users. People who are vetted are funneled through these quantum computer hubs. Only from one of those could we get a perturbation."

"You're right, but someone with a quantum computer is using what amounts to a jackhammer to bust their way in," said Li. "Look at this."

Li showed John what was going on, and his partner shook his head.

"We knew this day would come," said John.

"Yeah, but not this soon. We just went online two hours ago. How could they break the firewall and solve the algorithm so quickly?"

"It's the Party," said John. "They have unlimited money, remember?"

"What do we do? How long until they discover where we're setup?"

"I show it will take another sixty-three minutes for them to lock on our location. I think it's time to move on."

John and Li shut down their network and packed up their equipment within the hour, but it took over a day to get everything to a new location, and they hoped they could stay up and running there for at least a week or more.

However, that was not to be. They had to move three more times before they could modify their protocols and find a location they could keep secure—for a while. *****

CH 3

General Yi had a vast network of his own. This one spread from California to Maine and up through Nova Scotia. Both Canada and the United States had collapsed economically from the trillions of debt owed to China and other countries. When the world called in their marker and America couldn't pay, the U.S. faced a global war or surrender. They chose the latter.

In exchange for the forgiveness of the two hundred-twenty-three trillion in debt, China agreed to take 83 percent of the land in the U.S. and free access to Canada and its resources for the debt forgiveness of both countries. Private property rights were immediately forfeited, and the only remaining lands not owned by the Party in Beijing were in Alaska which was re-annexed by Russia. China desperately needed Siberian oil reserves, so the deal struck was to re-unite Alaska to Russia, nullifying the purchase made by Secretary of State William Seward for $7.2 million dollars in 1867.

"Our president wants them found," said Yi.

"We're working on it, general," said Colonel Wan Zu of the North American Patriots Intelligence Corp.

"That's not an answer I like," said Yi, scowling. "You know the president wants results—not excuses. We must find the source of this new outbreak. This will continue until we refine our technology to be able to find them more quickly and exterminate them. You understand this, yes?"

Zu saluted. "We will locate them, sir."

"By the end of the week. No later," said Yi. "We will call in bombing runs if we need to. I don't care how many civilians die. I want them destroyed."

*****

CH 4

Although all layers of the Internet were completely controlled and censored by the Party, the new architecture, LatticeOne, as it was called, now handled ninety percent of information searches even though there were only five percent of the websites on the Internet. This was exasperating to the Party leadership and the Chinese president. They wanted it all controlled.

Fleeing from the iron grip of the authorities, Li and John had created LatticeOne as an artificial system designed to change constantly, re-defining its algorithms on a continuous flow to make blockage of websites on the Lattice more difficult. However, although the equipment was relatively mobile, they were running out of options to keep it hidden from the authorities.

"Li, we've gone about everywhere we can without getting caught. But now there aren't many places left to hide. They've put monitors on twelve hundred locations we've been at to prevent us from returning. What do we do now?"

Li shook his head. "I only know of one more thing to do."

"What's that?"

"We respond in kind."

"What does that mean?" asked John, packing up the equipment for the last time.

"I've been working on something for a while. I didn't want to tell you for fear if you got captured, our last chance would be revealed. But now, I don't see any way around it, and anyway, I've finished it."

"What is it?" asked John. "I really wish you would have told me."

"I know, but it was just too risky. Not that you would talk on your own, but you know as well as I that there is no way to keep from talking when you're being tortured. When you're chained to a chair and you watch as different parts of your body are cut off, you eventually cave."

"I get it. So, what is your solution?" asked John.

"I will show you," Li said, smiling.

Li pulled out his micro-thin laptop that was still one of the most powerful anyone outside the government had. He booted up his screen and selected a file. The file opened and began reciting the thousands of lines of code Li had programmed.

"I think I see," said John, reading the lines. "But tell me what I'm reading."

Li explained it, but it was complicated. We'll have to wait for the next firewall attack. Then, this will kick-in. We'll see if it works.

Li and John moved their equipment to another bunker—this one cleverly buried under the Black Hills of South Dakota. But these weren't just any hills—above them were the obliterated faces of four former presidents. They were ripped from the mountain side soon after the new owners of the country came to power. All monuments to the founding fathers, all statues, all memorials were brought down—torn from their moorings or defaced so badly they could never be restored. In this case, they were below what remained of Mt. Rushmore.

"Okay," said Li. "Let's see what happens. We'll reconnect the LatticeOne program, and then I'll initiate my firewall algorithm. Let's go fishing and see what we catch, shall we?"

Indeed, the two enjoyed three days of calm during which their LatticeOne was able to provide people with the truth about what was going on in their country and the world. The news wasn't colored by judgement or interpretation – only the facts were permitted. The lack of interpretation meant people had to decide for themselves whether the story was important and what the implications were. In many cases, they had to analyze raw data too—not an easy task. But it freed them of the Party propaganda machines that told them the news they wanted them to hear, in a way they wanted them to hear and understand it.

"So far, so good," said John, monitoring the equipment.

"Yes," said Li, "but the time will come, and it will come soon. Be ready."

Another two days passed, and still nothing unusual happened. The Lattice was enjoying ninety-five percent of national traffic. People were clamoring for real transparency and honesty.

Yet, the following day, all that changed.

"Li, come here!" shouted John, sitting up and typing furiously on his keyboard.

"What is it?"

"Look at this. It's an attack on the firewall algorithm. It's from the Party. It's sophisticated—at a level I haven't seen before."

Li looked at it as it came in. "Holy shit!" he cried. "I don't know if my algorithm can stop that!"

"And if it doesn't?"

"Our equipment will be fried," said Li. "And if this is the level they've gone to, then they will be here before we have a chance to pack up and get out. We may be finished, John."

John watched things intently. He wanted to close the station and move out again, but he knew this time it was different. Within the hour— maybe less—they would hear transport planes flying in and troops disembarking to find and kill them.

"How long will your algorithm take?" asked John, nervously waiting.

"Let's watch and see," said Li.

They sat in silence, watching the screens in front of them which showed the traffic on the Lattice and the Internet. It also showed the capability of the government's internal net system which was highly encrypted and handled the traffic of everything from the Department of Labor crime reports to the National Security Council's spy reports on what was happening in the Ukraine. None of it was readable, but they were able to see the volume levels.

Minutes passed, and the Party server began digging through the precious algorithm that kept them hidden from all layers of the Internet and beyond the Party's grasp.

"How much time, until it breaks through?" asked John.

"I calculate two minutes, twenty-six seconds."

They waited. The minutes seemed like hours.

"I show thirty-three seconds," said Li. "We'll know then."

The seconds now ticked away. Time seemed to stop as if they were on the cusp of a black hole's event horizon.

"Nine seconds," said Li.

John looked up at the clock above him. The digital seconds were counting down.

"Time," said Li.

John held his breath, and after a few more seconds he asked, "Well?"

Suddenly, the traffic numbers to the Lattice plummeted to zero.

"Shit!" said Li. "How can that happen?"

"What does that mean?" asked John, now panicked.

"It means we're …"

But at the same time, the traffic for the Lattice instantly rebounded—bouncing back at the previous levels, and then surging to an all-time high.

"Look!" said John, pointing to the Internet numbers. "Now, they've fallen. Five … three … one … zero. Zero percent. The Prime Internet is down—completely down. No one can access anything."

Li smiled. "So is the government web. It's down too. Completely down."

"What happened?" asked John, excitedly.

"When they broke through the firewall, they encountered and embraced a virulent virus which I implanted. It was immediately uploaded into their system and infected the entire Prime Internet and then the government's systems. They all shut down. It will take them months, if not years, to find it. I buried it deep—very deep."

"Excellent!" said John, smiling.

But then they heard rumbling overhead.

"They're coming, aren't they?" asked John.

"I'm afraid they are," said Li.

"Do we stand a chance?"

Li shook his head. "No. We don't. The only thing we can do is initiate our backup plan. Sorry John. I love you like a brother. I'll have to see you on the other side."

"Goodbye Li," said John tearfully.

The troops blew the hatch to get into the underground bunker and began their assault on the control room. Sixty seconds later, there was another explosion. This one was so great that it made the first sound like a small firecracker.

The entire hill upon which Mt. Rushmore once stood crumbled into pieces. It collapsed on itself, destroying what was left of the four presidents and killing two more heroes below.

It was a loss for those at the top, but a triumph for the two at the bottom. It was a victory the four presidents would have been proud of.

*****

WEALTH

CH I

"Slavatorian Chairman Zhlatka? Seeing that we have defeated you and your species, we will commence with the games." The statement came from a booming, disembodied voice over an unseen speaker system.

"Games?" asked a tall, but muscular man dressed smartly in a midnight-blue military uniform with scores of colorful ribbons across his chest. He glanced over at a tiny, frail-looking woman no more than twenty years old standing next to him. She only shrugged but had a puzzled look on her face that matched his.

"Yes. We Slavatorians enjoy a good game now and again, and we understand that humans have held games for over three thousand years. Am I right? I believe you call them Olympics."

Brilliant overhead lights came on all around the two, and they suddenly realized they were standing on a round concrete stage surrounded by stadium seating packed full of Slavatorians. But the lights were so bright and shining directly into their eyes, and they were unable to see just how big the stadium was and how many were seated for the event. From the echoes and the noise, Colonel Carlyle figured there had to be more than three hundred thousand watching them at that very moment.

"Yes, we humans enjoy games," said the colonel, "but we only enjoy them if they are fair. How do we know if these will be fair?"

There was uncomfortable silence over the air waves, but then the voice returned.

"Fairness is in the eye of the beholder. Is it not? What we think is fair, may not equate to your understanding. Am I right?"

The colonel wondered if the questioning was a trap but answered anyway. "You are right. But if I don't believe they are fair, why should I participate?"

"I don't suppose you have a choice. You lost the war, did you not?"

The colonel bit his lip and, this time, didn't answer.

"You don't need to respond. We all know the answer. So, if you are the conquered, then you must do as we, the conquerors, ask. Correct?" asked the voice.

"If we're forced to participate in some stupid game," said a second man, a major with bulging muscles, wearing a black, tank top, and camouflage shorts, "then what are the rules to the game? You can't expect us to play if you don't have rules."

This was the remaining crew of the last assault craft captured by the alien forces. The *USS Tempest* had held out against all odds but was finally tracked down and forced into the hold of one of the giant alien cruisers. The six crew—Colonel Ivan Rostov, Major Jason Stefka, Lieutenant Lucia White, Sergeant Gondo Keita, and Corporals Amica Paulsen and Jeremiah Fetter—were captured and taken prisoner.

"Quite right," said the voice. "Here are the rules."

Instantly, an immense scroll of words on a page appeared just in front of the stage. It unfurled slowly as the narrator read the instructions. The script was plain with no embellishments, so it was clear and easy to follow along.

"… and in summary, the game is to be played by all parties on stage against one another. The one who accumulates the greatest wealth wins."

"And how long do we have to gain this wealth?" asked the colonel.

"The game must be played within the human space-time framework of one year—365.256 days. Whoever has tallied the greatest wealth during that time shall win."

"What will we win?" shouted a younger man dressed in dirty blue jeans and a torn collarless, plaid shirt. This was Gondo Keita, the sergeant of the group.

"I believe you have a right to know that," said the voice.

"Damn straight!" said the young man.

"If you win the game, you will win your freedom. How is that?"

"Our freedom? How can we win that if you control our planet and all walks of life on it?" asked the colonel.

"You must trust us," came the short reply.

"Trust you? After what you did during the war?" said the colonel.

"Yes, especially because of what we did during the war," said the voice.

"You were …" began the colonel, but the small woman next to him took him by the arm and shook her head.

"We were what?"

"Nothing," said the colonel, backing down.

"When do we start this game, then?" asked the lieutenant, the young woman standing next to him.

"I'm so glad you asked," said the voice. "You start … now."

And with that, the entire stadium went black.

*****

CH 2

Colonel Rostov had been in command of the failed One Nation collective armed force for four years while it fought the superior forces of the Slavatorians. He had been on the transport ship *USS Tempest* on his way to meet with General Clayton in a hardened bunker under the Antarctic when that base was struck by alien fire and destroyed. The *Tempest* was captured as it tried to make its escape.

The Slavatorians were an advanced race from the Perseus Constellation. For millennia they had fought other races in the galaxy and, most notably, those that offered protection to the inhabitants of Earth. However, in this matter, they were able to outsmart the Galactic Council responsible for guarding and watching over earthlings. By creating a diversion in another part of the galaxy, they attacked another developing planet, known as Gaia 2. However, while they threw three airborne divisions of assault spacecraft against this planet, the Galactic Council raced to defend it. In doing so, they abandoned their shield over Earth. It was then, that the Slavatorians sent the majority of their arsenal against the blue planet.

The war lasted only four years but could have been resolved much sooner had the Slavatorians wanted to destroy the planet completely. However, they wanted only to enslave the inhabitants and mine the rare resources for their use back home.

It was the final battle in the Antarctic which brought the conflict to an end. One Nation had moved all its graviton torpedoes—the most powerful in its arsenal—to the base in Antarctica. The Slavatorians were quick to discover them and launched their tachyon pulses at the land mass, destroying the entire surface and allowing the oceans of the Atlantic, Pacific and Indian Oceans to reclaim the South Pole.

The leadership of One Nation was quickly imprisoned, and most were executed. However, Rostov and his crew were spared as it was believed the colonel had the skills to lead and could lead the humans kneeling to their new masters and agreeing to become their slaves mining ore from the planet.

"So," said Major Stefka, "what do we do now?"

"We must first decide what 'wealth' means," answered Colonel Rostov.

"What? What are you talking about?" said Corp. Paulsen. "It's obvious what wealth is."

"It's obvious? Then what is your definition?" asked Rostov.

"Money. The one who creates the most money at the end of the year wins."

"*Huh?*" said the colonel. "What do the rest of you think?"

"I agree," said Corp. Fetter. "That's the way I was raised. It's what you own that makes you rich and wealthy. That means land or money."

"I see," said the colonel. "I come from a different background. In Russia we didn't own anything. Everything was owned by the state. So, how was our wealth determined?"

The other five looked at each other and shrugged.

"What if I suggested something different?" said the colonel. "What if I suggested spiritual wealth?"

"What?" came the chorus.

"Spiritual wealth," he repeated.

This was very strange coming from a military man, but Rostov was not an ordinary army man. All the same, the group laughed.

"No disrespect, colonel," said Corp. Paulsen, "but I don't think that's what they had in mind."

"You really think the Slavatorians believe in that junk?" asked Stefka.

"I don't know," said Rostov. "But what I do know is that I can defend it."

"I'm not going there," said Paulsen. "We're sure to lose and become enslaved if you do that."

"I agree," said Fetter. "You'll doom us and the rest of humanity to lives as slaves to these creatures. We'll be digging mines and our own graves for these things the rest of our lives."

"Well, that's the direction I want to go with this," said Rostov.

"Then I'm out," said Stefka, crossing his arms. "Anybody else with me?"

"Yep. I am," said Fetter.

"So am I," said Paulsen.

"Me too," said White, chiming in. "I'm not gonna' be anybody's slave. Ever!"

Rostov looked over at the only one who hadn't expressed an opinion. This was Sgt. Keita.

"What do you say, sergeant?"

Keita sat in thought, pressing the palms of his hands together. It took almost a minute before he answered.

"My family comes from a spiritual place," he said. "We had little growing up, but we were taught that it wasn't money that made you who you were, but the strength of your character. My pappa always said, 'There are three things that are important in life: love God, love yourself, and love your neighbor. If you can do that, you can do anything." He paused and looked at Rostov. "I'm with you colonel. You tell me where you want to go, and I'll follow you."

So, the human camp divided into two camps—one led by Rostov; the other led by Stefka. But it was not equally divided. Only Keita and Rostov were determined to follow the spiritual path. The other four pursued money, power, and materialism.

Only time would tell who was right. In fact, they would know in only 364 days. Time was ticking.

*****

CH 3

During the first six months, Stefka struggled convince the other humans throughout the globe to turnover their lands, money and valuables to him and his team. He told them the fate of humanity rested on them accumulating more wealth from Earth than the Slavatorians. He was convinced early on that he could reason with his fellow human beings to be unselfish and give up what they had so no one had to become enslaved.

But people resisted. They didn't believe Stefka and thought he was only trying to take what they had for himself and the other three team members.

"But you must!" he shouted at them. "You have no choice!"

"You're lying!" they cried. "We've heard this before. We have so little now anyway—after the war and all. Now, you even want to take that away from us!"

Stefka went to the Slavatorian Council and asked if he could use their military to force the people of Earth to comply, and, surprisingly, they agreed.

"By executive order, you will submit all your lands, your valuables, your money—everything you own—to me and the team," said Stefka, declaring worldwide martial law.

The Slavatorians put their armies into action throughout the globe, confiscating the wealth of every man, woman and child in the world and granting Stefka global powers over all of it.

"I am Emperor," Stefka declared once the transfer of wealth had happened. It had been less than a year, and already the absolute power of his position was affecting him. He felt powerful. His commands became the word of god and would not be challenged. He got everything he asked for and more.

"But what about us?" asked Paulsen, finding herself and the other two members of Stefka's team sidelined. Increasingly, they had no say in what was happening, and all the wealth was being deposited into specific locations designated by Stefka and guarded by his armies.

"Yeah," said White. "We all must share in this wealth. We helped you get this. We are a team, and teams fight together and win together."

Stefka laughed. "The Slavatorians only granted *me* the power to issue proclamations and collect title to the wealth of the world. You have no such power." He motioned to twenty Slavatorian guards standing with photon blasters.

"Seize them ... all of them. They are of no use to me now," he said with a sardonic smile. "Imprison them in the deepest cells. I never wish to see their pathetic faces again."

The wealthy and intellectuals were rounded up and imprisoned as well. Many who resisted were executed on the spot. No one who challenged Stefka was permitted to continue their disobedience and either disappeared, were imprisoned, or were executed.

The world cowered in fear. They now wondered if life would have been better serving under the Slavatorians.

*****

CH 4

Day 365

It was one year to the day since the challenge had been meted out, and the last hours were counting down for the precise moment that the earth had made one full revolution around the Sun. Stefka was proud of his success and the vastness of the wealth he had accumulated. There was no way, in his mind, that the Slavatorians could have accumulated anything comparable in wealth, as he had it all.

"This hearing must come to order," said Zlacto, the chairman of the Slavatorian Council. "We will now review the contest with the humans on the accumulation of wealth during the last 365.256 Earth days. As stated in the proposal and rules, the group that accumulated the greatest wealth would get to decide the fate of the humans. Therefore, I will turn the proceedings over to my vice-counsel, Epkok Monton. Vice-counsel, the floor is yours."

"Thank you, Mr. Chairman," said Monton, his image suddenly apparating in a hologram in the middle of the stage. Meanwhile, the three hundred thousand spectators in the stands quieted to hear his remarks.

"We understand that the humans took the unusual approach of dividing their team into two. Each decided to pursue the accumulation of wealth in a different way. Therefore, we must evaluate each separately to determine which, if either, accumulated greater wealth than the Slavatorian Council during this period.

"First, we will go to the two-person team of Colonel Rostov. We have determined that the colonel's team has accumulated wealth totaling only five ounces of gold—a paltry sum, and one which automatically eliminates them from the competition."

"I object," said the colonel. "Our measure of wealth was not determined in ounces of gold, which you are now stating. Such a measure was never discussed or presented during the outset of the competition."

Monton laughed. "But what other yardstick would one use? Throughout history, a being's wealth has been measured based on the land owned, the cattle owned, the money, jewels, precious stones, and other valuable materials owned. All these things are convertible into a tangible value that may be exchanged for some unit of gold. All things are measurable in gold. That is the only way to measure wealth."

Stefka smiled. He knew all along that this would be the yardstick used by the alien species. And with this established, he knew he had won and could become master and emperor of the blue planet and all who lived there.

"Your protest is denied," said Monton. "Next, we move to Lt. Stefka whose team was able to accumulate significant wealth during the year. By our estimates, Emperor Stefka has accumulated wealth to an extent no other being on the planet has. All told, we estimate his wealth at ..."

Monton glanced down at his screen.

"His wealth is estimated to be equivalent to 203,746 metric tons. In the old unit of measure—the dollar—this would total over 130.1 trillion dollars. That is a sizeable sum."

Stefka glowed. He could feel the energy of victory coursing through his veins. He would be the ruler of the planet. He would control the lives of ten billion people. He would determine what people could and couldn't do. He was dictator of all. Far from being enslaved himself, now he was positioned to become the enslaver.

But Monton continued.

"Now, let's look at the accumulation of wealth by the Slavatorian Council during that time," he said.

He projected on a screen the local star group within the galaxy showing many solar systems and planetary systems within one hundred light years.

"Here is a list of the planets the Slavatorian armies have conquered during that time."

The screen began populating and pointing out all the planets conquered by the Slavatorians. The list was long. There were numerous planetary systems they had subdued during that time and the names of each planet were listed in a long column that stretched many pages.

"All told, the Slavatorians conquered one hundred seven planets with all their lands, resources, money, and valuables. It all now belongs to us. The total value of this accumulation is ..."

He changed the screen, bringing up the new total.

"360.75 *million* metric tons of gold. That number is 1,772 times greater than the 203.7 *thousand* recorded by Emperor Stefka. Therefore, the humans lose. We will begin rounding them up for hard labor camps within three days. They will work for us in the deep ore mines, producing gold and other valuable metals for our needs."

"Thank you, vice-counsel Monton. This meeting is adjourned," said Zlacto, the chairman, pounding the gavel.

"I object!" shouted Stefka. "You said accumulation of wealth from Earth!"

Monton shook his head. "No." He immediately presented the scroll with the rules and unrolled it in front of Stefka. "Nowhere in this document does it limit wealth to Earth. This case is closed."

Stefka was devastated. Immediately, the guards came into the room and placed manacles around his wrists and ankles and led him away. They began to do the same with the colonel.

"No!" shouted Rostov, in protest. "I do not accept the verdict of this Council for the reason I argued at the beginning of this hearing."

"You have no choice," said Zlacto. "The ruling of this council is final."

"No, it is not," said the colonel. "First, I may state in my defense and that of Sergeant Keita beside me, that we have been striving for spiritual wealth during this past year."

"We do not recognize that," said Zlacto.

"If you measure our spiritual frequency, you will find that we have evolved to one compatible with five- or even six- dimensional spirituality. We are much closer to God and His frequency and spirituality than you are."

"Again, this meeting is adjourned. Your protest has no bearing on the outcome of this ..."

"Yes, it does," said the colonel, standing up to the bullying tactic. "In accordance with the Intergalactic Federation and their Council to which you *must* submit by galactic law, our case has the right to be appealed to their council. I demand such an appeal."

Zlacto looked uncomfortable, but he only banged the gavel harder.

"This meeting is adjourned," he barked.

"No, it is not," said another voice coming from an image now hovering in front of the meeting room. It was a disembodied head and face of the chairman of the Intergalactic Federation—Otbu Potus.

"The colonel has declared an appeal of this matter, and the Intergalactic Federation has accepted hearing it. This case will be heard no later than tomorrow in our chambers. We will all reconvene then."

The image of Potus dissolved. Zlacto was not happy. He got up and left the chambers abruptly.

*****

CH 5

It seemed like a blink of the eye and the parties regrouped in the vast chambers of the Intergalactic Council. Only the council members were there physically—the others joined via holographic projection through a wormhole connection. Although the hearing was done telepathically, a translator was provided for the human participants. In addition, no one was allowed in the surrounding stadium. There was no audience for this closed-door meeting.

"Case No. E390A4578," announced the chairman as it was translated by the tall gray being standing in the chambers.

The colonel and sergeant on Earth saw a holographic image before them. It now showed a pyramid of images with the Intergalactic Council Chairman at the top and the six associate members forming the row beneath him. There were seven members in total. On either side of the pyramid were images of the disputing parties. To the left were three pictures of the Slavatorians—the chairman of their council and two associates—and to the right of the column, the images of Lt. Colonel Rostov, Sgt. Kieta, and even Major Stefka was permitted to attend.

Each member of the Galactic Council was of a different species. Two were Pleiadeans, one was Siriun, one was Andromedin, and the last was Arcturiun. None sat in chairs but rather on a "cloud-like" disc where they seemed to float, hovering above the floor.

"Case E390A4578 will now be heard," said the chairman—a humanoid with blue skin but a normal-sized head. He was very handsome with a strong chin and jawline and deep-set, mustard green eyes. "Will the chamber attendant please read the case as it appears on the docket?"

The tall gray came forward. He was thin with spindly arms and legs and a narrow torso and had large, black eyes and cranium, but a small nose and mouth. He wore a navy robe and a black collar as he held a clear plate with markings which he communicated to the humanoids.

"Case E390A4578. The case brought by Colonel Ivan Rostov is against the Slavatorian Council. It states that the agreement between the parties was for a challenge to be undertaken over 365.256 Earth days. During this challenge, the winner would decide the fate of the human species and its role on the planet. Having lost the war, the humans were given one last chance to determine their own destiny.

"While this Council does not condone the prosecution of the war that took place in violation of Intergalactic Law by the Slavatorians, this Council is not being asked to make a decision on this matter. The lawfulness of the war will be decided in a separate hearing. This Council is being asked to rule on the challenge and the definition of 'wealth' in connection with the agreement therewith.

"Therefore, the Council will hear the arguments from each side regarding the goal which they endeavored to achieve. First, we will hear the arguments from the Slavatorian Council. Chairman Zhlatka, please present your position."

The holographic image of Zhlatka grew larger in the middle of the stage as he spoke. His reptilian face and yellow-slit eyes focused on his argument. It was done telepathically, but the gray in the chamber translated.

"The Chairman states that the objective of wealth—the accumulation of resources of value—is a universal one. He says all civilizations strive to improve their standards of existence—to make things easier and better for each member of their society. By accumulating the resources needed for this, they can accomplish this universal goal.

"Wealth, then, would include exclusive ownership and control over land, mineral resources of value to society and in developing technology, fresh water, animals used for performing work or for food sources, or any item that is widely or universally accepted as currency to exchange for goods or services required. He adds that 'ownership' of other species is also included in the equation of value.

"There is no disputing this definition, he says. It is an axiom. It is an immutable law of nature, so says the council chairman."

The gray concluded his translation and then turned to Major Stefka.

"Major Stefka was also party to the agreement. He has stated that he would be presenting his position, but only after a verdict is rendered on the case between the Lt. Colonel and the Slavatorian Council."

Stefka smiled slyly.

"Now, we will hear from Colonel Rustov."

In this case, the gray translated telepathically what was said.

"I want to thank the council for hearing my case," said Rustov. "My petition is that 'wealth' is not universally accepted as material resources. Rather, in its purest form—at the highest levels of spiritual vibration--it is considered growing in faith and developing compassion and love for all things and beings. Unconditional love is the heart of all things. It comes from the source of all things—God. Material things only benefit beings in the 3D material dimension, while spiritual wealth benefits beings in all dimensions. My friend, Sgt. Keita, and I embarked on a journey to accumulate spiritual wealth—not material wealth. By doing this, we grew closer to God who is the source of all. We hope the Intergalactic Council agrees.

"The humans claim they achieved a much higher frequency of love and kindness than that of the Slavatorians as of end of the challenge and thereby won the contest. He is asking the council to decide on the definition and, thereby, the case," said the gray.

The Intergalactic Council chairman's cloud chair rose higher as he sat on it.

"We have already reviewed the petitions as submitted," he answered, and we have made our decision.

*****

CH 6

Rustov held his breath. He knew the decision would determine the fate of the human species. Stefka too waited for the decision, thinking through how to position himself for maximum benefit once it was announced.

"We the Council find for the humans. We agree that wealth in its very essence is defined spiritually and not materially. To be higher in love means to have greater wealth. Therefore, since the Lt. Colonel and the Sergeant attained a higher vibration of love and forgiveness, they are able to decide the fate of their species."

"No!" shouted Zhlatka. "You are wrong! We will not accept your decision."

"You have no choice. I don't believe you wish to go to war against the entire Federation for control over one planet. We believe you have violated intergalactic law in warring against many other worlds during the past year and will be pursuing those allegations against you. Do not push us further on this matter."

"I have my position ready now," said Stefka, grinning.

The gray turned to look at the image of the former emperor and then to the Council chairman. "Do you have a verdict on the Stefka position?"

"We do," said the chairman.

"But I haven't presented it yet," said Stefka, confused.

"There is no need," said the Intergalactic Council chairman. "You forfeited your position when you did not file with the colonel. It is now moot and our decision regarding you has been made. You must obey the determination made by the colonel as to what happens to humanity and to you specifically."

"He is going to decide what happens to me?" asked Stefka, now trembling. "He alone?"

"Yes."

Stefka looked pleadingly at the Rustov, his face sorrowful and repentant. "Please!" he exclaimed. "Please have mercy on me!"

The colonel stared at the former dictator. Then, his eyes softened.

"It would be hypocritical of me to judge you and be anything less than loving toward you, my friend," said Rustov. "We have learned to become loving and forgiving. Therefore, we will not treat you any differently. Mankind was meant to live freely. As a great-document in human history once said—he should have the inalienable rights given by God of life, liberty, and the pursuit of happiness. In that vein, you will be granted the same, but will be held to that standard as you treat others. If you agree, you will be exonerated."

"I do," said Stefka.

"I think we're done here," said the Intergalactic Chairman.

"I believe we are," answered Rustov.

*****

CONTRABAND

CH 1

"We have a problem," said Defense Secretary Dan Rivers. "The country has seen an explosion of transporter systems during the last few years. Not only are people buying and receiving products through their personal transporter systems, but they are also buying and receiving illegal items through them. This must be stopped!"

The president thought for a moment. "How bad is it?" she asked.

"It's bad, Madam President. Not only are kids getting alcohol and drugs, but it's far worse than that." This was her Secretary of Homeland Security, Isaac Shapiro, who was there to backup what the Secretary of Defense was telling her.

"How so?"

"The illegal arms trade has exploded as well," said Rivers. "It's possible to send claymore mines, anti-tank weapons, RPGs and other things over these systems. Rogue governments are developing the capability to transport much larger weapons systems instantly from one location to another."

President Marstan smiled. "I suppose you will tell me the CCP is teleporting an aircraft carrier to New York harbor or something."

"No ma'am, but we fear they could teleport a nuke—a suitcase nuke into downtown Manhattan," said Shapiro.

"Is that possible?" she asked. Her mood instantly changed, turning the event more somber and contemplative.

"Yes," said Rivers flatly, waiting now to see her reaction.

Marstan sat back and stroked her chin. The vintage 1880 Resolute Desk lay before her, ready to take on whatever challenge it was given. It had seen much since Rutherford B. Hayes accepted it as a gift from Queen Victoria.

"What are the recommendations?" she asked, grasping for a life preserver.

"Madam President," began her Secretary of Homeland Security, "we would suggest one of the following approaches. Each has its pros and cons, of course, and I will outline each."

"Proceed," she answered, waving her hand.

The Oval Office's central projection system kicked on, and images quickly appeared in holographic form in the center of the room, as if dancing on the Presidential Seal prominently displayed on the carpeting.

"The first option," said Shapiro, "is to do nothing. If we do nothing, we must rely on our local law enforcement to detect and apprehend those smuggling illegal weapons into the country. Unfortunately, these forces are already spread thin working on other things, and their training is not up to the level we would need to ensure they could detect such a scheme. The FBI is the next layer. They are better trained and could work with local authorities. They have contacts in the field, but not as good as the local police. The third option would be to ban all teleportation of goods from foreign countries. Unfortunately, that would cripple our economy as most of our consumer goods are produced overseas. We could ban them from certain countries, but we all know those countries would only export them to countries on our approved list and get around our restrictions."

"It doesn't sound like we have many options," said the president.

"Oh, but we do have another option, ma'am."

"And what might that be?"

Shapiro explained his plan, and when he finished, she nodded.

"Do it," she said, "but I don't want to be involved. I don't want my fingerprints anywhere near that. There's too much going on between our two countries to get drawn into that one."

"Understood," said Shapiro. "Understood."

*****

CH 2

Shapiro arrived in Tel Aviv to visit with the Israeli prime minister. He was on a mission—one of top secrecy. Through his contacts he had learned that the Israelis had developed a technology to identify the teleportation signature of a nuclear device. The technology also enabled the user to block the atomized energy during its pathway through the atmosphere and into the reassembly chamber of the receiving teleportation system. Basically, it was the magic bullet the U.S. president was hoping for to stop a nuclear device from getting sent from a belligerent country into the United States and detonated on U.S. soil.

"Ah, my good friend," said Israeli Prime Minister Caleb Geller, opening his arms to greet Shapiro. "It is good to see you again."

"Yes, Caleb. It has been too long."

"Please, sit," said Geller, gesturing to the light silver couch along the wall in his office. "So, what is it that I can help you with?"

"My government understands that you are using a new technology to prevent certain destructive weapons from getting inside your border through the teleportation portals."

"Yes, the TeleSpectographer. It's a brilliant feat of engineering. Comes from our Science and Technology Institute here in Tel Aviv. We can detect a nuke and other WMDs from being used against us. No one else has it."

"I presume you have test data for it."

"I thought you might ask for that, so I have it here for you," said Geller, taking a folder from his desk and handing it to the secretary. "It's quite impressive, really. The device can identify and disrupt WMDs 94.7 percent of the time, and it gives a false positive only nine percent of the time. That's still too high, but better that than the other way around." Geller smiled as he explained.

"Excellent," said Shapiro. "After doing our own testing, we would like to purchase five thousand units."

"My!" said Geller. "It will take time to fabricate that many."

"That's fine. We will begin our own testing and take them as they are produced. My people will sort out the details with yours."

"We are also working on something else."

"What's that?"

"A way to teleport items without needing to have a receiving device on the other end. You only need to have the sending device. Based on the coordinates entered in the system, you can beam something directly to that point."

"Just like in the old *Star Trek* show," said Shapiro.

Geller chuckled. "I suppose so. Everything in that series becomes a reality sooner or later, it seems. But we are racing against the clock."

"How so?"

"We understand that the Chinese have hacked our systems and have obtained some of that technology. Our Mossad group has learned that they are well along in their own development. We don't know how soon they might be able to deploy such a system."

"Will your TeleSpectographer detect incoming WMDs through that system?" asked Shapiro.

"We don't know. Our guess is, maybe."

"That's not very reassuring."

"No, I understand, but technology is moving amazingly fast these days as you know. It only takes months, sometimes weeks, to leapfrog a new development and render it useless. We can only do what we can do. We're trying diligently to find out."

"And sabotage their efforts, I hope?" said Shapiro.

Geller only smiled. "It was nice seeing you again, Isaac. You should stop by more often."

Shapiro got up from his seat and extended his hand.

"I look forward to the first shipment," he answered.

*****

CH 3

Prime Minister Geller was not a fan of President Marstan. Earlier during their careers, they had clashed over the handling of the Palestinian situation and the giving up of Israeli land for peace. Settlements in the West Bank had continued under Geller, and Marstan had been most outspoken about their being stopped. Still, Israel and the United States had been allies for a long time. The bonds were deep, and one president wouldn't change that.

Shapiro boarded his government hyperplane for the two-hour trip to Washington, D.C. Still, with the time change, Shapiro was tired when he arrived at Andrews AFB just outside the city. It was dark, and he was looking forward to getting back to the regular grind after having spent two weeks shuttling amongst the major players in the Middle East.

Although he wasn't required to go through normal security stations, the secretary was required to cross through an army review post for a standard screening.

"Good day, sir," said the sergeant who was manning the post. He saluted and then motioned for the secretary's aid to deposit their bags on the belt that ran through the scanning booth.

"All clear," said the corporal looking at the images as the bags went through. "Oh," he then said suddenly, "what is this?"

The sergeant came over to the screen and the two whispered. Then, the sergeant approached Shapiro.

"I'm sorry to trouble you, sir, but we just need a quick look at one of your bags. It's standard protocol. I apologize for the delay."

"Be quick about it," said the secretary, brusquely. "I'd like to get home for supper."

"Yes, sir."

The sergeant took the suitcase and opened it. Inside was a black case.

"Would you open the case, sir?" he asked Shapiro.

"I ... I don't know what that is," said the secretary, surprised by what was found.

"Sir, just open the case."

"I don't know how. It's not mine."

The sergeant reached in and gently pulled the case from the luggage. On the sides were chrome clasps that slid within tracks. He pushed on them, moving them less than an inch before hearing the case unlock. Then, he backed away.

"I'll be back sir. Please wait here," said the sergeant. "This will only take a moment."

It was five minutes before the military man returned, but this time he was accompanied by another man—this one dressed in a dark suit. The civilian examined the case without opening it and put it back through the examination tube. The belt was stopped, and the image enlarged many times as the men pointed at certain spots on the screen and murmured amongst themselves.

The sergeant came over to where Shapiro and his aid were standing.

"Sir, we will need to hold your bag for further examination. You're free to go. Once we've finished, the bag will be delivered to your house."

"Great," said Shapiro, aggravated. "Just get it to me by tomorrow. I may have to go back out of town within the next few days."

Shapiro got home and crashed on his family room couch, not wanting to waken his wife. The next morning came early, and he took his shower, fixed a quick cup of black coffee, and hurried to the office. It was on the way there that he received an urgent message from the president's office. Diverted to the new route, the driver took them through Georgetown and down to Pennsylvania Avenue where they shot across to the White House.

"So?" said the president as Shapiro entered the Oval Office. "I take it your trip was successful?"

"I believe so," said Shapiro, standing in front of the president's ornate desk. "Geller said we would have the devices as soon as they can be manufactured."

"Good. I got a call from Geller this morning. As you know, he and I have had few conversations over the years, but today's was unusual."

"How so?"

"He said we have many enemies in the world and that we should remember who our allies are."

"That is strange," said Shapiro.

It was then that the president's com button lighted on her desk, and she picked up the line.

"Yes? ... Uh huh ... Uh huh ... I see. Yes, I understand." She hung up the phone.

Within moments two Secret Service agents came into the room. They approached Shapiro and looked over at Marstan who nodded at them.

"Mr. Shapiro," said one of the agents, turning toward the secretary, "you have the right to remain silent. Anything you say can be used against you in court. You have the right to talk to a lawyer for advice before we ask you any questions. You have the right to have a lawyer with you during questioning. If you cannot afford a lawyer, one will be appointed for you before any questioning if you wish. If you decide to answer questions now without a lawyer present, you have the right to stop answering at any time. Do you understand these rights as we have told them to you?"

"What is this?" asked Shapiro, standing up as he was being handcuffed by the agents. "What's going on here?"

"Apparently, you brought back more than you were allowed to through customs, Isaac," said the president.

"That's impossible. I didn't bring anything back."

The president clicked her control panel on her desk, illuminating the screen on the far wall. On it flashed images of the insides of the black case they had found in his luggage at the Andrews checkpoint. On one side of the case were wires connected to a battery with other electronic circuits intermeshed. On the other side were several vials of white powder.

"What is that?" Shapiro asked.

"I'm told that you brought back with you a bomb that if exploded would have resulted in the wide distribution of anthrax. The CDC examined it and reported to me that the contents of those vials contained enough anthrax to kill tens of thousands. Were you planning on coming to the White House with it?"

"No! Of course not! I would never have ..."

"Then how and why did you bring it back?" asked the president, staring coldly at him.

"I didn't know it was there. I swear!"

Moments later, there was another disturbance. The air in the center of the room began to swirl and a distorted image began to form in waves. It was a shimmering light that grew in intensity until it flashed so brightly that everyone in the room had to turn away. When they looked back, they saw another black case resting on the president's desk.

Immediately, the Secret Service ordered the president to leave, but she refused.

"I want to know what that is," she insisted.

Ten minutes later, two men in full, white bio-suits came in carrying cases of supplied air. They were covered from head to toe and handed others in the room their own respirators. Quickly, they began working on the case, unlatching the clasps and gingerly raising the lid.

"What is it?" asked Shapiro, still in the room.

"There's a note," said one of the Secret Service agents taking it from the opened case and handing it to another agent to read.

"What does it say?" asked Marstan.

"It says, 'Dear Madam President. Here is another gift from us to you. We just wanted you to know that you *do* have enemies, and they have the capability to reaching you wherever you are. Teleportation has come a long way, and we are now able to send anything anywhere. Just let this be a warning. Signed—*Your Greatest Enemy.*'"

"Who sent this?" asked the president, infuriated at the violation.

"The message also has a postscript," said the agent still looking at the paper.

"Go on ..."

"It reads: 'P.S. The powder in these vials is better used to bake your next batch of chocolate chip cookies. However, as for the next batch you might get ... you might not be so lucky.'"

*****

CICADA 3318

CH 1

It wasn't the first time it had been posted on the Internet. A century earlier, it had been posted too, but this time it arose with additional years tacked onto it, mimicking the 17-year cycle of emergence of its namesake—the cicada.

"What do you make of this?" asked Tom Ashton, a graduate student at MIT who was studying for his PhD in statistical analysis. He touched a key on his computer and projected the image as a 3D hologram into the middle of the apartment that he shared with another student, Jan Springer.

Springer glanced up from his reading. "What is it?"

"That's what I was asking you," said Ashton.

Springer got up from his chair and circled around the image, looking at it from all angles. "It appears to be a tesseract."

Ashton looked at the image again. "Yeah, you're right. It's a fourth-dimension square, isn't it?"

"What's it supposed to mean?" asked Springer.

"It's part of a puzzle. I read about it online. There's this group that sends these encrypted messages or ones with a hidden question that begs an answer. If it's anything like the ones from a century ago, it will test all of us to figure them out and make it through to the end."

"What's the end? You mean there's more than one?"

"Yeah, there's a whole series of them, but they don't all come out at once. The last time it took a few years before they all came out and got solved."

"Where does it all lead to? What did the one a century ago lead to?" Springer asked.

"Ah, that one. Well, let's look it up," said Ashton. "Computer, tell me about the Cicada Internet test of 2012."

"Pulling up information now," the computer replied.

Ashton read what was presented and shook his head.

"It doesn't appear that it led to anything," he answered. "There were several questions and clues scattered around the world. Some people made it through to the end and were invited to join a secret group, but nothing really came of it."

"Huh. Well, that doesn't seem to be very fun," said Springer returning to his reading.

"No, but I think I'm still going to try to figure it out," said Ashton.

"Why? Why waste your time?" asked his roommate.

"For the challenge, my dear friend. For the challenge."

*****

CH 2

Ashton grew deeper and deeper into the problems presented on the Cicada 3318 website—so deep, in fact, that his roommate worried he wasn't spending enough time on his doctoral thesis.

"What do your sponsors say about it?" asked Springer.

"They don't know," answered Ashton, "but they are getting annoyed that I'm not making better progress on my thesis."

"Well, you'd better quit screwing around with it, then. You don't want to risk losing your sponsorship."

"I'll be fine. I can do both. The Cicada problem I'm working on right now has to do with another of the dimensional geographic figures. This time it's a rectified five orthoplex."

"What the hell is that?" asked Springer.

"It looks like this," said Ashton, projecting the figure in a 3D hologram, even though it was a 5D polytope.

"That's an amazing figure," said Springer, gazing at it. "What are you supposed to do with that?"

"They want you to determine the vertices in nine-dimensional space. Supposedly, when you do that, there's a message that pops out as the colors of the vertices in this 3D model hide the clue, but not in 9D."

Springer laughed. "Good luck," he said before adding, "Perhaps you should get your PhD in complex differential geometry instead."

However, Ashton did not head his roommate's warning and spent even more time on the Cicada project—all but abandoning his thesis. Within three months, his sponsor—Professor Arkin—threatened him with cancellation of his program.

"Where are you going?" Springer asked him as he was heading out the apartment door with a suitcase as well as his backpack.

"I'm going to New York City for a day. There's a clue up there I have to see. It's posted to a corkboard displaying what's playing on Broadway right now. There are only two of us competing for the end prize—whatever that is—and I want to be the one who wins this thing."

"Wins what? You don't even know what it's all about?"

Ashton smiled. "That's what makes this so exciting. This is the last clue. I'll stop once I figure it out. It has to do with the breeding habits of the cicada and the pixels on this post in New York. I'll see you on Monday."

However, Ashton did not return on Monday. In fact, he didn't return at all.

*****

CH 3

Springer worried when his roommate didn't come back from his trip to New York City. He waited until Wednesday and contacted Ashton's parents who lived in Miami, but they hadn't heard from their son either. The police were called in to investigate in Manhattan, but few clues were forthcoming. It appeared that Ashton had disappeared.

Time went by, but the police weren't making any progress on the case. Springer felt they weren't giving it the attention it needed, so he took matters into his own hands. He wanted to know what happened to his friend, so he told his doctoral sponsor that he would be taking a semester off—a sabbatical—to try to track down the whereabouts of his roommate, Tom Ashton.

Starting in New York City, Springer went to the hotel where Ashton said he was staying before he disappeared. However, he never showed up there. Although the police detective refused to give Springer any information on the case, citing that it was an "investigation still in progress," Springer was able to gain access to some evidence through another contact he had inside the department.

Cameras at LaGuardia airport showed Ashton going through the terminal but never coming outside to catch a taxi or even a water taxi to Manhattan. One camera did spot someone who looked like Ashton peering at an electronic board near his gate, but it had been presumed he was only checking to see where his luggage was coming out on the conveyer belt. Yet, his bag was never claimed and was now in police custody.

Going through Ashton's Internet accounts and his file on the Cicada project, Springer noticed the image of the mysterious group's logo—the cicada—kept coming up. So, he went back to the airport on a hunch. He found the electronic board his roommate had stood in front of in the camera footage. Next to it was an advertisement—for the Cicada Bar and Grill. The logo for the restaurant was the very same as that in Ashton's files. The tagline for the restaurant was very strange:

"Curiosity is lying in wait for every secret." – Ralph Waldo Emerson 3318.

That's it, Springer said to himself.

He pulled up a map of Manhattan on his cell phone and entered a search for 3318 Emerson. It took only seconds, and the map showed the location with the building and surrounds. It was in an industrial park far north of the hustle and bustle of lower Manhattan.

Running back outside, he hailed a robocab.

"Where are you going?" asked the robotic driver, not even pivoting its head to address its new passenger.

"3318 Emerson," he answered.

The cab sped off along the electric rail, but it didn't just go into Manhattan; it continued north and crossed the George Washington Bridge into New Jersey. There, it headed south once again.

"Where are we going?" asked Springer, now more anxious about the destination.

"3318 Emerson," said the driver. "That's in New Jersey."

Springer looked again at his map. Indeed, he had mistaken the location for Manhattan. He was headed across the bridge, over the Hudson River and into New Jersey.

The taxi pulled into the industrial park—the very one Springer had seen on his screen. It was dark and looked abandoned. There were several rusted, steel buildings with parts of their roofs either collapsed or collapsing.

"Are you sure this is it?" asked Springer.

"Yes, sir. That will be 3,301 credits," said the driver.

"Are you kidding? It's exactly 3,301 credits?"

"Yes. Please pay with your electronic bracelet," came the monotone response.

Springer held up his black bracelet to be scanned, and the 3301 credits were instantly deducted from his account. He got out of the cab which quickly jetted off, disappearing after turning right at the end of the long cement drive.

Dusk was fast approaching, and Springer spotted a feeble, yellow light emanating from a dirty, twin-paned window at ground level. The window was so low to the ground that it was hard to tell from what floor it was coming.

Springer went to several of the smokey gray, steel doors but found all were locked. Then, he walked around the building finally finding the broad loading dock. There were several bays where old combustion engine trucks used to load and unload their cargos. Now, it was empty, abandoned, and forlorn.

The young student jogged up the rickety, metal staircase and up to the docking doors. All were locked too, but he noticed that one of the rusted doors held a chain with a lock that was sprung open. Undoing the lock and pulling the chain through the door handles, he pushed the door latch and opened it. At first, it fought back, not wishing to give up its defenses so easily. But soon it relented, swinging in and revealing a dark passage inside.

Springer continued down the aphotic hall, becoming increasingly anxious and then terrified of what he was getting himself into. His heart was racing as he approached another staircase. However, instead of finding more lights on above him, he found the light was coming from below. So, he moved down the staircase toward the eerie light source, grasping the metal railing as if it were the only life support for him in the entire world. Reaching the bottom, he saw a vast room that was cold and dark. Only a few overhead bulbs dangled from the ceiling joists and gave any light to the dismal place.

As he started into the room, his angst turned to fear. It was as if all his senses had been stripped from him. He could no longer hear, see, smell or sense anything. He had never felt so afraid in his life. Nothing he had experienced came close to the abject terror he sensed. He thought he had somehow stumbled into the *Twilight Zone*.

Had he only realized then that the Twilight Zone would have been a far better place.

*****

CH 4

"Hello, Jan," said a voice coming from behind him.

Springer turned and stared at an older man with dark hair but a gray goatee. He wore a smart, black, pin-striped suit and fashionable tie.

"Who are you?" Springer asked, shaking.

"It doesn't matter," said the man. "All you need to know is that I am the brainchild of the Cicada project. I was around one hundred years ago when the first experiment was conducted online, and I'm still here. We won't quibble with how that is possible. Instead, we shall focus on you and your roommate. Both of you are excellent candidates for our experiment which has been refined over the decades and is nearing perfection."

"What do you mean?"

"Your roommate participated and was surprisingly brilliant at solving our breadcrumbs of problems. You, too, with your deciphering of the code at the airport, were quickly elevated into the qualifying group."

"Lucky me," said Springer sarcastically.

"Yes, you are lucky, my young man. Here, let me show you."

The tall man with piercing black eyes, a long, narrow nose, and large ears, walked briskly into the vast chamber. In the center were rows upon rows of computer stacks and massive cables along the floor connecting them. There were no blinking lights or bleeping sounds— only a modicum of heat being released from the units as they worked their magic.

"What do these do?" asked Springer, looking around in wonder.

"They run things."

"What things?"

The old man laughed. "The world, of course. They run everything. Without them, life on Earth would be impossible. We humans would have long ago destroyed the planet and all life on it. These computers are the only things that prevent that from happening."

"How?"

"So, we're going to play the Where, What, Why and How Game, are we? All right. Then I'll tell you that a century ago a group of the greatest minds in the world assembled to discuss how to keep the planet from committing suicide—that is, how to keep man from killing it. We found that we couldn't do it by machine alone but needed constant interaction and monitoring by very smart people. Hence, we created the Cicada project to attract the most brilliant minds to help us do that.

"We took those minds and put them to work, helping to solve some of the gravest problems of the era. Of course, many of the solutions only led to other problems, but such is the nature of life, is it not?"

"Where is my friend? Where is Ashton?" Springer asked, going no farther in the room.

"Let me show you," said the man, continuing onward.

As they walked, Springer asked, "Why do you call yourselves Cicadas, anyway?"

"Very good," responded the man. "You've used your What, Where, How and Why so far. And your question about the cicada is a relevant one. You see the cicada is a master of camouflage and disguise, blending in with tree trunks, foliage and other of its environs. It is also resilient, having been around since the Late Triassic Period some 240 million years ago. But what is most intriguing to me is the mating song it sings, attracting a female from far away. Using the Internet and the clues, we did the same thing—like a Siren's song of sorts—to attract young, smart minds like yours and your friend's."

He continued walking through the labyrinth of machines until he reached a metal staircase which took them up to another level. When they reached the top, Springer found the new room dimly lit, but its permitter ringed with tanks.

"What are these?" Springer asked.

"Ah, here is where you've made your first mistake, young man."

"What? I don't understand."

The old man smiled, but this time it wasn't a kind, genial smile. This time there was an edge of darkness in it. "You've not covered two other questions. The first is When."

"When?" repeated Springer.

"Yes, we are moving to our new platform tonight. That is when we expect to link similar laboratories in Europe, Asia, South America, and Africa together with this one. Then, it will truly be a cohesive, united, global endeavor."

Springer still looked confused.

"Ah, and as to the *Who* question," said the man not waiting for the query to come. "I believe this should help you."

The man moved across the room to one of the large tanks. It contained a yellowish liquid and had tubes and lines running into it, but there was nothing else inside.

"What is this?" asked Springer, looking up at the man.

"Wrong again," said the man. "You mean *Who* is this?" He pointed to a brass label on the tank. It read: J.P. Springer.

Springer suddenly couldn't breathe. His mind was spinning, and his heart racing.

"But you may ask the *Where* question once more—as in Where is my friend Ashton? You see, he's right here next to you. He will be here for the rest of eternity, just like you."

In the tank next to Springer's was a human brain floating in a small sea of yellow liquid and hooked up to a myriad of tubes, wires, and electrodes. It too had a nameplate: Cicada No. 665. T.W. Ashton.

*****

ELEMENT 127

CH 1

"Who's to say there can't be an infinite number of elements on the Periodic Table," said Professor van Gleason, a man now in his nineties who had been at the forefront of some of the most scintillating discoveries of the twenty-first century. "I mean, we had already found elements or created elements synthetically up to 118 by 2002. But just as we broke-up the table for the unique characteristics of elements 57 to 71 and 89 to 103—the Lanthanides and Actinides—we must now break the table further into another subset which I call the Pesticides." He laughed. "Sorry, that's a joke I've told many times and it still cracks me up."

The audience of one hundred academicians and scientists in the auditorium laughed with him even though it was an old joke of his.

"No, I actually believe we should call element 121 when it is discovered Lavoisium, and those following through 137 the Lavoisienides, after the French chemist Antoine Lavoisier, considered by many the Father of Modern Chemistry.

"And while it is true that 57 to 71 fills out the 4f subshell of the electron orbits and the 89 to 103 fills out the 5f subshell, there are elements undiscovered that begin filling the eighth shell. Of course, these elements exist beyond 173, which are referred to as the supercritical elements. We just need to find them. Just because the Dirac equations *suggest* that elements beyond 137 cannot exist out of the Dirac Sea doesn't mean this is true. It is by no means axiomatic. We only need to change our approach to find them.

"While I may not live to see the day, others will. Soon, we will have a brilliant mind who will see the path to the higher elements, and it will not take the power of the sun to find them."

Professor Van Gleason lived for three weeks following this speech. Sadly, he died, not knowing whether his prediction would ever come true.

*****

CH 2

"You know, I think he was right," said Dr. Loenburger of the Munich Institute for Technology. "I believe there is a way to find higher level elements beyond 118. To date, our approach has been like taking a Styrofoam hammer to a walnut. Not enough brute force has been used to collide two heavy elements with ions to see what we get out of it. It will take the right energy level combined with the right elements to create them. We're dealing with fusion, not fission. We're dealing with 'sticking' matter together, rather than splitting it apart as they do on the rails at CERN."

"We need something that will create electrons in the 8s shell for elements 119 and 120," said Dr. Wyler. "Some say the Aufbau effect no longer applies at this level—that electrons no longer fill orbits based on the next lowest energy orbital. As we know, the velocity of electrons increases as one goes farther from the nucleus and into subsequent outer shells. Bohr's famous equation—$v = 2.188 \times 10^6 \times Z/n$ meters per second—enables us to determine this. As the velocity increases, so too does the electron's mass."

Both men knew that element 118 – Oganesson—had electrons in many orbitals around the nucleus. Orbitals 1s, 2s, 2p, 3s, 3p, 3d, 4s, 4p, 4d, 4f, 5s, 5p, 5d, 5f, 6s, 6p, 6d, 7s and 7p were all assumed to be filled with the remaining orbitals unfilled. A simple extrapolation from the Aufbau principle would predict the eighth row to fill orbitals in the order 8s, 5g, 6f, 7d, 8p; but after element 120, the proximity of the electron shells makes placement in a simple table problematic. Although a simple extrapolation of the periodic table, following Seaborg's original concept, would put the elements after 120 as follows: 121–138 form the g-block superactinides (which Dr. van Gleason wished to call Lavoisienides); 139–152 form the f-block superactinides, 153–161 form the d-block or possibly transition metals; 162–166 post-transition metals; 167 would be a halogen; 168 a noble gas; 169 an alkali metal; and 170 an alkaline earth metal.

"But Seaborg said we can't have elements over 130 because of their inherent instability," said Addison Conley, a graduate student assisting the two scientists.

"I think Seaborg is wrong," said Loenburger, "I know that Walter Grenier and several others agreed that higher numbers are possible. If you want to get up to 151 or even 183, we'd need electrons in shell 8—up to the g-block or suborbital. If that is possible and the shell is filled, we could get up to element number 218. That would take a new technology than what we have now. It will take a much higher energy level, less time and a shorter distance, that's all."

"Is that all?" Dr. Wyler laughed. "How can we generate that kind of energy burst?"

"A matter-anti-matter collision, but in a large enough amount to generate what we need—about 2.6 GeV in less than 10^{-12} seconds or one trillionth of a second."

"But that kind of annihilation could create enough energy to blow a hole in the fabric of space and time."

Dr. Loenburger shook his head. "No. That was also feared when the now-mothballed CERN collider went online, and nothing happened. My math shows that it is far from enough energy to create a black hole."

"You'd better hope so."

*****

CH 3

Seventeen years later ...

After years of politicking and lobbying world governments for the funding, the fusion project to create heavier elements eventually broke ground. A neutral country had to be picked as countries of the West and the East all contributed to its construction and operation. Like the UN and other world organizations, the CERN3.0 project was delayed with infighting and cost-overruns. Finally, nearly seventeen years later, the project broke ground and after another fifteen years was operational. By then, Dr. Wyle and Dr. Loenburger had retired, and it was left to two new doctors—Myerson and Grieg—to carry on the project.

Wyle's calculations were recomputed and vetted many times between the time lobbying for the project started and its completion, and all felt certain in his assessment that at black hole would not be created from creating a super-heavy element.

The magic day finally arrived in the same town that hosted the original two CERN LHCs. The third one was not a ring like the 26.7KM LHC1 or the 130KM LHC2 used to create fission. Instead, the new unit was a 60 square meter underground laboratory. Rather than using huge racetracks to accelerate particles at near the speed of light and smashing them together to find even smaller particles, this facility was built to bombard or fuse a light element into a heavier one, together to make one even heavier. But more energy was required than had been used to date, and it was hoped that the matter-antimatter annihilator segment would produce the quantities needed.

In this experiment, the two scientists were shooting a high energy beam of Molybdenum at lead. Lead, symbol Pb on the Periodic Table, has an atomic number 86, while Molybdenum (Mo) had a smaller number, 42. If successful, scientists hoped to create a larger, heavier element and reach a weight and composition of electrons needed for element 119 or above. In this case, they believed their combination of elements would fuse to create an element with atomic number 127.

"We just need ten," said Dr. Greig.

"Yeah, but ten femtoseconds are more than we've ever been able to get before," said Dr. Myerson. "It's a lifetime."

"Think of it this way," said Greig. "It takes a tenth of a second to blink, right? All we have to do is keep this thing together for a thousand trillionth of the time it takes to blink. How hard can that be?"

"That's what the IUPAC requires, right?" asked Myerson, referring to the International Union of Pure and Applied Chemistry which regulated such matters.

"Yeah. It's got to form an electron cloud before it counts."

"All right. Well, I'm ready when you are."

"Okay," said Dr. Myerson. "Engage."

The safety keys were thrown, and the buttons pushed to energize the magnets capable of propelling the Molybdenum element into orbit around the elliptical platform. Accelerating it to nearly 60 percent of the speed of light, the machine was readied to bombard the heavier lead atoms with it. Such a heavy atom required enormous amounts of energy, and the initial phase of the experiment used traditional magnets to propel the atoms. Once the atoms reached a velocity of 20 percent of the speed of light, more energy was needed; that would be when the matter-antimatter collision would be initiated.

"Engage the MA annihilator," said Myerson.

It only required touching a few more computer screens to initiate the annihilation and creation of a huge energy blast.

"We have an MA annihilation and 2.74 GeV. What do the impact instruments read?"

"We have impact, and ..."

But no sooner did the words leave Greig's mouth than something out of a class B horror movie occurred.

There was a split second when time froze. Then, a burst of light so bright and intense many in the surrounding neighborhoods and as far away as Lausanne which was nearly thirty kilometers across Lake Leman. Yet, just as fast as the light came, it seemed to be reabsorbed into blackness.

Simply, it was as if a hydrogen bomb had gone off. However, others more accurately described it as a window being blown out of a spacecraft traveling outside of Earth's orbit. There was a huge rush of air, like the scientists had built an enormous vacuum cleaner and had turned it on for the first time. Ripping trees from the ground, buildings from their foundations, and anything else standing or resting within a ten-kilometer radius of the laboratory, the incident laid waste to a vast swath of land. The area over three hundred square kilometers was devastated. But the strangest thing of all was that all the matter disappeared. It vanished on the very spot where the fusion occurred.

Some say that the fusion of such a dense element—estimated to be something close to 164 in atomic number, rather than the 127 the scientists were shooting for—created a portal. The density of such an element was likely 46 grams per cubic centimeter—this compared with lead which is $11.34g/cm^3$ or gold at $19.32g/cm^3$. This rip in space-time likely led into another universe or point within our universe. However brief, creation of the new super-heavy element did not create a black hole in the traditional sense, but the effect was the same. The incident happened within 100 femtoseconds, and when the element decayed, the portal closed as if nothing had ever happened.

As for Drs. Meyerson- and Greig, neither were ever found.

It would be another fifty-four years before heavier elements were created without causing such destruction. These were elements 127 – named Meyersonium and 128, Greigon. As for Lavoisium, that element 122, would have to wait another twenty years.

*****

WHAT'S YOUR CN?

CH 1

"They're ugly!" said fourteen-year-old Miranda Howard. "I'm not wearing one."

"You have to," said her mother, Patty. "It's the law."

Patty struggled to put the yellow armband around Miranda's upper arm. Only two inches wide, it held a visible screen with a digital number highlighted in red. Numbers below five were in red; those from five to seven in orange, eight and nine in blue, and a ten was in green. Orange numbers were concerning but would not get you in trouble. Red numbers would prohibit you from doing many things and a number of zero or one would blink rapidly, signaling you were at risk of being arrested.

However, the yellow band signaled that Miranda was a juvenile and wouldn't be harshly treated until she reached the age of "Awareness": eighteen. Then, her band would be changed from yellow to orange. At the age of twenty-five, the band was changed again from orange to red, and then at age thirty, it was made pure white. By that age, there was no leniency for having a score below a green ten and no leeway if it dropped even to a nine or eight.

"I don't care."

"Well, *we* care. We don't want you spending the next ten years in a prison for rebellious children. Do you?" asked her mother, trying to scare her a little.

"It sucks!" said Miranda. "I get this badge, and it already has a sucky number. Why can't I get a ten?"

"You haven't earned a ten yet, Mandy. It will take time."

"Bel Talanda got a ten. She's in my grade."

"Well, Talanda is Talanda. You're Mandy. You'll just have to work a little harder. We need you to get your score up to at least a five by the time school starts in September. I don't want you to soil the family name by going to school with a four. That's not going to be acceptable in this household."

"What can I do to change it?"

"We can start by buying you some t-shirts that say *Power to the People! Bread and Freedom!* or *From 1% to 99%*. You should get a point or so for that."

"I don't even know what that stuff means," said Miranda.

"It doesn't matter," said Patty, "What does matter are the Watchers that record and monitor all this stuff."

"Watchers?"

"Yeah," said her mom. "They setup cameras everywhere on buildings, the streets, inside stores … They take your picture wherever you go. They'll see what you're wearing, and they'll give you points toward your armband."

"I don't care. Those t-shirts are ugly too."

"Well, I'm buying them for you, and you're wearing them whether you like it or not. When your thirty-five, you can begin making decisions on your own—but not until then."

"When will I get the points?" Miranda asked.

"It takes a while for them to analyze your pictures and actions. If you do stuff they like they give you points too."

"Like what?" asked Miranda.

"Like going to your B&BLM meetings for your diversity sessions. Or joining the 99 Percenter Club. If you volunteer to speak at your next school convocation in support of the Youth Party, that will help. There are many things you can do."

"They burned last year's history books because they said they were lies. They said I'd get points for saying good things about the new book. Will that get my score to an eight?"

"I don't know if it will get you to eight, but it certainly won't hurt. Just make sure you don't disagree with anything your teacher says in class. They will take points off for that too."

*****

CH 2

Washington had adopted a new regime to cope with the growing unrest in the states. When a state governor was getting out of line, the Party Chairman, Li, would impose stricter measures to bring them back into the fold. If necessary, the governor would merely be replaced by a "sudden" demand by the people to recall the governor and elect a new one.

"How is the Citizen Badge Program going?" asked Li.

"We're running into some difficulties," said Won, his Minister of Propaganda. "There are still state governors and state legislatures that are trying to defy our mandates, sir."

"We can't have that, as you know. We must obey the dictates of the orders from the Chinese Communist Party. The CCP requires strict obedience—otherwise we will all suffer the consequences."

"Then we'll need to recall the governors of several states, sir. We'll have to start with the governors of the big population states—Georgia, Tennessee, Missouri, Indiana, Texas, the Carolinas, and possibly Florida."

"Do it."

"We'll need to create polling numbers ... fake polling numbers."

"Do it."

"And we'll need the media to pick up the results."

"That's easy. Threaten the station managers with 'issues' renewing their broadcast licenses or find something else. Hell, threaten an audit—that is always effective."

"Will do, Mr. Chairman."

*****

CH 3

School was going to start in three weeks, and Miranda was still at a four. Patty was worried. She had gone on the Internet to see if there were ways around it. On one website, she read where she could pay someone else on an exchange to switch armbands. If the other person in the same age group had a higher number and was willing to let it go, they could make money selling it to someone who needed it.

Patty gave it a try but found out that the armband frequency was calibrated to the cerebral implants required of all citizens at age five. The new armband wouldn't work with a different person, and no number would appear on the band making it less than worthless.

So, Patty kept looking. She found ads for upgrades but had also read warnings about deceptive ads and shams, so she avoided them.

Finally, the first day of school came, and nothing she had done—the t-shirts, clubs, or anything else—had made a difference in her daughter's armband score.

"What's your daughter's social security number?" asked the woman at the Ministry of Citizen Affairs.

"It's 6158-45-8921," Patty said. "There must be something wrong. You must not be collecting everything she's been doing to improve her score."

"Thank you, Ms. ..."

"Patricia Palmer," Patty answered.

"Yes, Ms. Palmer. I see here that your daughter has done some things to get off her Citizen Number of four, but I'm afraid it hasn't been enough."

"Not enough! She's worked hard on that."

"I'm sorry, but it's not enough. She'll need to work harder than that. There's nothing more I can do. Go to our website and look at other ways she can improve. Good luck."

The woman abruptly hung up.

Patty had no choice but to call the school to say her daughter was sick and wouldn't be able to come to school. She knew that would only last so long. So, she did the next best thing: she bought an upgrade.

On the Deep Web, Mandy found a site that offered upgrades for citizenship badge. It was offered by a not-for-profit organization, but she thought it was controlled by the Party.

> This month only—upgrade your Citizenship Badge one point for only $18,500. Upgrades of two points—only $28,000, and upgrades of three points $35,000.

It was a lot of money to pay for the upgrade, and it would only last for six months. Then, additional installments were needed. It was extortion, of course, but most families resorted to it to maintain a high social profile. Little did they know that the government kept the real scores on file and those were the ones they went by.

Patty bought the three-pack for $28,000 to protect against Mandy losing points somehow during the six months. She couldn't afford to keep renewing the one point at $18,500 and also couldn't afford to have her daughter kicked out of school. The $28,000 was even a stretch, but Mandy had no other choice.

The upgrade was downloaded directly to Miranda's badge, and soon after, the badge showed a stellar number: an orange seven.

Good enough, thought Patty. *At least that should keep her in school. I just have to stay on her about her activities and what she's wearing.*

*****

CH 4

Six months later ...

Mandy opened the online notices, and there was one from the U.S. Ministry of Citizen Affairs. Before she clicked the file document, she worried. *What could this be? Why am I getting this?*

There were two notices one never wanted to receive: one from the Internal Revenue Service and the other from the Ministry of Citizen Affairs.

The ministry notice read as follows:

> *Dear Citizen:*
>
> *We have received notice that one in your family has a Citizenship Number below five (5). This, as you know, is not an acceptable rating. Your family member must take the following measures to increase the CN to at least a level five but preferably above an eight (8) to be considered a loyal citizen of this nation.*
>
> *Failure to comply with this request may result in the cancelation of benefits bestowed on the individual. Among those benefits are:*
>
> > • *Ability to enter any merchant store, including food markets, grocery stores, and other critical needs stores.*
> > • *Ability to maintain any bank account in any financial institution.*
> > • *Ability to purchase any sources of entertainment either within or outside the home.*
> > • *Be subjected to annual fines of up to $250,000 per year.*
> > • *Be arrested and detained for up to one year for failure to maintain an acceptable CN rating.*
> > • *Have your identity listed on the federal posting for those in violation of the CN requirements.*
> > • *Other measures as appropriate and necessary.*
>
> *Although your family member is in the Yellow Group, we still require a minimum CN of five (5). That member may be denied access to schooling, medical treatment, and other benefits bestowed by the government.*
>
> *Please rectify this situation immediately.*

Sincerely,

Lois Tillson,
Minister of Citizen Affairs

Although Mandy had avoided the social stigma of having a family member with a citizenship rating below five, she had not evaded the feds.

Peggy was livid. The family had money from the premature death of their father—Joseph Warren—but that money was running out. They could not afford the stiff penalties that might be imposed by the government and would have to find ways to get Mandy's badge up to the proper reading.

Meanwhile, the subscription to show Miranda's badge at a seven was running out and Mandy didn't have the money to renew it.

"I will not!" shouted Miranda.

"You will!" said Peggy. "You'll do that and more."

"I won't," Miranda protested, crossing her arms in defiance.

"Too bad. There are some things you just have to do."

"I'm not doing it!"

"If you don't, I'm putting you in a state-run orphanage," said Mandy.

"You wouldn't."

"You're leaving me no choice."

During the next three weeks, Miranda posted pro-government posts on her social websites. She volunteered to help the party distribute electronic propaganda messages to senior citizens in advance of the 'election.' She agreed to be filmed and lie about her dedication to the Party and the cause to ensure that her friends went along with her and gave reverence to the Party Chairman. She agreed to be filmed worshiping to a statue of President Li surrounded by thousands of beautiful flowers, a blue sky and a brilliant sun shining down on all.

As her reward, Miranda's badge—which had dropped from seven back to four—was revitalized to a healthier six.

***

"I'm sorry Mandy, we won't be able to have dinner with you and Miranda next week," said Cindy Crofton, a long-time friend of Peggy's.

"Why not?"

"Well, let's just say that your situation is not one that we're comfortable with."

"What situation is that?"

"To be candid, Peggy. Your family right now has a 6.5 average. We can't socialize with anyone below an eight or it might bring down ours. The Party is cracking down, as you know. We are loyal patriots. Loyal citizens. We've worked awfully hard to get to an eight point five. That would suffer if we had dinner with you."

"But that's improving. We're doing everything we can to raise that!" said Peggy.

"Well, call me when you get above an eight. In the meantime, I really shouldn't be talking to you either. Take care Peggy."

Only an hour later, Peggy got another call.

"Patricia? This is Herb."

Herb Spencer was her boss. Peggy worked as a marketing advertiser for a popular fashion magazine in town, and Herb was the Editor in Chief.

"Yes, Herb. What can I do for you? You got my markups on the latest campaign, didn't you?"

"Yes. But that's not why I'm contacting you. You do good work—you know that. But Peggy, I'm going to have to let you go."

"What? I'm doing everything you ask. I'm getting it to you *before* you want it, and I'm suggesting things that could make things better. Do you not want my suggestions?"

"Listen, I know all that, but I received my monthly report on the CN score for my employees. It shows that your family CN is below a seven. We don't' permit anyone here with a CN below seven. I'm afraid you can't work here."

"But Herb! I don't have one below seven. Mine's an eight!"

"Peggy, it pains me, but this is something I have to do. I'm sorry."

Herb hung up.

If things didn't change soon, Peggy and her daughter would have no access to food, clothing, and most likely, shelter. If the landlord didn't come soon to evict her because of her CN rating, he would because she wouldn't be able to pay the rent.

Peggy was beyond inconsolable.

"Miranda, we're going to have to take a little trip," she said.

"Where are we going?" Miranda asked. "Do I need to pack anything?"

"No. I don't think that is necessary. It will be a short trip—just down the road. There's something down there I want you to see."

*****

CH 5

Chairman Li entered the meeting. He was wearing his CN badge just as all others were required. However, his always read an eleven. There were no other elevens allowed in the CB system. His was the only one. It was therefore worshiped, just as he was, as someone or something from a divine source. All others could attain a CN score up to ten, but that was it.

No one questioned the chairman's number. It was as it was. And those of party members were not questioned either. Those always stayed at ten no matter what they did or didn't do—almost. When one fell out of favor with the chairman, anything was possible.

But for most, the gravy train was alive and well within the government. People were rewarded and cursed depending on whether they willingly helped or hurt the regime. And like all other citizens, one's life or death depended on his or her CN score.

"You have not fulfilled your quota for the quarter, Phelps," said Chairman Li. Phelps was the Minister of Agriculture and food shortages were widespread, resulting in the deaths of thousands. Phelps crime was not that there wasn't enough food. It was that he had not properly prepared propaganda to justify the shortages or, better yet, deny and disavow any shortages at all.

"We have used your Minister of Propaganda to help us in …"

"I don't want to hear it!" shouted the chairman. "You have failed to properly advise the masses about how well our programs are doing."

"But people are starving in the countryside," said Phelps.

"Silence!" shouted Li.

Immediately, the Minister of Agriculture's CN badge changed. The number dropped from a ten to a four. This was unheard of—even for a party member.

"But!"

"No! You are failing the party!"

"I will change things. I will change the data and distribute it to the media to make things better!"

"It's too late for that," said Li.

Phelps bowed his head low. "I ask for forgiveness," he said.

With his ashen face looking down at his chest where his arms were crossed, Phelps saw his number drop further. Now it was two point eight.

"You are beyond redemption."

"I will resign," said Phelps.

"You will do more than that," said Li.

Li motioned for his guards who took Phelps from the room. Everyone knew what was to happen to Phelps, and no one spoke up to defend him.

"I believe we need a new Minister of Agriculture," said Li. "Any suggestions?"

*****

CH 6

The sirens and lights of the police cruisers flashed throughout the woods. The red and blue lights dotted the various tree trunks in the forest surrounding the shallow lake only a few miles from the city. Overhead, the iron bridge stood as it always had, spanning the distance between the two riverbeds. However, there was one thing that was different—a piece of the railing was missing—broken off from its mounting.

"Adam? What do you make of this?" asked the detective coming up to the police officer who was monitoring the operation from his squad car.

"It was probably about eleven at night when a small sedan veered off the bridge and plunged into the river. We don't know why. There doesn't seem to be any malfunction with the car. There were no skid marks suggesting it was trying to avoid an animal on the bridge, and there was no other car involved."

"So, who are the vics?"

"We've got a mother and her daughter. Their last CNs were below five, so I don't think we should spend any more time on it."

"No. Don't. Just document what you can and file it. They aren't worth any more time than that."

*****

YOU'VE BEEN BOOKED

CH 1

Jonathon Capshaw was about as ordinary as ordinary got. Of moderate height – about five foot eight – and medium weight – about one hundred sixty pounds – and average age – thirty-seven, he found himself in a mid-life crisis; yet he wasn't even aware of it.

Single, never-married, Jonathon had yearned to find the perfect woman with whom to spend the rest of his life but thought he just hadn't been at the right place at the right time. It probably didn't help that he still sported a goatee and short-cropped hair—a throw-back to the early twenty-first century. His clothes were decades out of style as he was still wearing straight-legged blue jeans, white shirts, and a muted, plaid sport coats. The current style of the young and hip was more in tune with the wild, LSD-induced age of the 1960s and 1970s—nearly two hundred years earlier—with bell bottoms, necklaces, and wild paisley shirts.

Parties were extreme, and so was the drug use. Most people did hash or cocaine after work and even harder stuff on weekends. Workweeks were only three days long, so the synthetic drugs on the market could be taken on a Wednesday night and last through Sunday. But Jonathon held to a strict moral code—one increasingly outdated and considered Stoic and Puritanical. He had never taken drugs and didn't use alcohol, even when he was with his drinking friends.

As for other friends, he had few. One of the best, most loyal, and understanding was Marcy Horwath. Marcy and Jonathon worked together in the virtual office of Stonemeyer and Stonemeyer, LLC., an architectural firm in the downtown loop area. Jonathon was a senior architect while Marcy was only a few years younger but working her way up the corporate ladder.

While Jonathon was short and diminutive, Marcy was thick-boned, long-legged and tall. She was in no way fat or overweight, it was just her genetic makeup coming from a mainly Hungarian background. Standing in flats, she was nearly six feet tall, over five inches more than Jonathon. Yet, she had a kind face, youthful and energetic with blue eyes that were full of life. In some ways, she could have been Jonathon's sister. She too had dark brown hair with strands of bleach blonde cropped close around

her ears, and although she didn't smile often, when she did, it was broad
and wide.

It was late on a Wednesday night when Jonathon was finishing the
review of a Halo-CAM blueprint for a new levitating work tower that was
planned for the center of town. The old banker's building of the First
American Depository had already been razed, and a new building was to
go up in its place. Air rights had been purchased above the old building
to allow the new levitating one to hover up to twenty floors above the
ground, but there could be no building below it according to local safety
standards. Carbon nanotube elevators would shuttle occupants and
visitors to and from the new building, but these were still being
constructed. In the meantime, shuttlecraft were to be used until the
elevators could be completed and installed.

Jonathon pressed the software button *Review Completed* and started to
turn off his computer. However, before he could begin the sequence, a
holographic bulletin popped out of his screen, floating before his eyes.

> *Notice: Mr. Capshaw.*
>
> *Flight Information:*
> *Spaceline: Galactic One*
> *Departure Date: Thurs., September 11, 2155.*
> *Departing: O'Hare Spaceport (ORD) at 8:23 AM.*
> *Return Date: Sun., September 14, 2155*
> *Arriving: O'Hare Spaceport (ORD) at 9:54 PM*
> *Reference No: FGLM5Y*
>
> *Flight is confirmed.*

What? What flight? he thought. *I didn't book any flight. At least I don't
remember booking any. I haven't been on a flight in years. It must be a
mistake.*

Jonathon queried the Galactic One website, and nothing came up. So, he
went back and deleted the message.

A week went by, and again on Wednesday night, he got another
message.

> *Notice: Mr. Capshaw.*
>
> *Flight Information:*
> *Spaceline: Galactic One*
> *Departure Date, Thurs., September 18, 2155.*

Departing: O'Hare Spaceport (ORD) at 8:23 AM.
Return Date: Sun., September 21, 2155
Arriving: O'Hare Spaceport (ORD) at 9:54 PM
Reference No: PCLM8Y

Flight is confirmed.

Again, he went to the spaceline website to see if there were really a flight scheduled for him.

Reference No: PCLM8Y
We are sorry. We have no record of this itinerary

No flights under this Ref. No. have been booked

He tried several times and got the same message.

Somebody is messing with me, he thought. So, he called Marcy.

"Hey, Marcy. You didn't happen to book me on a flight, did you? It leaves tomorrow from O'Hare."

"A flight? No, why? Why would I book you a flight?"

"I don't know. But I'm booked on a flight tomorrow morning, and I didn't make it."

"Well, I certainly didn't make it. Where are you going?"

"I don't know. I didn't make the flight," Jonathon said sarcastically.

"No, Jonathon," Marcy said quickly, reacting to his abruptness. "I didn't. I'm sure it's just a mistake of some kind. Now, was there anything else?"

"No, never mind. I'll see you on Monday."

Jonathon canceled the notice and blocked the sending address. He flagged it to go directly to junk in the future. *That was that*, he thought.

Week three, and it was a Wednesday night. This time, Jonathon wasn't surprised when he received the third notice. Instead of being perplexed, he laughed. He wasn't sure how the message had evaded his filter, but he knew there were tricks in technology that would allow it. Still, he looked on the Galactic One website to see, just in case.

This time, the itinerary popped out from the screen, hovering in front of his face.

Departure Date: Thurs., September 25, 2155.
Departing: O'Hare Spaceport (ORD) at 8:23 AM

I never booked this! he thought, again. *But maybe I'm supposed to go on this flight for some reason.*

Jonathon had never believed in Fate, but at this stage of his life he figured he would just "go with the flow" and see what happened. He told Marcy he would not be in on Monday and that he was going out of town. She never asked whether he was following one of his flight notices. Instead, she only said, "That's nice. We'll see you on Tuesday."

He took an air taxi to the spaceport and checked in at the Galactic One terminal desk. As the desk manager processed his papers and his departure documents, Jonathon looked on the electronic board behind the man to find his flight number and destination. But nothing was posted.

"This may sound stupid," Jonathon asked, "but where is this flight going?"

The manager finished processing the paperwork and finally looked up, handing him his documents.

"Your gate is Q456. Go through the access port and enter the queue at security area six."

"Thank you, but again where does this flight go?"

"You're joking, right?" asked the manager, rolling his eyes.

"Uh."

"You can't tell me you booked this ticket, and you don't know where it's going."

Jonathon grinned sheepishly. "Of course not. I was only kidding. Really."

After getting the 3-D body scan and chemical sensory chamber analysis which awaited everyone going through security, he took a helipod scooter to the launch gate.

"Mr. Capshaw?"

The attendant at the gate was dressed in an immaculate, navy blue uniform with gold trim and matching buttons. She had short blonde hair pulled back into a tight bun. Her eyes were large, hazel and dazzling with eyelashes that could create air currents. Her lips were full, and their rose color blended well with the light rouge she had used on her high cheekbones. She was stunning.

"Yes?" answered Jonathon nervously, intimidated by her beauty.

"You may come with me," she said. "You are our only first-class passenger on today's flight, and I want to make sure you're properly cared for."

"First class?" he asked. "But my ticket says coach?"

"Yes, but I guess it's your lucky day. The computer selected a coach passenger at random and your name was drawn. Isn't that great?"

Jonathon gave her a weak, suspicious grin and rose to follow her. Inside the craft, he found the first-class section lavish and spacious. His seat and enclosure had its own self-serve bar, shower facility, and entertainment cluster. The seat itself was thickly padded and stretched out into a full recline for sleeping with a clear canopy that came down over the head to drown-out cabin noises.

"Here are your quarters," she said, motioning for him to enter.

Jonathon walked inside, wide-eyed and amazed. He'd never experienced anything so luxurious in his life.

"Feel free to freshen up before we lift off. Departure is set for 8:53 now. It's been pushed back a bit due to some last-minute crew changes."

"I'm sorry, I just have one more question. What time do we get to ..." Jonathon acted like he was only trying to recall the name of the destination.

"We'll be arriving at our first stop at 20:46."

"What? Almost two hours?"

She looked at him as though she'd heard that reaction before. "I'm afraid so—aeronautical protocols, I'm afraid," she answered. "At the Orbital One, you'll be ferried to your main ship. Your itinerary should tell you where you're going from there."

The attendant closed the door behind her.

Orbital One? he thought. *Wasn't that the first of seven orbiting space hubs above the earth?* These had been constructed as transit points between sportports on the ground and terrestrial bases on other planets. Some of the later orbitals had been built to house destination resorts and provide for freighter ships transporting mining ores, supplies and other cargo to and from the bases.

After taking a quick shower, he was told to strap in for the launch. There weren't many restraints needed, as his seat molded directly to his body during lift-off and landing, preventing him from moving. Two yellow, magnetic shoulder harnesses kept him from leaving the seat entirely.

"We will be lifting off within three minutes," said the captain, his face appearing holographically in front of Jonathon's seat. "Please secure all belongings. Flight attendants, please secure the cabin."

Moments later, he heard over the ship's speakers, "Count down sequence has begun," said the captain, and the numbers on Jonathon's entertainment console showed a scarlet red ten before ticking off one-by-one to zero.

The force was minimal, only pushing his body gently into the seat behind him. The anti-gravity cyclotron began swirling below in the belly of the ship, engaging the dark energy which had been discovered a little over a century earlier but only recently understood well enough to use in space flight. Engaging the dark energy, the ship rose quickly and sped off toward its destination—the first one anyway.

*****

CH 2

The trip to Orbital One was not a straight line from launch pad to docking bay. A straight path to the orbital would have taken about ten minutes at the maximum sub-warp speed of 0.05W or five percent of light speed. However, most short-flight "puddle jumpers" as they were called, were only allowed to reach speeds of half that—about 0.025W. Those that traveled longer interplanetary routes were allowed faster speeds to cover the greater distances—some as fast as 0.2W or twenty percent of light speed.

The time seemed to pass quickly, even though clocks on board ran more slowly the faster the ships flew, and soon the captain announced, "Crew, prepare for docking."

Firing its forward thrusters, the craft gently bumped the docking station in the orbital bay.

"Passengers disembarking for Orbiter One should make their way immediately to the passport and visa chip scanning and verification stations," reported the lead flight attendant. "Those going to our next stop should stay on board. Attendants, I believe we only have one 'through,' so if that passenger would remain on board, we will get underway as soon as the rest of the passengers depart the shuttle."

Jonathon summoned the attendant.

"Am I staying onboard or getting off here?" he asked.

"You're our only 'through'," said the attendant. "That means, you're going on to the next destination. Just stay in your seat. We will be departing shortly."

Jonathon fidgeted nervously, unsure where he was going or what was in store.

"Would you like a cocktail?" asked another attendant, walking by.

"No, I'm sorry. I don't drink," answered Jonathon.

"Oh, well what about a juice, then?" she asked.

"Yes, that would be quite nice, thanks."

After bringing him a tall, thin glass with a blue liquid, she left him to ponder what it was. He took a sip and found it quite pleasing, somewhat sweet, with hints of apricot and a blueberry.

He had emptied only half the glass when the shuttle released from its dock and pushed away from the Orbiter. He remembered hearing the thrusters fire, but nothing after that.

"Mr. Capshaw? Mr. Capshaw?" It was the attendant pushing gently on his arm. "We've arrived at your destination."

Jonathon, groggy-eyed and disoriented, pushed up in his seat. "What?"

"I said, we're here, Mr. Capshaw. It's time for you to disembark."

The attendant helped Jonathon with his coat and small piece of baggage and led him to the exit. He glided through the opening and into another. There, an aero-company employee waved him into a square elevator with full wall digital screens showing pictures of glacier-covered mountains, turquois lakes, golden stalks of wheat blowing gently in a light breeze, and a tropical beach with two palm trees on one side. These two trees seemed to have found love in one another as their trunks bent lithesomely toward each other—their fronds lightly touching at the ends.

Jonathon strapped himself into the elevator and waited as it smoothly left its platform—to him moving horizontally, rather than up and down even though in space there were no such distinctions. By the time the elevator stopped, Jonathon found himself planted firmly on the floor— gravity having been restored.

Walking off the lift, he was greeted by a wide, colorful electronic sign which read:

> Welcome to Europa. We hope you enjoy your stay.

Europa? Thought Jonathon. He knew Europa was one of the four Galilean moons of Jupiter, discovered by the brilliant scientist in 1610. With its water-ice crust, it was one of the few objects besides Earth that held water on its surface. But at a temperature of minus 160° Celsius and no rocky surface where plants or animals could develop, humans had created self-contained habitats to survive on the icy crust. Tourist resorts soon developed, and Europa had become one of the "hottest" places to spend a holiday.

The attendant at the front desk of the resort checked him in. She was young, only in her twenties, and was pleasant and vivacious.

"Welcome, Mr. Capshaw. I see you'll be staying with us for two nights, is that correct?"

"Yes, I think so."

"Well, you are already signed up for several of our activities starting tomorrow. You're booked for the Mt. Fury Ice Expedition, the Afternoon Submarine Cruise, and the Jupiter Observatory. Was there anything else you wanted to do while you are here?"

"Uh, no, that will be quite marvelous, thank you."

Jonathon spent the next two days exploring the moon and gazing in amazement at the huge gas planet Jupiter with its iconic Red Spot—a huge storm over 1.3 times the size of Earth spinning near the equator at over 268 miles per hour.

At the end of his last day, he went down to the dining hall for a final meal before getting on his return flight home. With the assistance of gravity boots, he walked securely along the magnetic pathways that counteracted the near weightlessness of the small planetoid. Europa's 0.8% gravity made most things hover rather than rest in place, and serving meals and beverages on the surface was a challenge. Most came in sealed containers and were ingested directly through straws or from pouches.

This night's meal was a delicious lobster bisque served with a Chardonnay from the Martian settlement of Sonoma, named after the Californian valley. Jonathon had met several genuinely nice and wealthy guests staying at the resort. Tonight was no different as he sat down across from an older couple he found was celebrating their centennial wedding anniversary.

"That is marvelous," said Jonathon, raising his glass. "To the golden anniversary and may you have many more."

"So, what brings you to Europa?" asked the gentleman who was beaming next to his bride.

"I … I …" Jonathon began before realizing he needed a reasonable answer. "I was invited. It was a gift of sorts," he answered.

The man smiled. "Well, it was very nice of them to give it to you. Not many can afford something like this."

Jonathon smiled weakly. "Yes, they were very nice indeed. So, what made you decide on coming here of all places?"

"I've always wanted to go to another planet," said the man, "and when Essie said she'd like to come here, I put our deposit down. We retired many years ago and our kids, grandkids, and great grandkids are well along, so we thought we'd be adventurous."

"Good for you. I hope you've been enjoying yourselves."

As they finished their meals, the waiter came over carrying a silver tray.

"Mr. Capshaw, I believe there is a message for you." He lifted the lid, and underneath was a clear, post-card sized electronic reader. Jonathon picked it up and instantly it energized, spewing forth an image which floated like a cloud over the table.

"Jonathon," said the image of a human, coming into view. It was an older woman with long, gray hair that was coiled in braids around her head. She had kind, blue eyes, and a smile that radiated warmth and grace. "You probably don't remember me, but I'm your Great Aunt Janet—your Grandfather Henry's sister. My other brother, your Great Uncle Thomas, passed away last year and had no one to leave his estate to but me. If you are receiving this message now, you should be on Europa for a well-deserved vacation."

Jonathon sat with his napkin barely resting on his lap in total shock and wonder. The other couple at his table also looked surprised at his message but now were engrossed in what was unfolding before all of them.

"So, what does all this mean?" asked his great aunt in the message. "Well, your Uncle Thomas was a fine man and a world-renowned artist of which I'm sure you were aware. His paintings were sought after throughout the solar system. During his life, he managed to earn, save, and invest well, and with his paintings selling for millions of G-credits, he accumulated a significant estate.

"Jonathon, if you are receiving this message, it also means that I have passed on as well. As you are the only one left within our close family, Thomas and I wanted you to be our sole heir. And if you're wondering, the estate is worth over 23 billion G-credits."

Jonathon thought he would throw up. He had never imagined so much money in his life. However, his other reaction was "Why on earth would I need anything close to that much money?" But his aunt continued.

"But there is one thing I'd like you to do when you get back to Earth. You have been blind for too long about people who care about you. In fact, there is one there who cares for you deeply and you haven't seen it. I know you don't know this, but I communicated with this person often as we share a special mutual friend. But that is not important. What *is* important is you reach out. Will you do this? I hope you will."

His aunt went on to tell him more about the mutual friend and the one he had been blind to. She was firm, yet gracious, and she was clear about what she expected of him. In the end, he nodded and smiled.

"Well, what are you going to do?" asked the older woman at his table.

"I'm going home," Jonathon answered. "It looks like I have some things to do."

*****

Jonathon returned home, but within the first several months, little in his life had changed. He lived in the same apartment, drove the same hovercar, had the same outdated clothes, and the same old friends. However, there was one thing that had changed. He had done as his aunt had asked.

"So, Marcy," he asked as she curled up next to him on the sofa, "where do you want to go for dinner tonight?"

She smiled back at him. "It doesn't matter, Jonathon. Why don't we just get a pizza and have it delivered. We can watch old reruns of *Star Trek*. How's that?"

"Perfect," Jonathon answered lying back in the cushion and putting his arm around her. "Absolutely perfect."

*****

CHALLENGER DEEP

CH 1

"When will it happen?" Ivan posted on a very deep and dark website marked as *http://yz3xv6qupaj7qvmy90bv.blackonion*

"How much?" came the reply.

"Twenty. Bearer bonds."

"Where? When?"

"Fisherman's Wharf Marina, 1935 Thursday, tomorrow."

"Put half in locker 354 Greyhound Terminal tonight. Will collect rest there on Thursday after job is done."

"Roger."

***

It was called the Mariana's Web—the deepest part of the Internet. Well below the regular Internet where most people found stories of their friends, looked for jobs, shared pictures of weddings, and births, and generally survived day-to-day on the tools used for everyday life.

Below the regular Internet were the private sites that required special access codes to get into. These were used by private companies, government agencies, payment and collection firms and others. Still deeper was the Deep Net. Here lurked the quasi-legal stuff that was made difficult to trace by encryption and other means. Although some was legal, other activities were not. But it still didn't compare to what was in the deepest channels of the global access system. One was the Mariana's Web—named after the Mariana's Trench, the deepest oceanic trench on earth. It lay in the Pacific Ocean, eighteen hundred miles east of Taiwan. But even this was not the deepest part of the Internet. Within the Mariana's Trench lay the deepest point on earth—called the Challenger Deep. Nearly thirty-six thousand feet deep—or nearly seven miles below the surface of the Pacific Ocean—the Challenger Deep was the ultimate depth.

For the Internet, the Challenger Deep was as dark as it got.

*****

CH 2

"This is breaking news," said anchor Brandon Petty of the CNP network. "We have information that Senator Colleen Dubois was shot tonight as she and her husband were preparing their boat for sailing during this Memorial weekend. Dubois, who represents the collective of Caribbean islands from Puerto Rico to Trinidad, has been outspoken recently about the way the executive branch has been conducting its foreign policy with the countries of South America. She has been a major voice against the annexation of several countries on the continent after the rash of bankruptcies filed by nations on the mainland."

Petty paused a moment, listening to the producer talk to him in his ear buds.

"We understand, now," Petty continued, "that she was pronounced dead at the scene. Senator Dubois will be remembered for her work with ..."

The contract for hire to assassinate a U.S. Senator was on the higher Mariana's portion of the Internet—not even at the even more-debase Challenger Deep level where—it was hard to believe—more horrible and graphic things were posted.

Pete Collins was an investigator for an underworld organization that monitored what was going on in the world. Where authorities in governments avoided direct involvement in looking into these atrocities, Pete and his colleagues at QGo were determined to shine a light on the cockroaches of society and let the masses of the world—the *hoi polloi*—see what was really going on around them.

"Ted, what are you seeing?" asked Pete, using his organization's high-tech software to ferret out the most heinous of activities going on online.

"Of course, there's the assassination of the senator. That must be a high priority. But there are two others that are even worse."

"I'd ask you how things could be worse, but we've been doing this long enough that I'm certain you're right. Can we get assets out to look at them?"

"I'm not sure," said Pete. "Do we have assets in Eritrea?"

"No, why?"

"That's where this next one lies—Eritrea and other neighboring countries in Africa."

"Explain."

Pete told Ted what the posts were suggesting, and Ted shook his head in disbelief.

"That can't be happening. That's just … disgusting!"

"I know," said Pete. "But that's what you find in the Challenger Deep. Am I right? You've been at this a while now. How can you be shocked anymore?"

"I guess I'm just amazed at how horrible people can be. Even in my darkest dreams—my worst imagination—I couldn't think of such horrible things."

"Well, they exist, Ted. We both know that. Our jobs are to find the people doing them and figure out a way to keep them from ever doing them again."

"What if correcting the problem is worse than the problem itself?" asked Ted.

"I wouldn't be doing this job if I thought that," said Pete. "Would you?"

Ted shook his head.

"No, I didn't think so," Pete said. "So, what you need to do is find someone in Eritrea who knows something. We need connections. Use the money in the Cayman's account if you have to—that's why we have it. In most third-world countries, you'll need to use some to grease the palms."

"Hell," said Ted, "I have to do that in the U.S. too."

"Yeah, I know. When can you leave?" Pete asked.

"By the end of the week," said Ted. "I've got some things to get done before I leave."

"Let's not go beyond Friday. I'd really like to avoid many deaths."

"Many or any?" asked Ted.

"Many. I'm afraid it's already too late to avoid a death count."

"All right. I'm off to … to …"

"Eritrea," said Pete, finishing his sentence.

"Yeah. That place." *****

CH 3

The strongman leader of Eritrea was Tuma Afwerki, grandson of an earlier dictator of the country, Isaias Afwerki, who left the country in shambles to his eldest son who then passed it along to his son, Tuma. Tuma had continued his grandfather's and father's savage ways and kept his people the poorest in the world while he enjoyed wealth and splendor.

However, things were becoming more desperate there; the country was running out of water—clean water. Even Afwerki's family and military were struggling to find enough for themselves. People were dying by the thousands from dehydration and starvation. It was a global disaster. Yet few cared or paid any attention to it. It usually ended up on page thirty-five or thirty-six of Section B of the paper, but never the front page.

However, on the deepest part of the web, it was a hot commodity.

> Contact 986YH89.45TZ.689.0T. Will exchange four bulls and eight cows for 5G network.

On the surface, this looked innocent enough, but these were merely code words. The bulls and cows referred to men and women. The 5G referred to five thousand gallons, and the 'network' was the network of clean water. It was a slave trade transaction—exchanging humans for water.

This was happening on a grand scale in the Challenger Deep. There were bids and solicitations for slaves in far greater numbers—some in the hundreds—in exchange for food and water. The dictator of Eritrea was at the heart of it—kidnapping his own people and selling them to get what he wanted to maintain his lifestyle.

Ted located a mercenary cell in Djibouti, a neighbor of Eritrea, to assist in the operation. The cell was closely aligned—not with the Djibouti government which was rife with corruption—but with an underground organization called the FFC which supported QGo priorities.

"Can you handle the assignment?" asked Ted typing from his hotel room in Djibouti although over an encrypted line into the Challenger Deep network.

"Yes. We have assets in Djibouti and can infiltrate as necessary into Eritrea," said the agent.

"Good. We will provide you access to the five thousand gallons of fresh water. This will come on a cargo ship and be labeled vegetable oil. You know what to do. Let us know when the job is finished. We'll wire 25 percent now and the rest when the job is done."

It took time for the water to arrive, but when it did, the mission went into action within five days. Tuma was reached via the Challenger Deep and arrangements were made for the delivery.

The exchange was to take place on a dock in Assab along the Red Sea near the Gulf of Aden. There was no cover. It was wide open with two long man-made promontories extending out into the sea to provide docking for freight and other cargo ships. All around was an arid wasteland which stretched for miles east of the town.

It was June—*not* the hottest month of the year—yet the temperature was already approaching 110° F and was likely to top 115° that day. The sun beat down on the sands surrounding the dock, and the few full-time workers there came out from their hut to work thirty minutes tying up the freighter to the moorings on shore. It was the Liberian-registered freighter, *Aglaia,* that pulled into port with a length/beam of 268 and 33 meters and a draft of 8.6.

Off in the distance—peering out over the gritty sand dunes—were two white Range Rovers with four men, two using high-powered binoculars to evaluate the conditions and two behind them carrying an AK-47s, fully loaded and ready to go.

"How we know which container holds water?" asked one of the men, speaking in Tigrinya, a local dialect.

"They say it marked vegetable oil. We shall see," said another as he folded his binoculars. "We go and have closer look."

Not far away was another vehicle—an old Ford F150—dirty and rusted. It was non-descript and that's just the way the driver wanted it. He got out of the truck and turned the knobs on his own set of binoculars. These were high-tech and received secondary data from an overhead satellite. As a result, he had a 3D—almost 4D—view of what was going on in front of him. He too jumped back into his vehicle and drove off toward the dock as a thick cloud of dust billowed up behind it.

*****

CH 4

"We have a problem," said the man speaking Tigrinya.

"What is the problem?" asked another man on the other end of the radio.

"The ship captain say he cannot release container, unless manifest is signed by president of country."

"Right. Sure. That's not going to happen," said the other man. "Get the paper, and we'll have it delivered to the president at his palace for his signature."

The captain was instructed to give the authorization paper to one of the Eritrea security men to take back to the palace.

"Did you hear that?" asked Ted, listening in from Djibouti.

"I'm all over it," said Omar Berhane, the man in the Ford F150.

Through his binoculars, Berhane watched as the Range Rover pulled away from the dock, carrying the paper to be signed to release the cargo. Meanwhile, in an un-air-conditioned bus idling not far outside the secure harbor, were the slaves dripping in sweat and fear and manacled to their seats awaiting the exchange. He put his key in the ignition and fired up the Ford. He watched as the rovers left the dock and followed them a safe distance to ensure he wasn't seen.

"Are you in position?" asked Berhane, talking to others on the mercenary team.

"Yes. I see them. Will engage."

It all happened fast. Another non-descript pickup truck came toward the first Range Rover and let it pass. However, it swerved in front of the second one, colliding head-on with it. Jumping out, the men in the pickup riddled it with bullets before awaiting the first SUV to see the carnage and turn around. It was instantly surrounded by other trucks that came out from behind sand mounds. The men from the rovers were replaced with Berhane and another from his team. They took the authorization paper from the dead man's hands in the second Rover, pulling him out and hiding his body a short distance from the road.

Arriving at the palace, Berhane showed his credentials and went in. Although he checked his weapons at the security checkpoint, he kept with him a plastic gun made especially for missions like this.

"Your Majesty," said Berhane, coming into the president's office. It was covered with priceless paintings and gold fixtures, including a sparkling, grand chandelier hanging above him. He was quickly disgusted.

"Come in," said Tuma, not looking up from his desk. "What do you have for me?"

"I have the authorization they need you to sign for the water, sire. The slaves are positioned and ready for the exchange once we receive the water from the vessel. If you would just sign here." Berhane pointed to the spot.

One shot rang out. That was all it took.

Guards rushed in and began shooting. Berhane was killed instantly, as was his assistant. But the job had been done.

*****

CH 5

"Why did we fail?"

It was Pete asking Ted about what went wrong.

"We didn't completely fail. We only partially failed," said Ted.

"Partial failure is failure, Ted."

"We'll do better next time. Our failure was not getting our asset out alive. That was a shame."

"Yes, it was," said Pete. "Your next assignment is harder too. We can't fuck this one up. *Millions* of lives are at stake."

"Nuclear?"

"Nope."

"Bio?"

"Nope. It's a food supply."

"A food supply? Why is that our concern?" asked Ted.

"Here is the Challenger chain," said Pete.

> "We need to know tipping point," R3 posted on a website marked as http://uuz568ioy8898bniz26yyz.blackonion
>
> "Approaching within 9 days"
>
> "Effects?"
>
> "2-3M"
>
> "How long?"
>
> "4-5 days--quick"
>
> "Good. Engage Warp Drive."

"And what is the translation of that?" asked Ted, knowing Pete had already deciphered it."

"This one is a game changer. If they're able to do this in Uruguay, where it's being tested, then they'll use it on other South American countries and African countries where they don't have checks and balances. Millions will die."

"And the objective?"

"To overthrow the government. Once control is seized, they can move up the food chain—no pun intended—to attack Western Europe, Mexico, and America. Saboteurs are being installed in various points in the food chains of these countries to contaminate them. The enemy are the people paying-off food inspectors, so they'll look the other way when they spot diseased meats, *Salmonella*-tainted vegetables—you name it. In Mexico and Central America, it will be just as easy. In America and Western Europe, efforts are already afoot to get levels of toxicity raised so the impact on the civilian population will be devastating. It will take longer in America and Europe, but over time the toxicity levels will accumulate in the citizenry and the results will bear fruit."

"What does that mean?"

"It means, that within twenty years, ninety percent of people over the age of thirty-five will have dementia—ninety-eight percent over fifty. Our nation will become crippled by it, and all our resources will be spent caring for the two hundred million inflicted, leaving nothing left for military or other spending."

"*Shit!* You're lying to me, man. You've gone whacko now."

"I wish I were," said Pete. "If they succeed, it will be more horrible than you can imagine. If what they say is true, they will kill outright two to three million in Uruguay within five days."

"That's almost the entire population."

"Yes, out of 3.5 million total."

"So, what can we do?" asked Ted.

"This is the plan," said Pete. "This is about all we can do."

*****

CH 6

The food supply in Uruguay had always been tenuous. Thousands each year got sick or died because of contamination in the food system. From the farmers to the market, foods were not always traceable back to their source and certainly not back to the specific field from which they came. When someone got sick—from *E. coli, Staphylococcus, Salmonella, Botulism,* and others—the hospital would report the incident to the country's health department, known as the Ministry of Health or MOH. They, in turn, would obtain information on what the patient ate, where it was purchased, and the stock numbers that might lead to the source of the contamination. Unfortunately. This information was rarely complete, and when it was, it was rarely accurate.

However, many believed this was by design. People high up in government purchased their foods from state-run and approved stores and ate at federally sanctioned restaurants. These were given special scrutiny. With the puny investigation resources available in the MOH, there just wasn't the manpower to monitor the operations of every farmer, processor, and distributor. So, they didn't try.

Instead, orders were received from the presidential palace that "Operation Filter" was ready to be engaged.

"Is everything in place, then?" asked the country's president, Alphonso Mirez.

"Yes. Everyone is in line," said his chief of staff, Carlos Gama. "We've made it clear, so no one steps out of it."

"Standard bribes, then?"

"Yes, nothing more than we normally must do."

"Good," said the president. "And what about the healthcare system? What's the status of the hospitals and clinics in the urban areas?"

"They are stocked. It's the suburban and rural hospitals and clinics that have nothing. They have not received medical supply shipments in weeks. Most do not have even the basics like syringes, cannulas, needles, blood plasma, catheters, IV bags and tubes, antiseptic wipes, surgical sutures and staples, intubation sets, masks, or autoclaves for sterilizing equipment. We've set them back to the Stone Age, sir," said Gama, laughing.

"Good. I don't' give a shit about them. The votes are in the urban cities. If we control them, we control the country. Put in place food rationing immediately. Urban centers get twice the rations of the rural people, and the military get four times the rations. Understood?"

"Yes, sir."

"Remember, Gama. The leader lives and dies by his army. If you take care of your military and its commanders, they will take care of you."

"Who said that?"

"Machiavelli, of course. Who else?"

***

Later that same day, there was a rapid exchange of notes on a message board posted in the deep end of the pool—the Challenger Deep.

> When will it happen?" Imran posted on the website marked as http://iuiso345ilYYZ45091HOVB122.blackonion
>
> "Friday?" came the reply.
>
> "And the grease?"
>
> "Grease will be in accounts Thursday PM."
>
> "Retirement plans?"
>
> "Plans funded within 90 days—after completion."

The grease referred to the bribes paid to all the government officials involved in the plan, including all the directors who signed off on the reports of contamination from field officers. These would be disregarded. For his ultimate approval, President Mirez would receive the equivalent of USD $100 million deposited to his Swiss account, with another $250 million paid to his retirement account after ninety days. It would be transferred in Bitcoins, and therefore, untraceable.

Chaos began to unfold slowly as produce with *E. coli* and other pathogens flooded the rural marketplaces. Hospitals outside the major cities were inundated with cases, and they increased significantly every day, as if caused by a virus contagion that had gotten loose from a weapons lab.

Ted was across the Rio de La Plata in Buenos Aires watching as things unfolded only 135 miles away in Montevideo, Uruguay. Insiders kept him informed on what was going on, and he was relaying that back to Pete in their bunker in the U.S.

"What do you want to do?" asked Ted. "I don't understand why the president would do this."

"Control," said Pete. "If he can send a message to the people in the farmlands without losing votes, he knows it will spread to those in the cities too. The urbanites will feel thankful to him that they were spared and continue their support. It's all a matter of manipulation."

"But people are dying?"

"Yes, but I have information that the government has stockpiled antidotes and supplies in Montevideo, so they can be rushed out to 'save' the people. It only solidifies the idea that the government can save them."

"Well, they're right. People's health is the most precious thing they have. They will do *anything* to keep it."

"It's time we use the Deep Net to kick off our program. I'm working with agents down there who can help us," said Pete. "Hopefully, we can pull the lid off this scam for the world to see."

"Okay. What does that mean?"

"I'll get back to you tomorrow. But what I can tell you is be ready. If they do next what I think, they will unleash something no one is prepared for down there."

Ted received his instructions the next day. He read them once, and then again before shaking his head. He was tempted to contact Pete, but decided breaking protocol was more dangerous that late in the operation, so he started at once to execute the mission.

The first blast of press releases flooded the news stations and included a code which changed daily. This was a government code which authenticated the message as coming from the ruling agency. Without the code, the message was ignored.

*A#ty78%239hn*o31T*

Press Release: For Immediate Distribution

The Ministry of Agriculture announced today that all meat and poultry products produced between September 4 and October 13 this year are tainted and should be disposed.

Next, Ted contacted the president of the United Health Organization in New York. The UHO had replaced the WHO after a series of debacles on the world stage. The UHO president, Francois Caron, received the notice as it came through special backchannels known only to global operatives within the Challenger Deep organization.

> *Mr. President,*
>
> *Attached you will find documents validating the efforts of many across the globe to destabilize governments by tainting their countries' food supplies. The initial thrust—as a test of the program—is occurring now in Uruguay, and unless immediate efforts are made, two to three million may die from virulent bacteria.*
>
> *Contact us at this email address for more information:*

Ted had included the email address and waited for contact—but the contact never happened.

"What do I do?" asked Ted.

"I don't understand," said Pete. "I've been told that Caron was totally independent of the Deep State—that he truly cared about the welfare of the people."

Then, there was a knock on Ted's hotel room door.

"Just a minute, Pete," said Ted.

Pete could hear Ted in the background.

"Yes, may I help you?"

It didn't sound like he had opened the door but had merely gone to it and asked his question.

Bang! Bang!

Pete sat stunned, listening to it all unfold over the phone.

"Who is this?" came a gruff voice picking up Ted's line.

Pete hung up. Quickly, he packed up his equipment and left his flat. Within the hour his door was blasted from its hinges by five men dressed in black and holding HK MP5 submachine guns.

However, Pete was long gone.

*****

CH 7

The Challenger Deep Operation was terminated. Pete's whereabouts were never traced even though Interpol and the special force operations of the major powers were sent to look for him. Ted's body was recovered in Argentina but was immediately disposed of in a landfill just outside Buenos Aires.

Since the president had no intention of stopping the food contamination in Uruguay or to notify anyone of the seriousness of the problem, hundreds of thousands in the countryside died. Media outlets throughout the country were told that news of a food supply problem was "fake news" and should be disregarded. The outlets were warned that broadcasting the problem would lead to their licenses being pulled. So, nothing was said.

Stories on the Internet were quashed, and the media quickly circled the wagons in defense of the president. Once the death toll rose to a high enough level and suppression of the news was unavoidable, the media stated that the president was taking "unprecedented" measures to combat the problem and stop its advance. It was then that supplies were sent out to the rural areas to deal with the issue, and the presidential palace was praised for its speedy and decisive action. It was all part of a pre-planned script.

*****

Epilogue

Attempts to repeat the experiment in other countries failed. Tainted food products were discovered by other watch groups and the public notified.

How these groups were notified remains a mystery, but many point to a Challenger Deep posting that was encrypted. It was decrypted and circulated widely.

"A man-made plague incubated under our own noses," was posted on the website marked as *http://kl5v6tyj09987qvnx92b3.blackonion*

>*"Where?" came the reply.*

>*"Course no. Western Civ H400."*

>*"When?"*

>*"Two weeks."*

>*"Why?"*

>*"Global control. UR what U eat."*

>*"Who?"*

>*"DS, of course."*

>*"Attributions?"*

>*"In memory of Ted."*

*****

HAL'S PAWN SHOP

CH 1

Hal's Pawn Shop had been on the outskirts of town for over a hundred years. It had always been a tacky joint, but after so many years it had become one of Bradyville's landmark sites. The town wasn't large—only about two thousand people—but it had its own pawn shop all the same.

And it was a thriving pawn shop too, having been passed down from generation to generation within the Pendleton family. Hal had started the shop, and his sons and now grandsons had taken over running it after he died. It was up to Myron and Cliff to run the show.

Hal's Pawn Shop was unusual from another perspective. Its customers always got either what they wanted or what they needed. Customer satisfaction was very high for those who got what they needed, but reviews were mixed for the rest. The Pendletons never forced their customers to take their suggestions, but when they did, it was usually for the better. It was never assured that customers would ask for things they *needed*, however. Most often, they only asked for those they just wanted. But that was just the way people were, and the boys at Hal's Pawn Shop merely felt obliged to help.

"Howdy Marcus," said Myron, who was in a jovial mood. "Haven't seen you for a while."

"It's plantin' season," said Marcus. "You know that."

"Oh, yeah. I forgot. How's it goin'? What do you think the crop will be like this year?"

"Hard to tell. Depends on the weather, a' course. With all the forecasting tools and advances in computers, we still can't predict whether it will rain tomorrow, let alone in three months."

"Got that right," said Myron. "So, what bring you in?"

"Just lookin'," said Marcus. "You know me, I'm always looking for a bargain."

"Anything you want? Need?"

"Well, truth be known, I'd like an entertainment unit or something like it. I hear people buy these holodecks and then can't make the payments, so they bring the equipment in here."

As technology had taken over civilization, Hal's shop had attracted more and more high-tech gadgets and instruments. Although Myron and Cliff didn't know everything about everything they took in, they understood enough. The boys—like their father and grandfather—had a knack for knowing when there was a good "fit" for a customer. They also knew when there wasn't.

"Oh, we don't take stuff like that," said Myron. "The store owner will be knocking at our door wanting it returned. We'd lose our shirts."

"Yeah, I thought so."

"But we do get the smaller holodomes in the store."

"So, what do you have?" Marcus asked.

"First, tell me why you want it?"

Marcus began telling the story of the previous six months. He had been struggling. His wife of thirty years had left him, his crops had come down with a strange, fungal disease that had wiped out 20 percent of them, and within the last three weeks, his dog had died.

"Man, that's rough," said Myron.

"Yeah, but who am I to complain," said Marcus. "There are people in the world starving. That's the way I look at it."

Myron smiled. That was quintessential Marcus—always upbeat and positive regardless of what happened.

"So, you're looking for a new holodome surround system, *eh?*" asked Myron. "Do you really think that's a good idea?"

Marcus frowned. "Why not?"

"Well, it seems to me you need more time around other people, not less. If you get the holodome, you may never come out of your room?" Myron laughed disarmingly.

"I think I need a little alone time."

"I understand. I was just thinking you might want to think about Max over here."

Myron took Marcus down the aisle and over a row to a lifelike robotic dog that sat in the corner of the store. He was a bulldog type, and even with his battery turned off, his face and countenance seemed happy and comforting.

"Now that you can't get a real dog anymore … not with the ban on enslaving live pets and all … I thought you and Max might …"

"It's also about people getting bitten by dogs. They say it's an epidemic, but it's really heartbreaking. I'd love to get a new, live dog too. I'm just not sure about a mechanical one. I live on a farm, for God's sake! Why would I have a robotic dog instead of a real one?"

"Max is a great dog. He's a MX model, version 3.3. I know that's a little dated now, and that's why the owner brought him in. He just isn't modern enough for anybody anymore, but he does need a home."

Marcus thought about it but shook his head. "No, I want a holodome. I've always wanted one, and now without the wife, I'm going to get it."

"All right, then," said Myron. "I'll box it up for you and have it delivered tomorrow."

After Marcus left the store. Myron had his brother come out and help him box up the order.

"What do you think?" asked Cliff.

"I hope he just comes around," said Myron. "There's still a chance."

*****

CH 2

Marcus came into the store. He wasn't angry, but he did seem annoyed.

"Myron?" he asked.

Myron came out from the back room and smiled as he greeted his friend.

"Marcus, how are things going?"

"Not well, Myron. They made the delivery yesterday, but they delivered the wrong thing. They were supposed to drop off and install the Holodome IV unit."

"Yes, why?"

"They brought the robot dog instead. I told you I didn't want the dog. I wanted the holodome. Why did they bring me the wrong thing?"

"Oh, I'm sorry, Marcus. I guess they must have gotten their wires crossed. I told them *not* to ship that. I will send the holodome right out and get it all taken care of. Sorry for the inconvenience."

"Good," Marcus answered, getting ready to leave.

"But just to be sure—you are *sure* you don't want to keep Max, right. Have you turned him on?"

"*No*. He's still in his crate. He's in the back of my truck now."

"Okay, okay. I'll send the boys out to take Max off your truck. They'll drive out to your place either this afternoon or tomorrow with the holodome. How's that?"

***

Three weeks passed, and things seemed quiet in the small town. There wasn't much going on as fall had returned with its cool, fresh breezes and shorter days of sunlight.

Max still sat in the corner of the shop where he'd been resting for nearly a year. There, he seemed lonely and forgotten even though no energy was flowing through his system. There had been no interest in him since he'd arrived, and Myron hadn't been able to find him a new home. He was a pet in search of a home, and Myron only hoped he wouldn't have to euthanize him to the scrap heap.

It was on one of those cool, crisp mornings that Glen Goodman came into the shop. Glen was a long-time resident of Bradyville and had grown up with Myron's father. Glen had long-since retired. He was a well-known lawyer in town—in fact, the only lawyer in town. When he retired, the townspeople worried that they'd have no one to turn to if they got into a legal jam. Glen had reassured them that his friends at Owens & Murphy in the next town over would take care of them if anything should arise.

"Glen, how are you and the family these days?" asked Myron. "We haven't seen you at Rotary for a while. Is everything all right?"

Glen ambled into the shop with the help of a black cane. He'd used it even before he needed it, just to "start practicing early" as he used to joke. However, with his bad hip and growing arthritis it was harder for him to get around these days.

"As well as can be expected," Glen said. "At eighty-nine, I'm doin' great, though."

"You don't look a day over forty," said Myron smiling. "So, what brings you in? Is there something you're looking for?"

"Yes," said Glen, "guidance."

"Guidance? But you're an attorney. You're supposed to give that to other people—not ask for it yourself."

"I'm retired," Glen answered. "I now ask others for guidance all the time—for free, of course."

Myron laughed. "Okay, I won't charge you this time, but what I can help with?"

"It's Marcus."

"What about him?"

"No one's seen him in weeks. He's not been in town. He's not been working his fields. His crops need to be harvested, but he's not doing that."

"Has anyone gone to check on him?"

"Yes. But he is just holed-up in his holodome room and won't come out. He says he doesn't care about his farm. He only wants to shoot aliens. That's not like him. Something's wrong."

"Can the police do anything?"

"No, they say they can't. Marcus isn't committing any crimes."

"What about his doctor?"

"Doc Wildebrand said he's likely still depressed over everything that's happened to him."

"Yeah, I'd say so. Can't the doc get involved, then?"

"Nope—not without Marcus' consent."

"What about family members?"

"They can't get through to him either. His sister, Madeleine, brought him some homemade lasagna the other day and when she went back the next day it was still out on the kitchen table. He hadn't touched it."

Myron shook his head. "I was afraid of this," he said. "But what can I do?"

"I'm told there are things that can be done with holodome systems."

"What do you mean?"

"You *know* what I mean," said Glen with a wink. "I'm told you can—let's just say—*influence* them remotely. I saw it online too. You can modify the program so it does things that can … well, let's just say … influence the user."

Myron knew exactly what Glen was talking about, but to do that would be a violation of many laws and regulations. The Pawn Shop had always done the right thing by its patrons and steered them in the right direction. *But this is pushing it,* Myron thought.

"I can't do that, Glen. You of all people would understand that."

"Yes, I do. You are a God-fearing family, and I've always respected you for that. At my age, I'm a bit too practical, I guess. Don't get me wrong, I'm a believer too, but when things get this bad, I can't just stand around and see a good man throw his life away."

"I understand," said Myron. Then, he added, "I tell you what. Here's the name of a programmer in La Salle. I've given you some ideas, but the rest is up to you."

As Myron was going to the backroom, Glen called to him. "Say, Myron. What do you think about this big dog over here?"

"I think he'd be perfect," Myron answered.

*****

CH 3

Marcus sat crouched down in his bunker. The alien attack force was expected any moment, and he clutched his M23-B plasma gun in his hands ready for the final battle. To his right was the rest of his company, a mix of men and women playing remotely from other parts of the world, all of whom were nervous about the outcome. By the end of the day, they would know if their efforts to save planet Earth from the Cygnus 3 Reptoid Race would succeed in conquering them and enslaving humanity or they would be defeated and forced to return to their constellation empty-handed.

"Major?" asked Lieutenant Harshad from India. "How much ammo do we have left? Is more coming in?"

"No, I'm afraid we only have enough for one major defensive battle," said Marcus. "After that, we're out. We'll all be captured and taken prisoner or neutralized."

"I think I'd rather be neutralized than captured," said Harshad. "They say they eat their prisoners. Is that true?"

Marcus didn't answer. He had heard the same thing but didn't want to stir up any more fear than they already had. Moments later, his first lieutenant called out again.

"There … on the horizon … I see them. They're in battle formation!"

Marcus rose from his trench and peered through his digital holoculars. Indeed, fifty kilometers off, were twenty alien battleships that had suddenly appeared, coming out of warp speed and hovering in formation over the North Atlantic coast.

Bark! Bark!

What the heck? thought Marcus looking over into the muddy, grungy trench where they had dug in to brace for the attack. There, nuzzling up against him was a tiny puppy--a small bulldog. It was terrified—its eyes wide open and its tail tucked between its back two legs. Thunderous noises were going off all around them with bombs exploding, laser pulses crackling through the air, and the high-pitched hum of the alien spacecraft spinning effortlessly in front of them and ready to administer complete annihilation.

"It's okay, buddy," said Marcus picking up the puppy hologram in his arms. The young pup seemed reassured once he fell into Marcus' arms but continued to whimper.

Then there was a screeching sound that pierced the blanket of grinding, groaning trucks, missile batteries, and defensive energy generators all around them. The dog barked again, but then suddenly ran out of the trench and into the open battlefield.

"No! Don't!" shouted Marcus watching as the battleships began unleashing their deadly plasma cannons and MAM (matter-anti-matter) missiles.

Marcus rose from the trench.

"Where are you going?" asked Sergeant Marta Rios, also with the company. "You'll be killed!"

The little dog scrambled out into the middle of the field as the energy blasts began raining down, vaporizing everything they hit.

"Come back!" screamed Marcus, scrambling out of the trench.

He started running after the little dog as it scampered on its short, stubby legs. Its mouth was open, and its tongue out and panting. But despite the danger, its tail was wagging as if he were having the time of his life.

"Come back here!" Marcus shouted again, now chasing after the little guy.

Suddenly, there was a brilliant burst of light. The crack of sound made from the expanding air around the energy field was so loud, anyone within a half mile would have been struck deaf by it.

"Major!"

But it was too late. When the smoke cleared, all that was left was a big, blackened hole in the middle of the field. Some fifteen feet across, it was all that remained of the major and his dog.

*****

CH 4

A week later, the door to the Pawn Shop opened.

"Marcus! It's good to see you again. You've surfaced!"

"Yes. I'm out and about once more," he answered, still a little disoriented by the sudden change from game room to real world. "It was good seeing everyone at Rotary last night."

"It was good seeing you there as well," said Myron. "And how's Max?"

"Max is great. I don't know what I would do without him. He's been a godsend to me—getting me out of the house and back into the swing of things."

"Good. I thought so."

Marcus smiled at Myron. "So, how did you know?"

"How did I know what?" Myron asked.

"How did you know I would end up with Max instead of the holodome?"

Myron smiled. "It's what we do. We know our customers ... sometimes better than they know themselves."

*****

ALGORITHM 42

CH 1

The dream of having one algorithm that could control all aspects of society had become a reality, and the massive computer program that was put in place to run everything—from hovercraft flight patterns, to building environmental controls, to dispatch for robo-cops, robo-ambulances, and robo firefighters—was already installed and running. Based on audio and visual commands, citizens throughout the city, the state, the nation, and the world, could access basic government functions via their computer. No more human intervention was required.

However, all this had happened over one thousand years ago.

By now, the program had evolved to assume even more functions, and the ability of life on the planet to move forward without it was in doubt. While other planets were being terraformed and converted into Earth-like places for humans, Earth itself had been kept from degrading into a cesspool of pollution and filth because of this computer—this program—this Algorithm 42.

Named after the answer to the *Hitchhiker's Guide to the Galaxy* question, forty-two became the moniker attached to this algorithm. It was no matter that in the story the supercomputer spent 7.5 million years to calculate the answer. What was important was, by then, no one remembered what the question had been.

Likewise, no one knew exactly how Algorithm 42 worked either, but few, if anyone, cared. The program worked, and that was that. Of course, that was that until it didn't—work, that is.

"What's wrong?" asked Alden Wimsbey, the Minister of Technology for Earth Quadrant One.

"I don't know," said Dr. Jacob Gnesh, the Director of Operations for Global Sanitation. "Suddenly, some of the regular routines aren't working anymore. Garbage isn't being picked up in Central America. There's a problem with the routing of orders from the central line to those in the Republic of Meximerica. There's also the …"

The director, Archibald Puck, prattled on for another few minutes about all the things going wrong in the world because of the algorithm.

"That can't be," said Gnesh. "It's been working flawlessly for 453 years."

"Well, it's not working now. Get your team in there to take a look," said Wimsbey. "We need to get this fixed as soon as possible."

"But we've not tinkered with the algorithm in a thousand years," said Gnesh. "We can't just go in and change it."

"What happened 453 years ago, then?" asked Wimsbey. "What did they do then when it errored?"

"It was human error. There was nothing wrong with the algorithm."

"I see. Well, maybe that's the problem now too."

However, it wasn't. After reviewing the program, the scientists found that it had changed on its own accord in iterations over the years. The changes were tiny, imperceptible, but over time they added up. Finally, they had affected the way the sanitation program ran, causing problems.

After a month of intense study, the team came back with a recommendation: modify the program back to its original form.

"I agree," said Wimsbey. "Let's make the changes straight away."

The order went out to make the first changes to the code, and the team went to work logging in to make them online.

"Jack, I'm trying to login to the mainframe and access the source code ledgers, but I'm having problems."

"What kind of problems?"

"The computer is kicking me out. I can't get beyond the first firewall," said Dr. Frank Wilkins, deputy director to Gnesh.

"Try the B2 Protocols. They should get you in."

A few minutes later.

"I still can't get in, Jack."

Gnesh went to the computer terminal and attached the headset to his own brain. He began thinking of the proper sequence of codes needed to get into the source layer and expected them to register and be implemented. But he too found that he was blocked.

"I'm going to try the C1d protocol."

Gnesh pulled off the head probes and re-adjusted them. Then he got a copy of the C1d protocol and plugged it into the system to upload. Immediately, he was stopped. He pushed the buttons a few more times to get it to load, but the same error message came up: *Error! Illegal Action.*

"Damn it!" said Gnesh.

He tried one more time.

"Damn ..."

Wilkins didn't hear the last words and looked over at his colleague.

"Jack! What's wrong?"

Gnesh's eyes were opened wide and unblinking, but his body was trembling as if it were suffering from some electric pulse. His brain sensors showed they were still connected to the grid and trying to make commands to change the program.

"Jack!"

Wilkins grabbed Gnesh and pulled him off his chair. He laid him down next to the console before leaping up and slamming his hand against the neuroconnection lever.

"Call 912. Get emergency in here, now!"

Gnesh's body began convulsing—now shaking violently. Wilkins covered him with a blanket to keep him from going into shock, and they rushed him to the hospital.

It was another two days before anyone could visit him in the hospital. His vitals had stabilized, and he had regained consciousness by the time Wilkins entered his room.

"How are you feeling, Jack?" asked the associate director, coming to Gnesh's bed.

"Better, I think."

"Good. You look better than you did when we strapped you into the hoverEMT unit."

Gnesh smiled. "Good. How's the software change going?"

Wilkins was quiet.

"Not well, I take it."

"We're working on it," said Wilkins.

"Have you been able to get into the program?"

"No."

"When do you think you will?"

Wilkins shrugged.

"That's not encouraging," said Gnesh.

"No. I'm afraid it's not."

*****

CH 2

Five years later, the team was no closer to penetrating the firewall barrier put up by the algorithm than they had been earlier. In fact, now things were worse. As if in retaliation, other programs began failing, including those for water treatment, emergency police and fire services and street camera surveillance. Equipment used in other areas such as hyper-tollbooth monitoring and hovercraft speed cameras were also out.

"What is happening?" asked Dr. Gnesh, who was still involved with the project.

"I don't know," answered his new associate, Dr. James McAllen. "Everything we do is countermanded and blocked by the computer. It's as if the algorithm knows what we are about to do or anticipates it. It's like it can read our minds."

"Hmmm. I wonder ..."

"It's crazy, I know," said McAllen.

"No, Jim. It may not be."

"So, what are you thinking?"

"I wonder if it has evolved to the point that it *can* read our thoughts."

"No. There's no way that ..."

"No way? Really? After a thousand years, you don't think an algorithm could evolve too? You don't think it could rise to telepathy?"

"No."

"Well, you may be right," said Dr. Gnesh. "Then, again, I think you're wrong. I think it can, and I think it has."

"Okay. If it has, then what can we do?"

"We must wear lead helmets ... of sorts."

"What?"

"We must shield ourselves from the invasive probe of Algorithm 42. I suggest using a degraded plutonium hyperbarrier," said Gnesh. "It's what they used during the last war to deflect missile warheads from sensitive targets on the ground."

"How would that work?" exclaimed McAllen.

Yet, with all the concern, they were able to fabricate a shield of sorts from the omnipresent eye of Algorithm 42. It was an uncomfortable, but necessary cap that Gnesh insisted be worn by every member of the team.

"Let's see what happens now," said the director.

Almost immediately, the new solutions being developed by the team began to take hold. Each had more impact than any before. But then, there was another snag.

"Doctor, you have to see this," said McAllen.

Gnesh came over to the holographic monitor. The image was suspended in mid-air with all the dimensions of a 3D picture. The doctor rotated the image and looked at it from different angles.

"We're approaching this wrong," said Gnesh. "All of our computations are using Base 10."

"Yeah, so?"

"If you recall the Hitchhiker's Guide to the Galaxy, the question to the answer of forty-two was what?"

"I don't know."

"What is six times nine?"

"But that isn't forty-two," exclaimed McAllen.

"You're right. It isn't. It's fifty-four."

"I don't understand."

"We need to calculate our modifications to the algorithm using a different base. It's not ten. It's never been ten. Algorithm 42 was never developed using formulae in Base 10."

"Then what was it?"

"Base 12. It should all be based on 12, not 10. That's why it's resisting. It believes we are an alien or hostile race or form that is trying to prevent it from doing its job. If we use Base 12, it will know we are the creators ... of the ones who created it."

"How are you getting to Base 12?" asked McAllen.

"It's simple, my good Holmes. Gnesh smiled. His brilliance knew no bounds. "What do you get when you subtract fifty-four from forty-two?"

*****

CH 3

"I must say," said the Global President, Modicum Turley. "I didn't think it was possible to modify the algorithm and bring it back to normalcy. I was afraid it would spin out of control and leave us with no alternative but to try to shut it down completely."

"Mr. President, that would not have worked either. It would not have let you shut it down. It would have stopped you," said Gnesh.

"Not possible," said Turley with all the hubris he was used to displaying. "I have final authority of these sorts of things."

"With all due respect, sir. The system runs things. Even with our small modifications, it *allowed* it. Let's not have any misconceptions."

"I can't stand for that."

"Well, that's the truth. We can only do as much as it allows. It's calling the shots, sir. Not us," said Gnesh.

"Then what do we do going forward?" asked the president. "Should we find another algorithm to replace it?"

"Perhaps," said Gnesh, "however, as I always say, 'deal with the devil you know rather than the one you don't'."

"What's that supposed to mean?"

"It means that we know we can deal with this algorithm if we use Base 12 as the code. If we create another, we don't know what it might do."

"True. But what if Algorithm 42 evolves to a point that it no longer accepts or acknowledges Base 12 commands?"

Gnesh smiled. "Let's just hope someone with a human brain evolves faster than it does."

*****

ALEXANDRIA

CH 1

Dr. Alford Peabody had been exploring the thousands of islands of Indonesia for over fifty years. In total, there was said to be over seventeen thousand such islands that constitute the country—the best known of which was Java.

However, Peabody had worked his way east and had studied the primitive peoples throughout the Tenggara and Timor-Leste region that resided in the Savu Sea. Although only two villages he found had never seen a white man before and were totally isolated from the rest of the world, most were well connected to the government in Jakarta on one of the main islands.

But Peabody wasn't just any anthropologist; he was one of some renown. He had written extensively about the cultures amongst the many tribes living on the islands and the impact of Islam on the ancient religious practices of the people. Like Christianity before it, Islam had dislodged the traditions of the tribes and forced conversion to the Muslim faith. According to the Muslin faith, turning away from Islam was an act punishable by death. This dissuaded many from making a change.

Peabody's small boat approached a tiny island set just east of the Leti archipelago. It was such a small dot of land that a foreigner hadn't visited it in decades, if not centuries. The tribe there still practiced the ways, customs, and trades of their forefathers—fishing and farming.

There was no main town as the population held less than two hundred inhabitants on the entire island. Yet, as Peabody's boat pulled to shore, men from the village were alerted to the foreigner, and by the time he waded onto the sandy shores, there were nine sturdy, muscular men waiting to see why he had come to visit.

The professor had brought with him a pocket translator—one that could decipher seven regional languages used on other islands nearby. One of these, Leti, was thought to be the language of the island, and fortunately for Peabody, it was.

"Take me to your leader," said Peabody wading ashore. He smiled and chuckled subtly at the cliché. But when the men of the tribe only stared at him, he repeated it. "Take me to your chief—you know, the one who is in charge here."

One man nodded and strode off apparently assuming the visitors would follow him. He walked up a single, tread-worn path cut into a green and lush hill which lead to the village. Grass huts appeared on the next rise, just outside a thick and foreboding wall of tall trees that formed a perimeter to guard the nearby tropical jungle beyond.

Arriving in the village, Peabody was surprised as a young boy hurried up to him, offering something in his small hands. The boy was no more than seven or eight and held an impish smile. He was missing two of his front baby teeth, and his adult ones had yet to grow in. His dark hair was straight and brushed over his forehead in a continuous bang. The boy was excited to see the foreigner and said something quickly in his Leti language; however, Peabody had to look to his machine and wait for a translation.

"Sir? Would you like to buy this key?" the translator asked, converting what the boy said into English.

Indeed, in the boy's hand was a metal key. It was odd, as the shape and composition were not something that could have been made in the village. Made of some luminous, smooth metal, the key had a rounded head and two prong-like bodies coming from it. The prongs had many tiny holes drilled into each—something that would have taken special machinery to craft.

"What is this a key to?" asked Peabody, turning it over and looking at it carefully.

The small boy listened to explorer's translator device, amazed by the sound coming from it. He nodded that he understood and said, "I don't know. I found it in the hills up there." The boy pointed to another series of hills—these twice as high as the ones Peabody had hiked to get to the village.

"What do you want for it?" asked Peabody.

The boy pointed at the translator, but Peabody shook his head. Then, the boy pointed to a necklace of turquoise stones the professor had around his neck. Peabody had worn that necklace for more than twenty years, and no one had ever asked for it in return for something. It wasn't valuable, but figured it was more valuable than some worthless key the boy had dug up in the hillside.

However, taking pity on the boy, Peabody smiled and nodded, taking the necklace off and giving it to the boy who handed him the key. The boy was ecstatic, running off proudly and yelling at the top of his lungs about the great deal he'd gotten from the visitor.

Only two huts down, a door opened, and an elderly man came out of another abode. He had long, stringy hair down the middle of his back and many rows of yellow and orange necklaces that lined his chest. Around his waist was only a simple, white cloth tied in a knot in front. On his head, he wore a feathered headdress of colorful feathers and plumes ranging the entire rainbow spectrum. He held no bones in his nose or earlobes, but he did wear a heavy striping of white paint across his forehead and on his cheeks. His gray beard was thick and bushy like his hair and filled his face—only his eyes and nose were easily recognizable from the rest of the portrait.

"Where are you from?" said the man through Peabody's translator.

"I am from a land far from here," said Peabody. "Have you had any other visitors from outside your island?"

"Yes," said the man, turning and going back inside his hut. There, he sat down on the earthen ground and crossed his legs as if in a yoga position. "Others here, but it was long ago. No one here remembers but it has been told by our ancestors."

"I do not mean you any harm," said Peabody. "I only come to listen and to talk to you about your culture and people."

The chief didn't seem to understand those concepts, but he was amenable to having the explorer and his small band stay a while.

"Thank you for your hospitality," said Peabody. "I look forward to talking to you and others during the next few days."

"There only one rule," said the chief. "You may not go beyond the second hill. That is sacred ground. If you go there, you will be killed. Do you understand?"

Peabody drew back. He'd never been threatened like that before, but he nodded in agreement before leaving with the warriors.

The chief directed one of his warriors to take Peabody and his party to another hut nearby. It was larger than most others in the village except for the chief's. Made of grass with a dirt floor, the hut had a hole in the center off the roof to allow smoke from a fire to drift up and clear the dwelling.

The next few days were busy for the professor as he talked to the chief and others in the village. Peabody recorded a great deal about the way the people lived, hunted, married, kept law and order, developed their sons and daughters, and worshipped. They prayed to the gods of the earth, the water, and the sky—all the things they could see. But they were protective of the sacred grounds not far from their village. All told him the same thing: the grounds were holy and must not be defiled by him or anyone in his party.

When Peabody returned to an audience with the chief, he asked him more about the holy grounds and why they were considered sacred.

"These were the lands bestowed on our people by the gods," said the chief. "Although I have never been there, my father and his father told stories about an enormous building there. It was made by the gods themselves and the gods lived there until many thousand years ago when they returned to the skies." He pointed upward toward the roof of the hut.

"Who were these gods?" asked Peabody, recording everything.

"They came down in swirling houses that were shiny and blinked with brilliant, colored lights like the sun. They didn't come out of these houses in the sky, but suddenly appeared on the ground. They said they were from those houses."

"I see," said Peabody.

"They had big heads and big, dark eyes—almost black. They were large beings too—almost twice as tall as our people. They were giants compared to us and strong and mighty. They carried small weapons with them for protection. When they shot them, nothing came out but whatever they were shooting at instantly fell to the ground dead. They shot many animals with them. They said they killed them for food."

"How did you and your people treat them?"

"They were gods. We bow to them—me and my warrior chieftains. They gods. Must show them respect or they be unhappy with us."

"What about the city then? They must have come out of their houses in the sky to live there?"

"Yes," said the chief. "Some left and used their houses to move huge stones into place on the Sacred Mountain. That's how they built them. Then, when they finished, there were those who stayed. The others left in the floating houses. They have not come back."

"Do you know how long ago that was?"

"I do not know. My father didn't know either, but it was a very long time—hundreds of generations ago."

"And they lived on the sacred ground? Did your ancestors interact with them?"

"Yes. My ancestors worked under them. They dug in the earth for minerals the gods wanted. They had no choice but to work. Our leaders—kings—did not fight the gods because they were too powerful."

"Why did they—the gods—leave the Sacred Mountain?"

"We do not know. One day, some came back in their swirling houses in the sky, and the gods on the mountain suddenly disappeared. Then, the swirling houses vanished too. The stories tell us that it all happened within a day."

Peabody chuckled.

"What is so funny?" asked the leader, slightly offended.

"Nothing. I am exceedingly interested in your story. Thank you."

"One more thing," said the chief. "They said we are not to live on the Sacred Mountain or go there. It is forbidden. They said they will return one day and wish for it all to be as they left it. There cannot be anything changed or turned, or they will unleash their wrath on the village below."

"Your village," said Peabody.

"Yes, my village," answered the chief sternly.

Peabody left with more questions than he had before. As he walked to his hut, he glanced out toward the taller hills that marked the boundary of the sacred land. *It would only take a few hours,* he thought. *They would never know I was there.*

*****

CH 2

Just as the sun was coming up in the east, Peabody was already hiking up the first hill toward the sacred grounds. He expected to find something amazing and astounding as he walked the crest of the second hill where the grounds were to begin, but he found no such thing—only another hill that lay beyond.

Two hours later, he was still hiking, getting farther and farther from the village and its people. The rare and unusual town of the gods was only supposed to be a short distance, but he was finding out quickly that it wasn't. Into the third hour, Peabody began to have second thoughts about his trip. Many more hours, and he would have trouble getting back to his hut before the evening supper with the chief, which was another requirement of his stay. But he decided to press on, despite the risks.

Finally, he reached a particularly steep, high hill and was able to look out across a steep ravine spanned by an ancient wood and rope bridge. There in the distance was a group of buildings. They were magnificent— standing like the temples in Egypt. They were structures like he had never seen before; only those of Angkor Wat in Cambodia were even remotely similar.

One building in the center stood tallest of all—some four hundred feet in the air. He was awestruck, wondering how anyone could have built such structures in the middle of jungle so long ago. Stone was not plentiful, and it would have taken a Herculean effort to move them to that spot.

But Peabody had another problem. If he continued to the sacred city, he would not be able to return to the village and the chief in time that evening. He was risking everything by pushing onward. Yet, his curiosity overwhelmed him, and he pressed ahead.

It was be a decision he would find no time to regret later.

*****

CH 3

That night in the village, the chief waited, and when Peabody did not show up for supper, he sent his guards to the hut to find him. He wasn't there.

The chief knew where he'd gone, and he sighed, knowing what he would have to do when the foreigner returned. It was not something he would relish, but it would have to be done to protect the traditions and ways of their people. *If one person were allowed to violate the rules and go to the sacred place, then anyone could,* he thought. The chief could not allow this.

***

By nightfall, Peabody reached the sacred city. As the sun began to set, he strode along the wide avenues and tall, stone buildings that resembled those of ancient civilizations found elsewhere on Earth. Of course, it was all overgrown with vegetation and most of the buildings had deteriorated from the winds, rains, and flora and fauna that had taken over much of where the city had been. Yet, it was clear that the area had once been the home of a thriving community.

Peabody lit a makeshift torch he had created from a sturdy stick and dried moss from trees nearby. He held it out and let the fire catch, bursting into a full flame. Then, he entered one of the many enormous structures built as part of the central city hub. All the edifices had entryways over nine feet tall, suggesting that whoever had lived there had been a tall people. Indeed, these could have been the very giants the chief had mentioned in his talk about ancient folklore.

Even though the buildings looked archaic, their insides contained the remnants of an advanced society—particularly in the era they were built. There were stone ovens, wells for water, rain capturing systems on the roofs, stone covers in the roads suggesting an underground sewer system, roads lined with stone to avoid the mud that bogged down carts, grooves in the roads, suggesting chariots or carts were used, and many other signs.

In addition, there were mosaics in the dwellings—both on the floors and walls. Peabody could see the residue of fresco-like paintings of extraordinary detail, and the broken remains of exquisite pottery and sculptures. These ranged from human and animal forms to other more geometric designs—again suggesting an advanced knowledge of mathematics and geometry.

Peabody continued, holding out his torch and moving to one of the largest buildings in the complex. There, he entered and looked up. The ceilings were nearly seventy feet high, and lining the walls were wooden shelves. There were thousands of shelves, and they were all perched on the walls nearly to the top of the high ceiling. He moved closer to see what was on the shelves, and it was then that he gasped.

"My god," he murmured. "It can't be!"

Stacked high on each shelf were scrolls and books. Ancient clay tablets were also stacked neatly in rows and columns as if a librarian had just been through the area moments earlier to organize and maintain it.

Peabody picked up a few. They were inexplicably intact. He couldn't explain how such relics could survive in the hot and humid environment of Indonesia. They should have rotted away eons ago, yet they were there.

The first scroll he examined was fragile but not crumbling. He carefully unrolled it. The heading was in Latin: *Democritus of Abdera--On the Planets*. The next: *Democritus of Abdera—The Causes of Atmospheric Phenomena*. A third: *Agrippina the Younger--Homer's Catalogue of Ships Archimedes'*, and others. There was Aristotle's book on Pythagoras; a letter from Callinicos to Cleopatra on *The History of Alexandria*; Cato the Elder's *Origines* and *The History of Rome*; Eudemus' *History of Mathematics* and *History of Astronomy*; Homer's *Margites*; Lucan's *Orpheus* and his *Medea*; Protagoras' *On Truth*; Quintilian's *On Cicero's Republic* and *The Physical Defects of Mankind*, and many, many others. All were lost works—lost masterpieces. They were those thought not to have survived the burning of perhaps the greatest library of works ever built--one more than twenty-five hundred years earlier.

My God, thought Peabody. *These are the manuscripts and lost works from the Library of Alexandria.*

At its zenith, the library housed nearly 400,000 works and required over one hundred people to manage them. Established by Alexander the Great in 334 BC, the library was just outside of modern-day city of Cairo, in Alexandria, on the shores of the Mediterranean. The library was a magnet for special works created from scholars throughout Europe and the Middle East. Priceless works were thought lost during the fire that was ordered by Theophilus the patriarch of Alexandria in 391AD. However, this fire did not destroy the structure. The final act of destruction came from Caliph Omar in 640AD who stated that any volume that contradicted the Koran would be destroyed—and so they were.

Or maybe not.

Peabody looked up at the towering walls filled with shelves chocked full of dusty manuscripts and scrolls. *What else might be here?* he thought, tingling with the realization that he may have stumbled on one of the greatest finds in human history.

After several hours, his eyes grew heavy. His torch was going out, and he lay down on the stone floor to fall asleep. Tomorrow would be another day.

*****

CH 4

The rays of the morning sun streamed in through a low opening in the stones. Peabody cleared his eyes and awoke to marvel at the daylight scene of the spectacular library all around him. It was even more magnificent now than it had been the previous evening. There were not thousands of books and manuscripts—but *millions*. It was something that nearly brought the experienced scientist to his knees.

Peabody left the library and headed directly for the tallest building in the complex. It resembled the Mayan temple of Chichen Itza in Mexico. The long, stone staircase in front rose hundreds of steps to the top where the stone cupola stood lined with forty or more columns.

By the time Peabody reached the top, he was out of breath and needed to stoop over to catch his wind. Surveying the temple, he found it sealed; there was a heavy, stone door blocking the entrance.

Peabody pushed and pulled on the door, but it would not move. It was frozen in place, either by nature and time or by a human or some other hand. He thought about his options, but there was nothing nearby to pry it open.

So discouraged, he reluctantly began the long trip down the way he had come. Yet, only a few steps down, he stopped and smiled. Digging into his pocket he pulled out something he'd almost forgotten about.

I wonder? he thought.

The professor went back up to the door and looked it over more carefully. This time, he spotted a small hole in the center, waist high. It was caked with sand and dirt and appeared much smaller than it really was. Carefully, he began digging out the sediment with his fingers until the opening grew wider. In fact, he discovered there were two openings—just the right spacing for the two-pronged key he had bought from the young boy in the village.

But just then, he heard noises coming from below at the base of the temple. There were at least ten warriors hurrying toward it and then running up the stairs toward him. They were the chief's men and obviously sent to find him and bring him back to face his fate.

Fumbling with the key, he pushed it into the holes and locked it into place. He turned the etched metal rods and heard a distinct *click*. But by then, the warriors had almost reached the top.

Quickly, he pushed on the stone door which grudgingly gave way. Using all his might, he pressed his shoulder against it and watched it inch open, slowly … painfully slowly. But time was running out.

"Stop!" shouted one of the warriors nearing the apex—the words translated by Peabody's machine. The door opening was not yet wide enough for him to slip through, and when the spears began flying toward him, he obeyed, stopping and turning toward his attackers. Peabody held up his hands as if he were being arrested in New York City for spraying graffiti on subway car.

The warriors swarmed, and the leader grabbed him harshly, holding his arms to take him back down the stone staircase.

"Wait!" cried Peabody, using his translator. "You do understand that if you take me back to the village, the chief will have you killed too."

The men looked at him curiously. The leader shook his head. "No. Chief would not do that."

"Why? Aren't *all* people forbidden from coming here?"

"Yes, but chief ordered us to come and bring you back."

"Do you believe the chief will allow you to live after seeing this place? He hasn't seen this place. If you returned, you would threaten him with what you've seen here. The people of the village will believe you and wonder why you lived to tell them about it. The chief would fear you will become more favored by the gods than he. He will have no choice but to have you killed—along with me."

The leader looked at the door which now tempted him inside. It was ajar, and what was inside beckoned him. He eased his grip on Peabody and went to the door, motioning for several of his men to help him push it open. It moved and swung freely open.

*****

CH 5

A thick, gray mist swirled inside the door and, thus, inside the temple. The leader motioned for his men to wait, and he cautiously walked inside before quickly vanishing. Everyone stood a few minutes, but when their leader didn't return, they looked at each other wondering what to do. After hesitating, another man cautiously went through the opening too. But when he didn't return either, the other men in the party were frightened and ran, hurrying down the long stairs to the bottom of the temple pyramid. Two stumbled and rolled part of the way after tripping in their haste. The others barely made it to the grass before they too were tripping over each other to escape.

Then, the explorer returned to the temple opening. He stuck his hand into the swirling, gray mist but felt nothing. Suddenly, the cloud parted, and standing in front of him was a huge figure—one over eight feet tall. It was broad-shouldered, with a large head and black eyes. Its skin was pale and smooth, and it appeared to have small openings for a nose and larger ones on either side of its head where its ears might have been. Long and sinewy were its arms, reaching down below its waist, and Peabody could see that it had six fingers on each hand. Dressed in an ancient, lavender and gray tunic with strands of gold around its neck and wrists, it was an imposing, even frightening, sight.

Calming himself, the explorer took a deep breath. "Hello," is all he could think to say. Yet, his translator converted the word into a sound he had never heard before, and the language and dialect showing on its screen was comprised of strange symbols that were also unknown to him.

Suddenly from outside and below around the temple, Peabody heard more loud voices. He peered out through the doorway. In the distance, he saw hundreds of warriors running toward the base of the temple and starting up the stairs.

Panicked, he glanced back at the figure, which finally spoke to him. But the translator struggled to find an English translation. The sounds from the being were not words but rather a series of clicks and beeps. So, Peabody spoke again.

"Who are you?" he asked quickly.

"That matters not," said the figure, converting suddenly to English. "What matters is whether you will choose to come through this portal or remain here."

"Where does the portal lead?"

"To our ship which is orbiting just beyond your planet Mars. We are a benevolent society, and we wish only to help mankind. However, you have free will. You may choose to stay and face certain death or come with me and take your chances."

There was no emotion in the being's voice—at least not like a human feeling. It was flat and without intonation or inflection.

Peabody looked back down the stairs. The warriors were starting to throw their spears at him once more. One bounced off the stone wall next to his head. At that moment, the decision wasn't hard.

Peabody jumped through the opening. The mist closed in around him, and the door slammed shut. He and the secrets of the sacred grounds and Library of Alexandria vanished with him.

On the floor of the temple lay the key. One of the warriors picked it up and looked at it.

"What's that?" asked another warrior in Leti, watching as the first turned it over in his hand.

"Junk, I think," said the first.

He took the key and threw it out of the doorway. They listened as it bounced down the stone staircase landing somewhere outside. They merely shrugged and closed the temple door.

***

300 years later

A young boy from the village was with a group of friends. They had snuck off to the sacred city—an area prohibited by the local village chief. They boys explored the ruins for a short time, knowing they needed to rush back to the village before night fell and they might be caught.

Uton rounded the corner of the Great Wall which enclosed the tall, majestic temple in the city center. He was trying to find his friends so they could return to the village together. But something was shimmering on the ground in front of him.

He picked it up.

"What's that?" asked Lobon, one of the boys in the group, finally finding his friend.

"I don't know," said Uton, "but it looks valuable."

"It's junk," said Lobon. "Just leave it."

"No, I'm keeping it. If it's not valuable now, it looks like it's something that could be in the future."

*****

OMNIBIT

CH I

The world had worked for thousands of years by trading goats and chickens for rugs and clothing. The next stage was the use of precious metals like gold and silver to exchange for other valuable goods and services. Then, these metals were stamped into coins by a ruler or patriarch with his image to guarantee proper payment. These coins were eventually replaced with paper notes from banks that guaranteed and backed the slips with hard currency or precious metals. As trade expanded beyond state borders, local bank notes weren't known outside their own region and weren't considered valid tender. So, states created their own currency notes, replacing those of their local banks. These too were supported by real commodities. Once the states combined into a federation, the federal government banned state currencies and authorized only notes made and guaranteed by the federal government. Finally, the backing of paper currency was abandoned as well, leaving only the intentions of the state to defend the value of its paper money. Gold and silver no longer backed the paper. This became known as fiat money.

But this wasn't the end of the string. Paper money was replaced first by personal checks and then by credit cards, debit cards, and other means to convey liquidity. Finally, the world had evolved to bits and bytes to represent money and wealth. These crypto currencies replaced all paper and precious metals and became the new "gold standard." However, there was little backing the value of this bit-coin products and little way to validate their worth. However, as crypto-currencies came and went – being invented and abandoned—a new dominant method of payment came into being: *OmniScan*.

OmniScan was created by a genius, Antoine Vaseer, who had developed an unbreakable algorithm as the basis for creating the Internet currency. He, and he alone, knew the solution. It was all a big secret, and Antoine Vaseer wanted it to stay that way.

*****

CH 2

It was thought that Vaseer's formula for determining the total available OmniBits in circulation was based on the rare element of scandium or a combination of thorium, thulium, lutetium, tantalum, and rhenium. Of course, there was some uranium and gold also factored in to allow the currency to grow, as the others were so rare few new sources were ever found on Earth.

But Vaseer's formula was locked away in a high security vault in Geneva, Switzerland, and was only accessible by two people on Earth. In the event of Vaseer's death, his will would be read in the presence of only those two people. He had known the two men since his days at Columbia University and had full trust in them and their ability to safeguard the formula. The world's economy depended on it.

However, it would be those very two men who would be the first to violate that trust.

*****

CH 3

Aaron Romstein had grown up rich. His grandfather had created and sold an energy distribution company for billions. This wealth had affected his children and now his grandchildren. Both generations had become lazy and entitled. However, of all the descendants, Aaron was smart and creative, and he knew a good deal and opportunity when he saw one.

Romstein and Vaseer were roommates at Columbia and had stayed in touch for decades after graduation. Also in their college group was another long-time friend, Richard Kirk. Romstein and Kirk formed a business partnership shortly after leaving the university. Although they did quite well, they left a trail of bodies behind in their business dealings. Burning bridge after bridge by screwing over their employees, vendors and even some customers, the two eventually found themselves embroiled in several lawsuits that threatened to bankrupt them.

Vaseer was unaware of their difficulties and was eager to enter into an agreement for them to watch over the formula. Vaseer was a righteous man and had become more faithful as the years went by. His two friends had taken the other path, and by the time the partnership was forged, the two groups couldn't have been further apart ideologically. In the agreement, Vaseer turned over the formula to the two together with his ability to access it. He never wished to be accused of manipulating the algorithm for his own personal gain.

But as the litigation costs rose and the settlements to complainants increased from millions and tens of millions to hundreds of millions, Romstein and Kirk became desperate to find new sources of funds. It didn't take them long to seize upon the opportunity to cash in on their agreement with Vaseer.

"Let's manipulate the OmniBit," said Romstein. "We can buy or short it as we need to and change the formula, so the price goes up or goes down to make us more money."

Romstein and Kirk flew to Zurich, Switzerland, where they took a taxi directly to the DSM Bank downtown. Showing their IDs to the bank vice president, they were taken to the central vault. There, they found the lockbox—number 3303—and entered their primary key, while the VP entered his secondary key to remove the small box from its place in the wall. Pulling it out, the bank officer placed it on the viewing table in the middle of the vault. Again, he used the two keys to unlock the box and open the lid.

"Excellent," said Romstein smiling as he stared at what was inside. There was only one item in the box: a thin, white envelope.

Eagerly, Romstein grabbed the blank envelope, ripped it open and read the letter inside.

> *2 beaten egg*
> *1 cup milk*
> *2 teaspoon paprika*
> *1/2 teaspoon poultry seasoning*
> *4 teaspoons garlic salt*
> *2 teaspoon black pepper*
> *2 cup all-purpose flour*
> *2 cups beer*

> *This is the recipe—that runs the world—or not. If you find this, it means that you violated the terms of the agreement. You were not supposed to open the lock box until after my will was read, which means I am still alive at this reading.*

*****

CH 4

When Vaseer found out about the betrayal, he was outraged. He couldn't believe his two best friends would back-stab him as they had. Immediately, he contacted his attorney and brought charges against Romstein and Kirk to add to their legal woes.

However, three years later, Vaseer had a heart attack in his office at the university where he taught mathematics. He died a few days later. It was at the reading of the will when the truth was revealed.

"Thank you all for coming," said Warren Hersch, Vaseer's attorney, and administrator of his estate. "I will proceed with the reading of the will."

Hersch cleared his throat. "This is the last will and testament of Antoine Louis Vaseer, this day July 9, 2092."

Hersch went on through the legalese and into the details of the will. Then, he came to the last section.

"And furthermore, as for the OmniBit Algorithm …"

Everyone in the room sat up, listening more intently.

"The details behind the algorithm can be found in deposit box 42 at the DSM Bank of Zurich. As of the reading of my will, there is only one person who has access to this box, and they will remain anonymous. If they die before my passing, arrangements have been made for access to be granted to another."

People in the room looked around at others sitting there to spot any reaction by someone who might be the one to whom access had been given. However, no one seemed overtly calm or unsurprised by the announcement. But Hersch continued.

"I know many of you will wonder about the contents of the envelope discovered by my former partners. I understand that the letter was destroyed. Therefore, I can announce to you what was in that letter. It held a value greater than that of the algorithm itself. Had my partners only known."

"What was it?" asked many in the crowd.

Hersch smiled as read further. "I purchased this from a colonel many years ago, and always thought it might come in handy someday."

"What was it?"

Hersch looked up. "It was the recipe for Kentucky Fried Chicken—one of the best kept secrets in the world. The recipe itself is rumored to be worth nearly a trillion dollars."

Hersch laughed. "If they had only known."

*****

GLOBAL CURE

CH 1

Dr. Maria Martinov sat on a banker's box in the dimly lit downstairs archives of Omni Inc., the research company for which she'd spent the last seven years of her career. A brilliant scientist in her own right, Dr. Martinov was working on a project to isolate proteins specifically targeted as the cause for Type 2 diabetes. Following up on previous studies on the KSRP protein and its role in insulin signaling pathways, Maria was making good progress.

"Nope, not this one," she muttered under her breath as she flipped through the old, paper records of research conducted by other scientists at the lab.

In this case, she was looking for experiments conducted by Dr. Boris Novrowski during the 1950s and 1960s in connection with his work on diabetes. He was a renowned scientific researcher who had dabbled in many different areas, including cures for diabetes, cancer, and Alzheimer's. He had died in 1974, apparently of natural causes at his home in West Palm Beach, Florida. Yet, there were many who were suspicious of the cited cause of his death.

Novrowski's work spanned little more than twenty-three years from 1951 until his death in 1974 at the age of only fifty-four. He had breakthroughs on many different fronts—from chemical compounds, to natural remedies, to the beginning of the genetic revolution and discovery of genetic defects as possible triggers for disease. Yet, the county coroner had proclaimed that Novrowski had met his fate from a simple coronary infarction—he had suffered a heart attack.

Maria continued going through the records one-by-one, pushing each aside and hoping she would uncover the elusive study she knew should be there. And although many of the paper records had been scanned into the computer database of the company, she had found no such file in the system.

"Nope. Nope. Nope …"

Then her eyes scanned the heading of the next folder.

File No. NOV01892-4

Date: 2 March 1971

Title: Promising Success from DCA on Cancer Patients

Maria thought it was intriguing enough to spend a moment and get sidetracked by reading what the paper had to say.

Abstract:

Based on preliminary results and testing of over 325 patients with moderate (Stage III) to advanced (Stage IV) forms of esophageal, Colona rectal, and stomach cancers, the results brought by administering doses ranging from 75 mg to 100 mg of dichloroacetate (DCA) was remarkable. Of the patient population, 92.3 percent showed marked reductions in cancer masses with 83.8 percent having complete disappearance of cancer traces and no regression after two years.

The study results must be pursued vigorously, as this compound has also shown similar success in lung, breast, brain, bone and many other cancers.

The abstract continued, giving details of the experiments and the outcomes. Behind the paper were hundreds of pages of documentation supporting the claims and the conclusions.

Hours passed, and Maria continued reading until she suddenly looked at her watch: 7:15 PM.

"*Shit!*" she exclaimed, seeing how late the hour was.

Quickly, she slipped the abstract into a folder and hurried to her office to pack up her things and drive home. She was saddened not to have found Novrowski's work on diabetes, but she was now more intrigued by what she had found on his cancer work—something she had known nothing about.

Once at home, she booted up her computer and began searching for more information on this strange compound and what research and experimentation had been done with it since it was first identified nearly seventy years earlier. Her first queries picked up on the Novrowski trail, trying to find other work sourced by the scientist on the subject. However, of the few initial search results that came up, all gave her the same messages.

Error 404 Website Not Found, or

This Website has been taken down for violating this platform's rules and regulations.

She struggled to find a site that would tell her something—anything—about his work in the area. Finally, she pulled up her second search engine and dove into waters in which she had never swum before—the Deep Web.

Pulling up onion sites, she finally found several that gave her the information she knew had to be there.

DCA Proved to have Remarkable Healing Abilities

Thirty-year Study Shows DCA Effect on Cancer Cells

Novrowski Didn't Live to See the Fruits of his Work

All the articles explained in detail the positive results that were replicated from other experiments using DCA on cancer cells. Armed with the extensive information offered from the Deep Net, Maria went to see her boss the next day. Dr. Leonard Stimpson was in his early seventies and had been with the company for nearly forty years. As Director of Research and Development, Stimpson had seen many fads and promising solutions come and go without success. At the same time, he had overseen many which had been remarkably efficient at curing or, at a minimum, slowing a disease.

"Hey, Maria, it's been a few weeks since you've stopped-in to chat. How is the diabetes project going?" asked Stimpson.

"That part's fine, Dr. Stimpson. But that's not why I'm here. I want to talk to you about something else, actually. It's something I found in the records room in the basement."

Maria handed the director her folder with a summary on top that outlined what she'd found. Behind it were pages of detail and clinical support that she had extracted from the Deep Web. Stimpson opened the folder and quickly scanned the summary and attached abstract. Within a minute, he closed the folder and pushed it back across his desk to her. He was no longer smiling.

"Maria, I think it's best if you shred this. It will not be helpful to you or your career. Do you understand?"

"But it suggests there *is* a cure for cancer. Isn't that how you read this?" she asked.

"Maria, I'll say this one more time. Do *not* pursue this. Let it go."

"But ..."

"Maria. Let it go."

Stimpson swiveled his chair back toward his computer screen, clearly trying to convey that their meeting was over. At first, Maria hesitated to get up. It wasn't until he looked at her again—this time glaring at her—that she got the message.

"As I said. I think we're done here, Maria."

*****

However, Maria decided that she was not done.

The meeting with Stimpson had done nothing to dissuade her from pursuing the matter. In fact, in had emboldened her. She continued looking into the Novrowski paper and the background surrounding his mysterious death. She knew where there was smoke, there was fire, and she wouldn't give up until she saw the flames.

Novrowski's report on the effects of DCA came out in 1972 and was widely criticized—even denounced. He was demonized by the medical community and big pharmaceutical companies saying his methods were unsound and his findings were inaccurate. However, things didn't stop there. In early 1973, the American Medical Association filed charges against him as a medical doctor accusing him of intentionally misleading the public with respect to a cancer treatment. The state attorney general in Florida filed charges against him as well, followed by a federal investigation into his laboratory work. The company, Omni Galactic, was the very same one Martinov and Stimpson worked for.

In February 1974, the feds charged Novrowski with falsifying laboratory and experimental results, and the company fired him from his position. Even though the results of his work were replicated in two other experiments at that time, his career was destroyed. The findings of the other experiments were suppressed. Out of work and void of a career, Novrowski resorted to writing articles under a pen name for local journals and periodicals. In October of that year, he was found in his home in Sarasota, Florida, dead.

However, this was not the end of the story.

Novrowski's assistant, Dr. Cynthia Kline, was also discredited during this period. Although she was able to find work at another laboratory— Pinnacle Research, in Miami—she was terminated a year later in 1975. She too was found dead—hers occurring in March 1976 of an apparent suicide. Although she had no prescriptions and led a healthy lifestyle, she was found with 30 mg of a benzodiazepine which required a doctor's prescription. The usual dosage for that particular drug was 2 mg. Not only that, but other associates who worked with Novrowski were also discredited—their careers and lives ruined. Quickly thereafter, all mention of the work was expunged from the company records, and the last of the papers were packed away in the basement of Omni—intended never to see the light of day again.

But Maria wouldn't be stopped. Without a family to protect, she persevered.

It wasn't long before she found several strange things occurring. Her cell phone had strange clicks that weren't there before. Her Internet connection continued to go down, losing her access to the Internet. Eventually, she found it necessary to leave her home and access a WIFI through the local coffee shop down the street. Even that soon caught up with her as she began noticing gray sedans following her from her home as she walked. Within days, the coffee shop owner came to her table and pulled the plug on her computer.

"I'm sorry, ma'am, but we don't allow illicit web searching on our system," he said.

"But I'm not doing anything wrong," she answered, surprised at the accusation.

"Yes, you are," he countered.

"I'm just looking up medical research," she said, "not porn or other stuff."

"Sorry. You must leave. You are not welcome here."

Maria left the shop and began her walk home. As she crossed the street, she spotted a gray sedan parked just down the block. It was then she heard the tires squeal and saw the blue smoke billow up from behind them as the car tore down the street toward her. She looked down her side of the street but found no alleys to jump into to escape. Panicked, she began to run but only heard the car zooming from behind her, closing in. *She needed someplace to hide! Someplace to escape!* But there was no place to go.

Realizing she was doomed, she turned to face the car and did the unthinkable. She ran *toward* it.

Seeing his victim sprinting toward him, the attacker aimed the sedan directly at her. He steered it right down the middle of the street, his engine roaring as the car grew close, then closer, and then …

At the last minute, Maria dove to the side of the street, rolling across the pavement to the other side. The sedan barely missed her, and instead, grazed the front glass window of a flower shop, smashing it and sending splintered fragments everywhere.

Maria got up and ran as fast as she could in the opposite direction carrying her backpack. She reached the church grounds with its small cemetery and leaped up the six brick steps that took her through two mausoleums and across another wide, grassy patch before reaching another parallel street. She heard the car from the next block, backing out of the flower shop and racing toward the intersection ahead of her. As it careened around the corner, she pushed herself up against the cold, granite side of one of the last mausoleums in the cemetery hoping to hide. To her relief, the car passed, not seeing her.

A few minutes passed, and Maria listened. All was quiet.

Hearing nothing more, she walked rapidly down the alley between two other buildings, finally making her way to the train station. There, she hid, waiting for the next train. When it arrived, she jumped out from her hiding place and climbed onboard just as it was leaving. She watched out the window as the gray sedan pulled up to the station and two men in dark suits got out. The doors to the train closed. She had just escaped, but not by much.

*****

CH 3

Maria had no family living in the U.S., so she decided to withdraw her entire savings account and leave. Her parents lived in Switzerland even though they originally immigrated from Poland. Her father knew many people around the world from his career as a producer in Hollywood and had made a fortune in California. Her parents had relocated to Switzerland after he had retired. Now, she boarded a plane bound for Geneva.

As she approached the terminal desk, she worried her passport would be listed in the "No Fly" database—something that was becoming more common during those times. Carefully watching for any signs of hesitation, Maria observed the agent as she looked up her flight and validate her passport. Then, after swiping it through the airline system, she smiled, printed the boarding pass, and handed it all back to her.

"Have a nice flight," she said joyfully.

"Thanks," answered Maria.

The flight was direct from Miami to Geneva, and when she arrived, she headed to her hotel downtown which was within walking distance of her next stop: The World Health Organization on Avenue Apia.

Walking into the headquarters, she explained who she was and asked if she could see the director of research for virology studies, Dr. Anna Matshioti. Normally, this would have been impossible, but Maria had dropped the name of her boss, Dr. Stimpson, in her message. Stimpson and Matshioti had been close colleagues when both had worked at Walter Reed Hospital in Washington.

"She says she'd love to meet with you, but she's tied up until tomorrow. She can see you at 1300 hours," said the cheerful woman at the desk. "Can you come back then?"

Maria nodded. "Yes. That would be fine."

"And where are you staying?" asked the woman.

"I'm staying at the ..." she stopped, checking herself. "On second thought, I'm not sure where I'm staying. Just note that she can reach me on my cell."

Maria didn't trust anyone, and the less information she provided, she thought, the better.

Leaving the WHO building, she caught a taxi back to her hotel—the Intercontinental—not far away. But when she checked in, the hotel asked for a credit card. Fearing being tracked, she said she didn't have one.

"I'm sorry, ma'am. We can't allow you to stay here without putting down a credit card. That's our policy."

It took another hour to find a hotel that didn't require a credit card, and she took the elevator to the nineth floor, room 914 which held a small, single bed with no amenities. Exhausted, she quickly fell asleep.

It was early in the next morning when the phone in the room rang.

"Ms. Martinov," said the voice, using Ms. Instead of Dr.

"Yes?" Maria answered, groggily.

"There is a man in the lobby here to see you. He says its urgent."

"It's two in the morning!"

"I know. I'm sorry. But he said it was a matter of great urgency."

"Tell him I'll be right down."

Maria got out of bed and started to put her clothes on. Then, she stopped.

Who knows I'm here? Who knows where I'm staying? I didn't tell anyone, she thought.

Realizing she'd been compromised, she threw her belongings back into a suitcase and took the stairs to the mezzanine floor. There, she peered around the corner into the lobby to see the man who was waiting for her. Indeed, there was a man wearing a dark, navy suit and yellow tie. He was well-dressed, but as she looked at his shoes, she noticed they were standard government issue—unremarkable black, lace-ups. He wore an overcoat, and whether he was carrying a gun, she had no idea.

Not taking the chance, she slipped out the back door where the trash was taken out and found another taxi that was heading in her direction. She waved it down and hopped in the back seat.

"*Où allez-vous?*" asked the driver, turning on the meter.

Figuring she had been tracked to Geneva through the flight records, she said, *"Gare Cornavin,"* which was the central train station.

Moments later she was boarding a train out of the city and out of the country. *****

CH 4

"Hello, Dr. Stimpson? This is Dr. Martinov. I wanted to tell you that I am resigning from the company, effective immediately."

"Oh, I'm sorry to hear that Maria. Did something happen that made you decide to leave?"

The image of Maria came over the video line, showing her lying in a hammock and sipping on a cool beverage. In the background was the sand and surf with seagulls flying about and playing with each other along the moistened beach.

"Yes. I found that letting over 770 million people die of cancer during the past seventy years is something I cannot live with. I am dedicating myself to refining the experiments of Dr. Novrowski and bringing his cure to the marketplace."

"I see," said Stimpson. "Can I ask where you are? Perhaps we can meet and talk about this."

"No, I'm afraid that's not possible," she answered.

"Then where are you, Maria. You're putting yourself at great risk, and I can help you."

Maria laughed. "Sure. That's almost sincere."

"You can't do this, Maria," said Stimpson, more sternly.

"I can, and I will," she said determinedly.

"They will stop you, you know," he said, now threatening her.

"Yes. They have already tried, but they won't succeed. Big pharma and the global elites who fund them will never find me. Big pharma's profits will be crushed when they face the cure I will unleash. Research labs that survive and bury research findings to protect their grant money and donations will dry up, and the elites who want to reduce world populations through eugenic type practices of selective breeding and selective treatments for the rich and politically connected will be outraged but helpless to stop me."

Stimpson laughed. "You ... you think you can do all that? My little Maria? You are not sane. You will be killed. You will be prevented from this.

Cancer research is a multi-billion-dollar market. We can't have that disrupted. People will lose their livelihoods, and ..."

"... and the elites will lose a few billion too. Why should I care? Why should we care about the millions who die every year from cancer—a disease that can be cured and should have been cured decades ago?"

"That's not for you to decide."

"Oh, but it's okay for *you* to decide? What about the lives we could save? DCA or other compounds are inexpensive and can't be patented; that's why the drug companies won't let this go."

"There is a lot of power and money behind them. No, they won't let this go, and that's why you'll never succeed."

"Well, it disappoints me to see that you are on the wrong side of this," said Maria. "I used to look up to you."

"Ha! Flattery! It's useless."

"Yes, and so are you. Good day doctor."

Maria hung up just before enough time would have elapsed to reveal the path taken by her call. Anyone tapping the line and trying to trace the call would have been disappointed anyway. She had bounced it off many different nodes throughout the world. It would have been a daunting task to find her.

She shut off her phone and lay back in her hammock. But there was no brilliant sun shining overhead. Instead, the background lighting went off and the irritating florescent basement lights came on. Behind her was a green screen, and the projectors on either side were programmed to create whatever landscape she wanted. The options were endless, and tracking them down would only become a wild goose chase.

"Maria," said an older gentleman coming over to her, "I'm glad we found Giuseppe here to help you out. He's been a friend of mine since our time in Los Angeles. His studio here is perfect for you. You should be safe."

"Thanks, Dad," she answered smiling. "I just need time to finish the studies and find an avenue to get them published."

"I know just the person," said Bull Martinov, her father.

"Who's that?"

"He's Director of the Underground," said her father.

"Oh, no! The Resistance? That won't do any good. They'll track me down like they do all the Resistance Fighters. They'll stop me—even kill me like they did to Novrowski!"

"They won't."

"How can you be so sure?" she asked.

"He's the twin brother of the president."

"What? You mean …?"

"Yeah, the new president is one of us. We all just hope he can bring the world back from the brink. We're praying for it," said her father.

"Do you think he can do that?" his daughter asked.

"It's our last hope, dear. But with a cure for cancer, the world will be a lot farther along the path."

*****

ABOUT THE AUTHOR

Gage Axtin is a pseudonym used by the author for books published under the science fiction genre. This is the fourth book in the *Crossed Circuits* series. He lives in the Chicago area with his family and has written many other anthologies and novels.

CROSSED CIRCUITS V

Mr. Axtin's next volume, *Crossed Circuits V*, is expected to be published in 2021.